TRUTH BE TOLD

Kia Abdullah

ONE PLACE. MANY STORIES

HQ
An imprint of HarperCollins*Publishers* Ltd
1 London Bridge Street
London SE1 9GF

This edition 2020

1

First published in Great Britain by
HQ, an imprint of HarperCollins*Publishers* Ltd 2020

A catalogue record for this book is
available from the British Library.

ISBN: Hardback: 978-0-00-831472-9
Trade Paperback: 978-0-00-831473-6

MIX
Paper from
responsible sources
FSC
www.fsc.org   **FSC™ C007454**

This book is produced from independently certified FSC™ paper
to ensure responsible forest management.

For more information visit: www.harpercollins.co.uk/green

This book is set in Sabon

Printed and bound in Great Britain by
CPI Group (UK) Ltd, Croydon, CR0 4YY

Praise for Kia Abdullah

'A superb legal thriller that fairly crackles with tension'
Guardian

'A topical and gritty story'
Observer

'Just as impressive as the courtroom drama is Abdullah's portrayal of five deftly differentiated British-Asian families, and of the relationship between two disparate women who both become isolated pariahs'
Sunday Times

'A thought-provoking and sparklingly intelligent novel, with the welcome bonus of an unguessable ending'
Daily Telegraph

'A fresh and compelling read'
Sunday Post

'With razor-sharp insight into the lives of her characters, Kia Abdullah gives readers much more than a courtroom thriller'
Christina Dalcher, *Sunday Times* bestselling author of *VOX*

'Taut, gritty and compelling'
Louise Jensen, million-copy bestselling author of *The Sister*

'Intense, shocking and so real you can literally feel its heartbeat . . . the best book I've read this year'
Lisa Hall, author of *The Perfect Couple*

'Kia's novel is an excellent addition to the court-based criminal dramas we've come to love . . . It's a great read and draws you in with fast pacing and real characters'
Nazir Afzal OBE, Former Chief Crown Prosecutor, CPS

'I was blown away by *Take It Back*. From the explosive premise to the shockingly perfect ending, I loved every word'
Roz Watkins, author of *The Devil's Dice*

'Brave and shocking, a real welcome addition to the crime thriller genre. Kia's is a fresh voice and a thrilling novel'
Alex Khan, author of *Bollywood Wives*

Kia Abdullah is a novelist and travel writer from London. She has written for *The New York Times*, the *Guardian* and the *Telegraph*, and is the author of *Take It Back*, named one of the best thrillers of the year by the *Guardian* and the *Telegraph*.

Kia frequently contributes to the BBC commenting on a variety of issues affecting the British-Asian community and is the founder of Asian Booklist, a site that helps readers discover new books by British-Asian authors. Kia also runs Atlas & Boots, a travel blog read by 250,000 people a month. For more information about Kia and her writing, visit her website at kiaabdullah.com, or follow her at @KiaAbdullah on Instagram and Twitter.

Also by Kia Abdullah

Take It Back

For my little sis, Shafia

PART I

CHAPTER ONE

The Hadid family was an effortful one. Even minor occasions and trivial achievements were marked with a rigid persistence. Birthday cards arrived precisely on the day in question, except on Sundays when they would tip through the letterbox one day early. Wedding anniversaries were marked not only by the couple concerned but the entire extended family, great blooms of pink mandevilla arriving in steady procession. Lavish bouquets were dispatched routinely: congratulatory lilies for passing a test, good-luck orchids for a summer job, get-well roses for a lightweight cold. These gifts were cordially acknowledged with thank-you notes, each of which then garnered a phone call; a three-act play that ran on repeat.

Family news was issued systematically to ensure that everyone received an update. When Kamran interviewed at Oxford and his mother forgot to tell an aunt, she took it as a personal slight and needled them for weeks.

Kamran understood that his family made sense of the world through this codified means of connection, so when his housemaster pointed at a bouquet of flowers, instead of feeling pleasure, he only felt a sense of duty. He collected it with resignation, the sturdy ceramic pot held securely against a hip, then thanked the master and headed back to the third floor, his footsteps echoing off the wood-panelled walls.

At seventeen, Kamran was a senior and no longer had to share his room, unlike the boys in lower years. He set down the flowers on his desk, a Victorian construction of quarter-sawn oak. He opened a drawer, shaking it free of its mahogany boxing, and took out a piece of paper. Hampton's coat of arms was printed along the top, a golden lion on a royal blue shield with the words *Alere Flammam Veritatis* inscribed underneath. *To feed the flame of truth.*

Kamran's mother insisted that he use official stationery when writing to their relatives. She was of second-generation wealth, garnered by her father's steelwork business, but aspired to older money – hence Kamran's enrolment at Hampton College followed by his brother, Adam.

Set in a sprawling wooded estate, the boarding school was eight miles west of their family home: a stucco townhouse in Belsize Park where the boys were received each break like kings. Sometimes they would arrive on a Friday to find the house filled to the brim. Kamran and Adam would swap a glance before slipping into character of 'the two good sons'.

When greeting his uncles and aunts, Kamran would recall second-hand reports of other Asian families: their raucous laughter and flavoursome food, brash debates that verged on rude. He had seen the evidence on Instagram Live: brothers jostling over the last piece of chicken, set to a mother's gentle chiding, cut by a father's sterner scolding. Together, they sounded like family. The Hadids in comparison were more composed; a little more 'clenched', a friend once said.

Kamran's mother, Sofia, was obsessed with saving face. A great beauty at the age of forty-six, she had a laughably strict style of dress: slim chinos that tapered at the ankle, tailored tops with navy-and-white stripes, structured jackets with embellished buttons, complemented by pearls or diamonds but never both in tandem. Her dark hair fell in coiffured curls, framing her fine-boned features.

Kamran could tell that she was proud of them in the fussy way she arranged them for pictures: Kamran to the right, Adam to the left and herself ensconced in the middle. There was a neat symmetry to these photos: the brothers an identical five feet ten and their mother three inches shorter. It was strange to define a family this way – well groomed – but he couldn't deny it; he too liked the way they looked.

Kamran bore a clear resemblance to their mother: fine features with high cheekbones and a delicate, elegant jawline. Adam, at sixteen, took after their father with his large, heavy-lidded eyes and lips that were overtly full next to Kamran's more subtle appeal. Their mother liked nothing more than showing them off at weddings, her only regret that she had named her sons the wrong way around.

'You should have been Adam,' she would say to Kamran. After all, didn't 'Adam and Kamran' flow off the tongue more smoothly than 'Kamran and Adam'? It annoyed her, this slight hitch in their naming, especially as she had spent so long selecting ones that kept to Islamic tradition but could also pass for Western.

Still, she couldn't be prouder of them – a fact she shared with a finely tuned mix of vanity and humility. Seeing her spar with an aunt was akin to watching ballet. Sofia might start with a passing comment, a reference, say, to Kamran's interview at Oxford.

Aunty Rana, their father's sister, would reply with a lament on fees. 'But it was worth it,' she would say with a shrug. 'Yusuf *did* after all get a First and look where he is now.'

Sofia would volley back, 'Fees are certainly annoying. We're not *made* of money after all. I hate it when people assume that. Take Mack's Jag. He works so hard but just because he drives a Roadster, the garage assumes he's dripping with cash.'

A tight laugh from Rana. 'Why doesn't he take it to the official factory? That's what Aadil does.'

The children would watch these contests with tense amusement. Perhaps this is why they received such frequent congratulation. Their smallest achievements were shamelessly embellished – a keen swimmer recast as an Olympic hopeful, a piano recital hailed virtuosic. Neither side wanted to seem ungracious and so they bestowed each triumph with outsize praise, prompting this empty rally of thanks.

Kamran smoothed the piece of paper and began to write with his Cartier pen. In neat letters, he thanked Aunty Rana for her wishes following his interview. The note was polite but impersonal and he finished with an expansive 'x', their customary substitute for truer intimacy. He placed the note inside its envelope and sealed it with a sponge-tipped pen, knowing it would prompt a phone call to thank him for his thank you. Wearily, he returned to the office downstairs.

Finn Andersen received him with a smile. With wavy blond hair, broad shoulders and an easy, affable manner, Finn was the sort of boy who featured in Hampton's brochures.

Kamran placed his envelope in the silver pail reserved for outgoing post. 'You must be looking forward to tonight,' he said.

Finn glanced at his calendar. 'Tonight?'

'Your fancy party in the Hawtrey Room?'

'Ah, of course. Yes, I certainly am.'

'I hear that everyone gets a bit "tired and emotional".'

Finn laughed, his blue eyes squinting winsomely. 'That's what I hear.' As assistant to the housemaster, Finn was invited to Hampton's spring fundraiser where powerful alumni gathered to reminisce and write generous cheques after copious drinks. Hosted in the lavish Hawtrey Room at West Lawn, the party was an opportunity for invited pupils to network in a semi-formal setting.

'Well, have fun,' said Kamran. 'I'll see you later.'

Finn nodded. 'I certainly hope so.'

Kamran headed back up to his room. His duty was officially done and now he was free to play. At 6 p.m., their spring exeat would begin; a scheduled weekend that granted them leave. Barrett, a broad-chested boy in the same year as him, had invited some friends to the Cotswolds. Kamran was thrilled that his mother had permitted the trip and began to pack with alacrity, humming a half-formed tune.

From his wardrobe, he pulled out a standard-issue suitcase. With a sturdy brass handle and buttery leather in a dark green olive, it was one component of the Hampton aesthetic: well-turned-out young men, all smartly tugging the exact same case.

Kamran folded his pile of clothes into one half of the suitcase: chinos in khaki, black and dark navy, one polo

T-shirt in white and another in black, a knitted jumper and a pair of jeans. Barrett's parents were away, but from what he heard, these weekends in the country were civilised affairs: whisky in the drawing room with pungent cigars, as if priming already for their grand collective destiny. Hampton was, after all, breeding ground for the country's most powerful men. Here walked the sons of moguls and royals. These boys with their plummy accents and cheerful confidence were future kings and leaders. Kamran was comfortable in their midst. He may be of a different race but he dressed as they dressed, spoke as they spoke and held the same values and graces. He knew that it wasn't colour but class that set you apart at Hampton. You could spot the social intake by a mile. They pronounced their 't's and rounded their vowels in an effort to fit in, but they did not know how to hold a fork and were flummoxed by silver service. Kamran pitied them. No matter how they tried, they would never be accepted. Instead, they were treated with a bemused paternalism, as if too dim to withstand challenge. Of course, Hampton did not tolerate bullies, so the worst they ever faced was a hearty 'pleb' on the rugby field. It was fitting, thought Kamran, that at Hampton, even insults were traded in Latin. He closed his suitcase and wheeled it to the door. *Carpe vinum*, he thought as he checked his watch with a smile.

Zara Kaleel gazed at the four-tier chandelier looming above the altar, its mass of golden arms like snakes on Medusa, each curved and spindly, topped with a tongue of light. It cast a ceremonious shadow across the cavernous room, making it somehow colder. She was perched on the edge of a pew, wary of being asked to speak after her silence in the meeting last week. She squared her shoulders and crossed her legs, her right foot positioned in a demure *en pointe*. Places of worship put her on edge.

There were seven of them tonight in this sorry assembly of miscreants and misfits, all dotted across St Alfege Church as if sharing a pew might unglue a wound. Zara recognised three of them: Sam, the part-time teacher; Kerry, the wounded writer; Ed, the ex-criminal on the cusp of surrender.

As feared, Chris, the session leader, nodded at Zara. 'Would you like to address the group?' he asked, his Irish accent soft and lyrical.

Zara felt a spike of unease. How was it that she had spent years orating in open court but was anxious at the prospect of addressing this room? She raised a hand in polite refusal.

Chris angled his head to the right, entreating her to speak.

She faltered for a moment, caught exposed in his hopeful stare. 'Okay,' she said finally. 'I'm Zara Kaleel.' She pressed a nail into the pad of her thumb, leaving half-moon crescents that slowly plumped back. 'And I am an addict.' The words were strangely hollow, as if she were playing a role. 'I have been clean for three weeks.' The word 'clean' held a hitch, laden with sarcasm or irony as if she were somehow superior to this charade of recovery.

She had read that acceptance was a pertinent step and she agreed that this was true, but mainly for people who were *really* addicted. Zara hadn't fallen so deeply. In fact, she had stopped taking Diazepam regularly nearly five months ago and hadn't touched it for a full three weeks – except that one Thursday when she needed to sleep. She wasn't *really* an addict but those words formed a vital part of admission to this club and so she deigned to say them.

Unlike in the movies, there was no round of applause to praise her for her courage. Instead, the group waited in silence. In the front row, Ed turned in her direction. His hair fell in strings from the swamp-green canvas of a baseball cap and he stared at her with deathly grey eyes.

Zara wondered if she had made the right choice. Her options had been to see a therapist or join a Narcotics Anonymous meeting. She had balked at the thought of therapy; the shock-white exposure of sitting in a room, bleeding intimacies into soft upholstery as a stranger sat by and watched. She had agreed to attend this NA meeting; to come to church on a Saturday evening and say that she was a junkie.

Chris nodded sagely. 'Thank you, Zara. Can you share some of your story?'

She wrapped her woollen cardigan around her and folded her arms tightly. With her long dark hair in a messy bun and her skin make-up free, she looked many miles away from the barrister she used to be. 'I first started using about six years ago.' She uncrossed her legs and shifted in her seat. 'At first, it was because my job was stressful.' She paused, not knowing how much to share. 'I was a lawyer and it wasn't unusual to take medication to keep yourself going. I took it for several years on and off without any problems and then…'

Ed in the front row gave her a gentle nod.

Zara felt oddly touched by the gesture. She averted her gaze to the altar and focused on the folds of rich purple velvet. 'Then my dad died in 2017 – three years ago now.

He… we hadn't talked for six months because…' Zara shook her head. 'Anyway, I didn't get to say goodbye.' She tried to remain neutral as if reciting facts in court, but felt the dull, aching beat of ceaseless remorse. 'After that, I started taking Diazepam more frequently and I did some things I'm not proud of.' She flashed back to a newspaper headline: **FOUR MUSLIM TEENS RAPE DISABLED ENGLISH GIRL**. 'I let some people down and now I'm here.'

'Because you choose to be?' Chris was clearly more perceptive than Zara had believed.

Her lips curled in a plaintive moue. 'Because I have to be.' Chris waited and she shifted beneath his gaze. 'After I quit chambers, I took a job at a crisis centre working with victims of sexual assault. I had a difficult case last year and things have been… erratic ever since.' She gripped the edge of the pew in front. 'My boss told me to seek help if I wanted to keep my job.'

'Has that helped?'

She half shrugged. 'Well, I'm here, so that remains to be seen.'

Chris smiled. 'Okay. Thank you for sharing, Zara. You've been very brave.'

You've been very brave. Was recovery really this cheesy? Zara imagined how Safran would react when she told him about her NA meetings. She pictured the amused curve of his brow and the familiar lilt of his laugh. She – Zara the Brave – in recovery. *What a joke*, she thought. *What an abject hoot.*

Kamran heard a sharp rap on the door and opened it to welcome Jimmy. An athletic boy of Malaysian heritage, he, like Kamran, hailed from a wealthy family and dovetailed comfortably with the Hampton aesthetic. His thick dark hair was scrupulously styled and his manner was calm and confident.

'You heading to the Batts?' asked Jimmy.

'The Batts? But we're meeting Barrett in a minute.'

'No, we're not.' He gestured at Kamran's phone. 'I thought he texted you? His parents' trip got cancelled so we're not going up there after all.'

Kamran groaned. 'I didn't get the message.' He drew out his phone and checked his texts. 'The signal here drives me crazy.'

'Well, there's no harm done. We're heading to the Batts instead. Rumour has it that some old cad has smuggled in a keg.'

Kamran arched a brow. 'In that case, fuck this then.' He tipped his suitcase over and grabbed his blazer from the back of his chair. Together, they raced down the stairs into the warm May dusk outside.

The Batts, a large clearing hidden by a copse of trees, was located on the south-eastern boundary of the school grounds. It provided a refuge from their various housemasters, tutors and matrons. Access to drink, drugs and women was strictly controlled at Hampton and these covert soirees provided a rare and welcome chance to indulge.

Kamran's house, West Lawn, was located at the western extreme of Hampton's grounds. Eleven other boarding houses were dotted around the complex, each with around seventy boys; fourteen from each year. West Lawn was the centre of his life at Hampton, and his closest friends – Jimmy, Barrett and Nathan – were all housed there too.

Soon, the four of them were gathered on the Batts, joined by their boisterous peers. Jimmy handed Kamran a foamy beer, which he tipped to his lips in glee. Raised in a Muslim family, albeit a liberal one, he still felt a subversive thrill whenever he chose to drink. The beer was warm and sticky, but he gulped it down in hearty swigs. As the sky blotted dark with ink, the mood grew loose and merry.

Kamran spotted his brother, Adam, playing beer pong with some seniors. He headed over and lightly touched his shoulder.

Adam turned and flinched in surprise. 'What are you doing here?' he asked.

Kamran gestured towards his friends. 'Barrett's parents aren't leaving after all, so I'm coming home with you tomorrow.'

Adam's face flushed. 'Oh, right.'

Kamran pointed at the beer pong table. 'Sorry to ruin your fun.'

'Nah, you're not ruining anything,' he said gravely.

Kamran laughed. 'Adam, I'm kidding. You're sixteen. You can have a drink if you want to. Just go easy, okay?'

He nodded solemnly. 'Yeah. I will.'

Kamran headed back to his friends, vowing not to bother his brother. Adam was naturally pensive and a night of fun would do him good. As the younger sibling, he likely felt more pressure to perform. Kamran was a skilled fencer and popular at school. The thing Adam seemed to enjoy most was spending time with horses and yet he refused to play polo – 'a cruel sport' he'd say with that dreamy, absent air of his. He had joined the cricket team at their father's behest, but lacked a natural flair. Adam was too self-conscious in a team. He needed to learn to let go, and perhaps this party would help him.

Kamran passed a group of juniors that were climbing a large sycamore tree. Janus Keister reached the top branch, then pulled down his pants and mooned his friends.

'Very on brand, Keister!' yelled a boy, then chuckled at his own wit. Another group of juniors had fastened their ties around their heads and were running around shouting in Greek. Apparently, this is what passed for fun at Hampton. Kamran laughed as he watched, then joined his friends for a second drink.

Zara smoothed the Estée Lauder serum on her skin, taking care not to rub too hard in the hollow beneath her left cheekbone. The bruises had long healed but it was still delicate and she often felt a faint pain when she pressed it absentmindedly. Five months had passed since the attack and though she had clicked back into her heels and pulled on her armour of poise, she still felt a queasy vulnerability whenever she ventured from home. She had to harden herself to do it, as if she were duelling with the very act of existing.

It all started with Jodie Wolfe, a sixteen-year-old girl from East London who walked into Zara's office last July and accused four classmates of rape. In what would become a tabloid frenzy, Jodie – white, disabled, beleaguered – named her attackers as Muslim. The firestorm that followed took something from them both.

Zara, herself a Muslim, was denounced a traitor – rhetoric that led to a physical attack. It was on the most banal of evenings, during a late-night trip to pick up dry cleaning, that she had heard those fateful footsteps – two sets echoing her own. Her memory held the next moments in a murky midnight blue: her scream snuffed by the force of a palm, the crack of her cheek on brick, the giant flowers blooming in her vision, her body jolting upwards. A kick to her stomach when she fell to the ground and, then, the single most terrifying moment of her life: a bottle of clear liquid emptied on her face with the threat that it was acid. She had blacked out then, sinking into dark relief. When she woke, the doctors told her it was vodka, not acid, but the horror of that moment – the sadism in her attackers' eyes – changed something permanent inside her.

Ten days later, a video clip surfaced that seemed to prove the four boys' innocence: Jodie whispering to Amir, the ringleader, entreating him to touch her. Disgraced, Jodie said that she had lied and the case was swiftly thrown out of court.

Weeks later, a second clip emerged showing the events that followed the first. This one proved indisputably that the boys were, in fact, guilty. The case was reopened but Amir was set free and his friends were issued nominal sentences given their young age and clean rap sheets.

Zara had no way of knowing if it was this final infraction that led her to the precipice, or if she would have arrived there regardless following her attack. She found herself taking Diazepam with more zeal than ever before, mixing it with alcohol with dangerous frequency if only to collapse into dreamless sleep, free of violent memories.

She reached her nadir in February when she roused in her

car one day to the blare of horns deep inside Rotherhithe Tunnel, a narrow, suffocating tube that burrowed beneath the Thames. She had veered out of her lane into the path of oncoming traffic – extraordinarily lethal in such a small space. She snapped to rigid attention and drove home with a manic focus. Once safely inside her Greenwich flat, she let herself dissolve. It was *shame* that she felt more than anything – not only for being so weak but for putting someone's life at risk.

Safran had forced her to take a break after hearing what had happened that day. He had bundled her into his car and driven her to Dartmoor. They took long, bracing walks in the February cold and saw wild horses gallop on the moor. The memory of that week made her well with sorrow. Sharing a home with her friend made her see how lonely she was. There was comfort in knowing there was heat in the house, in seeing the grains of salt fanned across the table, in the curtain that wasn't folded quite the way she wanted, or the haphazard way he left his shoes on the landing. They had spent evenings in front of the fire, eating comfort food and watching TV. Every laugh from her he took as a small victory.

Their colleagues from chambers had often wondered if their friendship went further given their easy manner and the way they looked together: he, tall and athletic with sleek good looks; she with her haughty cheekbones and naturally full lips. Their chemistry was never sexual, however. They were more like comrades in arms.

Over the course of the week, they had watched the first season of *Breaking Bad* – he appalled that she hadn't yet seen it – and in the bright, warm tones of the Albuquerque desert, she found a strange and calming comfort. Perhaps nothing was elemental and everyone was in danger of change. Perhaps that's why she, Zara the Brave, still felt this strange anxiety even at home on a Saturday evening.

She paced to the kitchen and poured herself a cool glass of water. She sat on her large cream sofa, legs tucked beneath her thighs, and watched the hand on her large wall clock as it counted down the minutes to night.

Were those gunshots? Kamran wondered idly. There was no way to tell over the riotous noise. The babble of boys mixed with tinny music that played from someone's phone. Shouts and screams rose like flares that joined to form a din. Kamran felt unsteady on his feet, but where he'd usually stop, he carried on drinking, knowing that tomorrow he was free from duties.

Besides, he had never been truly drunk, not *stinking* drunk. He felt a tinge of envy when his friends would talk of hunching over a toilet bowl, the sheer abandon of knowing what was coming but going ahead and doing it anyway. It felt like an important part of living, a rite of passage to adulthood, and the fact that he'd never done it needled him unduly like it might if he'd never kissed a girl or not yet lost his virginity. Thankfully, *that* wasn't a worry. He thought of his family's cruise at Christmas and his fumbles with Maya, the ballet dancer. He thought of her long legs, shiny from the buttercream that she kept in a jar in her cabin. He thought of her lithe thighs and ready lips, her warm mouth and the downy film above it.

'She certainly taught me a thing or two,' he had joked with Jimmy on his return to Hampton, his voice gruff with newfound swagger. In truth, he had weaved with nerves and trembled beneath her fingers. She, a year older than he, had lulled him into security, telling him over and over how handsome he was, how desperately she wanted him. He didn't care that she was bored or looking for something to do that might annoy her wealthy parents. He succumbed to her that evening and every evening for the rest of the trip, begging Adam to cover for him.

He hadn't been with a woman since. The girls from the comp nearby certainly made him flutter, but given his schedule at Hampton, he had little chance to indulge. There was plenty of time for that, he supposed. He was approaching his final year of study and would soon be starting at Oxford. All those girls from their single-sex schools – what an utter treat.

Kamran knew the sort of man he aspired to be – a strong and faithful one, loyal and fair like his father – but first he wanted to have some fun; to drive it all from his system. He would give himself ten years, he'd decided – from eighteen to twenty-eight – to sample the fairer sex. After that, he would look for a wife and have three kids and buy a nice car like his dad. Until then, he would seize his youth with all his might.

Kamran accepted another beer, its hoppy smell mingling with spring wisteria. It was warm and gummy in his throat but he chugged it down regardless. A group of juniors rode by on bicycles in close pursuit of a small white rabbit, its bushy tail flashing a desperate SOS. Kamran willed it to escape and was pleased when a boy wobbled and fell, his legs tangling in the cold blue metal. Giddily, he stood and remounted the bike, wobbling down the hill towards his quarry. Nearby, a separate group of boys dipped a pint with various body parts to feed to one of their friends. Further on, a group was pouring a keg straight into the mouth of a boy lying prone. Above the noise and chaos, the night took on a certain romance: strange and heady, sweet and surreal.

Kamran accepted another beer and the sky began to spin. He laughed out loud at something absurd. He heard the Hampton anthem and a chorus soon joined in. He loved this place. He really, truly did.

The night bled into a snatch of memories: him walking giddily home, fumbling for his keys, the jangle as they fell to the floor, the jarring sound making him giggle. The way his head pulsed as he brushed his teeth and how the room seemed to stretch and contract. Pulling off his clothes, falling into his sheets, swiping at some crumbs and then sinking into sleep.

It was deep and dreamless until he felt a body against his, the powerful arm curled around his chest, the hot whisper in his ear, the eager hand encircling him. It seemed inky and unreal, with the opiate quality of an erotic dream. Each touch, in isolation, felt entirely unthreatening: a fingertip brushing against his navel, dipping inside so slightly; lips on the curve of his shoulder blade, warm and hypnotic. It was only when he felt the full heft of weight that something triggered inside him: a distant alarm or warning that this might really be happening. But where his subconscious might have roused him, it lay only mute and submissive, blunted by the alcohol coursing through his bloodstream. He felt a bewildering mix of pain and pleasure and heard sounds in a voice that was somehow familiar. He tried to reach for meaning, to latch onto reality, but only sank back to a deep, dark sleep.

*

Sofia Hadid read the email with a febrile sense of defeat. Jonathan Walmsley, the CEO of her father's company, had dispatched her ideas with a cold and clear diplomacy. He appreciated her input, he wrote, but it wasn't the direction the company was heading. If she should have any similar ideas, however, then she should please feel free to contact him.

She knew he disliked her meddling, that he wondered why she couldn't keep quiet like her sister, Noreen, and the other silent partners. What he didn't know was that Sofia had been her father's first choice as successor at Arshad Steel. It was only after she got married and pregnant that his preference seemed to shift. What hope did women have when their own fathers eschewed them for men?

For years, she had tried to prove her worth, sending him plans and proposals and strategies for improving efficiency. 'Focus on family,' he would tell her. 'It's the most important job in the world.' A gentle way of saying that she was no longer needed.

She took her thwarted ambitions and applied them to her role at home. She created a project called 'Hadid Family' in Basecamp, the project management software used by Arshad Steel. She added profiles for Kamran and Adam, her brows creasing at the lack of poetry in the order of those syllables.

She created a space where her children could share what they needed, as well as their goals, ambitions and worries. She even interviewed them bi-annually for a 'deep dive' into their lives. Mack thought it ludicrous, but why couldn't motherhood be approached like a job? If managers cared enough to formally check in with staff, why couldn't a mother follow suit? All too often, parents lost sight of their children;

assumed that because they saw them every day, they would spot a private aching. This is how children slipped from their grip and she refused to let that happen.

Besides, Basecamp was useful in other ways. It helped her keep track of her staff, especially since they worked different days and patterns: Julio the gardener on Monday, Magda the cleaner on Wednesday, Oliver the driver whenever he was needed since he was on full-time hours, and Nevinka the cook who was there every day.

Sofia used to have a live-in housekeeper when the children were small but now it seemed a tad indulgent. It would be useful though when the boys came home and the house-clean was already two days old.

She had received a message this morning, a taciturn text from Kamran saying he would not be going to Barrett's after all and would now be arriving with Adam – news that pleased her immensely. Her children were her greatest joy and biggest achievement. They *had* to be. What else could she show for her wealth?

When she heard the door rasp open, she swept over to them with open arms and ushered them in with a kiss.

'Hi, Mum.' Adam hauled his suitcase inside.

Sofia frowned. 'Where's Oliver?'

He shrugged. 'We told him we'd get our own cases.'

A cut of annoyance tightened her smile. 'Well, that's fine but it's two flights to your room.'

'Mum, we can handle it.'

There it was: that spike of impatience. She was only trying to help. 'So!' she said brightly, a two-letter palate cleanser, making way for warmth. 'How are my boys?'

Adam nodded. 'Yeah, fine.'

She looked to Kamran and noticed the film of sweat that glossed his upper lip. 'Are you ill?' she asked.

He tugged at a collar uncomfortably. 'No, I'm just tired.'

'You don't look well.' She grasped him by the elbow and turned him to the light. 'Shall I call Dr Hepenstall?'

He pulled away from her grip. 'No, I'm fine, Mum.' He gave her a listless smile. 'Honestly. I just got too hot in the car.'

Sofia was wary of pressing further so let them take their leave, listening as the twin creaks of their feet traced a path upstairs. One door closed and then another.

She checked her watch. It was approaching lunchtime so she headed to the kitchen to prepare their meal. She unwrapped the intricate platters of food prepared by Nevinka: *chana chaat*, a flavoursome mix of chickpea, mint, yoghurt and tamarind combined with onions and pastry; succulent lamb *kofta* meatballs; layers of *biryani*; and *kheer* for dessert, rice pudding topped with almonds and pistachios. Her sons loved homemade South Asian cuisine and it was important to her that they were connected to their culture. She arranged the platters on the large oak table and set out plates and cutlery. She drew three glasses of icy water and placed them neatly to the right of each setting. She took another glance at her watch, then settled down to wait, ignoring the airless press of boredom.

Kamran sat on his bed in a daze, a sturdy king-size with a sumptuous white duvet, goose down pillows and four extra cushions in burgundy and gold. He remembered pleading with his mother in Liberty to leave the cushions behind, but she had firmly insisted. 'It looks nice,' she'd said. 'You're barely home anyway and when people come round, they want a tour. It'll look nicer this way.'

He lay back on the cushions now to stop his stomach churning. Was he hung over, or was this the noisome texture of disgust? He could scarcely believe it had happened – was briefly convinced it had not – but the numb-white glaze of shock told him he couldn't be sure. Lying there, he felt his mind cut away from itself, so that even as he succumbed to paralysis, some stronger authority inside himself rose to marshal his strength.

It dived down for memories, grasping at them like seaweed from silt. The dull twinkle of stars in the sky, high-pitched jeers and raucous shouts. Adam playing beer pong and laughing in that nervy, restrained way that he did. Jimmy or maybe Nathan pushing another drink at him and Kamran glugging it freely, buoyed by youth and liberty.

He traced his walk home: passing beneath a Victorian lamplight, pausing to watch a hundred mites dance in the glow it cast to the ground. He'd seen one of Hampton's peacocks and hoped it would splay its feathers, knowing it would not. He had stumbled along the path, a sliver of safety in the baleful dark. He was drunker than he'd ever been, drunker even than that last night on the cruise when Maya had traced her tongue down the curve of his back, wrapped him in her mouth and did things with her delicate fingers he would never have dared imagine. He'd got hard thinking about it, swaying on the green. At West Lawn, he had thumbed in his key code, his fingers leaving five smudges of sweat. He had grappled with his keys outside his bedroom door, then slammed it shut and flinched at the noise before remembering that most of the boys had gone. He'd pulled off his shirt and trousers, and climbed into bed in a stupor.

He tried to draw outlines in his mind and fill in the inky blanks. He remembered a hand tugging at his underwear, the black band of his Tom Ford boxers skimming across his buttocks, hot breath in his hair, a heady, intense feeling and the murk of a vital question: had he wanted it? Had he known what was happening and relented anyway? Did a dark, perverse part of him react to the transgressive nature of it? He remembered asking a question if not out loud then in his mind: *what is happening?* The answer was swallowed by darkness and the fact that he hadn't fought. *He knew he hadn't fought.*

'Boys,' his mother's singsong voice called up, snapping him from his thoughts. Kamran stood and lightly slapped each of his cheeks, bolstering himself for battle. He looked in his mirror and smiled, dialling the wattage up and down until it looked easy and natural. 'Coming,' he called and joined Adam on his way down.

At the table, he picked up a *kofta* and popped it in his mouth. 'Thanks, Mum,' he said between bites, feeling the gummy meat settle between his teeth.

'So – talk to me,' she said.

He nodded, assuring her he would as soon as he finished his mouthful. He remembered being fifteen and a conversation in their car. He and Adam were coming home from school and she had asked them how they were. 'Fine,' said one. 'Yep,' said the other. She had pulled up on the side of the road. 'We're not doing this, okay?' she'd said. 'We're not going to be a family that doesn't talk to each other. We're going to communicate. So I'm going to ask you again: how was your day?'

Kamran had humoured her, not telling her that he too had seen that movie where Ethan Hawke pulls over his kids and gives them a similar speech. Perhaps cinema was as good a place as any to learn the nebulous art of parenting.

He swallowed his mouthful, knowing he couldn't fluff this performance. 'Things are good,' he said. 'I got a send up in fencing class. Mr Storr said I'm winning more pressure points than any other pupil. He might even select me for Grenoble.' He segued to a monologue, changing his voice here and there like an actor on a stage: plummy for Mr Morewood, a trill for Mrs Brodie, a Dutch lilt for Nathan and a cut-glass accent for Jimmy. Beneath it all, his stomach dredged with nausea. He took another bite and imagined what would happen if he blurted it out now.

'I think I was raped.'

'Mum, I think I was raped.'

'Hey, Mum, by the way, I'm pretty sure I was raped.'

He gulped a mouthful of water. 'Mr Wycombe said I'm on course for top boy in his class.'

His mother reached out and ruffled his hair. 'My boy. I'm so proud of you.'

He prayed she would look away, for his smile was a filament about to break. She held his gaze and he pretended to work something loose with his tongue to explain the strange contorting of his face. How does one deal with grief that wasn't caused by death?

She continued to ask him questions and Kamran dutifully answered, silently second-guessing himself – the angle of his elbow on the table, the fullness of his laugh – as if he'd forgotten how to be her son. He wanted to confide in her, needed surely to tell *someone*, for if he continued pretending now, he would have to pretend for the rest of his life.

CHAPTER TWO

Zara sensed someone watching her and glanced up from her screen. Sure enough, there was a boy in the doorway: mid-teens, lean but athletic with fine-boned features that verged on feminine.

She stiffened in her seat, an involuntary reaction to this Asian male stranger. The last one that found her alone had smashed her face against a wall.

'Ms Kaleel?' he asked hesitantly.

'Yes,' she replied, also a question.

'My name is Kamran Hadid.'

'How may I help you?' She relaxed a little beneath his mild manner.

'May I shut the door?' he asked.

She studied him. 'If you tell me what this is about.'

He paused, a nervous shimmer of energy. 'Something happened to me.'

She recognised the wilt in his speech. 'Okay,' she said gently.

He shut the door and pointed at a chair in query.

Zara nodded.

He sat down and pressed his palms into the soft black pleather. 'I think I was raped,' he said.

Zara exhaled. She reached for a pen and a light blue form. 'Okay. Kamran, I work as an independent sexual violence advisor here, also known as an ISVA. What I'm going to do is take a few details and then we can assess the best way to help you.'

'Okay,' he said with a hesitant catch in his breath.

Zara discreetly glanced at the clock, knowing that her next client was due. She took some basic details, then asked Kamran if he identified as trans.

'No,' he said with a crease on his brows.

Zara placed an 'X' on the form and then set it on the table. 'Okay, in that case, what we need to do, Kamran, is refer you to our sister clinic which is also a SARC, a Sexual Assault Referral Centre.' She caught his spike of doubt. 'The clinic has facilities to help boys like you.'

He grimaced. 'But... can't I tell you?'

Zara smiled sympathetically. 'I'm afraid this clinic is specifically designed for women but, Kamran, you will receive the same level of care from them. If it's easier for you to confide in a female counsellor, I can organise one for you at the Paddington SARC.'

'It's not that.' A flush laced across his cheek. 'I know you worked with that girl last year and I know that you're Muslim so...' He shrugged with the slightest lift of a shoulder. 'You'll understand what this means.'

Zara felt a jolt of unease. She had no interest in identity politics – not after Jodie's case – but also bore a sense of duty.

Kamran gathered his hands in his lap. 'I told myself to forget it; it's only been two days and I need time to work things out, but...' He blinked. 'Things like this don't just go away. You have to deal with them. That's true, isn't it?'

'I believe so,' she said. 'Kamran, I can see if they have a Muslim counsellor at Paddington. I'm really sorry but we only work with women here.' She watched the cold drain in his eyes. 'Listen, I'll put you in a cab right now and have you there in no time.'

A knock on the door startled them both. 'Zara, your eleven o'clock is here,' said Monica, an Artemis House administrator.

She nodded her thanks. 'Kamran, let me get you a cab.' She handed him the filled-in form. 'I'll call Lisa at the Paddington SARC. Give her this when you get there. I promise you they'll be discreet.'

He nodded dumbly, then remembered his manners and added, 'Thank you, I appreciate it.'

She hated to do it, but Artemis House was a women's facility. Their entire support structure and funding was based on the fact that this was a safe space for women and trans women. They just didn't have the infrastructure to assist men as well.

She picked up her phone but then set it down again. 'I'll be back in one moment,' she assured Kamran. She strode to Stuart's office and knocked on his open door. 'Hi, just a very quick one,' she said. 'I have a seventeen-year-old boy here reporting a rape. I know what our policy says but I wondered if there was any scope for exceptions. He's Muslim and said he'd like to speak to a Muslim counsellor.'

Stuart grimaced, his cheeks rounding in regret. 'Sorry, Zara, no cigar. Legally, we just can't do it given the terms of our funding.'

She nodded. 'That's what I thought.' She thanked him and headed wearily back to her office.

*

The acrid smell of the pine tree made Kamran feel queasy. He pressed a fist against his nose to try to block it out.

'Paddington, is it?' asked the cab driver.

'Yes, sir,' said Kamran. He had wasted an hour journeying across London to go and see Zara in Whitechapel. Now, they headed west on City Road and he watched mutely as the red-white-blue storefronts of shoebox chicken shops morphed to the racing green of artisanal crêperies. The hum and beat of life outside seemed foreign and unknowable. There was a value, wasn't there, in knowing the pattern of your days; in knowing the pattern your *life*? He had it all mapped out for him: Oxford, an MBA, a high-ranking role at his father's company, marriage, three kids and a manicured lawn. He was about to upend his life for what? An illusory chance at justice?

They hurtled closer to Paddington and as the world outside pressed against the glass, Kamran felt his nerve desert him. He leaned forward, the seatbelt catching on his shoulder. 'Actually, I'm sorry, sir, but can you please take me to Hampton School instead? It's on Hampton Hill.'

The cabbie met his eyes in the mirror, then pecked his chin at his GPS. 'The address here says Paddington.'

'I know. I'm sorry. I can pay you extra.'

He frowned. 'Fine,' he said and reached out and started the meter.

Kamran leaned back in his seat, feeling the forceful lift of relief. He'd been mad to think that reporting the rape was the correct thing to do. Gripped by mania in the small hours of the morning, he was convinced that the only way to exorcise this feeling was to spew it into the world; to cleanse himself through confession. Now, turned away from Artemis House, he willed himself to draw upon sheer brute force. Happiness, after all, was a wilful act. '*Faber est suae quisque fortunae*,' his father liked to say. 'Every man is the architect of his own fortune.' Kamran believed that was true and with enough strength and patience, perhaps he could correct his life back to its original course.

At Hampton, he headed straight to West Lawn, walking briskly to avoid being stopped. As he entered the building, he heard a voice from the housemaster's office.

'Busy morning?'

Kamran looked up and halted. He stared at the shock of blond hair, the easy smile and gleam in his eye. 'Yes,' he replied, a visible heat rising in his cheeks. His gaze dipped to the floor, then back up to Finn.

'Good to hear.' His smile widened lopsidedly. 'I had fun the other night.'

Kamran flinched. '"Fun?"'

Finn laughed ruefully. 'You're right. We *did* get a bit "tired and emotional".'

Kamran hovered there for a beat, reaching for something appropriate. 'I should go,' he managed and headed for the stairs.

Back in his room, Kamran examined past contact with Finn, casting a searchlight over fields of memories to find the one that mattered; the one that sent the false message.

Finn had an easy, roguish charm that manifested as flirtatiousness. Had Kamran reciprocated unwittingly? He thought of their last meeting before he left for the party and held each word to scrutiny: 'tired and emotional', 'have fun', 'see you later'. There was no hint of suggestion.

'I certainly hope so' and that winning grin. Had there been a deeper meaning that Kamran hadn't caught? What *really* happened on the night of the party? Would he ever know?

Erin Quinto slid a sheet of paper across the desk, the spikes of her cuff glinting in the sun. 'I have the boy's home address in Belsize Park, his school address in Hampton and a landline number for his family, but no direct details for him. They don't list them in the school database.'

Zara scanned the piece of paper. 'So there's no way to contact him?'

Erin raked a hand through her short black hair. 'Not via official channels.'

'And unofficial ones?' Zara knew that Erin, freelance investigator at Artemis House, was notoriously resourceful.

'Just a protected Instagram account. You could add him on there, or... I could dig further.'

Zara recognised the code for 'something illegal'. 'No,' she said. 'I'll add him on Instagram but I'll have to check with Stuart first. I'm already on thin ice with this.'

Restive with guilt yesterday, Zara had called the Paddington SARC to check on Kamran's case but Lisa, her contact there, said he hadn't attended. Zara had searched for 'Kamran Hadid' online and found an article on Tatler. com picturing him and his elegant family at a black-tie gala – but still no contact details. She told herself that a boy like Kamran had a support system in place but she knew that wealth and privilege were no fit antidote to corrosive shame.

'HadidMajor is his Instagram handle,' said Erin, adding

a scrawl to the sheet of paper. 'And Hadid M is his name.' She stood. 'Let me know if you need more help.'

'I will. Thank you.' Zara studied the piece of paper, tracing a finger across the creamy texture. She remembered the look in Kamran's eye: the cold drain when he realised she wouldn't help him, the monotone politeness of his quiet goodbye. Haunted by the dire statistics around male mental health, she knew she had to check on him.

She stood and marched to Stuart's office.

He looked up, his unruly blond curls bouncing with the motion. 'Oh no, I recognise that look.'

Zara held up a palm. 'Hear me out.'

'Lawyers,' he said with a rueful smile. 'God, they love to talk.'

'*We*,' she corrected, for Stuart was once a lawyer too. He had left the bar eight years ago to found Artemis House, initially using family money but now reliant on external funding.

'What is it?' he asked good-naturedly.

Zara sat down. 'I mentioned yesterday that a seventeen-year-old boy came in to see me. I put him in a cab to Paddington, but he didn't turn up there. I'd like permission to follow up with him.'

Stuart frowned. 'If he didn't turn up, it means he wasn't ready to talk.'

'But he did turn up,' said Zara. 'He was ready to talk but we turned him away.'

'You put him in a cab to where he needed to go. You couldn't have done more.'

'That's not true, Stuart. I *could* have done more if we weren't throttled by rules.'

33

Stuart sighed. 'The rules are there for a reason.' He pushed back his chair to face her more squarely. 'Zara, you're on the frontline and I know that that's where the work happens, but without all the rules and bureaucracy, there wouldn't even *be* a frontline. We get funding from twenty different women's groups. They would be up in arms if they knew we were misdirecting funds and they would be well within their rights. We can't do it.'

Zara felt a spike of frustration. 'But Stuart—'

'No.'

'Okay, well, what if I did it in my own time?'

He shook his head. 'That's blurring the lines. How do we separate the two? If you receive a desperate email from him at 10 a.m., would you not answer it till six? What happens if we get audited? We can't mix the two.'

Zara scowled. 'He was *ready*, Stuart. He was ready for help and we turned him away. He didn't show up at Paddington so where is he? What's going through his head? What's he going to do? That will be on us – not some unseen bureaucracy but on *you* and *me*.'

Stuart exhaled. He studied her for a moment, then held up his hands in surrender. 'The best I can do is grant you unpaid leave and you work as a truly independent ISVA.'

Zara immediately rose to her feet. 'Thank you, Stuart. I'll confirm my leave as soon as I speak to him.'

'Zara.' He stopped her at the threshold. 'What is it about *this* kid?'

She pressed a hand against the doorframe. 'You know what's strange? I'm so critical of tribalism. I think it's such a base instinct but I see in him the men I grew up with and

I know what something like this would do to them.' Her lips formed a mirthless smile. 'It would erase their sense of self, their honour, their *worth*. I need to show him that these aren't lost.'

Stuart nodded and righted his tie. 'Very well, then,' he said. 'Off you go.'

Zara arrived at Hampton late on Thursday and paused at the gates in her silver Audi to give the guard her name. Kamran hadn't responded to her request on Instagram and she had grown increasingly worried. It had been two days since her meeting with Stuart and though he swore he couldn't involve himself, he had pulled some strings to get her in.

The guard checked his tablet, sliding a pout from one corner of his mouth to the other. 'Ah, there it is.' He opened the gates and waved her through.

Zara drove across the crunchy gravel, a rose-yellow sweep of California Gold. She parked by a stretch of manicured lawn, noting the Bentley and Rolls Royce. From her car, she had a clear view of Hampton House: a colonnaded entrance approached by a grand symmetrical staircase that traversed three levels of terraces.

Inside, she was met by a silver-haired man in rimless glasses – MR LISMORE, his nameplate said.

'May I help you?' he asked with a perfunctory smile.

'Yes. I'm here to see one of your pupils.'

He glanced down at his list. May I take your name, please?'

'Yes, of course. Zara Kaleel.'

'K,' he said, tracing his finger down a printed list. 'K. K. Ah, there you are.' A shadow passed over his face. 'Ah, but

Ms Kaleel, it says you are here to see Kamran Hadid but he's on authorised leave.' He tapped the piece of paper. 'I'm surprised no one thought to inform you.'

Zara frowned. 'Leave? Does that mean he's at home?'

'I expect so. Perhaps if you tell me what business you have, I can call Mr Morewood and—'

'That won't be necessary. You've been very helpful.'

'But—'

'Thank you,' she said, flashing him a smile.

He returned it instinctively. 'You're welcome. Thank you for coming all this way.'

Back in her car, Zara considered her options. She could drive to Artemis House and forget about Kamran, she could wait a few days and revisit Hampton, or she could visit him at home. *And what?* she thought. *Tell a Muslim family she was there to discuss the rape of their son?*

Maybe he was fine, she reasoned. Maybe he had called a helpline and was working through the trauma. She recalled the spike of doubt, however, when she had told him to go elsewhere. Zara grimaced, then keyed his address into her GPS and headed to Belsize Park.

There, she drove along streets of stucco townhouses that rose in storeys of three. Uniform black doors were flanked by fluted pillars, each marked with discreet numbers. She turned into Kamran's street and parked by number sixty-two. She climbed the three stairs to the door, then rang, waited and rang again.

After a moment, a woman opened the door. She was tall and elegant, dressed in a white silk blouse with a pussy bow collar and pale grey trousers that tapered at the ankle. Zara recognised her from *Tatler* as Kamran's mother.

'Ms Hadid, my name is Zara Kaleel. I'm here to talk about your son, Kamran.' It only lasted a second but she saw how the woman looked her over, assessing Zara's neat high bun, slimline trousers and light cream jumper, deciding in an instant that she was one of them.

She opened the door wider. 'I'm sorry. I wasn't expecting anyone. Hampton usually call.'

'I'm sorry to drop in on you like this.' Zara was careful not to lie.

'Please come in.' The woman stepped aside.

Zara walked in, hit by the fresh scent of coffee and bergamot. She followed her host into a large living room, tastefully decorated in fawn and cream, with snatches of brass and verdigris blue.

'Ms Hadid, I—'

'It's Mrs, but please call me Sofia.' She gestured at a sofa. 'And please take a seat. Would you like some tea?'

'No, thank you. I—'

'Coffee? Water? Juice?'

Zara smiled politely. 'No, thank you.' She pointed at a chair. 'Won't you join me?'

Sofia Hadid took a seat. 'I informed the registrar that Kamran hasn't been feeling very well. I know absence is regarded poorly but he really is in a bad way. Just a few days should do it.'

Zara nodded. 'I'm very sorry to hear that.' They exchanged banalities for a minute or two, then Zara began amiably. 'Sofia, I should say that I haven't come from the school to see how Kamran is.' She picked her words carefully, knowing they gave her plausible deniability if she were accused of lying her way in. 'I've come to see him about an incident involving a fellow student.'

Sofia bristled. 'What incident?'

Zara waved a casual hand. 'Just some tomfoolery that happened last week.'

'But how does it involve Kamran?'

'I'm not sure it does. I'm just trying to get a full picture.' She paused, her voice light and casual. 'He probably wouldn't have seen anything, but I'd be remiss not to ask.'

Sofia nodded thoughtfully. 'In that case, I'll see if he's able to join us.'

'I'm happy to pop up and see him,' Zara offered quickly. 'It's important not to strain him if he's feeling unwell.'

Sofia hesitated. 'Oh, he won't be presentable up there. I'll just go and bring him.'

Zara nodded, not wanting to push. 'Thank you.'

She marvelled at the vagaries of this job – and indeed this city. She thought of her last big case and Jodie's cramped quarters at the Wentworth Estate. The acrid smoke, the slushy stairs and the stale smell of urine. This was practically a different world – one of tasteful accent walls and vintage mandolins, early years classics and grand wooden beams. Zara wandered to the mantelpiece, clearly invited to do so by the various awards and trinkets. She looked at photographs of Sofia, ten years younger, with a seven- or eight-year-old Kamran. He brandished an award proudly, his legs draped over his father's shoulder. A younger boy, presumably Kamran's brother, stood glumly by their father's thigh. Next to the photos was a neat line of greeting cards. She glanced behind her, then picked up the first one.

'Dear Kamran. I was very sorry to hear that you're unwell. I hope these flowers will cheer you up,' it read, signed by 'Aunty Rana'. Another, also from Rana, congratulated him on his interview at Oxford.

Zara heard footsteps on the stairs. She set down the card and turned around. Kamran appeared behind his mother, dressed in a grey T-shirt and navy blue jogging bottoms. His hair was dishevelled and dark circles pooled beneath his eyes. He greeted her with a polite smile, but then recognition hit: a lance of fear cut across his face, the press of panic clear in his stance. His gaze darted to Sofia but when he saw no worry or anger there, he fell smoothly into character.

'Hi, Ms Kaleel.'

'Hello, Kamran. I'm sorry to disrupt your morning. I wanted to have a quick chat.'

'Of course.' He sat in the chair furthest from the window, his wan face falling into shadow. He turned to Sofia. 'Mum, my throat's feeling a bit sore. Do you mind making me a honey tea?'

She beamed. 'Of course, my love.' She glanced at Zara. 'Are you sure I can't offer you something?'

Zara nodded as if acquiescing. 'I'll agree to a cup of tea – thank you.'

'Is Earl Grey okay?'

'Yes, wonderful.' She waited for Sofia to leave, then turned to Kamran.

'What are you doing here?' he asked in a savage whisper. He flung an arm at the door. 'I haven't told my mother.'

Zara held a finger to her lips. 'Kamran, the Paddington

39

SARC told me you didn't go there. You need to have a medical exam.'

He sighed, a harsh plosive of frustration. 'I changed my mind, okay?'

'Why?'

'Why should I bother? What's the point?' A frantic note rose in his voice.

'Kamran, you need help.'

'Yes, and that's why I came to you.'

Zara flinched. 'I'm sorry for sending you away. My hands were tied, but I'm here now.'

'Why?'

She blinked. 'Because I want to make sure you're okay.'

'I *am*. Now go!'

'Kamran, will you at least come in for a medical exam?'

'No. Please go!' He glanced at the door, the note of panic notching higher in his voice. 'Please.'

'Will you give me your email address so I can send you some material?'

He shook his head. 'I don't need any material.'

'You can ignore it if you want to but I promise it will help.'

Sofia's footsteps sounded in the hall.

'Please,' pressed Zara.

His eyes flicked to the door and back. Panicked into relenting, he recited it to her in an urgent whisper.

Zara exhaled. 'Thank you.'

Sofia entered the room with a tea tray, an ornate silver confection with delicate leaves adorning each corner. She set it down and took a seat next to Kamran, draping an affectionate arm around his shoulders. 'He'll be back up and running in no time. Won't you, Kamran?' She placed a palm on the nape of his neck. 'Nothing keeps you down for long.'

Kamran nodded brightly. He answered Zara's cursory questions and confirmed that he knew nothing of any incident.

Zara studied him as he spoke. The haunted look had lifted and he now looked bright and hopeful. Here was a family play-acting for each other. What would happen if the pretence failed?

She took a sip of tea and heard the front door open. Footsteps in the hall approached the living room. A man, tall and powerfully built, paused at the threshold. He was in his early fifties and dressed in khaki trousers and a dark green jacket. 'Oh hello,' he said, spotting Zara. His baritone voice came from deep in his throat. 'I'm Mustaque Hadid – Mack.'

Zara stood to greet him, but he interrupted.

'Oh, no please sit. I hope you'll excuse me. I just need to...' He indicated the item in his left hand.

Zara balked, noting the long black barrel of a hunting rifle.

'I like to lock this away as soon as I'm in,' he said, giving her a little bow before trudging down the hall. She heard a door close in the bowels of the house.

'Please excuse Kamran's father,' said Sofia smoothly. 'He goes hunting every Thursday in the Wessex Hills. Gets insufferable if he cannot.'

Zara nodded. 'Of course.'

'The boys go with him sometimes. Adam can't stand it, of course, but I suppose you know that given his stance on

Hampton's fox-hunting.' She laughed. 'Such sensitivity is not becoming in a man.'

Kamran pulled away from her. 'They laugh and have fun, Mum, and don't respect their quarry. You can't blame him for not enjoying it.'

Sofia smiled stiffly. 'We all have to do things we don't enjoy. The sooner Adam understands that, the better.'

Zara returned her smile politely. 'Well, I have what I need.' She drained her tea, though it was still too hot. 'Thank you for your time.' She stood up to leave.

'You're welcome,' said Sofia. 'Of course, if you can warn us next time, I can make sure Kamran is more… presentable.'

'Of course. I do apologise.' She promised Kamran she'd be in touch and followed Sofia to the door where they exchanged a final goodbye.

Outside, Zara glanced up at the house. It was strange; it wasn't envy she felt but pity. How tiring it must be to be perfect.

Inside the house, Kamran sipped his tea and watched his mother clear away the tray.

'They usually call before they send someone,' she said absent-mindedly. 'The house is a state. What must she think of us.'

'The house is fine,' he told her.

'It's not.' She gestured at the rug. 'Magda cancelled yesterday. Her granddaughter's ill again.' She tutted. 'Why don't people take responsibility for their own children?'

Kamran's hands tensed into fists as he listened to her fret. Part of him wanted to tell her out of spite, just to shut her up.

Kamran loved his mother, thought highly of her class and grace, but was exhausted by her pedantry. 'I'm feeling a bit cold so I'm going to head back up,' he said.

'Do you want a hot water bottle?'

'No, Mum, I'm fine. I just want to rest.' He softened his tone to add, 'Thank you.'

He headed up to his room and burrowed in his bed, the expensive sheets cool on his skin. He threw off his duvet, walked to his wardrobe and pulled out a thick fleece blanket. He lined the inside of the duvet with it and curled up underneath. He knew it would make him sweat but maybe that's what he needed: to bleed out all the rage buried beneath the surface.

Why had he given Zara his email address? He'd decided, hadn't he, to move on? How much pain could it possibly cause when he wasn't even sure what had happened? He willed himself to remember but could recall only snatches: inky movements in the dark of night, strong arms that made him feel safe, a careening feeling of loss of control and in the morning, that shock of blond hair in his bed. Finn's strong jaw peaceably asleep, his bare chest rising and falling. Kamran's own body naked beneath the sheets. His head, thick and blurry; his tongue, stale and cottony. The mêlée of emotions: confusion, disgust, revulsion, but beneath it all, a morning erection that didn't die away. He had fled the scene, practically running to the gym where he headed straight to the showers. He'd questioned his basic convictions; thought of Maya on the cruise and her long, dark legs. He knew what he was and what he wasn't, so why had he woken with a boy in his bed?

His thoughts jangled in the spin of his mind as he stood beneath the shower and scrubbed until his skin bloomed red, great patches of colour that spoke of rabid shame. All those times he'd paused at the housemaster's desk; all the smart rejoinders and their witty repartees. Had it all been flirting? The thought of it made him retch with guilt.

CHAPTER THREE

Zara sagged on the mat and swiped a string of hair from her face. It stuck there stubbornly and she pinched it with her nails to peel it away. She watched the pair in the centre: a willowy redhead and Barry, their instructor. He, a heavy-set man with a bullish neck, squeezed an arm around the woman's waist, a vein straining beneath his flesh.

'Hi-yah!' she yelled dramatically and slammed her elbow into his liver, bending forward as she did so to slip from his grip. She whooped, then turned and high-fived him.

Zara glanced at her sister. 'Really?' she mouthed.

Lena pressed the air with a palm, asking her for patience.

Zara rolled her eyes. She knew that this class with its shouty statement of female empowerment was merely a means to make money. The truth was that a ten-week course on self-defence couldn't teach you to protect yourself. She had felt the unbridled power of a man who hadn't pulled his punches, hadn't shown mercy, had held every inch of his strength against hers and she'd known she couldn't fight him.

Lena had enrolled them in the fortnightly class when Zara had recovered. Months later, she remained unmoved.

She – five feet four and slight – could go to all the classes she liked but she could never overpower a man.

Women could fight for equality in boardrooms and courtrooms but at the basest level – in hand-to-hand combat – men would always win. Perhaps this was why so many used soothing words and revealed their skin to manoeuvre the men in their lives.

What would happen, wondered Zara, if appeasement were offered earlier? If society treated men more gently, perhaps they would be gentler. Instead of placing them in the hard, small cage of masculinity, could we allow them to feel more deeply? She remembered Sofia's words: 'Sensitivity is unbecoming in a man.' Hadn't Zara thought the very same thing? Hadn't she dumped Sameer at uni because he was too needy? Because he followed her around like a dog, wouldn't let her go alone to the campus shop to collect painkillers for her period? She remembered the exact moment she decided to leave him: when she tried to adjust her hair and his hand went with hers, not wanting to lose her grip. He had cried when she told him and hadn't that made her feel queasy? Hadn't she wondered why she'd wasted five months of her life on him?

Even now, she felt a shiver of distaste when dining with a nervous date: his hand shaking as he poured the wine, a film of sweat on his forehead, nervous chatter as he perused the menu – and so wasn't she part of the problem too, feeding the fragile egos that had slammed her against that wall?

Barry now had the woman on her knees, standing beside her and gripping her neck. There was a gleam in his eye. He was enjoying this. The redhead struggled and he held her there a moment too long, before letting her unseat him. This was a charade. Put them both in a deserted alley and there was no way she would fight him off.

Kamran stared at the name on screen: Zara Kaleel. The message had arrived last night and he'd sent it straight to the bin, but found himself returning to it. He thought of her in the news last year, so quick and confident. He had confided in her because he knew she would understand. She – like him – couldn't just be who she wanted. She had to answer to her community. It's true he was cocooned from the sharpest edge of it, but he still felt its pinpricks poised on his skin. He had to be discreet and despite turning up at his home, Zara understood this. With the dredge of distress in his stomach, he held his breath and opened the message.

> Kamran, here are some resources that might help you through what you're experiencing. I've made an appointment for you to have a medical exam tomorrow and to meet with me and a SOIT (Sexual Offences Investigation Trained) police officer on Monday 11th May. She is excellent and I trust her. We can take your report and decide what to do after. I hope you will come. We'll be waiting.

Beneath it lay two sets of dates, times and locations – each on a neat new line. He checked his watch. He had already missed the medical exam but Monday was in two days and he could still meet the police officer. He would be back at Hampton but could claim a trip to the family doctor.

Kamran caught himself, startled by his readiness to

47

formulate a plan. It shook him, for it exposed what he wanted at heart: a chance to tell someone what had happened to him. But what would it cost him and the people he loved? Would he upend their lives for nothing? Kamran reread the words on screen, then reached out with a trembling hand and archived the message.

Downstairs, Sofia sat at the breakfast bar, her head cocked at the ceiling as she tried to glean if Kamran was at least watching TV. Met with silence, she attempted to busy herself on her laptop. She navigated to her email and reread the reply from Jonathan Walmsley. She understood the message couched in his genteel words: your ideas are useless. She slumped and closed her laptop, but then immediately straightened at the sound of footsteps.

Her husband walked in, his gait unmistakeable. He had a natural confidence which had no doubt played a vital part in growing his family's company: an international purveyor of medical supplies. Behind the boorish exterior, he was a deeply astute businessman, knowing just when to use an expletive to put someone at ease or rein in his humour when faced with someone prim.

'Morning, hon.' He gave her a kiss on the cheek and though he was clean-shaven, he still felt rough on her skin.

'You're not in the office today?' she asked, noting his casual outfit: a pale yellow polo shirt paired with khaki trousers.

He picked up one of the croissants that Sofia had arranged on the breakfast bar and took a wide bite, sending flakes of pastry sweeping across the granite. Absently, he brushed them off the counter. Sofia tensed as she watched the flakes dust the spotless floor.

'No. I told you, hon. I'm meeting Al about the Medicare deal.'

'Oh.' He hadn't told her. 'Is there anything to worry about?'

Mack drained the coffee pot into a mug and took a hearty swig. 'Of course not.' He shrugged his broad shoulders. At fifty-six, he maintained a strong physique and towered over her at six feet three. 'It's under control.'

She sensed he was ready to leave and spoke her next words quickly. 'Do you think I should call the doctor about Kamran? He's not looking very well and I'm worried about him.'

Mack rolled his eyes good-naturedly. 'He'll be fine, hon. Stop mothering him.'

She bristled. 'I hate it when you say that.'

'I know you do.' He brushed her chin with a finger. 'But I love it when you sulk.' He leaned in and kissed her lips, leaving behind the bitter blast of coffee. 'I've got to go.' He picked up a second croissant. 'But I'll be home for dinner.'

Sofia watched him leave and then put on a fresh pot of coffee. As she poured herself a cup, she remembered their first date all those years ago; how she was dismayed by his aggressive manner in dealing with the waiter. He had crooked his finger at him and asked for the menu as soon as they'd sat down.

When the couple at the next table spent many minutes laughing and joking with the same man, Sofia had felt strangely inferior. The waiter was good at his job and changed his demeanour for Mack: attentive, dignified, restrained, not presuming to make recommendations like he did with the couple next door. Sofia had smiled tightly and ordered the gnocchi with truffles, the least messy dish on the menu. She didn't want slippery linguini messing up her lipstick or, horrifyingly, the white crepe-overlay of her tasteful gown.

Luckily, things improved over the course of the meal. Mack was a natural storyteller and regaled her with tales of his childhood, his ever-complaining mother and taciturn father, mimicking them with comic skill. She couldn't help but laugh at the pin-perfect impression of archetypal Asian aunties.

Sofia knew that laughing made her nose look wide and she placed her hand above it, shielding it from view. That night, Mack had kissed her so hotly and every inch of her sang for his skin but she was well aware of men like him: bold, presumptuous, bored by easy conquests, and so she had leaned away from him, heart strobing in her chest. Over the next four dates, she teased him, each time offering a little bit more. God, she'd been beautiful at twenty-six. Now, twenty years later, age was unavoidable. She looked after herself assiduously and, with her clothes on, could pass for ten years younger. When naked in the mirror, however, the dimpled skin across her stomach and doughy band around her hips gave away the truth.

She and Mack had settled into a charade of sorts. When she bent over to pick something up, he'd make a growling sound, might even grab her with feigned lust, pretending he still wanted her. When he caught her topless in their bedroom mirror, he'd raise his brows lasciviously and she'd bat him away playfully, both knowing that neither had the energy or desire to take things any further.

He had been so amorous when they were younger and for many years into their marriage. Did sex drive switch off like a bulb or was it now aimed at someone younger? She often suspected that he had a mistress: a twenty-something waitress or pretty receptionist and wondered if she really cared. She loved Mack, genuinely, but in maturity had come to accept that sex was merely sex. If Mack finding satisfaction elsewhere meant that her family stayed intact, then so be it. Her priority was her children and making sure they were happy and safe. As long as that was true, everything else would be okay.

Zara entered Bow Road Police Station and made her way to an interview room. She knocked and entered, hit by the smell of stale fast food. Mia Scavo stood and shook her hand. The officer wore formless clothes in black and grey and her light blonde hair in a trademark bun: severe and scraped back with not a loose strand.

'Thanks for this,' said Zara.

'Not at all.' Mia gestured towards a chair. 'I take it you're ready for another big case?'

Zara gave her a rueful look. '"Ready" might be an over-statement.'

Mia tapped her pen against her notebook. 'Have you heard from Jodie at all?'

'No, but I did hear she's starting college in September.'

'That's good.'

They fell silent for a moment. They had last worked

together on Jodie Wolfe's case and remembered its multiple blows: first, Jodie's admission that she had lied, then the realisation that she had not, followed by the final strike: Amir, the ringleader, set free and the others handed nominal sentences. In a few short months, they too would be free. Given the conviction rates for rape, this one was a win but the wounds from the case still smarted.

'It was worth the fight,' said Mia, knowing what Zara was thinking.

'I know,' she replied quietly. 'We take what we can get.'

A knock on the door cut in and Zara looked up to find Kamran at the threshold. She stood and guided him in. 'I'm glad you came,' she said, feeling a wash of relief. A part of her had thought that he wouldn't turn up at all and though that would absolve her, she would always harbour some guilt.

Kamran took a seat. 'I… I missed the medical exam last week.'

'I know,' said Zara. 'That's okay.'

'But I called them this morning and they let me go in, so… that's done.'

'On your own?'

He lifted a shoulder. 'They had someone there to help.'

Zara felt a swell of sympathy. 'Okay, thank you. I'll coordinate with them.' She introduced him to Mia and explained that she, a SOIT officer, would take his statement now.

Kamran nodded, a long muscle twitching in his jaw.

Mia eased into the interview, first asking about his school, friends and hobbies, before broaching the assault.

'It was the start of our spring exeat,' said Kamran. 'I was supposed to spend the weekend at a friend's but it was

cancelled at the last minute, so I went to a party instead.'
He grimaced. 'Hampton is strict during term time but they
loosen the reins before breaks.'

'Were you drinking?' asked Mia.

Kamran nodded. 'Yes.'

'Do you know how much?'

His shoulders stiffened with guilt. 'I started with a few
beers – three maybe – but then there was other stuff. It's
a tradition at Hampton that you swipe something from your
parents so there was all sorts there: whisky, cognac, port.
Someone even brought some sherry.'

'After three beers, how many other drinks do you think
you had?'

Kamran's gaze dropped to his lap. For a moment, he
studied the arc of his nails. 'Another four or five maybe. I'm
not certain.'

Zara watched from the sidelines, knowing this would be
used for leverage if it proceeded to court.

Kamran continued. 'Initially, I tried not to drink too
much. My brother, Adam, was there and Mum always tells
me to set an example because he'll follow my lead. I don't
think she understands that he's his own person.'

'Did you talk to him?' asked Mia.

'Briefly. At the start of the evening. I told him not to drink
too much.' Kamran's face twisted in a grimace. 'Do as I say,
not as I do.'

Mia made a note. 'Okay, Kamran, can you walk me
through the evening in as much detail as possible?

He nodded. The party had been loud, he remembered. The
boys were in a boisterous mood, which is why he was amused

by the neat row of bin bags propped against a tree. Even in the throes of abandon, the boys couldn't escape the stamp of their school. Hamptonians were meant to be fine young gentlemen: phlegmatic, restrained and respectful. Littering wasn't a part of that ethos. He remembered the loud game of beer pong and Adam looking characteristically solemn. He hadn't seen Finn at the party; he would have been at West Lawn, swilling drinks with friends of his own.

Kamran added detail where possible: clouds sulking at the edge of the sky, the hundred mites in amber light. The way you could, at this extreme end of the campus, hear the faint thrum of traffic; a reminder that there was a wild and boundless world right outside these walls.

At Mia's request, he recalled what he, Jimmy, Barrett and Nathan had talked about that night. There was nothing unusual: pressure about their grades, how Nathan's parents were likely getting divorced but were going to Vahine Island anyway for a last-gasp attempt at saving their marriage – the first-world problems of first-world people. Things like rape weren't supposed to happen to boys like him. This wasn't a part of his upward trajectory.

Kamran led Mia through the excesses of the evening to that moment in any party where people start to depart and no one knows if the mood will turn intimate or desolate; whether you will have a deep conversation with someone fun or end up in a bathroom crying. He, in a stupor of drink, chose not to take the risk. He headed home: westwards to West Lawn.

Had he seen anyone along the way? He pictured the expanse of grass. There were figures shifting in the dark but nothing of note or threat. He had continued along the path, lamplight splashing in pools on the concrete. His brogues were soundless on the ground and he remembered thinking that Hampton was made for silence. Silence in the libraries, silence in the halls, silence even in lessons when the only sign of life would be magpies crowing outside.

At West Lawn, he had tapped in his personal key code: 21 007, a fact that pleased him greatly.

'Hadid,' he would say to his friends in the early days. 'Kamran Hadid,' pretending to unholster a gun.

Jimmy would laugh. 'A brown Bond? That'll be the day.'

That night, he entered to silence. He glanced at the housemaster's office and crept up the stairs to his room. He fumbled with his key, his fingers limp and clammy. Eventually, he slotted it home and turned it with a creak.

He shut the door with his left leg, the ball of his foot tapping the wood and closing it too loudly. Their doors didn't lock automatically. Had he locked his? He remembered the clang of the metal key: a £50 fine if he lost it. He tossed it on the dresser and it fell to the floor in a jangle. He emptied his pockets and pulled his shirt off over his head. He brushed his teeth and splashed his face with water. What after that? His head vibrating and blooms of bursting black. Were they in his eyes or in his head – he couldn't tell. What happened after that?

Kamran slackened in his chair. 'I can't remember.'

Mia circled some text in her notebook. 'You said you don't think you locked your door? How certain are you about this?'

'I'm not certain. I just don't remember doing it.'

'Did you close the door?'

'Yes. I remember it being too loud.'

Mia made a note. 'Okay, you said you remember taking off your shirt. Did you take off your trousers?'

Kamran considered this. 'Yes. I think I just wore my boxers to bed.'

'Are you sure?'

He hesitated. 'I'm not certain but I think I did.'

Zara watched, knowing that the sequence of events had to be exact. Mia had to scour the surface until every last detail held up to scrutiny. A full picture now would prevent the possibility of a harmful surprise.

'What happened next?'

Kamran winced. 'I can't remember. I'd drunk so much, my head was turning black.'

Zara stiffened. She knew that jurors would hear this, some of whom would blame the drink. Reasonable men and women understood that consent should be proactive and explicit, and would agree as much in the clear wash of day, but behind closed doors, they held darker thoughts; that if you got so drunk you couldn't move, maybe, just *maybe*, you were asking for it.

Mia pressed Kamran on, pushing him through the murk to his next clear memory.

'There was someone else in the bed,' he said. 'I remember them pressing into me.' He bit his lower lip, working loose a piece of dry skin.

'Kamran, I need you to tell me exactly what you remember. It's okay if there are gaps, but tell me what you do know.'

He dug a thumbnail into the chipboard edge of the table. 'I remember feeling vaguely awake as if I were in a dream.

I remember a body behind me and...' His shoulders rose and
fell with the effort of finding words. 'I felt fingers hooking
into the elastic band of my boxers. He... he had a hand on
my thigh and I remember it was warm.' Kamran paused.
'I can't say exactly what happened but I know he reached
forward and touched me.'

'Where?'

'My penis.' His voice took on a powerless tilt.

'What happened after this?'

Kamran flushed with colour. 'I... I grew hard.' His eyes
flicked to Zara. 'But I read that this was normal.'

Mia nodded but made no comment. 'What happened next?'

Kamran faltered. 'He—'

Zara watched him try to find the right word. Entered me?
Violated me? Raped me?

'It's all jumbled up in my head.'

Mia waited.

'He tried to push inside me but it was like he wasn't really
trying.'

'What do you mean?'

'I don't know. I think he tried once or twice and then we
fell asleep.'

Mia made a note. 'Did he penetrate you?'

Kamran nodded. 'Yes, but only a little bit.'

'Did you feel any pain?'

'Yes, but it's all hazy in my head.'

'And did he ejaculate?'

'Yes. He—' Kamran grimaced. 'When he couldn't do
what he wanted, he sort of rubbed himself on me and then
I think he came.'

'Did you?'

Kamran drew back in his seat. 'No.'

'What happened next?'

'I fell asleep.'

'What's the next thing you remember?'

Kamran recalled his waking moments. Victims often spoke of 'before' and 'after', two epochs divided by trauma. Had he known that morning that something was wrong? He had turned in his bed and there it was: a shock of blond hair, the bulk of a stranger's body and the sharp jab of horror. He'd bargained with himself: maybe Finn had entered the wrong room and fallen in his bed in a drunken stupor. Maybe nothing had happened at all. Maybe he'd undressed in the dark and hadn't realised there was someone in the room.

He had stared at Finn in the crisp light of morning and felt the press of nausea. Something *had* happened, he knew. Finn stirred by his side and that's when Kamran froze, unsure what to do. He dressed and fled before Finn could wake, heading to the gym and straight to the shower.

Had he wanted it? He'd got hard, hadn't he? Kamran stayed under the hot shower until he heard the voices of the polo team. He wrapped himself up quickly and locked himself inside a cubicle, his breath coming much too fast. Something had happened and Kamran hadn't asked for it.

'By the time I returned, he was gone.'

'Did you tell anyone about it?' asked Mia.

'No.'

'Have you spoken to Finn about it?'

'No.'

'What happened after that?'

'I picked up my brother. We met our driver and went home.'

Mia closed her notebook. 'Thank you, Kamran. You've done a very brave thing coming to report this.' She explained that the police would now start to gather evidence.

Kamran worried the cuff of his sleeve. 'Can I choose not to bring a formal complaint?'

'Yes.'

'What happens then?'

Mia set down her pen. 'We store the evidence we have in case you change your mind.'

'Nothing happens to Finn?'

'No.'

Kamran digested this. 'Can I think about it?' He looked at Zara, a hesitant wilt in his gaze. '"Rapist" is such an ugly word and I... I just need to think about what I'm saying.'

'Of course.' Mia asked him to take a few days.

They finished and Zara beckoned him up. 'Come on, I'll drive you back.' Outside, she cast him a sidelong glance as they walked to her car. 'Have you told your mum?'

'She wouldn't understand.'

'I think you'd be surprised.'

He frowned. 'My mum, she... she shields us from the world. I'm seventeen and I've never used the London Underground alone.' He got in the car and clicked in his seatbelt. 'I once told Jimmy that I wasn't sure we'd cope in the real world and do you know what he said? "The whole point of Hampton is that we never have to deal with real people in the real world." I realised he was right.' Kamran's lips twisted bitterly. 'That same week, my mum read a statistic that fourteen million people in the UK were living in poverty and you know what she did? She laughed. "That's not true, is it?" she said. "Look around. It's clearly not true!"' Kamran shook his head. 'A woman like my mum should never have to learn that something like this happened to her son.'

Zara felt a swell of sorrow. 'She will understand, Kamran. You don't have to feel embarrassed.'

He exhaled softly and turned away from her – a gentle closing of the conversation – and remained that way for the rest of the drive.

Zara dropped him off at Hampton and as she said goodbye, she felt her conscience needle. 'You don't have to be *embarrassed*,' she had said. Why was it that she seldom used that word with women but reached for it first with Kamran as if it should be the foremost emotion in a man who'd been raped?

She watched him in the early evening light, a brittleness in his shoulders, a cold varnish in his eyes. 'Kamran, don't lose yourself in this, okay?'

He regarded her blankly. 'I won't,' he said and she could tell from the dart of his eyes that he was aching to take his leave.

'I'll see you soon,' she said. She watched him walk across the green until his silhouette vanished in a dip.

Zara checked her watch, then headed back to East London, speeding along the A501 to beat rush-hour traffic. She drove to her mother's house, perched on a side street in Bow. Zara's childhood home was a squat two-storey building with a small, neatly kept front garden. She unlatched the black cast-iron gate and made sure she shut it again. Her mother preferred it that way, the gate's low whine announcing visitors a few beats before the doorbell.

Sure enough, Fatima peeked through the downstairs window, pulling aside a bright white curtain. A moment later, she opened the door.

'*Assalamu Alaikum*,' said Zara, kissing her mother's cheek.

'*Walaikum assalam*,' she replied.

It was strange, this merciless passage of time. Last year, she had vowed to be kinder to her mother, but it was easier thought than done. It was true that she was more patient now and a little less defensive, but still they lacked the easy facility of mother-daughter relationships. Zara knew that this was partly due to the choices she had made. In refusing to stay in her arranged marriage and quitting her job in chambers, Zara had flouted her mother's wishes and they had never quite recovered.

'Go and sit,' said Fatima, gesturing towards the living room. 'I'm going to read *Asr*, but your sisters are here.' She headed upstairs for prayer.

Zara greeted Lena and Salma. 'Is Rafiq here?' she asked.

'Not today,' replied Lena.

Zara visibly relaxed. She knew her brother disapproved of her life – an unmarried Asian girl living alone – and though they were making amends, their truce had proved uneasy.

Lena handed her a cup of tea. 'Are you still on for our class next week?'

'If we must,' said Zara.

Salma, the eldest, cut in. 'Is this the self-defence class?'

'Yeah,' said Zara. 'But I still think it's a waste of time.'

Salma watched her. 'Let's hope you'll never find out.'

The three of them fell silent. Zara's gaze dipped low as she blinked away the memory: her scream snuffed by the force of a palm, her body jolting upwards, her sisters in a funereal huddle outside her hospital room.

Salma pushed forward a plate of biscuits to break the spell of her words. 'So what are you working on now?' she asked.

Zara took a moment to find an answer, still caught in the memory. 'It's, uh, it's a tricky one,' she said, folding away the image.

'Oh?' Salma had an analytical mind and always took an interest in her work.

Zara cupped her hands around her tea. 'I can't say too much,' she started, 'but I was in the office last Monday when a client – well spoken, polite, clearly from a rich family – came in to report an assault.'

'Okay.' Salma waited, the case seemingly lacking the requisite drama.

'He said he was raped by someone he knows.'

Salma paused mid-sip. '"He"?' She winced. 'Please don't say it was a child.'

'No – well...' Zara hesitated, wary of revealing too much. 'He's seventeen.'

'Who did it? A teacher?'

'No. A pupil,' she conceded.

Salma frowned. 'A pupil? Then why didn't he fight back?'

Lena interjected. 'Would you ask the same question if it was a woman?' She was the most sensitive of the three sisters: *Little Women*'s Beth to Salma's Meg and Zara's Jo.

Salma huffed. 'No, I wouldn't, but a man's clearly more able to defend himself.'

Lena's lips tightened to a line. 'If you say so,' she said obliquely.

Salma rolled her eyes and turned back to Zara. 'What do you know about the other guy?'

'The rapist?'

Salma made a peculiar expression, her brow arched in doubt. 'Yeah, "the rapist", I suppose.'

Zara's head tipped to one side. 'What do you mean "I suppose"?'

'Well, it doesn't sound like there was any force.'

'And neither was there consent.'

Salma raised a palm. 'No, I know that. Obviously it is "rape" technically, but it's not a violent, terrifying one. I don't think you can compare it to what women go through.'

'What about women who get date raped?'

'Well, that's different,' Salma insisted. 'Women are physically weaker. I just don't think it's the same with a man against a man.'

Zara digested this. The shame of male rape was caused exactly by statements like this. The stigma of weakness was thick and cowing. 'I don't think that's right,' she said, 'but to answer your question: I don't know very much about him yet.'

'Is he gay?'

'I can't say for sure.'

Salma shook her head with wonder. 'God, it must be hard. I'm glad we don't have to deal with that.'

'What do you mean?'

'Well, there's no such a thing as a gay Muslim, is there?'

Zara blinked. 'I don't think—'

'I mean, I know they're out there,' Salma interrupted.

'But what I don't get is why people like that cling to religion. I don't have anything against gays obviously, but if you *are* gay, how can you still be Catholic or Muslim?'

Zara studied her sister. There was no malice in her tone, just a curious ignorance. 'It's more complicated than that.'

'I don't think it is,' said Salma. 'You're either this or that. You can't be both.'

Zara tried to decide if it was worth fighting this battle, for she knew she wearied her sisters. They were gentle in their joshing – 'Zara the Brave comes to the rescue!', 'Zara the Brave will conquer you!' – but there was some truth behind the humour. Her refusal to let things lie or concede an inch of ground often made their debates exhausting.

Zara took a sip of her tea, then met Salma's gaze. 'Okay, what if one of your boys – let's say Yakub – turns sixteen in a few years and tells you that he's gay. How would you react?'

'Well, I mean…' Salma flexed her shoulders as if gearing for a fight. 'I would accept it.'

'So there would be no angry arguments, no tears, no tantrums?'

Salma hesitated. 'Well, there would be tears but only because I'd be scared for him. Life is hard enough and this would only make it harder.'

Zara nodded. 'Okay, but there would be no cataclysmic event? No kicking him out of the house? No disownment? No sending him to Bangladesh?'

Salma flinched. 'Of course not. What do you take me for?'

'Okay, so he would still live in your house, cook with you, go to school, take out the bins as normal?'

'Yes.'

'And he'd do what his brothers would do? Play football? Go to the cinema? Spend too much time online?'

Salma's lips curled in a half smile. 'Yes.'

'Would he still celebrate Eid with you?'

She shrugged. 'Yes, of course.'

'Would he still go to Friday prayer with his brothers?'

'Yes.' There was a tiny catch in her voice.

'Would he go to *janazahs* at mosque?'

'Yes.'

'Would he still give *zakat*?'

'Yes.' Now, her voice was small.

'You would want him to be a part of that?'

Salma was silent. Her features blanched with sorrow. 'Yes, I would.'

'Would you deny him any of that or expect him to remain at home?'

Her eyes grew glassy. 'No.'

'Okay,' said Zara gently. 'I guess *that's* how you can be gay and Muslim.'

Salma swiped discreetly at her eyes. 'God, I can tell you were a lawyer.' She laughed but it was a blare of a sound, designed to mask something deeper. She picked up her cup of tea and hugged it to her chest.

Zara gently pushed the plate of biscuits back towards her sister.

Kamran pulled the blanket tighter and bunched the folds around his neck. There was something unremittingly cruel about having to be in this room. This, his supposed sanctuary, was also the scene of the crime and though he had washed his sheets three times, they still felt befouled.

He tried to give shape to the weight of his trauma. He thought of it as a thick bar of fluorescent light that hummed from throat to groin. Real healing would dim that light, snuff out sections until it grew dark – but how could he heal if he couldn't remember? Instead, he would push down the pain until it was a sun-bright penny lodged in his gut. That's where he'd let it burn.

A thought slithered into his mind, making his stomach clench. Perhaps the only way to understand what had happened was to talk to Finn. Together, they would talk and together they'd forget. After all, it was one drunken night. Isn't this what happened at boys' schools? Experimentation? Liberation? Wasn't this just another experience?

Kamran traced his hands along the underside of the blanket: soft white fleece that sometimes came off on his clothes. He pushed his fingers into it, marshalling his strength. He took a bracing breath and tossed the blanket off him, the sweep of his arm feigning courage. He walked across the room, a stony chill on the soles of his feet, and pulled on his shoes and blazer. He glanced at the wall clock. It was 4.30 p.m. on a Thursday afternoon. Finn would be manning the housemaster's office for at least another half hour.

He picked up his knobby metal key and walked into the hall. He felt a vinegar sting in his throat and swallowed once, then twice, to clear it. He descended three flights to the housemaster's office and knocked on the open door.

'Come in,' called Finn before looking up.

Kamran stepped inside, his loafers clicking flatly on the polished wooden floor.

Finn smiled. 'Hadid Major. How may I help you today?'

Kamran closed the door behind him. 'May I sit?'

Finn gestured generously. 'Of course.' As assistant to the housemaster, he was used to pupils asking for his time.

Kamran sat in a chair, a large Chesterfield of squeaky burgundy leather. He traced the padded armrest, his fingers dipping in the seams between.

'Problems?' asked Finn.

'I... I've come to talk about Friday.'

'Oh?' Finn checked his desk calendar. 'Friday the eighth?'

Kamran tensed. 'Friday the first. I want to talk about what happened.'

Finn smiled accommodatingly. 'Okay.'

Kamran waited. 'I want you to tell me what happened.'

Finn frowned. 'With what?'

'With us.'

His chin tilted at an angle. 'With us?'

Kamran felt a flare of anger. 'Stop playing the idiot. Look, I don't want this to go any further. I just want to understand what happened.'

Finn sat back in his chair, his lips poised in a patient smile. 'Kamran, do you want to tell me what you're talking about?'

'Friday night!' His voice was high and bitter. 'You were in my fucking room!'

Finn tensed, his features strained with alarm. 'Look, before you say anything else, I want to tell you that I—'

'You what? That you're a faggot!?'

Finn blanched. 'Don't use that ugly word.'

Kamran felt his conscience spark but it was snuffed out by anger.

'What happened?' asked Finn. 'Did someone spot us or—'

'How could you do it?' spat Kamran.

Finn held up a defensive hand. 'Look, it takes two to do what we did.'

Kamran jabbed a finger at him. 'Don't you say that. Don't you *dare* fucking say that.'

'I... what do you want me to say?'

'Tell me what happened. Tell me *exactly* what happened.'

Finn grimaced. 'You know what happened.'

'No, I fucking don't!' He clenched his fingers around the arm of his chair. 'I want you to tell me.'

Finn exhaled quietly. 'Okay, well, firstly, we were both drunk. You know I went to the spring fundraiser.'

'How much did you drink?'

'Too much.'

'How much?'

Finn hesitated. 'About seven drinks.'

'What do you remember?'

'I don't. Not really. I was coming back from the party. It was about two. I went to your room and—' He shrugged. 'Well, I don't need to spell it out.'

Kamran stared at him. How could he be so casual about it? 'Are you gay?' he asked.

Finn made a small sibilant sound. 'Well, yeah. What do *you* think?'

'You disgust me.'

He flinched. 'Don't say that.'

Kamran felt a spike of emotion: a profound urge to hurt him.

Finn scooted his chair forward. 'Listen, I'm sorry.' He laid a hand on Kamran's wrist. 'I know what your family would say and you might not want to admit it, but you *know* it was consensual.'

Kamran shook off his hand. 'Don't fucking touch me.' He jolted up from his chair, his armpits sliding with sweat. 'Don't you *ever* touch me again.' His skin burned with a white-hot hate. 'Stay the fuck away from me.' Kamran fled from the office.

What had he expected? That Finn would break down and cry? That he would deny everything? His insistence that Kamran consented was a violation of a different type: of not knowing his own mind.

But wasn't it true in a way? Hadn't he been so drunk that night that he hadn't even locked his door? And hadn't he reacted in the past to Finn's overtures? A hot embrace on the rugby field, a reciprocal smile to his charming grin?

Is this what women go through? he wondered. A painstaking examination of each innocent action; holding cloth to light to find a sullied patch. Had Finn targeted him specifically or had he walked down the hall, twisting every handle? Was there a chance that Finn had really been drunk and not known what he was doing? Had he simply fallen into a bed only to find a warm body waiting?

Kamran put himself in Finn's shoes; pictured himself stumbling into a room, falling into a bed, finding a sleeping woman there with soft limbs and warm breath. Would he be tempted too? Would it feel like an act of violence or just like coming home? If he found Maya in his bed, wouldn't he too take off her clothes? Was he a potential rapist too?

Rape. The word was so harsh, so emotive. It almost did a disservice to the victim. It made the crime sound *so* heinous, the stench of it *so* strong, that one loathed to impose it on bright-eyed men, especially ones who looked like Finn.

But Finn *was* a rapist and what happened *was* an act of violence. It was true that Kamran did not fight, but neither did he consent. Finn had walked into his room uninvited and put himself inside his body, turning Kamran into a rape victim. The label was a noose round his neck, making his throat clot with muscle.

It takes two to do what we did.

How dare Finn say those words? How dare he cast Kamran as a co-conspirator? Had he done this before? Was he relying on the fact that his victims would stay silent, cowed by the spectre of shame?

Kamran felt the tang of metal in his mouth, the acid flavour of fear. He realised that he had to do it. He *had* to seek justice. There was no easy route from this. He picked up his phone and drafted a message to Zara. Gripping it in his fist, he left the room and headed to the green. He walked away from West Lawn until the signal grew stronger. He watched the bars grow one by one and then, with the beat of his heart going too fast, he took a deep breath and pressed send. The message contained four words that were sure to upend his life. *Help me stop Finn.*

Zara leaned forward so that the lamp suspended on a stem above her head didn't shine directly on her. The restaurant was a blocky, overlit affair with art-deco prints in black, white and green. Idly, she leafed through the menu. Safran had texted her to say he'd be late. It was the lawyer's burden, she knew. They were punctual in matters of work but often at the expense of friends. She remembered her time in chambers and how friends would lay bets on how late she would be. It was sad that she rarely saw them anymore, their time squeezed by careers and kids. In fact, Safran was the only friend she saw with any frequency.

As she waited, her hands went restlessly from her lap to her glass to her knife. She straightened her napkin so that it sat flush against the menu, inching the fork just so. Since she'd stopped taking Diazepam, she noticed herself doing this more. She had always liked neatness and order, but never before would she set her alarm five or six times in a ritual, nor would she reread an email three times before sending it off. Sometimes, she found herself reading a line over and over, especially when it came to lists. She would tell herself to stop being ridiculous and yet she'd repeat the phrase, telling herself 'one last time, one last time'. At first, she thought it was simply withdrawal but after five weeks it still hadn't passed. At least it followed a sequence, she reasoned. Though the act itself was irrational, the neat rituals were entirely predictable and so she didn't seek advice. It was, after all, just a state of mind.

She glanced at her watch and ordered a lime and soda, but instead of taking a sip, she spun the glass in her palms and morosely watched the crowd: media types and city bankers. Finally, she spotted Safran who cut his way across the room and met her with a hug.

'Sorry, sorry,' he said, stripping off his coat and tossing it on the back of his chair. 'There was an emergency.'

She raised a hand. 'I get it.'

He smiled, his left dimple dipping in his cheek. 'Thank you.' He nodded at a waiter who hurried over to take their order. Safran had a way about him, an easy manner that made others keen to please him.

He loosened his tie and slung it over his coat. 'So guess what?' he said.

'What?' Zara smiled instinctively.

'I'm going on a date with a doctor tomorrow.'

'Really?' She feigned confusion. 'When did Leonardo DiCaprio date a doctor?'

Safran grinned and conceded the jibe. In chambers, they'd had a running joke that Safran's exes were DBD: Dumped By DiCaprio. Like the actor's, Safran's girlfriends were usually tall, slim and blonde. 'Well, this may surprise you,' he said, 'but actually she's Pakistani.'

'No!' Zara's jaw dropped in mock surprise.

He gave her a sheepish look. 'Okay, don't laugh, but I saw her at a wedding and made the mistake of telling my brother that I thought she was pretty. He told his wife who told her mum who told an auntie and suddenly, the girl's being proffered like a slice of lamb.'

'Well, it's your own fault for being such an eligible barrister.'

He laughed. 'Maybe I'll like her.'

'Maybe you will.' She felt a shimmer of discomfort at the prospect of Safran meeting someone serious. What would follow? Marriage? Kids? The natural wastage of another friendship? There was nothing romantic between them but she relied on him more than she liked to admit. He was a source of logic and calm; the person she'd call if in trouble. She thought of all the friends she had lost. One by one, they were pulled away by life, work and parenthood and then there was just her, no one to call for an impromptu coffee. Safran was the only one.

'Hey,' he said, coaxing her back. 'You okay?'

'Yeah.' She swallowed. 'I'd be really happy for you, Saf.'

'Let's not get ahead of ourselves. Marrying an Asian doctor is such a cliché.'

'And being an Asian lawyer isn't?'

He laughed. 'I'll give you that.'

They ordered food – grilled steak for him and a sea bream fillet for her – and ate with the unselfconscious gusto of old friends, sharing memories and anecdotes from their time in court.

After the meal, they took a stroll in the mild May air, drifting naturally towards the river. The Thames was steely in the fading light and birds wheeled in the sky above. HMS *Belfast* stood like a shield as they descended the steps to the riverbank. The air was smoky and the chatter from the nearby restaurants added a comforting hum.

'How's the family?' asked Safran.

'Oh, you know,' she said.

'No, I don't.'

She smiled faintly. 'They're fine. I saw them earlier this week.'

'Was it okay?'

'Yeah, but I got into a bit of a thing with Salma.'

'Oh?'

'Yeah. It's so fucking weird being Muslim.'

He stopped and turned to look at her. 'What do you mean?'

'I wish people came with a barometer, so you could tell by looking at them how conservative they are. Will they judge you for drinking? Or wearing jeans? Or showing a bit of wrist? Where do their lines of liberalism lie? Do they have sex outside marriage? Or do they expect you to be in niqab? Like, how comfortable can I be with you? How much of myself can I show to you?'

Safran studied her. 'Where's this coming from?'

Zara gestured eastwards vaguely towards her mother's home. 'Salma. She was saying you can't be both gay and Muslim and I was surprised by that.'

'Why? That's not such a radical thing to say.'

She glanced up at him. 'You don't think?'

'No.' He leaned his elbows on the cast-iron gate. 'I'm going to sound cynical but the world is built of cliques. I'm not saying that's right but it's true. Some cliques are relatively small – like Old Etonians – and some cliques are huge – like Muslims – and in this drive for inclusion, we want to say that anyone is welcome anywhere and anyone can become anything but that's not true. If you didn't go to Eton, you can't be an Old Etonian. If you're gay, then it's hard to also be a Muslim.'

Zara arched a brow. 'See, this is what I mean about a barometer. I thought you were more liberal than that.'

He shook his head. 'It's not about conservative versus liberal or tolerance versus intolerance. It's just logic.'

74

'So if someone told you they were a gay Muslim, you'd think they were wrong to call themselves that?'

He shrugged. 'They can call themselves what they like. I don't have an issue. I just think we need to stop trying to bend things to our will when they clearly don't fit.'

Zara was surprised. Safran often played the contrarian but usually from a place of empathy.

He saw the look on her face and softened his tone. 'Look, I'm talking from a logical standpoint. If you're gay and you want to fall in love and have sex and enjoy the fruits of being alive, maybe you're better off without the Islamic faith.'

Zara was affronted. 'That's a cold way to look at it.'

'Maybe,' he said mildly, 'but I also think it's true.'

Zara studied him, confounded by his casual dismissal. She wanted to debate and fight, but could see from his unruffled stance that his conviction was immovable. What chance did they have at progress when even men like Safran held tightly to tradition?

She turned to the Thames and watched the slate-grey waves fold onto the shore. There, standing next to her closest friend, she wondered if you ever really knew anyone at all.

CHAPTER FOUR

Finn laced up his trainers and then checked his phone for the fourteenth time. **Hadid M is offline**. Finn's texts – two last night and one this morning – still remained unanswered. He felt a stirring unease but urged himself to stay calm. Kamran was confused and that was understandable, but surely he'd be discreet. Surely, there was no need to worry.

Finn opened his fitness app and loaded his favourite playlist. If there was one way to clear his mind, it was out on a gruelling run. He set off, striking the pavement in long strides, his muscles in full force. He felt fit and strong, finally back to his pre-Christmas shape. It was disheartening how quickly it had melted away, softened by endless help-ings of creamy potatoes and succulent hunks of meat. He remembered Johnny Hallsbrook from the swim team pressing a finger into the doughy band of flesh around his stomach. 'Overindulged this Christmas, eh, Andersen?' he had goaded with a smile.

Finn had immediately restricted his calories but it took a whole four months to shift the weight. Still, he felt good now and stronger than before. He knew that other athletes envied his physique. Maybe that's why they noted the slightest decline, often with evident glee. It was all in jest, though. It was *always* in jest and if you received it otherwise, well, then you needed a thicker skin.

He pushed on along the loose circle from West Lawn past the golf course up towards the Music Halls. He could run five thousand metres in sixteen minutes and though the words 'Olympic hopeful' were mentioned to him often, he ran because he loved it. It kept him energised and cleared spaces in his mind, akin to a form of therapy.

He pressed on past the Music Halls, glancing down at his smart watch and picking up his pace to make sure he hit his target. As he emerged from a line of oaks, he spotted Mr Morewood waving at him from Hampton House. Finn raised a hand uncertainly, but then realised that the deputy headmaster was asking him to slow. He glanced at his watch and reluctantly paused the lap. This would mess up his records. He slowed to a jog and then a walk. Next to Morewood stood a pair he didn't recognise: a woman dressed in a smart navy suit with her hair scraped back in a high blonde bun and an older man with a doughy face whose copper-coloured overcoat matched his reddish hair.

Finn crunched across the gravel and paused by the trio. 'Hello, sir.'

'I thought you might come this way,' said Morewood.

Finn glanced at the woman and then back to the deputy head. 'Is everything okay?'

Morewood nodded. 'Can you come to my office, please?'

Finn gestured at his attire. 'Like this, sir?' Usually, he would wear a tie and blazer when entering the masters' offices.

'That's fine.' Morewood was brusque. 'Come along.' He

led them into Hampton House and up a flight of stairs to his office, footsteps echoing off the sturdy mahogany. The room held two large desks: one loaded with papers and the other for receiving guests. Its scent was not of musty academia but of freshly cut lemongrass, just like the hotel in which Finn stayed last year – Raffles in Phnom Penh.

Morewood asked his guests to sit and they did so in an awkward configuration: him behind the desk, Finn opposite and the two strangers flanking him.

'Finn,' he started gravely. 'These people have sought permission to talk to you. They are from the London Metropolitan Police and are investigating a complaint.'

Finn glanced sideways at the woman.

'This is—' Morewood paused. 'I do apologise. I forgot your name, officer.'

'I'm DC Mia Scavo.' She scooted her chair back so she could face Finn more squarely. 'And this is DC John Dexter.'

Finn felt a tang of unease, but kept it from his features. 'It's nice to meet you, Officer Scavo.' He gripped her hand in a firm shake and offered the same to Dexter. 'Is everything okay?'

'We'd like to ask you some questions,' said Mia.

Morewood cut in. 'I believe your parents are in Switzerland, Finn?'

'Yes, sir.'

'They have given their permission for the police to talk to you as long as it's conducted on school grounds. As Hampton's child protection officer, I'll be sitting in.'

'Yes, sir.' Was this to do with his father's business? Last year, there had been trouble with the police – a smear campaign, his father had said – but as far as he knew, it was all resolved.

Mia explained that the interview would be recorded.

Finn nodded. 'Of course, officer.'

'We would like to talk to you about the night of May first,' she started.

'Okay.' Finn's throat felt prickly.

'We hear you were at a party on campus. Hampton's spring fundraiser?'

'Yes, that's right.'

'Can you tell us about that party?'

Finn shifted in his chair. 'Is there anything in particular you would like to know?'

Mia smiled but it was free of warmth. 'No, we just want to know what happened.'

He swallowed. 'Well, the parties are known for being rather lively. It's fair to say that Hampton keeps its pupils on a tight rein and these parties are a chance for us to relax.'

'Go on.'

Finn felt self-conscious in his shorts and vest and was wary of the sweat cooling on his skin. A biscuity scent rose from his shorts and he worried that the officers could smell him. He placed his hands in his lap, his fingers dipping inwards into the crease between his thighs. 'Well, I arrived shortly after 9 p.m. and talked to some of the boys there. It was a nice mix. Sometimes you get entrenched in your own house so it's nice to swap notes with other Hamptonians.'

Finn recalled the events of the night: the drink, the revelry, the sheer intoxicant that was life as a master of the universe. Mia asked for examples of the 'revelry' and he described seeing a pupil urinate into a plant pot, of a group of alumni lifting a junior up to the chandelier to see if he could swing on it. He spoke fluently, knowing that his fellow pupils would face no recrimination. The Hampton beaks were well aware of what went on at the fundraiser.

Mia gestured at the lawn outside, segmented by the window. 'I believe there were several similar parties happening around campus?'

Finn nodded. 'There were several events but the fundraiser is the most sought after. It goes on the longest and has a certain notoriety.'

'So it's safe to say that everyone had gone to bed by the time you finished?'

'Probably, yes.'

'Don't some pupils sleep in the same house as the party? Doesn't it disturb them?'

Finn shrugged a shoulder. 'The party is on the top floor and West Lawn is made of four-hundred-year-old stone walls. Nothing gets through it.'

'Okay, what time did you leave the party?'

'About 2 a.m.'

'Had it wound down?'

'No. But I was tired.'

'What did you do after?'

Finn felt the icy creep of realisation. Had Kamran gone to the police? 'I went downstairs.'

'To your room?'

He couldn't admit the truth, could he? What could he tell them? That it was a premeditated liaison? A one-time drunken fling? A complete fug in which neither was responsible? What would be the least questionable? He swallowed and felt the hard ridge of his throat. 'Yes.' He gestured outwards. 'At least I thought it was my room.'

'It wasn't?'

He grimaced. 'No.'

'What happened next?'

'I undressed, got into bed and went to sleep.'

'Did anything happen that was out of the ordinary?'

Finn's skin prickled with a fresh film of sweat. What had Kamran told them? 'I... I felt someone else in bed with me.'

'Did you know at this stage that you weren't in your own room?'

'Yes,' he admitted.

'Whose room were you in?'

'I was in Kamran's room. Kamran Hadid.' Finn looked at Morewood and then the officer. 'Did he report this?' he asked, his tone disbelieving.

Mia ignored the question. 'What did you do once you realised it wasn't your room?'

'I stayed there,' he said softly. 'I could feel someone next to me and I... reacted. I can't be sure but I think we did some things.'

'Why can't you be sure?'

'I was drunk and he was too. Neither of us knew what we were doing.'

'What do you remember?'

'I'd had a lot to drink. I can't remember much.'

'Okay, but what *do* you remember?'

Finn faltered. 'I think I took off his underwear and I touched him. I was drunk and he was too.'

'Did it go any further?'

Finn took a shallow breath. 'Yes.'

'Did you have intercourse?'

Finn nodded. 'It's all a bit of a blur but, yes, I think so.'

'What's the next thing you remember?'

'I woke up and he was gone.' Finn winced at the memory. He hated waking up alone after a night like that.

'Did you see him after?'

'Not that day.'

'But since then?'

'Yes, but nothing happened. It was a one-night thing.'

'He tells us you spoke to him yesterday?'

'I—' Finn tried to think. 'Look. Have you actually spoken to him? He'll set you straight. We were both drunk and we didn't know what we were doing.'

'Yes, and he has given his version of events.' Mia hitched up the cuff of her sleeve. 'Tell me, Mr Andersen, did you at any point obtain Kamran's consent?'

Finn's lips parted. 'Kamran's consent? But we...' He stopped and the implication of her words hit him – an electric jolt of comprehension.

'He says you came into his room, got into bed with him and touched him without his consent. Is that true?'

Finn blinked dumbly. He ran through the whir of that night, pausing on each frame: the wet press of his palm on skin, the heat caught between his lips. 'But... he didn't say no.'

'Did he verbally consent?'

Finn's mouth goldfished open. 'He didn't say no.'

'Finn,' urged Mia. 'Did he verbally consent?'

'We were drunk. We...' He trailed off. How could this have happened? How could he not have known?

'Have you two had sex before?'

Finn flinched. 'No!'

'Did you want to?'

'I—' He considered lying, but only for a beat. 'I've thought about it but only in passing.'

'Had he?'

Finn grimaced. 'No. I don't know.'

'So Kamran has never indicated that he wanted to have sex with you?'

Finn stopped, caught in the laying of a trap. He looked to Morewood. 'Sir, do I need to call my parents?'

The teacher regarded him sombrely. 'I suggest we call them and ask if they would prefer to have a lawyer here.'

Mia cut into their exchange. 'I'm not trying to catch you out. I just want to get to the truth.'

Finn tried to slow the frightening pace of his heart, to quieten the blare of his thoughts. He grappled for the least disruptive path from this. 'If I'm honest, officer, I wasn't thinking clearly. I stumbled into a bedroom, got into bed and found another body next to me. I didn't do a calculation of how much Kamran has or hasn't indicated that he wanted to have sex with me. I just reacted and so did he. He was making sounds like he enjoyed it, so I carried on without thinking.' Finn was unnerved by how calm he sounded. How could that be when panic was strafing right through his body?

Mia pressed him for details and, question by question, mapped out a picture of exactly what happened: where Finn touched Kamran, what sounds he made, how long it lasted.

83

Finn answered slowly and methodically, keeping a firm grip on the leash of hysteria, refusing to let it free. He could not comprehend how this had happened. Why hadn't Kamran refused? There was no violence, no coercion, no persuasion, no seduction. It was just two people's bodies reacting to each other. How could that be rape?

Had Kamran stood in that office and believed that Finn had raped him? He remembered the shadow that passed over his face on hearing those innocuous words: 'I had fun the other night'. Had he thought that he was mocking him?

Finn felt his composure waver, a sheet of metal in gale-force wind. 'I didn't mean to do it,' he said. 'I thought he wanted it.'

'That's not how consent works.' Mia leaned towards him. 'Finn, based on your account of the evening, Kamran did not give you his consent, which means that what took place is legally defined as rape.'

Finn stared at her, features fixed in horror.

'Please expect to be hearing from us.' Mia stood and addressed the teacher. 'It would be expedient to have Finn's parents here.'

Morewood stood too. 'Yes, but, officer, does this really need to go further? Clearly, it was two boys in a drunken tryst and one expressing buyer's regret.'

Mia regarded him coolly. 'I don't think that's clear at all, sir.' She nodded at him tersely. 'I suggest you leave the conclusions to us.'

Buyer's regret? Finn listened through a narcotic glaze that stretched the room to slow motion: the sparkly pile of insect wings scattered on the windowsill, the dry sigh of a paperback that peeled away from its neighbour and landed face first with a soft pop. There – set to the bleed of orchestral music that carried across the green – Finn felt the cracking apart of the world as he knew it. And for what? One drunken misjudgement. One irrevocable mistake.

Sofia Hadid stripped off her tennis whites just as her husband walked in. He wolf-whistled at the sight of her naked body and she tossed him an indulgent smile as if she appreciated this half-hearted expression of desire.

'Good game?' he asked.

'Yes.' She held her bathrobe up against her body.

'Did you invite Elizabeth Sergeant?'

'No,' she admitted.

'Hon, I thought I asked you to invite her. It would be good for my dealings with David if you got to know his wife.'

'I'll invite her next time,' she said with a trace of impatience. She found herself resenting his presence. Mack ran a large company but seemed to always be in and out, on his way to golf or a meeting – busy and not busy all at once.

'I'd appreciate that,' he said, his tone souring the plea.

'Fine,' she said tersely, ending the conversation. She walked to the bathroom and though she knew he no longer watched, she pressed her elbows into her hips to mask the two lumps of fat and slowed her pace so her buttocks wouldn't wobble.

In the shower, she lathered a cold, clear gel across her thighs and stomach, and scrubbed in a circular motion, moving up towards her heart. As she worked, she heard Mack whistle tunelessly in the bedroom, his idle cheer sparking irritation. If he didn't have commitments, why couldn't *he* stay at home? Why couldn't *he* look after their staff and tend to their children's needs?

It bothered her that she was so often dismissed as Mack's stay-at-home wife. She resented having to pretend that he was smarter; to smile demurely when people pointed a finger at him and shook their heads and said, 'That guy. That guy is a jammy one' when the idea being lauded was actually hers.

She turned up the heat and closed her eyes, letting it ease her frustration. She had to remember that she loved being a mother and a wife. Even when the house was empty and the endless march of hours felt lonely, she would rather this life than any other, including all the ones she had imagined in youth: scientist or CEO, maybe an inventor.

She switched off the shower and wrapped a thick towel around her hair and another around her body. She heard Mack's footsteps leave the bedroom, then echo down the hall. The front door slammed just as the phone started ringing. With a sigh, she walked to the bedroom, her feet marking spongy damp patches on the carpet.

'Hello, this is Sofia Hadid,' she said, stripping her voice of annoyance so that it sounded polite and prim. It was Mr Morewood from Hampton and Sofia grew alarmed as she heard him speak. Kamran had been involved in an incident, he said, but he would not explain the nature. 'It's best that you come to Hampton, Ms Hadid,' was all he would repeat. Sofia immediately called Mack but it rang through to voice-mail once, twice, then thrice.

Fighting a blare of panic, she dressed quickly, picking out a charcoal pantsuit with stark, tailored shoulders along with a white silk blouse. She blow-dried her hair and added a slick of lipstick as well as a string of pearls. She snapped on her Cartier watch and chose a bag that matched her lipstick: two flashes of colour in a monochrome sea. She slipped into her black Louboutins and called their driver, telling him to be quick. Oliver knocked on the door within minutes.

Silently, they slid across London streets out towards Hampton Hill. She could feel Oliver's eyes flicking to her in the mirror, no doubt aware that something was wrong. It annoyed her that he could tell. She yawned audibly – trying to signal nonchalance – and leaned back to watch the streets. Inside, her heart was wound like a drum. 'Don't worry,' Mr Morewood had said. 'He's safe.' As opposed to what? What danger could befall him in the leafy haven of Hampton?

She resisted the urge to tell Oliver to hurry, forced herself to blink and smile and stay quiet and calm. After an eternity, they drove through the gates of the school and parked by Hampton House. She strode up the symmetrical staircase and gave her name at reception. A silver-haired man whom she recognised as Mr Lismore escorted her up to the deputy head's office.

Kamran was seated in a chair in the corner. She went to him and cupped a hand across his cheek. 'What happened? Are you okay?'

Kamran pulled away from her. 'I told them not to call you.'

'Why?' She looked to Mr Morewood. 'What happened?'

'Ms Hadid, I'm sorry to have worried you. Won't you take a seat?' He waited. 'Now, before I begin, I should say that if Hadid Major had chosen to come to me first, we could have done this all in a less dramatic fashion. Alas, he went directly to the police so it's entirely out of my hands.'

Sofia felt a spike of alarm. 'The police?' She looked from Kamran to Morewood. 'Please tell me what happened.' Her voice held the slightest tremor.

Morewood launched into an explanation and as Sofia listened, she felt her world begin to tilt. 'Is this true?' she asked Kamran as if it might be some cruel cosmic joke.

He was entirely calm. 'Mum, it's okay. I'm okay.'

'How is it okay?' She looked up at the teacher, aware of the note of hysteria climbing in her voice. 'How could this have happened?' She pressed her nails into the crease of her palms to force herself to focus. Kamran needed practical help, not a frantic mother. 'Should I take him home?'

Morewood offered a tight smile. 'It would be better if he stayed at Hampton. We find that the stronger the sense of normality, the better for all involved.'

Sofia nodded, her senses dulled by shock. 'May I have a moment with him alone?'

'Of course.' Morewood stood and gestured magnanimously at the room. 'Please take your time.'

Sofia waited for the door to close, then pulled Kamran up into her arms. He was motionless, shoulders stiff and unyielding. It was hard, this awkward dance of parenthood. When her children were younger, it was easy to hug them and love them and show them unmetered affection, but as they grew, it became almost embarrassing, as if holding them too tight might be seen as gauche.

She stepped back and searched his face. If this were a daughter, Sofia would cry and rage and wrap her up in cotton wool and never let anyone near her, but she knew she had to approach this differently. She couldn't shroud her son in comforting wool; she had to build him up instead. Sofia needed to comfort him without letting his strength cave in.

She swept a lock of his hair aside. 'How do you feel?' she asked.

'I'm okay.'

'It's okay to not be okay,' she told him.

'Is it?'

She swallowed. How well her children knew her. 'What do you need?' she asked. 'I know some excellent therapists.'

He looked at her as if she were a stranger. 'I don't want a therapist.'

'Do you want to come home?'

He shook his head.

'Should I tell your father?'

'Would you rather not?'

Sofia hesitated. 'Perhaps it's for the best he doesn't know yet.'

He lifted a shoulder. 'Fine.'

'Do you want to go out to dinner? I can ask Mr Morewood for leave.'

'I just want things to go back to normal.'

Sofia frowned. 'If we pursue this case, they won't be normal for a while.'

'So what should I do?'

'Take your time to make sure that this is what you want to do.'

'And if it is?'

Fine lines creased her forehead. 'Then of course I will help you.'

Kamran wilted in relief. 'Thank you.'

Sofia swallowed the pain of seeing him worry. She pulled him back into her arms, not caring if it was embarrassing. 'At least come home this weekend?' she asked. He nodded and as she felt his chin dig into her shoulder, it was all she could do not to weep.

The creak of footsteps upstairs joined the faint hum of a lullaby: Lena preparing her son for a nap. Salma was in the kitchen helping their mother wash up, leaving Zara alone with her brother. The two sat in uneasy silence. Their relationship had suffered a years-long battle: he trying to assert his authority and she refusing to heel. Unlike her sisters, Zara could not operate in that delicate space of women who knew better than the men in their lives but who indulged them nonetheless. These women would issue sarcasm so sweetly that only they registered it – like a tone too high for men to detect. Zara couldn't do it; lacked the patience and maturity to be so forgiving. Instead, she would lock horns and be snippy and defensive. Paired with Rafiq's unyielding pride, it made for frequent clashes.

Tensions had eased somewhat after the attack on Zara last year. The two siblings had settled in a fragile truce, exchanging pleasantries like passing neighbours. After a full minute of silence, Rafiq cleared his throat and asked her how was work.

'Fine.' She reached for something else to say so it didn't sound like a rebuff. 'I'm working on an interesting case.'

'Yeah, Salma mentioned it. I hope you're on the right side this time.' He said it lightly as if in jest but Zara caught the undertone.

'What do you mean by that?' she asked.

'Nothing.' He brushed a piece of lint off his knee. 'Forget it.'

Zara bristled, knowing he was alluding to Jodie's case. 'It's clearly not nothing,' she said.

He flicked a hand in the air. 'Well, last year you went up against those Muslim boys and the case became a mess.'

Zara clenched her jaw. 'Yes and it turned out that those boys were guilty, you remember that?'

'Yeah, I know,' he said defensively. 'It was still a mess though.'

Zara bit the inside of her lip. 'I'm on the victim's side, which is where I like to be,' she said tartly, expecting her tone to rile him – had intended it, even – but he held up a hand serenely.

'Fine. I get it. I wasn't trying to have a go at you.'

Zara watched him sit there, rigid and aloof. She wondered who he'd be if he didn't feel the need to be the 'man of the house', to take an imperious tone with his wife, or rear at the smallest slight. Would he be fun and carefree or gentle and calm? Would he hold himself more loosely and have a quicker laugh? Maybe it wasn't just Zara who was injured by tradition.

'Are you happy?' she asked abruptly.

Rafiq watched her, defensive, thinking it a barb. When he registered her expression, however – open, bare, sympathetic – his features softened. 'What sort of question is that?' he said.

She bit down the compulsion to change the subject and pretend she had never asked. 'You seem angry and I probably seem angry too and...' She swallowed. 'Maybe that's because we haven't been happy for a long time.'

Rafiq didn't speak.

'I mean, Dad died three years ago and ever since then we've kind of just been... struggling.'

Rafiq's eyes seemed to grow glassy but Zara couldn't be sure. He seemed to be reaching for words, veering perhaps between flippancy and sincerity. Zara watched and felt a tug of sympathy. Who did Rafiq confide in? When he couldn't get a grasp on his life, who did he ask for help? She noted the subtle quiver of his jaw.

'You get over these things,' he said gruffly.

'Do we?' she asked.

His expression was accusing as if she had intended to wound him. 'Yeah, we do,' he said.

He straightened when Salma and their mother entered the room, the latter bearing a plate of fruit that she placed fussily next to Rafiq.

'Eat,' she urged. 'The apples are fresh from the tree and the cherries are from your auntie at number twenty-six.'

'I will.'

She raised the plate to him. 'Eat, eat,' she said.

'Okay, I will.' He picked up a slice of apple and bit it in half.

Zara listened to the fresh crunch of it, then she too reached for a slice.

Kamran pressed his toes in the thick cream carpet of his room in Belsize Park. His mother's banal décor and the white sky outside washed the room in featureless light. His parents had this rambling house and yet the only place he felt at home was his compact room at Hampton. Here, his mother dashed away any trinkets, saying they made it harder to dust. She rearranged his books in height order no matter the author or genre, always pulling them forward so their spines sat flush in one neat line.

Now, even his space at Hampton belonged to someone else. He thought again of the night it happened. Everything seemed flushed in midnight blue, the walls soft and porous, the furniture reduced to shapes and shadows. Would he always be stuck in that night?

There was a soft tap on the door and Kamran straightened, ready to receive his guest with a smile.

Adam hovered at the threshold. 'Hey. Can you talk?' he asked.

Kamran nodded.

Adam closed the door and sat in a soft white chair by the bed, angled askew as if left there casually but actually measured by their mother who had pushed and pulled it an inch here and there until it was positioned perfectly. He took the cushion from behind his back and tossed it on the bed. 'What's going on?' he asked.

Kamran neatened the cushion. 'With what?'

'I know something's going on. Mum never asks Hampton for term-time leave. I heard you both whispering yesterday. What's going on?'

Kamran watched his brother and struggled to find the words. How to carve out this horror and minimise the hurt? The two of them never spoke about sex. Even after he'd slept with Maya and boasted to half the school, Kamran was oblique with Adam. It just wasn't part of their family fabric. And now he had to tell him what? That his brother had been raped?

'Something happened,' he started.

Adam stilled. 'Is someone sick?'

'No, it's nothing like that.' He swallowed. 'Something happened at Hampton – on the night of the party.' He remembered the raucous laughter, beer bottles sinking in melting ice, Keister's cheeks held aloft from a tree. 'Remember I told you not to drink too much?'

'Yes.'

'Yeah, well, I should have listened to my own advice.' Kamran threaded his fingers in his lap. Then, he began his second retelling, rendered in a deadpan monotone.

Adam's breath fractured as he listened. 'Do you know who it was?'

'Yes.' Kamran's voice dropped to a rasp. 'It was Finn Andersen.'

Adam balked. 'But I *know* Finn. He... he wouldn't do something like that.'

'Well, he did,' said Kamran. 'I've spoken to him.'

'You have?'

'Yes. He said it was "fun".'

Adam flinched. 'He said that?'

Kamran nodded, feeling the vinegar tang of hate in his mouth.

Adam's eyes wheeled from the wall map to the door handle to the bookshelf to the bed, then finally settled on Kamran. 'Are you okay?' A tentative hand twisted towards his abdomen.

Kamran grimaced. 'Yeah, I think so.'

Adam's chest swelled with effort. His eyes filled with tears and he batted at them angrily. 'I'm sorry,' he said, his voice cracking between the words.

Kamran watched his brother break down and though he felt a kick of annoyance, he reached over and rubbed his shoulder. 'Come on, don't do that.'

Adam swiped at his eyes. 'Why did he do it? Have you two...?'

Kamran recoiled. 'No! Of course not.'

Adam took a shaky breath. 'Are you gay?'

'No. For Christ's sake, how can you ask that?'

His face crumpled. 'I'm sorry, I just can't believe this happened.'

Kamran reached forward and drew his brother into a hug. He let him cry instead of snapping like their father might.

A memory rose in his mind: Adam six and Kamran seven, out on their first hunt with their father. It was October and the leaves were crackly beneath their feet. The cold air snapped at Kamran's buff and he pulled it up to his nose, the breath inside misting warm. His thick twill coat was designed for hunting and he liked the way it sat heavy on his chest. He squared his shoulders and aped his father's walk, the cocky swagger and the easy way he cut through the bush. They walked for an hour and their father got testy, telling them to shush with increasing intensity. When Adam paused to touch a flower, their father pulled him up and pushed him forward. Immediately, Adam began to tear up. Kamran felt annoyed at his brother, as if his weakness tainted them both; made the team seem weaker.

They trudged on until Mack turned to them with electric urgency. He signalled them to quieten and watch. There was a gentle rustling and the bush parted. A deer walked out: a tawny roe with a cotton-wool tail. Their father beckoned them closer and told them to stay still. He braced the rifle on his shooting sticks and centred the deer in his sight. Kamran watched, his heartbeat revving in his chest. His father's finger lingered on the trigger, a subtle, deadly caress. Kamran's face grew blanched in alarm. He felt the world slow as Mack's finger tensed on the trigger.

'No!' he shouted.

Mack squeezed the trigger and the gunshot cracked through the air – but it was too late. The deer had skittered away, vaulted into motion by Kamran's warning. His father bellowed with frustration. He turned to Kamran and bounced a tight tap off the back of his head. 'What's wrong with you?' he shouted.

Kamran flinched and a socket of shame opened in his stomach.

'Why are you crying? You're not a baby.' His voice was clipped and angry.

'I'm sorry.'

'Sorry's no good now, is it?' He threw his hands in the air. 'Well, this has been a waste of time.' He tossed Kamran a handkerchief. 'For God's sake, stop whimpering.' He glowered at Adam. 'Get your things. We're going home.'

Something passed between the brothers that day: an understanding that they could not show weakness in front of their father – and though Adam sometimes wavered, Kamran never failed.

Now, behind closed doors with his weeping brother, he felt something twist in his gut. He tightened his arms around him and squeezed him on the shoulder. 'Don't cry,' he said. 'Come on, don't cry.'

*

Zara parked her car and basked in the welcome silence, no longer in earshot of central London. She had one last meeting and looked forward to going home and collapsing on her sofa. It was striking how much she had changed. Years ago, before her father's death, her days were filled to the seams. Safran used to joke that her life was like a parody of a CEO's diary: 6 a.m. wake-up, a forty-five-minute workout, fruit for breakfast, a commute to the office with a podcast in French, a quick talk to her clerk for any new cases, a trip to court, burning the midnight oil. On nights off, she would read up on case law or enrol on an online course, anything that kept her mind whirring, kept her learning, stopped her from wasting a single precious minute.

This all changed with her father's death, one white-hot point of pain with a wasted year on either side. Before it, there was her failed arranged marriage and six-month estrangement from her father. After it, a year of coasting before quitting life in chambers to work with women more broken than she was – and yet they hadn't fixed her. Swathes of days passed in sombre procession with evenings now spent at home, staring at her numbing TV. It was a soothing ritual and she felt no compulsion to change it.

She wound up her windows and locked her car, the sun still warm on her back. She strode up the symmetrical staircase into the reception of Hampton House. There, she gave her name and was escorted up to meet the deputy head.

'May I offer you some tea?' asked Mr Morewood, his tone chill and official.

'No, thank you.'

'In that case, how may I help you?'

'I'm here to talk about Kamran Hadid's care plan.'

'Ah.' He opened a notebook and traced a finger along the central seam. 'May I ask in what capacity you're here, Ms Kaleel?'

'I'm Kamran's counsellor.'

'And what does this mean?'

Zara offered an icy smile. 'Based on Hampton policy, a pupil has a right to an external counsellor. He can also request special provisions so that he may receive a standard of care.'

Morewood appraised her. 'Ms Kaleel, do you really think a court case will serve the boys well?'

She considered this. 'I think the truth will.'

'We have an internal mediation process which we can use to resolve disputes.'

'With independent supervision?' asked Zara.

Morewood hesitated. 'Well, no, but—'

'In that case, if Kamran wants to pursue a legal route, then that's what we must do.'

'Must we?' He steepled his long fingers. 'Ms Kaleel, boys will be boys and when emotions run high, they often do things they regret. This was an unfortunate incident but we are more than equipped to review it internally.'

Zara knew what this review would conclude: a blameless ruling that would surely allow Finn to stay in the school. She responded evenly. 'Mr Morewood, I think it's best we follow a legal course. This is what the complainant wishes and I suggest that Hampton cooperates.'

He forced a smile. 'Certainly.'

'Can you please make sure that Mr Andersen is separated

from Kamran and Adam Hadid? He should not have access to anyone who might act as a potential witness.'

Morewood drew in his breath, sharply as if in pain. 'Finn and Kamran are housed in the same building. Uprooting one would be terribly disruptive. We can move Kamran if that's what he wishes. Of course, it would not be fair to move Finn as *he* has not brought the complaint.'

Zara watched him for a second. She was well used to these plays at power. When she was younger, men like Morewood – who were of a certain age and spoke a certain way – could cut through her confidence like a knife in butter. With experience, however, she had learned that you could not pander to their egos or try to ease their scorn. Instead, you had to hold your ground and wait for them to yield.

'Kamran needs routine,' she said. 'It's easier if Mr Andersen is moved and it's best that Hampton does this voluntarily.' She did not articulate what the alternative might be but it was enough to move Morewood.

'Very well,' he said. 'Of course, it would be impossible to say they wouldn't encounter each other in the school's common areas.'

'That's fine. Please just make sure that Mr Andersen does not speak to my client.'

Morewood nodded once, stonily.

Zara secured additional provisions including a meeting room for her and Kamran and dates when they could meet. 'Thank you for your cooperation,' she told him when they finished. She stood and offered her hand, which Morewood shook a tad too firmly. 'I'll be in touch,' she promised.

'I have no doubt,' he replied drily.

She smiled and headed back to the symmetrical staircase outside Hampton House.

Finn kicked his trainers into a corner, next to his roommate's plimsolls. He knew he would feel better if he forced himself to run, but after his latest meeting with Morewood, he failed to find the will. The deputy head told him that he would be moving to Rendale House on the opposite end of campus. Finn barely knew anyone there and though he was told it was temporary, he knew it could last for months. How quickly things had escalated. He was desperate to talk to Kamran, but his phone had been confiscated and he was told that all his correspondence was subject to monitoring. Any contact with the Hadids would lead to suspension and so he accepted exile instead.

He would have to strip the room and move his belongings to somewhere new. He looked at the antique telegraph mounted on his half of the wall. It was brass, early twentieth century and had the words HENSCHEL CORPORATION, AMESBURG, MASS printed in a small gold square on the back.

'It's American, I'm afraid,' his father had said when handing over the present. Finn had been nine and in full swing of a naval phase, convinced he'd be a sailor. His father delighted him with stories of Norwegian explorers: Leif Erikson, Fridtjof Nansen, Roald Amundsen and his favourite, Thor Heyerdahl, who had rafted across the Pacific.

It saddened Finn that he and his father barely spoke anymore. There had been a perfunctory email that morning, explaining that he still had business in Geneva but if Finn needed them, they would drop everything and fly straight over. He knew his parents meant it but also that they'd be inconvenienced if he were to say yes. His father was a celebrated CEO, always on the speakers' circuit, and his mother would hate for him to let people down. She revelled in having status. She felt that her gay son lent her a certain cachet and used him often as a source of amusing anecdotes.

Finn heard her at a dinner party once trilling about his coming out. 'We overheard him on the phone to a friend worrying about what we'd say. His father left him a note: "Son, we've known you were gay since you were six years old. Just don't forget the OJ."' Her high-pitched warble of a laugh, her cloying need to be seen as progressive, her performative broad-mindedness. She wore his sexuality like an ornament; an heirloom brooch of fancy provenance.

Now, he was in a predicament that could not be spun into an amusing story no matter which way you told it. 'Haven't you heard this one? Finn might be a rapist!' Guffaws of laughter and trebles all round.

Could Kamran's claim become public knowledge? If he could only talk to him and explain. *But explain what?* After all, Finn had more questions than answers. Like, *why did I get so drunk? Why did I assume that it was okay? Why didn't I check?* Or *why didn't you push me away? Isn't it true that we're both to blame?*

Ed's voice carried across the cavernous room, set to the tinkle of the grand chandelier. 'People find it odd when I say that; that I want to live my best life to honour my victim, but to me it makes sense. If I can make something of myself, if I can maximise the value of my life, then I can honour his. That's why I can't slip back; it would dishonour him.'

Zara watched him speak and marvelled at how little you could tell of someone. Ed, the ex-criminal in her NA group, worked at *Inside*, a newspaper for Britain's prison population. He had served a nineteen-year sentence after killing a man in a botched robbery at the age of twenty-three. Now, here he was, making amends.

Ed sat down and the group leader, Chris, called for another speaker. Zara raised a hand, shaking off her cowardice. If Ed could admit a fatal mistake, couldn't she too find some courage?

'I'd like to speak tonight, Chris.'

He looked up with a surprised smile. 'Please do.' He beckoned her up.

Zara stood gingerly. 'I don't tell strangers this,' she started, 'but in 2016, when I was twenty-seven, I had an arranged marriage.' She placed a bracing hand on a pew. 'I don't like to talk about it because I feel like people make assumptions about me that aren't true. I'm a strong person and... it's important to me that people know that.' She cleared her throat. 'I saw the rest of my life stretch out in front of me and I knew that it would suffocate me. I didn't want to be this man's wife. I didn't want to raise this man's child – and so I walked out.' She exhaled. 'The last time I spoke here, I told you that I didn't see my father for six months before his death. The reason is because I left my arranged marriage and I told him I wasn't returning. He—'

Tears filled her eyes, shaping her lashes into dark, wet clumps. She tried to extract the words that sat like razor blades lodged in her throat. 'He told me that if I didn't go back to my husband, my brother would come round and hack me into pieces.'

The words punctured something in the room. Immediately, she wished to retract them. Spoken here in the harsh acoustics of the church, with little logic or context, they sounded unforgivable. What Ed and Chris didn't know was that Zara's father was a good man. He had loved her fiercely and it was only in that moment of madness – under the spectre of dishonour – that he'd reverted to a baser instinct: to threaten violence when a woman said no.

She couldn't possibly impart the nuances of him in the space of this short confession. Instead, she said something she hadn't yet admitted. 'Those words closed off something inside me. I've never been naturally chirpy but I was... present.' A small, bitter laugh. 'After that, it felt like a wall came down and since then I've been...' She tightened her grip on the pew. 'Alone.' She looked up, staving off tears. 'Which is why I'm here.' She took a ragged breath. 'That's all I'd like to say today.' Her hands closed into fists, her palms warm and puffy. Ed in the front row nodded at her. She nodded back and then sat, overwhelmed by her kinship with the strangers in this room.

CHAPTER FIVE

Sofia ensured that Kamran had his favourite breakfast: eggs Benedict with smoked salmon and a side order of chestnut mushrooms served with a tall glass of orange juice – freshly squeezed, she instructed Nevinka. She brought the tray up herself, opened the windows and neatened the room. She sat on his bed, making herself ruffle his hair, making herself not be awkward.

Kamran was taciturn. He pulled apart the salmon into fleshy strings, then listlessly pierced the egg and let the bread grow sopping wet.

'Eat something,' she urged, immediately regretting the words. Kamran needed more than banalities. He needed direction but she didn't know where to take him.

He took a polite bite, chewing for an age before swallowing, his eyes bulging slightly as if the act pained him.

'You don't have to eat it if you don't want to.'

He smiled joylessly. 'Thank you,' he said and set his fork down.

She watched him for a moment and in the tension of his features, saw that he ached to be left alone. She gathered up the mess and walked to the threshold, pausing for just a moment. He turned away from her, his body stiff and defensive. She hovered for a moment longer, then closed the door and headed downstairs. In the kitchen, she loaded the dishwasher, which she did conscientiously for Nevinka. As she rearranged the items within, she heard an urgent rap on the door. She strode to the hallway and checked her reflection in the mirror, twisting a lock of hair so that it curled beneath her chin. She opened the door with a steady smile.

A young man stood on her doorstep. He was slight with short brown hair, wide-set eyes and a slightly piggish nose. She noticed that his dark grey jumper was bobbled and the shirt collars underneath – a black and white check – flopped through lack of starch. He wasn't from Hampton, she was sure.

'May I help you?' she asked.

He glanced in the hallway behind her. 'I'm sorry to disturb you. I'm Owen Greer, activist and reporter.' He held out his hand.

She shook it instinctively.

'Ms Hadid, I wanted to talk to you about your son, Kamran.' He smiled sympathetically. 'I know what happened to him.'

Sofia felt the wrench of dismay. How did they find out so quickly? And who else would they tell? 'What do you want?' she asked.

The reporter lowered his voice, feigning intimacy. 'I'm working on a campaign feature about the taboo of male rape.'

The words made her flinch.

'I'm examining the mental effects on victims and want to ask for your permission to interview your son.'

She felt a bolt of anger and imagined herself slapping this man, leaving dark red marks across his cheeks and pushing him off her doorstep. Instead, she said, 'Thank you but we're not interested.'

'Ms Hadid, if I could just explain the purpose of the campaign. It's to help boys like—'

'No, thank you. Goodbye.'

He placed a hand on the door, not pushing but with enough tension to stop it in its tracks. 'Please, Ms Hadid. This is a taboo that needs to be brought to light.'

'Please step back,' she said, her tone lanced with a tricky bite.

He did, but continued to speak. 'Kamran needs to know that he's not alone. It's not just an article. There's a support group too.'

'No.'

'Just listen to what I—'

'No,' she snapped. 'Leave us alone.'

He started to object but she slammed the door. She pressed her forehead against it, praying he wouldn't persist. Would Kamran's case become public knowledge?

'What on earth was that?'

Sofia startled at the sound of Mack's voice. She had liked that baritone once. Now, it seemed far too loud, too often intrusive. She turned towards him. 'Nothing important.'

He stepped into the hall. His khaki-coloured cords and Argyle jumper were far too hot for May and a film of sweat glazed his upper lip. '"This is a taboo that needs to be brought to light",' he quoted. 'It doesn't sound like nothing to me.'

She wilted against the door. She had hoped to tell him on her own terms.

'"Kamran needs to know he's not alone"?' he said. 'What's happened?'

Sofia ushered him into the living room. 'I think you should sit down.'

He opted for a cream button-back armchair. 'Okay, I'm seated.'

She joined him, palms pressed together as if in plea. Perhaps she *was* pleading – for discretion, for understanding, for empathy. 'Kamran's got in some trouble at school.'

Mack frowned. 'But he never gets in trouble. You make sure of that.'

She swallowed. 'I couldn't help him this time.'

'What happened?'

Sofia smoothed a hand across her skirt. Usually, she could predict her husband's reaction: a loud, fulsome laugh when happy; a dismissive snap when not; a breezy riposte when slightly troubled followed by a game of golf. This time, she had no idea what he might say or do. 'Someone attacked Kamran.'

Mack tilted his head to one side. 'And?' He waited. 'Kamran knows how to take care of himself. I made sure of that.'

'No, not a fight. He—' The words gummed in her throat. 'He was sexually assaulted.'

Mack grew still, his features pinched with confusion as if he hadn't heard the words. The air seemed to thicken around them and, then, there was a yielding: in the subtle bow of his shoulders and the hard burl of his Adam's apple swallowing away emotion. 'Assault?' The word hung in a vacuum of white, sterile and untouchable. 'A teacher?' he asked breathlessly.

'No.' She swallowed. 'A student.'

'A student?' he repeated. 'But how?'

Sofia shared the details of the little she knew, watching Mack grow rigid, a sickly dampness spreading on his skin.

'They had *sex*?' he asked with a note of incredulity.

'I don't know the details. I didn't ask.'

'What do you mean you didn't ask?'

Sofia grimaced. 'The teacher said he was assaulted. I didn't want to ask him how far.'

'That's *exactly* what you ask him!'

'Mack—'

Her husband rose to his feet. 'I want to talk to Kamran.'

She held up a hand. 'Not now. Not until you have a chance to think about what you'll say.'

Mack strode to the foot of the stairs. 'Kamran!' he shouted, his deep voice echoing off the walls.

'Mack,' Sofia tried to intervene.

'Kamran! Come down here, please.' He climbed three stairs and shouted again.

There were footsteps and then a door opening softly. 'Yes?'

'Come down here, please.'

A beat of hesitation. 'Yes, sir.'

Upstairs, Kamran shut his door with a hollow press. He headed down the stairs, stooping with pre-apology. He knew he looked feeble with his thick woolly cardigan and dark eye bags – not the sort of son of whom Mack would be proud.

'Come on.' His father waggled his fingers at him, then led him to the living room. He waited until they were all sitting down. 'Your mother told me what happened.'

Kamran shrank into his seat, freighted with a viscous shame. He hadn't expected her to tell him so soon.

His father watched him, knee bouncing impatiently. 'Listen, son. I want you to tell me what that boy did to you.'

Kamran felt the air clamp like a hand on his mouth but he knew that his father had no patience for weakness so he squared his shoulders and spoke. 'He tried to have sex with me.'

'Tried or *did*?'

'Mack,' Sofia attempted to stop him.

He raised a finger at her. 'If someone hurt our son, we need to know what happened.' He waited for Kamran to answer.

'Tried,' Kamran lied.

His father's features were taut with stress. 'So he didn't manage to...?'

'Dad, I've already spoken to someone about this.'

'But did he hurt you?' he asked urgently.

'No.' Kamran's voice held the slightest tremor.

His father studied him. 'Are you gay?'

Kamran flinched hard, knowing he had to get it right to crush any doubt in his father's mind. If he didn't react with enough repulsion, Mack would start to doubt him. 'Dad! Of course I'm not.' He loaded the words with scorn.

Mack slackened with relief, the tension uncoiling. 'There's nothing wrong with it,' he said, 'but no Hadid has ever been gay and I doubt it would just happen now.'

Kamran shook his head. 'I'm not,' he said emphatically.

'Okay.' He exhaled. 'So what do we do about this?' he asked Sofia.

'I think we should discuss this later,' she replied.

Mack gestured at him. 'He's a grown boy. We can include him in this discussion.'

Kamran caught his mother's eye. He nodded softly, giving her permission.

She grimaced. To Mack, she said, 'We should find out any day now if the police will be charging the boy.'

'What are the chances they won't?'

Kamran knew what he was really asking: what are the chances we can forget this thing? What are the chances I can leave our son in your capable hands and head on out to play golf?

Sofia shook her head helplessly. 'I don't know. We have to be prepared for it to go either way.' She glanced at Kamran. 'I've booked him to see someone at the Fairview Clinic. Freya Coutts mentioned that her son went there after his recent episode.'

His father frowned. 'To see a therapist?'

'Yes.'

He made a derisive sound. 'Kamran doesn't need to go and see some quack. We can help him here.'

Kamran watched the exchange. 'I don't need a therapist, Mum,' he said quietly.

'You see?' His father walked over to him, gripped his shoulders and massaged them a touch too hard. He curled one hand in a fist and glanced a mock blow off Kamran's chin. 'This doesn't change who you are, okay? It's one of a million things that have happened and will happen to you and you have the power to decide what you do with it.'

'Yes, sir.'

'You know what I always say: *Faber est suae quisque fortunae.*'

Kamran nodded. 'Every man is the architect of his own fortune,' he said by rote.

'Exactly!'

Kamran took a tremulous breath and stepped back from his father. 'May I be excused?' he asked, saying the words in a rush before his voice could falter.

Mack gestured at the door magnanimously. 'You may.'

Kamran left the room but paused on the stairs when he heard his mother speak.

'Mack, he needs to talk to someone,' she said, her voice intense and low.

'Well, you're his mother. How about he try *you?*'

'That's not fair.' His mother was stung. 'I wasn't taught how to deal with this. Were *you?*'

There was a silence, laced only with the sounds of the house: the faint whir of the ceiling fan, the engine hum of the fridge.

His father was weary. 'I just don't think that crying to some stranger will help him.'

'Well, what *do* you think will help him?' she snapped.

'A sense of routine. Our respect instead of pity.'

'He needs more!' she shouted.

His father was silent for a moment. 'Okay, sweetheart,' he said quietly. 'If you think that he needs to talk to a therapist, then go ahead and arrange it.'

She made a low, choked sound of frustration. 'You think he will go now that he knows how you feel? That boy does everything you say!'

Kamran listened to his parents argue and felt the cold wash of regret tauten the pores of his skin.

His father was speaking now, in a rare placatory tone. 'He will be okay, sweetheart. He just needs some time. Look, it's not like it was a teacher.'

Kamran flinched. He felt repulsed by the thought of assault by a teacher but also a queasy envy. Would that harsher crime lend him a greater reprieve? Would it ease the stifling pressure that kept him cinched in a single piece? Could he collapse on this very stairwell and allow himself to weep?

Zara walked up the steps of Bow Road Police Station and headed to the lift. After two years in her job, she knew the station well. She was familiar with the waxen cast of the fluorescent lights and the plastic feel of the floor. She was here for an update from Mia and hoped that she had some news, maybe even some precious evidence that would work in Kamran's favour.

'You have to press it to get it to work.'

She turned to the source of the voice and watched him call the lift.

He met her gaze with a grin. 'I'm sorry. I was trying to find a better way of negging you and that's the best I could come up with.'

She stepped into the lift. '"Negging?"' she asked.

He cringed. 'I'm sorry. Negging is when you insult a woman just a tiny bit so she'll want to impress you. It's not something any decent guy would do. It's just that I went to an all-boys' school and never learned to flirt properly.'

Zara surprised him with a smile. 'A compliment is usually a good place to start.'

'You're beautiful,' he said, then winced. 'Too much?' He watched her face, then pressed a palm to his temple. 'Definitely too much.' He cleared his throat and tried again. 'I love the texture of your voice.'

Zara was taken aback. '*That*,' she said, 'is a good compliment.'

He pumped a fist in the air as the lift creaked to a stop.

'My floor,' she said.

'Wait. Can I know you?'

She fought another smile. 'Keep working on your compliments and maybe.' She stepped out.

He held the doors open. 'Look, I'm only here for the day and I don't trust serendipity, so please tell me how to find you.'

Zara hesitated. She took in his athletic build and warm, hopeful smile and tried to get a gauge on him. He wasn't assertive like Michael Attali, the last man she had dated. She remembered his banker's arrogance, his firm hand on the small of her back, the way he steered her through a crowd as if he might be her owner.

Finally, she said, 'I'm Zara of Artemis House.'

He grinned. 'I'm Matthew of Cavill House.' He watched her expression, then paused. 'Wait, is Artemis your surname?'

'No,' she said. 'It's where I work.'

'Oh.' He winced good-naturedly. 'I thought we were doing a *Game of Thrones* sort of thing. My name is Matthew Cavill. There is no house.'

She laughed and gestured at the corridor. 'I've got to go.'

'Okay. I'll find you.' He paused. 'But not in a creepy way.'

She nodded, then turned and headed through the double doors, feeling a strange lightness. She didn't know if he would find her and neither did she really care but for those few brief moments, he made her feel like someone else.

She turned into the corridor as the lingering smile ebbed from her face, then paused by an open office. She knocked and entered.

Mia Scavo glanced up from her desk. 'Hey, come in. I'll just be a minute.'

Zara took a seat at a wide Formica table that dominated the space like in a conference room. Four desks were squeezed along the walls, one apiece for Mia and Dexter and two other constables.

Mia spread open a rose-red folder, its textured cover like smudges of blood. 'Good news. Finn Andersen's fingerprints were found on Kamran's headboard.'

'How many?' asked Zara.

Mia glanced up. 'Five. Is that important?'

'Were they anywhere else?'

Mia flicked a page. 'On the doorknob, both external and internal, and one set on the desk.'

'That's it?'

'Yes. Why?'

'I just want to make sure they're not secret lovers and this is a tiff gone bad. I was worried we'd find his fingerprints everywhere.'

Mia frowned. 'You have doubts about Kamran?'

'No, I just wanted to make sure.'

They both remembered the sickening punch of Jodie saying she'd lied. The need to tread carefully was a lesson hard learned.

'Well, there's no danger of that,' said Mia. 'His prints weren't anywhere else.'

'Okay. This is good but it's of limited use. Finn hasn't denied being there.'

Mia's head tipped to one side, a token of concession. 'You're right and honestly if this were a female complainant, I think the CPS would have kicked it right back but male rape is becoming a cause célèbre. You remember that report last year that said they were dumping weak cases prematurely? Well, now they're pursuing them aggressively, including this one. Finn is going to be charged.'

Zara felt a shiver of unease. Crusades were rarely bloodless. She listened to the rest of the case particulars. 'What other evidence do we have?' she asked.

Mia tapped the folder. 'Witnesses corroborating what time they left their respective parties and CCTV footage showing Finn entering Kamran's room.'

'No medical evidence?'

'No bruising or other injuries.'

'So this is a pure case of "he said, he said"?'

'Yep.'

Zara sighed. She knew how rare it was to secure a conviction in a case like this. Kamran and Finn were of even height and even build, so the question was inevitable: if Kamran didn't want it, how did Finn force him? This wasn't a case of a woman and a man with a clear physical imbalance, nor was there a history of coercion or control. There was no tangible act of violence; no grip around a neck, no fist in a face. Would a jury cast this as rape?

'It's going to be tough,' said Zara. 'Have you dealt with male complainants before?'

'Yes, but mainly in the context of long-term abuse.' She gestured at Zara. 'You?'

'No. We've been trained to work with them but I never have. Stuart has granted me this one reprieve.'

Mia smiled. 'He's a good man.'

'One of few.'

'You think so?' Mia arched a brow. 'That he's one of few?'

'You don't?'

Mia leaned back in her chair. 'I think it's very easy to bash men – and don't get me wrong, they often deserve it – but I also think that we do it too casually, almost as a bonding exercise.' She tossed her pen on the table. 'We hear about rape culture, and you and I have witnessed it more than most, but to say that all men are innately violent or that rape is in our very *culture* worries me. I can't think of a time where violence against women was encouraged in the West. In fact, we try very hard to stop it, which gets lost in all the rhetoric.' She flicked a hand in the air. 'I mean, do you even *like* men?'

'That's a very broad question.'

Mia held her gaze. 'Not really.'

Zara considered this. 'I—' She tried to find her answer.

'We've got to treat men like humans, Zara, even if some do inhuman things. The majority of men are good and kind and I hope that we – not you and I but *we* as a society – can find our way back to that.' She grimaced. 'If you're going to work with male victims, you need to *like* men.'

Zara absorbed this. 'You're right,' she said. 'But do *you*?'

Mia's smile was small and plaintive. 'Yeah, I do.' She studied Zara for a second, then closed the rose-red folder, her tone changing to a more professional tenor. 'Will you talk to Kamran and tell him we're charging Finn?'

Zara nodded. 'Yes. I'm seeing him right after this.'

Mia squared the edges of her folder. 'We need to make sure he's in it for the long haul.'

Zara stood. 'I know. We will.' She hesitated for a moment. 'Thanks for the talk,' she added.

'Any time,' said Mia as the two shook hands.

Zara left the station and headed to her car. On the drive to Hampton, she felt a strange preoccupation. Did she *like* men? In the past, she had been frustrated by women who whimpered about the perils of men, feeble as Victorian housewives, bereft of any agency. And then two men attacked her and she came to understand why those women walked with watchful eyes or flinched so hard at sudden noises or backed straight out of a man's path – but how far could you fall? Refuse to ride the Tube? Refrain from standing up to a man for fear that he might strike you? That couldn't be the answer. Zara's approach was to toughen up; to inure herself to the menace of men, but what if she had got this wrong? What if she had to soften herself and learn to *like* them instead?

She thought of Kamran as she entered the grounds of Hampton. She knew that he was vulnerable but it was also true that if she compared him with Jodie, she thought of him as far stronger with his cut-glass accent and impeccable manners and how – at seventeen – he would use words like 'mordant' and 'propitious' without even blinking. Zara had to reach past that veneer and seek the boy inside.

She walked up to a meeting room on the second floor of Hampton House, secured as part of Kamran's care plan. It was dotted with plush green chairs with ornate mahogany frames and covered by a pale green carpet with – to her surprise – a few dark stains. Floor-to-ceiling sash windows opened to a manicured lawn and a serpentine pond beyond it. She smoothed her hair and crossed her knees, always adjusting herself to places like this.

Kamran knocked on the door a minute early and apologised for being late. He looked brochure-ready in his smart grey trousers, white shirt, black tie and navy woollen blazer. Zara gestured at the chair opposite. He sat and crossed his legs, then immediately uncrossed them again, spreading them wider so that his knees rested a foot apart. 'Thank you for coming,' he said.

'How are you?' she asked.

His eyes darted leftward. 'Okay.'

She studied him for a moment. Gently, she asked, 'And beneath the "okay"?'

He looked at her with a cold electricity. His lips parted as if to speak but then settled back to a silent seal.

Zara waited. 'It can be difficult to articulate what you're feeling now,' she told him. 'Can I ask if you would describe it as a physical sensation or an emotional one?'

At first, it seemed he wouldn't answer but then he cleared his throat. 'I think it's a physical sensation. I...' He held a hand across his collarbones. 'Here's where I feel weak... like I just want to curl in.'

'Why?'

'I... I feel ashamed.'

Zara watched the haunted shift of his gaze and felt a beating sorrow. 'Ashamed about what?'

He blinked. 'Ashamed that I didn't see it coming. Finn and I, we... We've touched before physically: play-fighting on the rugby field. I don't know if I gave the wrong impression.'

'Kamran.' Zara leaned forward, forcing herself to speak slowly for she knew her ferocity would only subdue him. 'Even if you *had* flirted with him, or kissed him, or even had sex with him before, that doesn't give him the right to do what he did without your explicit consent.'

Kamran's tone grew sour. 'But what if I *did* consent?'

Zara grew still. 'What do you mean?'

Kamran kneaded his palm with a thumb. 'I think I remember him saying "you like it?"'

Zara held her breath, feeling it bloat in her chest. This was new information. 'Did you say anything?' she asked gingerly.

Kamran looked at her, his face pinched with worry. 'No.'

'Are you sure?' Zara's voice belied her alarm. 'If you did, you can tell me now.'

'I'm sure.'

She exhaled, the pressure in her chest easing.

'But—' Kamran shifted in his seat. 'I didn't say no.'

Zara picked her words carefully, needing him to absorb them. 'Kamran, Finn came into your room, climbed into your bed without your consent, had intercourse with you without your consent and when you woke up, you felt violated. Those are the facts you understand to be correct, yes?'

He nodded.

'That meets the legal definition of rape. If those facts are true, then Finn Andersen raped you.'

Kamran blinked rapidly, shoulders rising with the effort of keeping his composure.

Zara gave him a moment to gather himself. 'I need to ask you something,' she said, her tone low and serious. 'I've received news from Mia that the Crown Prosecution Service will pursue the case based on the evidence you've given. They will need you to testify.'

Kamran balked. 'They... it's going to go to court?'

'Yes, they're going to charge Finn.'

'And put him in jail?' His voice took on a tinge of panic.

'That's unlikely for now,' said Zara, not wanting to spook him. 'There's a good chance he'll be given bail, which means he will continue at Hampton until the week of the trial.'

Kamran paled. 'I... I don't know if I can do it.' He stood up and walked to the window. 'It doesn't seem right.' He held out his hands and looked at his splayed fingers. 'I'm okay. My body is okay.' He pressed a palm against his chest. 'My mind is okay. I can't ruin his life over this.'

Zara watched him. She was touched by his concern for Finn, but also knew that it might dissuade him. 'Can I be honest with you, Kamran?'

He turned to face her. 'Yes.'

'I'll be frank. Few rape cases without objective evidence result in a conviction, so unless Finn confesses that he knew you didn't consent, there's little chance of him going to prison.'

A shadow fell on Kamran's face. 'Then what's the point?'

'The point is that you receive some closure.'

'But is it worth it?' Kamran gestured hopelessly. 'I mean, *look* at him. He's not a rapist.'

'But he is,' said Zara tenderly. 'Kamran, popular culture might have us believe that rapists are men in dark clothes in silent alleys but the vast majority are men known to the person they attack: their friends, their colleagues, their peers.'

Kamran gripped the radiator behind him, the columns cool and silent, offering no comfort. 'It will go on his school record. Isn't that enough? If he does it again, they will know.'

'Listen, Kamran. You should not do this out of duty to an imagined future victim. What I'm trying to say is that there is value in pursuing this for yourself.'

Kamran pulsed on his feet as if readying to sprint. 'I can't. If I do this, he'll always be a rapist and I'll always be the boy who was raped. I don't want that.'

Zara spoke gently. 'No one at all is going to make you do anything, Kamran.' She needed to give him space to make the right decision. 'I want you to think about closure and what that looks like to you. In twenty years' time, will you be coming back to this year, this month, that night, and wishing you had seen it through or will you have put it behind you? If it's the latter, then I promise I'll support you.'

'I can put it behind me,' said Kamran instinctively.

She studied him. 'Is that how you really feel?'

He nodded, but it was a jerky, defensive movement.

'Okay,' said Zara, but she knew he needed time. The reason some victims came forward decades after their rape is because someone – a parent, a cop, a lawyer – was all too ready to accept their reticence. If Kamran thought about his choice – *really* thought about it – and arrived at the same conclusion, then he had the best chance of moving on. Zara had to give him that. 'Can we agree to sleep on it?' she asked. 'I'll ask Mia to hold off on charging Finn and you can decide if you want to testify. How does that sound?'

'I just want to get on with my life.'

'I know, Kamran, and I promise you I will help you do that. I'm asking you to think about it for a couple of days. It's Tuesday today. If you feel the same on Thursday, we'll call it off. Okay?'

Kamran's breathing slowed and his eyes took on a glassy focus. 'Okay,' he said softly.

Zara patched a smile over her sense of gloom. As with all her charges, a small part of her hoped that perhaps he would decide against it. The justice system was not kind to victims of rape, but Kamran had to be sure and decide for himself.

She watched him in the pale mid-afternoon light – the curve of his brow and the set of his jaw, a boy on the cusp of manhood. She thought of the myriad things he would have to negotiate: romantic advances, footing the bill, pretending to be assured, pretending to be impermeable. This young man would have to grow up, but someone had taken something from him and now his armour might always be weak. She felt a rush of warmth for him. She would help this boy. Whatever happened, whatever he chose, she swore she would support him.

The vague sound of the Hampton orchestra wafted across the green, midway through its Wednesday practice. The music hall, set on a slight hill, was grand and ornate in incongruous Art Nouveau.

'It's as if Gaudi and Dali got drunk together and decided to design a building,' his mother had said when she first saw it. She was always saying things like that and Kamran didn't know if it was a sign of inherent knowledge or an endless need to prove herself. He suspected it was the latter.

He perched on his sill and listened to the orchestra, watching the building intently as if he might actually see the music. The sun bled through the surrounding trees, hot wind gusting through heavy leaves. Kamran usually loved spring. It suited his natural disposition: optimistic, bright and hopeful. Now, he felt at odds with it. Now, he sat through his classes in a grim and wordless silence and snapped harshly at his friends when they acted loud or pushy, just as he had with Jimmy when he'd knocked on his door only moments ago and asked him to an impromptu party. It was this dark curtain of a mood and the threat of it never lifting that drove him to consider what Zara said in yesterday's meeting. Would he always return to that night, freezing himself in time? He was terrified of the black dog of depression, had heard whispered stories of Uncle Shahin and how he couldn't even make a cup of tea.

He felt a sudden need for his mother. 'It's okay to not be okay,' she had told him – so unlike her. But it was true that she came through when he really needed her. She would set down her detached efficiency and envelop him in her arms. In cynical moods, he pictured her looking in a mirror: 'Siri, load program motherhood.' In reality, he knew that Sofia loved him fiercely; would walk to the ends of the earth for him in her precious Louboutins. Wouldn't she prefer that Kamran see this through and not have it recur years later? And what of his father? Could he stomach the fact that his son had been raped? He had dealt with it cursorily, delegating the decision to Sofia – but if this went to trial, could he really confront the truth?

In the music hall, the sounds of the orchestra grew louder. Kamran recognised it as Shostakovich's 'Leningrad' Symphony – the rousing sound of courage – and all at once he knew what to do. He walked out to the green and sent a message to Zara, telling her once and for all that he was in it for the long haul.

He heard a voice behind him and spotted Jimmy on the concrete path.

'Are you coming after all?' he called.

Kamran exhaled softly. 'Yes, I am,' he called back. *Siri,* he thought as he headed to his friend. *Load program self-destruct.*

Nick Boynton cupped a hand over his brows and squinted down at Finn. 'So what's going on?' he asked.

Finn avoided eye contact, gazing instead across the field and the Tartan track encircling it. Both were still strewn with athletes. 'I'm just having a bad run,' he said.

Nick thumbed his lips in thought, carefully choosing his words. 'Look, man, I pay attention to the margins – you know that.' He plucked a stopwatch from his pocket as if to prove his point. 'The others haven't noticed because you're still beating them comfortably, but *I've* noticed.' He watched Finn for a moment, his heavyset brows in a crease. 'You've been off your game for two weeks. Today, you were *five* seconds slower than your average time. Is there something I should know?'

Finn's lips parted but he did not speak, not trusting his voice to hold.

Nick sat down on the bench. He was slighter than Finn – possibly the least athletic of the track team – but his fine-tuned ability to bring the best from his men saw him elected as captain. 'Come on, man. If you don't want to tell me as your teammate, then tell me as your friend.'

Finn felt a knot of pressure tighten in his throat. 'I'm in trouble,' he said. He let out a long, slow breath.

Nick's eyes, large and bovine, now narrowed in confusion. 'What kind of trouble?'

Finn tried to smile to lighten the mood but it cracked into a sob, revealing the full rush of his pain.

'Finn, what's going on?' Nick scrabbled in his pocket and pulled out a white handkerchief. He spun around on the bench so that his back was to the field, tugging at Finn to follow suit – a tender attempt to create some privacy.

'I'm sorry, man.' Finn's voice was gruff.

'Don't be sorry.' Nick pressed the handkerchief into his palm. 'Listen, you don't have to say sorry for crying.'

This small show of empathy made Finn want to weep. 'I'm scared,' he admitted.

Nick shifted on the bench anxiously. 'About what?'

Finn grimaced, as if swallowing a painful seed. 'I did something and now I'm in trouble.'

'What did you do?'

Finn balled the handkerchief in his fist. 'I didn't mean to. It was a mistake but Morewood told me today that I have to go to court. He said he'll come with me but my parents aren't here and I don't know what to do.'

'What happened?' Nick's voice was soft and breathless.

Finn only shook his head.

Nick studied him for a moment, then asked gently, 'Do you need a lawyer? My dad can help. He—'

'No.' Finn gestured vaguely at the horizon. 'My parents are taking care of it.'

'And where are *they*?'

Finn faltered. 'They're... busy,' he managed.

Nick raised his brows a touch to show he understood. 'What can I do?'

Finn exhaled audibly, expelling pent-up tension. 'I just—' He drew a palm across his face, skimming away his tears. He didn't need anything from Nick. Knowing he was there was enough. He faced his friend and tried for a lighter tone, his voice wavering beneath the effort. 'You can help me get my times back up.'

Nick watched him plaintively. He tipped the stopwatch at Finn. 'I'm already on it, mate.'

Finn laughed but it was too harsh to be convincing.

Nick twiddled with the stopwatch, rotating it in his hands. 'Do you want to talk about what happened?'

Finn shook his head. 'No. I... I don't want to talk but I need someone to listen.'

Nick's smile was sad. 'Yeah. I get that.' He was silent for a moment. 'Seriously, though, Finn, if you need to talk or whatever, you know where to find me.' He gestured at the track behind them.

Finn nodded. 'Thank you.'

'I can hang for a while if you'd like?'

'No, no.' Finn's tone grew strangely formal. 'You go on. We'll catch up on Friday.'

'You sure?'

'Absolutely.'

'Okay.' Nick stood up. 'You can keep the handkerchief.' He shook Finn's hand, then stepped over the bench and headed off the track.

Finn felt the squall in his mind calm down. After receiving the news from Morewood this morning that he was being charged, Finn had spent a feverish hour researching statistics, finding a sickening succour in headlines about the essential decriminalisation of rape. In the UK, less than a third of such allegations tried at court against eighteen- to twenty-four-year-old men led to a conviction. Finn was even younger and had a high chance of acquittal.

He never imagined that that night would end like this; never thought that Kamran would go to the police. And now he had to plead innocent and he had to do it convincingly. His future depended on it. *I am not guilty*, he repeated like a mantra. It was the only message that mattered. The only version of truth.

CHAPTER SIX

Zara pressed at a spot just below her shoulder blade. She rubbed the knot of muscle and thought wistfully of the fortnightly massage she had at Chalfonts on Fridays near her chambers. What would they make of her now? Zara no longer had weekly manicures or monthly waxes and trims. Her hair, though long and thick, had a dusting of split ends and she no longer touched up her make-up at the first sign of shine. 'Mid-powered lawyer,' Safran had joked when she adopted this mellower aesthetic.

It was true that a strong image served as a form of power. When Jodie's case was in the news, hadn't she pulled on her Lanvin suit and slicked on heavy mascara? Would she resort to similar armour when Kamran's case was seen in court? He had texted her on Wednesday and the reaction had been swift. Finn was charged on the very same day and the date of the trial was officially set: four months from now on September the seventh. A handful of court reporters had caught wind of the story and though it hadn't yet gone national, Zara feared that it would. Two handsome boys caught up in a rape trial at an exclusive all-male boarding school. It was the stuff of tabloid dreams. The thought of another high-profile case made her feel uneasy.

She opened a tab on her browser and searched for news on Hampton. There was one new result since the last time she looked: a video of Seth Dawson, an author and self-styled 'culture warrior', on a morning TV talk show. The segment was titled 'the noose of continuous consent'.

Dawson had thick silver hair and a salt-and-pepper beard that lent him an air of authority. He was a calm, considered speaker with none of the bombast of other pundits.

'There is a broad range of behaviours that can be described as sexual misconduct, from poor decision-making and impaired judgement to coercive control and violent predation,' he explained. '"Campus rape" usually fits into the first two categories. Those involved might feel regret after the event, but let's be honest about what this is: an ambiguous and often alcohol-fuelled sexual encounter caused by flawed decision-making – *not* predatory behaviour.'

Dawson shook his head impatiently. 'Stopping to ask for permission before every sexual act is unintuitive and retrograde. Overzealous activists have persuaded young people that a casual drunken fling was actually premeditated rape.'

Zara digested this. Dawson's words played right into Kamran's doubts about what had happened on the night of the party. She hoped he would not see it. The last thing they needed was a skittish witness.

Kamran surveyed his room at West Lawn. 'Mum?' he called out. He ducked back out to see if she had wandered down the hall. He had told her earlier that the trial was set for September. She had spoken slowly, as if rifling through her vocabulary for the best permutation of words. She had told him she would be there for him and support him all the way. *Siri, load program empathy.*

'Mum?' he called out again.

Sofia walked out of the bathroom, holding a bottle of pills. 'What on earth is this?'

He looked at the bottle blankly. 'Nothing.'

She shook it, the tap-tap echoing tinnily. 'It says Zopiclone on the bottle. Where did you get these?'

'I read they were good for helping you sleep.'

'Where did you get these?' she repeated.

'The internet.'

She tensed in alarm, then gripped him hard and steered him to the bed. 'Kamran, tell me you haven't—'

'For God's sake, Mum. I bought them because I couldn't sleep.'

'Why didn't you speak to the nurse?'

He pulled his arm from her grip. 'Because everything would get routed to the housemaster and it would go on my file and become a big thing for ever. I didn't want it on my record.'

She sagged. 'I don't like the idea of you being here all by yourself all day.'

'Mum, I can't leave now. It's an important year.'

She gripped the pills in her palm. 'Promise me these were just for sleeping.'

'They were just for sleeping, Mum. I haven't even opened them.'

She searched his face, combing for traces of doubt. Finally, she nodded, deciding to believe him. She tucked the bottle away in her bag as if it might serve as a talisman.

He gestured towards the door. 'Come on, Mum. Let's go.'

Together, they picked up Adam and filed into the waiting car. Sofia sat up front with Oliver, an act she saw as benevolent, with Kamran and Adam paired in the back. They wound towards Belsize Park to their picture-perfect house on their picture-perfect street. Funny – it never felt like coming home. As they drove, Kamran felt Adam's fingers find his and squeeze them in his fist. He looked at his younger brother and nodded, an unspoken answer to an unspoken question. *I'm okay*, it said. *I'm okay.*

Zara walked into the restaurant on Red Lion Street and was surprised to find that Safran was waiting. He stood, pulled out her chair and gave her a kiss on the cheek in one fluid movement.

'You're already here,' she said.

'I am indeed.' He loosened his tie and rolled up the sleeves of his crisp white shirt. 'I've ordered you that dodgy American *syrah* you like.'

She hesitated. 'Thanks, Saf, but I'm actually not drinking at the moment.'

He tilted his head quizzically. 'Oh?'

She squirmed a little. 'I've been going to NA meetings.' Her gaze flicked away from his. 'For work mainly,' she added quickly to allay the indignity of seeking help. 'It's to make sure I'm off the Diazepam – just a formality really, but they insist on me being teetotal and I thought I may as well try it.'

Safran pouted pensively. 'Am *I* still allowed to drink?'

Zara broke into a smile. 'Yes, Saf, you are.'

'Well, thank Christ for that.' He poured a glass of water and slid it across the table to her.

She accepted it, grateful that Safran hadn't pressed the issue. 'So—' Zara changed the subject. 'How did it go with the doctor?'

Safran groaned. 'She is a goddess sent from the foothills of *jannah* itself.'

'But?'

'But she's uptight. Doesn't drink. Doesn't swear. Doesn't even gossip; says it's bad for the soul.'

Zara feigned confusion. 'Isn't that what Muslim boys want, though? After years of fun with DiCaprio's exes, to settle down with a nice girl?'

Safran poured himself some water too. 'I want a teammate; someone I don't have to pretend with. I'm thirty-six now, Zar. It's time to settle down and I don't even know where to start.'

She frowned. 'You've never had trouble with women.'

'Yeah, but I'm still single.' His lips twisted in a cheerless smile. 'I mean, it doesn't *really* bother me, not yet, but it's starting to.'

'Sorry, Saf. I'd love to help but I'm hardly one to give advice.'

He looked at her. 'No,' he said blankly. 'You're not.' His bluntness made them laugh and they settled into an effortless evening. Copious dishes of *mezze* appeared at the table: piping feta parcels, juicy vine leaves and generous portions of *pide*.

Safran told her about his current case: a bribery allegation against an executive who accepted a million pounds in exchange for influencing the awarding of contracts by a multinational construction services company.

Zara smiled playfully. 'Well, whatever you think of what I do, at least it's not boring.'

'I'll give you that,' he said. 'So tell me – what are you working on now?'

Zara glanced over her shoulder to make sure they had privacy. It was in a restaurant like this that she had unwittingly talked about Jodie's case next to a reporter. When she was sure that no one was listening, she told Safran about Kamran's case.

'That's a bold decision by the CPS,' he said. 'It will be a miracle if they secure a conviction.'

'Yes, but it's worth trying.'

'Do you think the accused is a rapist?'

Zara arched a brow. 'Don't you?'

Safran lifted a shoulder. 'I don't know, Zar. It's a tricky one. I think kids – especially seventeen-year-old boys – make mistakes. From the sound of it, there was no coercion or premeditation; just ill judgement.'

Zara frowned. 'Okay, so if someone climbed through your window at night without your permission, got into bed with you, put themselves inside of you and you were too drunk to say no, that isn't rape?'

Safran waved a hand impatiently. 'That's not the same thing. They're in a heady environment. They have identical bedrooms. He was confused, went into the wrong one, found a warm body there and things happened.'

'I don't get you, Saf.' Zara's voice grew clipped. 'Just when I think I've figured you out, you say something like this.'

He shrugged, completely non-defensive. 'From your position, we have to conclude that the accused is a monster. From my position, we assume he was a misguided kid who made a stupid mistake. I think we need to stop assuming the worst of young men, as if they're all out to hurt someone. They were drunk, they fooled around, it was confusing.'

'You think it's as simple as that?'

'From what I've heard so far? Yes.'

Zara fell silent. Safran was her voice of reason. Would the jury see it the same way as him? Just a heady drunken encounter between two confused schoolmates? 'Christ,' she said softly, feeling the weight of the question press heavy on her shoulders. She reached for her glass, wishing it held something stronger than water.

Mack greeted Kamran with a slap on the back. 'There's my boy,' he said cheerfully. 'I've got a treat for you both.' He handed him his hunting jacket. 'I've arranged a sunset hunt.'

Kamran felt his stomach drop. 'That's great, Dad, but could we go tomorrow? It's been a really long week.'

'Which is exactly why we should go today: put a full stop on it so you can enjoy the weekend in peace.' He looked from Kamran to Adam. 'Go on now,' he said. 'It'll do you good to get out.'

Kamran swallowed a sigh. 'Yes, sir,' he said, knowing there was little use in arguing.

The three of them sat in the truck in a sour silence. They were headed to the Wessex Hills and though it was prime weather for hunting – clear skies, still wind – it was the last thing Kamran wanted. His father noticed and tried to counter it with false cheer that only increased the strain. His banter – which was intended in good humour – seemed to verge on bullying as he flicked Adam's cap for being too big and tugged at his belt for hanging too loose.

He drove in a cavalier, freewheeling style, revving straight over dips in the ground, making them jolt in their seats.

Dad, thought Kamran, *is what you get when nothing bad happens to a person.* He'd read once that everyone has trauma, but his father had led a life of privilege: a private school education, Oxford, an MBA at Harvard, then back to Britain to a hedge fund before joining the family company. His life ran in neat lanes, switching from childhood to adolescence to adulthood to middle age, all with clean transitions: no bumps, no setbacks, no ruinous events. Perhaps that was why he found it so hard to empathise with weakness. He would tut at the mental health debates on early morning TV, shouting, 'They're kids! They don't need therapists! They just need parents who will play with them!'

Anxiety was his *bête noire*. 'Everyone is anxious these days!' his voice would boom from downstairs. 'Is Nevinka anxious about cooking? Is Oliver anxious about driving? Am I anxious about living? No! Because we're not—' He would pause then, always forgetting the word. 'Snowflakes!' he would shout triumphantly and then laugh. 'Never has a word better fit a generation,' he would say. 'Snowflakes!'

Perhaps if his father had been born poor or disabled or just *ordinary*, he would have greater empathy. 'If Dad were American,' Adam once said, 'he would be a Trump supporter.' Kamran told him that was ludicrous, but feared that Adam was right. If you had never known pain or trauma or hunger, perhaps your capacity for empathy was just naturally smaller.

His father parked in a clearing and cut the engine to a merciful stop. He opened the door and bounded out. Kamran stepped out too and their eyes met in the dusky light.

His father paused, his hand awkward on the lip of the roof. 'Your mum tells me that the case is going to trial.'

'Yes, sir,' he said quietly, feeling painfully exposed.

A muscle twitched in his father's jaw. 'Well then, let's get ready to fight.' He pulled out a .243 sako rifle and handed it to Kamran.

Kamran gripped the stock of the rifle, his knuckles paling from the pressure.

'When taking a shot, why do we aim for the broadside?' asked his father.

Kamran answered by rote. 'Because it gives us a bigger target – easily thirty centimetres.'

'Precisely. And why don't we aim for the head or the neck?'

Adam dived in. 'Because they're small targets and you can easily miss by a few centimetres and cause the deer immense pain without actually killing it.'

'Excellent.'

Adam beamed, raising a swell of affection in the pit of Kamran's chest.

Their father glanced at his watch. 'Right, we've only got an hour after sunset, so let's get going.'

They headed into the woods, the engine-whir of crickets stirring a tense adrenaline. They picked their way past thickets and branches, Kamran careful to follow his father's footsteps so as not to make a sound that hadn't been made already.

On reaching a clearing next to a stream, their father

signalled at them to stop. Across the water stood a deer, a roebuck with a glossy rust coat. He beckoned them closer and told Kamran to take aim.

The deer snapped to attention, frozen in high alert.

Their father drew a finger to his lips, features tight in a grimace. Kamran knelt to brace the rifle, feeling the seize of pressure in his chest. Behind him, Adam shifted to give him space. As he backed away, a twig snapped beneath his feet. It may as well have been a gunshot, for the deer jolted in panic and fled into the thicket.

Their father groaned with frustration. 'I told you not to move,' he told Adam, the whisper harsh with venom. He exhaled, a plosive popping of air in the silence. 'Come on,' he said, head jerking forward. 'We'll track it.'

Kamran glanced at Adam with a slight shake of his head. *Don't worry about it.*

As he followed his father, Kamran wished that the woods would quieten. The sounds – the rasp of a nearby breath, the call of sudden distress – cast a sense of malevolence, making him unnerved. He gripped the rifle hard, calmed by its solid bulk.

They reached a second clearing and came upon a group of deer: a male, female and kid. Their father beckoned Kamran forward and pointed at the male. 'A clean broadside shot.'

Kamran glanced at the female, tending to the kid. 'But—' he pointed at the pair.

Mack's face creased in disgust. He tapped his head: two twitchy beats on his temple. *Don't be so stupid*, it said. *Think*. He had often told them that deer did not live in family groups in the same way humans do, but what was this if not a family? He flicked his hand in the air. *Well?*

Kamran raised his rifle and centred the deer in his sights. For a mad moment, he contemplated turning ninety degrees and pointing the barrel at his father instead. He watched the deer for a moment, breathing slowly to calm his pulse. Then, knowing he had no other way out, he gently squeezed the trigger. The gunshot cracked through the air and felled the deer in an instant. Its two companions fled and Kamran slid the safety back on.

'*Shabash!*' His father slapped him on the back. 'That was a fine shot.'

Kamran felt a bilious rush travel up his throat. He turned around and doubled up, praying he wouldn't retch. He sucked in great swallows of breath and swiped at the sweat on his forehead, feeling strangely faint. Adam next to him had tears in his eyes and the sight made him strangely mad. *You're not the one who has to fucking do it*, he wanted to spit. *I am. I do it so you don't have to.*

'All right,' called his father. 'Come on, stand up, son. You've done the deed, so let's finish it.'

They made their way to the kill, Adam dwelling by their bags, pretending to keep guard. As they extracted the carcass, his father tested him with further questions. 'What is the primary purpose of gralloching?' 'What are three ways to reduce contamination risk?' 'What do we look for when we inspect the carcass?'

Kamran answered mechanically, accepting his praise with modest nods. When they readied to leave, he offered the front seat to Adam who immediately waved it away. His brother preferred his own company; needed solitude to refuel; would rather go to the lake at Hampton than dwell in his shared room.

Kamran climbed up next to his father and they drove into the darkness, three men returning from battle. He watched the landscape and thought of the deer in the back of their truck felled by a shot to the heart. Sometimes, an injured deer would run a hundred metres before succumbing to death. Stalkers could tell where it was hit by surveying the blood on the ground. Bright red indicated arterial blood, light and frothy meant a hit in the lungs, dark and thick was a shot to the liver and watery spelled trouble: a shot to the stomach or intestines. He thought of those seconds before death – the fear, the panic, the agony. Given the same choice, he would undoubtedly rather a bullet in the head.

Finn stood on the rust-red track and savoured the feel of the surface. The rough texture of the Tartan on his soles was comfortingly familiar: a tether amid the turmoil. He could not believe how fast his life was changing. He had appeared in court the day before to plead not guilty of rape. Morewood had escorted him in the absence of his parents. They had called before the hearing. 'Are you sure you don't need us?' they asked. 'Please call us if you change your mind' – putting the onus firmly on Finn.

It riled him when he read fawning accounts of Scandinavia and its forward-thinking parenting, or when people's faces lit up as they took in his blond hair and blue eyes and realised he was Norwegian, the *ne plus ultra* of strength and masculinity. He was embarrassed by the way he impressed people merely by existing. A handsome young white man, the world eager at his feet. And now what? It was reaching up to seize him with the tar-black claw of despair. He could not let it capture him. This track was his lifeline – the one place he could outrun what chased him.

He tightened his laces and moved through his warm-up exercises ahead of Friday practice, fluidly completing twenty reps of each.

He spotted Nick nearby, one foot propped on a bench, a finger sliding around his heel to straighten his trainer's Achilles notch. Finn walked over and said hello.

Nick righted his foot. 'Hey,' he replied.

Finn glanced around them and saw two of their team-mates, Laurence and Hugo, walk onto the track. 'Listen, I just want to say thanks for Wednesday and I'm sorry about the waterworks.' He shrugged awkwardly, his laugh uncertain. 'I was in a weird place but I'm all right now. I want to regain those seconds I've lost.'

Something passed over Nick's face: a rupture of discomfort. He ushered Finn away from the track onto a bank of grass. 'You haven't heard,' he said, his voice a grim monotone.

'Heard what?'

Nick swallowed. 'People know what you did.'

'What do you mean?' asked Finn.

'On the night of the spring fundraiser.'

The air drained from his lungs. 'How?'

Nick shifted on his feet. 'A monitor at Hampton House heard Mr Lismore on reception talking on the phone.'

Finn balked. 'The staff know?'

Nick rubbed a thumb across his lips 'Maybe not all of them, but some of them.'

Finn covered his face with his hands and tried to slow the pulse of panic. There was no way to stem this tide. If a handful of pupils knew now, the rest of them would know tomorrow. 'Does the team know?' he asked, but when he looked over to Laurence and Hugo, he saw that the answer was clear. The two boys stood shoulder to shoulder, their faces hard with livid distaste. 'It isn't true,' he told Nick. 'It's not.'

His friend nodded peaceably. 'I do need to talk to you.' He hesitated. 'I've been asked to tell you to take a break from the team.'

Finn blanched with shock. 'What? Why?'

'You're representing Hampton at tournaments, Finn. We can't bring someone charged with a crime, especially one like yours.'

'Nick, you can't do this.'

'It's not up to me.'

'Please. You've got to do something. This is the only thing I have.'

Nick tutted. 'Come on, man. Don't be dramatic. You're good at loads of things.'

'But not like this!'

'I can't help you, man.'

Finn felt the pull of panic. He could not lose this; would go insane if he did. He shook his head and pointed at the track. 'I'm not going,' he said. 'I'm racing.'

Nick looked at him plaintively. 'Finn, you can't.'

'I can and I am.' He headed towards the track but when he reached the outer lane, Hugo stepped in his path. 'Go home, Andersen.'

Finn stared at him. 'Are you serious?'

'You know the track is reserved for the team.'

'Yes and I'm in the team.'

Hugo raised his brows at Nick.

'Finn, mate. You're not on the team,' called Nick.

He tried to force his way onto the track, but Hugo pushed him off with more violence than expected.

Finn looked from him to Laurence, overcome by something he couldn't unpick: shock, resentment and fury. These were his teammates; they *knew* what running meant to him. 'I'm going to Morewood about this.'

Nick held up his hands. 'The orders came from him, man. He doesn't want you at public events. Don't you get it? Your name will get out there. People know who you are. You're only going to disrupt the team.' He gestured at the school grounds. 'You can still run, mate. Just not here.'

'I don't have to compete,' Finn pleaded. 'Just don't kick me off the team.'

'Look, it's not just Morewood,' said Nick. 'The team doesn't want you here either.'

'And you? You're the captain. They have to listen to you.'

Nick exhaled. 'I don't think you should be here either.'

Finn felt the words like a blow to the gut. 'But I didn't do it.'

Nick's voice dropped low. 'Mate, you as good as admitted it to me.'

'That's not true,' he said breathlessly.

'You said you did something you weren't supposed to. You said you made a mistake...'

'No. Nick, please—'

'Go home, mate. You're disrupting practice.' He turned his back to Finn and blew his whistle. 'Come on, lads. Let's hustle.'

Finn stared at the track, inert with disbelief. In his feverish research into figures and statistics, he hadn't factored this. If Nick – their intelligent, mature, compassionate captain – had cast him out so bluntly, others would surely follow.

Finn stepped back, wanting to hide the voltage of his pain. He raised a hand in parting, convincing himself that they were still friends.

Kamran hovered by a large green Chesterfield chair, hand resting uncertainly on one studded wing.

Mr Morewood did not look up. Instead, he continued to write in a diary, the scratch of his pen nib the only sound. After a moment, he nodded at the chair. 'Sit,' he instructed.

Kamran obeyed, gingerly gathering his hands in his lap.

'Mr Hadid, I understand that news of your case reached our pupils this week. I have spoken to Mr Lismore on reception and am assured that he did not divulge the information, contrary to rumour.'

Kamran nodded.

'I will continue to investigate but I fear that the culprit may never be found given the nebulous nature of the rumour mill.' He paused. 'May I ask if you have faced opprobrium in the days since?'

'Opprobrium,' repeated Kamran. The word sounded comical on his tongue, like 'hippo' or 'hyperbole'. What qualified as opprobrium? The 'is it true' and 'what can I do' repeated by friends and teachers? The covert offers to beat up Finn? The furtive stares and glances? 'No, sir. No opprobrium,' he answered.

Morewood set down his pen. 'Mr Hadid—' He paused,

then laced his fingers. 'Kamran,' he tried again. His voice was gentler, but uncomfortable in this stab at intimacy. 'I know how overwhelming this must be for you. I think it's extremely important for you to process what happened and to find closure with professional help.'

Kamran shifted in his seat.

'I strongly believe that Hampton's mediation service can help you do this most effectively. If you were to use our internal review instead of the more aggressive route, I would personally guarantee confidentiality and you would bypass the intense scrutiny that comes with reporters, courts, judges and juries.' He gestured at the window and the grounds outside. 'As you know, we have a psychologist at Hampton as well as a doctor, three chaplains and of course your housemaster and tutor. We have the mechanisms here to help you while protecting you from the glare of strangers. If you want to follow this course, I can make the arrangements post-haste.' He offered a pained smile. 'I do believe that this is the best course for you and your family.'

Kamran felt the pressure of Morewood's gaze. He knew what would happen if he agreed: a seemingly balanced pro-cess that would ultimately rule against him. He was aware of the legacy of abuse at public schools, and how Hampton would do everything it could to distance itself from history.

'So – what are your thoughts?' asked Morewood.

Kamran tried to think what Zara might say if she were in the room. 'I trust the law,' he said weakly.

Morewood sighed. 'Oh, son,' he said, heavy with condes-cension. 'I have to be honest: I think you're in for a very big shock.'

Kamran dug his fingernails into the pad of his palms. 'I appreciate the warning, sir.'

Morewood studied him. 'If we deal with this internally, we can take immediate action and it would all be over in a week or two. There would be no fussing about for the entire summer.'

Kamran felt his conviction waver. If he stayed there much longer, he knew he would yield. 'I would rather focus on school, sir, and let the police deal with it.'

Morewood huffed. 'Very well,' he said, his tone now cold and formal. 'In that case, Mr Hadid, you are excused.'

Kamran stood. 'Thank you, sir,' he said quietly. He left the office and felt his energy desert him.

Outside, he leaned against a wall, churning with anxiety. Never before had he defied a master. He needed to eat – or vomit. He didn't know which. He slid onto a cold marble stair, feeling his stomach seize. He had always suspected that the case would go public, but that it had happened now, months before the start of the trial, gripped him with paralysis. *It's not long now,* he thought. It's not long until the end of term. But then what? A tense summer with his mother and father, and months of pretending that nothing was wrong. He remained on the stair for a while, trying to gather the will to stand.

Finn picked at the lip of the parcel tape, then smoothed a strip over the cardboard box. It was the final day before summer break and he had come to collect the last of his belongings from the housemaster's office at West Lawn.

He watered the dragon plant on the floor, making sure to

pour equally over the patch of soil. He gently touched the tips of two shoots. 'Be strong, little fellas,' he said. The act brought tears to his eyes. When he was appointed in the role, the plant was languishing behind a cupboard, ostensibly days from death. He photographed it and ran a Google image search to find its name and origin. It couldn't get too cold, so he had taken it from the draughty corner and placed it in the sunlight, watering it assiduously once a week until it began to flourish. It was strangely therapeutic, tending to something alive. He had assumed that, like his father, he would lack paternal instinct. He had never had a pet, neither had he craved one, but tending to the plant had stirred a strange instinct: to nourish and protect. Leaving it here for the summer filled him with a sickly sorrow.

He sank into a chair and watched the tiny green shoots. *I did that*, he thought. *That's what I did. That's who I am.* He heard footsteps pause in the doorway and glanced up absently. Their eyes locked and Finn bolted to his feet.

Kamran hesitated. In his hands, he held a small cream envelope, tied with a gauzy ribbon. He raised it an inch. 'I just need to put this in the post.'

Finn stepped back, bumping into his chair, which skittered across the wooden floor. 'Sorry, I'm not supposed to be here. I was just packing the last of my things.'

They held each other's gaze and Finn felt a swell of emotion. He was desperate to plead his innocence; to beg Kamran to see reason, but he knew how much trouble this could cause and so he chose to say nothing. He hefted the box into his arms and turned towards the door.

'You know I had to report it,' said Kamran.

Finn opened his mouth to speak, not knowing if he should apologise or demand an apology. After a beat, he said, 'We're not allowed to talk to each other.'

'I know that.' Kamran's voice was strained. 'But I want you to know this isn't easy for me either.'

Finn swallowed. 'We're not allowed to talk to each other,' he repeated. He left the room, his blood pulsing a sonar beat. He strode out onto the green and headed back to Rendale House, holding back tears so no one would see.

Kamran spotted his friends gathered on the green and forced himself to smile.

'Hey, guys,' he said brightly.

'Hey,' replied Jimmy.

'All right?' said Nathan.

Kamran shifted on his feet, wiping his soles on the grass only for something to do. 'Are you all packed up for the summer?'

'Yeah,' said Barrett. 'All set.' His head bobbed in a pronounced nod as if motion alone might carry the conversation.

'So what's going on?' asked Kamran.

Barrett shrugged a shoulder. 'Oh, you know. This and that.' He looked to the others. 'Jimmy was just saying that he'll be thinking of us poor bastards when he's sunning himself in Malaysia.'

There was a forced round of laughter.

'And what about you? You'll be in the Cotswolds, right?'

'Yeah.' Barrett toed a stone in the grass, dislodging it from its cocoon. 'You could come up and see me if you wanted.'

Kamran started in surprise. 'That would be great,' he said, breathless with relief, buoyed by solidarity.

'Okay, I'll check when we can borrow Justyna.'

Kamran laughed. 'We don't need to bring your maid, man. We can clean up after ourselves.'

'No it's, uh...' Barrett fidgeted with his lapel.

'What?'

He shook his head. 'No, it's nothing.'

Kamran studied him. 'Tell me.'

'It's just that my old lady wants an adult to be there.'

Kamran frowned. 'But you're always there with just mates.'

'I know.' Barrett squirmed. 'She's being paranoid.'

'Why?' Kamran looked to Jimmy and Nathan as if they might offer an answer. Then, it dawned on him. 'Wait, does she think I'll accuse you of something?'

Barrett scoffed. 'Don't be daft, mate. It's not like that.'

'Then what is it?'

'Honestly, it's not a big deal. She *wants* you to come.'

Kamran felt mortified. He was appalled by Barrett's words and belittled by his clumsy effort to shield him from the truth.

Jimmy cut into the silence. 'Or you could come and see me in Malaysia. It beats the Cotswolds any day.'

Kamran tensed his jaw, but waved a casual hand in the air. 'It all sounds great, guys, but I don't think my mum will let me. She wants me to stay at home this summer.'

'That's too bad,' said Barrett with discernable relief.

'Thanks for the offer though.' Kamran stepped back from the circle and patted his pockets in a purposeful manner. 'Well, I better get on with packing then.'

'If I don't see you, then have a good summer, man,' said Barrett, extending a hand. Kamran shook it, neither of them making eye contact.

Nathan offered his hand too. 'Take care of yourself, mate.'

Jimmy gestured in the direction of West Lawn. 'I'll walk you up,' he said, falling in step with Kamran. After a few paces, he gestured over his shoulder. 'Sorry about them.'

'It's okay.' Kamran was thankful for Jimmy but also bothered by the apology, for it implied an ownership over their friends that he could no longer claim.

Jimmy slowed his pace. 'How are you feeling about summer at home?'

Kamran felt a pellet of dread settle in his stomach. 'It's going to be hard,' he said.

'And how are you feeling full stop?'

They walked a few paces in silence. 'Worried,' admitted Kamran.

'About the trial?'

'Yeah.'

Jimmy stopped as they approached West Lawn. 'Listen, man, you're doing the right thing. I'm proud of you.'

Kamran was mute with gratitude for he needed Jimmy's support. Unlike Barrett and Nathan who shifted uncomfortably if they swayed too close to the night of the party, Jimmy asked questions directly. 'Are you okay?' 'Are you scared?' 'How are you feeling?' 'What do you need?'

With others, Kamran kept up a pretence. His laugh still came easily but it had a hollow texture. He still bantered with Adam on their journeys in the car but it held a contrived quality as if they were playing tennis and could not drop the ball in case it shattered the illusion that everything was normal. Even teachers treated him differently, warily glancing at the classroom door to ensure that it was open if they happened to be alone.

'I meant what I said about Malaysia,' said Jimmy. 'We could stay in the villa, go swimming every day, relax, just get away?'

Kamran smiled wistfully. 'I wish I could but there's no way Mum would let me.'

'Okay, but we'll stay in touch?'

'Yeah, we will.'

Jimmy drew him into a fierce hug. 'I love you, man.'

The words surprised him and he took a moment to steady his voice. 'Thanks, man,' he said gruffly. 'Me too.'

'Take care of yourself this summer, yeah?'

Kamran nodded. 'Yeah, I'll try.'

'I'll see you in September.'

'Yeah,' said Kamran, feeling the dry heave of his gut. 'September.'

PART II

CHAPTER SEVEN

Zara looked out over Aldgate East from her fourth-storey window. The area seemed to literally depress at the first sign of cold. It was unusually chilly for September and the streets seemed discoloured, people hunkering in their coats as if hiding from an unseen foe. In the distance, she could see the Shard reaching towards a monochrome sky. Fanning out from the skyscraper was a battery of squat grey buildings with hardly a tree in sight. It stirred a sense of melancholy, making Zara feel restless on this Friday afternoon. She stood and paced the length of her office as if that might ward off this feeling. She thought of the Diazepam she would take on days like this and bit down the urge before it formed fully.

Kamran's trial was starting on Monday, which made her feel ill at ease. Over the course of the summer, the case had drawn a worrying level of attention. It was used by activists as a cautionary tale in their 'yes means yes' campaigning while tabloids prepared for the trial with glee: a posh boy raped at his boarding school. It was perfectly seasoned for scandal. Zara recalled Jodie's trial – the headlines, the protests, the riot – and prayed that Kamran would be spared the same violence.

She checked her watch and headed out to meet him now for his familiarisation visit at Inner London Crown Court. This was one of the more elegant courts in the city, tasked with processing serious crimes that couldn't be tried at the Old Bailey. She drove past the iron gates and parked outside the building. With its expansive façade of Portland stone, the court was akin to a stately home.

Zara entered through a revolving door and passed through security: a quick unzip of her bag, a customary swig of her water and the emptying of her pockets onto a round metal plate. On the other side, she met Mia and Kamran and walked with them to courtroom one. It was a vast square with enormous Diocletian windows and a cavernous domed roof. Its blood-red carpet and leather seats gave it an air of portentous ceremony.

Zara explained to Kamran the layout of the room. The judge's bench was an elevated platform that presided over the court. The seat in the centre where the judge would sit was the only one with cushions – one orange and the other green. Opposite the bench was the dock where Finn would sit behind bulletproof glass. The witness box was to the right of the dock and the jury to its left. Above the dock was the public gallery also behind bulletproof glass.

A door to the courtroom opened and Andrew Leeson walked in, the CPS barrister who had tried Jodie's case last year. He was tall and slim with a long face and fine blond lashes that gave him an effeminate air. Zara stood and greeted him warmly.

She introduced him to Kamran, with Mia as a witness. The two could meet only briefly lest Leeson be seen to coach him. Zara watched them and was taken aback by Kamran's ease as he amiably sparred with Leeson. Was this the value of a public-school pedigree? Did he recognise one of his own? It was strange: Zara was in her domain and yet seeing the two together – their comfort and facility – *she* felt like the outsider.

Mia sat down in the jury box and Zara went and joined her. Leeson readied to leave and they watched the men shake hands. Kamran wandered around the courtroom, leaning over the judge's bench to try to see behind it, gazing up at the ceiling as if he might need to describe it. Perhaps he was committing it to memory so he could pre-construct a nightmare and arm himself for the days to come.

He joined them on the red leather seats, his legs stretching further than theirs. 'The women you work with, do they get over it?' he asked softly.

Zara glanced at him. 'Some do,' she said. Sitting side by side lent them a certain intimacy; a closeness that wasn't cloying.

'Which ones?'

Zara considered this. 'The ones who accept the outcome.'

'And those that don't?'

What could Zara tell him? That they were haunted by spectres at night, that they locked their doors three times, that they felt a deep disgust for surrendering to victimhood, that they – strong, bold, independent women – were weakened by the whims of a man?

'We eventually learn to,' said Mia.

Zara turned to her, surprised.

Mia lifted a shoulder. 'It shouldn't be a shock. Eleven

happen every hour.' She caught Kamran's eye. 'Sorry, I shouldn't be telling you this.'

'No, please,' he said, his voice thick with urgency. 'Please tell me.'

Mia focused on the judge's bench. After a beat, she said, 'I was a newly qualified officer and was keen to show I was "one of the lads". I was drinking but not too much. I knew when to stop.' She brushed a strand of hair from her eyes.

'A fellow new recruit offered to drive me home and I was thankful for the offer. When we got there, he said he was desperate for the toilet and asked if he could pause for a pit stop. I knew him fairly well and didn't think anything of it so I let him upstairs. I made the mistake of turning on the TV while he was in the bathroom. He came out and said, "*Glengarry Glen Ross*? That's my favourite film!" and sat down on the sofa. It was 1 a.m. and I was tired but I was—' Mia weaved a hand in the air. 'Polite. And so I sat down, thinking maybe he'd leave after a few minutes but he stayed, laughing and shouting at the TV, really engaging with it and I thought, *maybe he just really likes the film*.' She snickered. 'God, we rationalise so much.

'It was about halfway through the film and in my head I'm thinking, *how do I get rid of him?* and part of me is thinking, *well, at most it's an hour and he'll be gone* and so I sat there with all these thoughts when he got up and switched off the light, saying films are better in the dark. I knew something was up then and I said that actually I was tired and I wouldn't last the film. "That's okay," he said. "Just let me watch this scene. I love it so much." So we watched this scene together and I'm thinking he's going to leave but he starts leaning towards me. I freeze because I'm young and haven't figured out what's what yet and he just lunges at me. I push him off, not too violently because I want to let him down easily and he holds my wrists, whispers a stream of compliments as if trying to put me in a trance and I push back and he tells me not to be a tease and he... he takes what he wants from me. And you know what he tells me the next day? "I had fun last night."'

Zara sensed Kamran startle but did not interrupt Mia.

Her voice was now bitter. 'Like he doesn't even know what he did.' She turned towards Kamran. 'I know what you're going through: negotiating with yourself – "Well, how bad was it really? Do I really want to do this?" – so let me tell you something: even if it doesn't go your way, you will know that you stood up and you told the truth. I didn't and that still haunts me.'

Kamran took an audible breath. 'Thank you,' he said quietly. 'I'm sorry.'

'Me too,' said Mia.

The three of them sat there for a long time, stirring only when a cleaner walked in, her shoulders ducking apologetically, making herself as small as possible.

'Thank you,' said Zara as they stood up to leave. Outside, the air snapped with cold and it roused them from their melancholy.

Kamran pointed at a black saloon. 'Oliver will drive me home.'

Zara nodded. 'I'll pick you up from Hampton on Monday. If you need anything over the weekend, call me, okay?'

'Okay.' Kamran slid into the waiting car.

Zara watched it leave before turning to Mia. 'Did you drive?'

'No, I was dropped off.'

'You want a lift?'

'Yes. Thank you.'

'Do you want to talk about it?'

Mia shook her head, staring at the saloon's wake. 'No. But thank you.'

They got into Zara's car and without letting herself double guess it, she reached over and squeezed Mia's hand. She nodded in response – an unspoken thank you. They drove through the streets in silence. It was close to 7 p.m. but Mia asked to be dropped at the station.

'I'll walk you in,' said Zara.

Mia didn't argue. They walked side by side up the stairs and stepped into the station where the warmth hit them in a milky wash. Mia's office was empty but the fluorescent light was still on.

Zara paused in the doorway. 'Are you going to be all right?'

Mia nodded. 'I'm fine. I don't tend to tell people because...' She wrung a hand in the air. '"Victim" is such an ugly word, you know? It's debilitating and I don't want to wear that label.'

'I get it.' Zara smiled tenderly but didn't reach out for a hug. Instead, she held out her hand and Mia shook it firmly.

Back outside the station, Zara was startled by a familiar face: an athletic man with a broad smile.

'Hi!' he said brightly. 'I'm Matthew of Cavill House. We met here in June.'

She recalled their exchange and an instinctive smile spread across her face. 'Yes, I remember. I believe you were trying to "neg" me.'

He groaned. 'I know. What an arsehole.'

Zara moved so that they faced each other on the same step. She hadn't thought about him since their meeting in June but was surprised by a strange lightness: the weight of the day lifting.

'I tried to email you,' he said. 'I used all sorts of variations of your name followed by Artemis House dot com and they all bounced back.' He caught himself. 'God, that sounds creepy, doesn't it?'

She laughed. 'It does a bit, yes.'

He gazed down at her. 'Are you going somewhere?'

'Home,' she replied.

'Could I take you out for a drink?' He asked it haltingly as if poised for defeat.

Zara took in his smile: easy and open and calm. It felt so uncomplicated standing there with him in the amber pool of lamplight. She considered it for a moment. 'Okay,' she agreed.

He did a double take. 'Really?' He held up a stack of files before she could change her mind. 'I just need to run this in. Please don't go anywhere.' He rushed up the stairs and into the station.

Zara waited on the last step, her back pressed against the cool iron gate, and felt a sense of ease. If her brain stopped whirring for even just an hour, she would call this day a win.

Finn loved the hour before curfew when the gentle bloom of night made Hampton close to magical. As he watched it now, however, through the glaze of his bedroom window, it filled him with an aching loneliness.

He was a senior now, which meant he no longer shared a room and all the extra space seemed to only magnify his solitude. It was so profound, so familiar, that it made him well up with tears.

Finn was used to not having his parents around. During breaks, he flew to Switzerland only to spend it with the gardener's dog who would lick his hands for peanut crumbs and sidle beneath his legs on the warm white rug. How he had yearned for a brother in childhood. Boarding school had been a revelation. The pupils were the same on the surface – well spoken, well mannered – but look a little deeper and there was a dizzying range of difference. There was Henry who collected first editions and had a copy of *Quaint Fragment* worth ten thousand pounds, bought for a bargain in a second-hand bookshop. There was Evan with his pocket watch and slicked centre parting reminiscent of a textbook Nazi. There was pudgy Charlie who spelt his name with a 'y' and was convinced that the moon landing was a pure conspiracy. Hampton gave them space to be who they were.

It was true that the seniors ruled the school and there was always a bit of joshing, but all in all, the boys at Hampton were gentlemen in the making. They shared a comradeship that made them feel like a family, just as the brochure promised it would be.

So what did that make him? A wolf among sheep? The thought filled him with oily unease. Finn watched the shadows deepen outside. Then, compelled by some unseen force, he picked up his phone and clicked on a name: Hadid M.

He knew it would break the conditions of his bail and could possibly land him in custody, but he *needed* to talk to him. He needed to plead forgiveness, to state yet again that he hadn't meant it. Tomorrow was his day in court and how could he sit there calmly if his conscience was still smarting?

He typed out a message. 'I know I'm not allowed to contact you, but can we talk?'

Hadid M is typing... read the message on the screen. It stopped, then started, then stopped again.

Please, typed Finn. **I just want to talk.**

Hadid M is typing... appeared again.

Please just tell the truth, said the message. The status disappeared indicating that he was no longer online.

Finn felt a pulse of frustration. He folded into himself, head on his knees as if bracing on a plane. He pressed hard against his ears to squeeze out the panic. The only way he would get through the trial is if he stayed calm and remembered his lines. It was a confused drunken encounter. He didn't know what he was doing. He thought that Kamran was willing. There was no sign of resistance. They were equally inebriated. And that detail he had to cling to: the door was unlocked. The door was unlocked and if it had been shut, this wouldn't have happened at all.

Sofia rifled through Kamran's medicine cabinet, checking each bottle obsessively. She stared at the dark green suitcase in the corner, fighting the urge to throw it open, to thumb through the shirts and trousers, to pull out Kamran's washbag and rifle through it for pills. She wanted to believe that he was sensible but you heard stories of mothers who never knew their sons at all; sons who took drugs or had a gambling problem or coerced a girl into sex. Every man who did something terrible was somebody's son and she wasn't so self-involved that she thought herself immune. She fretted until she forced herself into a decision.

Kamran was busy helping his father load firewood, so she knelt by the suitcase, unzipped it swiftly and pulled out his navy washbag. There were plasters, deodorant, Compeed, hand sanitiser. She paused, then pulled out a pack of condoms. It was a pack of ten but when she opened it, there were only four inside.

She braced her knees on the floor as her thoughts began to sway. Hampton strictly controlled access to students. There were no girls allowed on campus so where had Kamran used these?

She heard movement next door and placed everything back in the suitcase. She zipped it up swiftly and left the room. Moving down the hall, she knocked on the adjacent door.

'Come in,' called Adam's voice.

She walked in and sat on his bed, fiddling with her wedding ring. 'So Oliver is dropping you both at Hampton tonight.'

Adam glanced up. 'Yeah, I know.'

She hesitated. 'Adam, can I ask you to do something?'

'Sure.'

She stopped herself from chiding him for using that word. It was so *American*. She gathered herself and said, 'As you know, Kamran has asked me not to go to court tomorrow.'

'Yeah, I know.'

'When he leaves Hampton for court, can you go to his room and check his medicine cabinet. You still have the spare key?'

Adam frowned. 'Why?'

'I found some pills last time and I want to make sure that he's okay.' She smoothed a crease on the lap of her skirt. Then, she asked, 'Is your brother sexually active?'

Adam squirmed visibly. 'How am I meant to know? Why don't you ask him?'

A blush laced across her face. 'Sorry, I shouldn't have asked.'

He pulled away from her. 'No, you shouldn't have.'

'But you will check his room?'

He shrugged mutely.

'Please, Adam, it's important.'

He sighed. 'Okay, fine.'

'Thank you.' She hated to pitch him against his brother but she was doing this for Kamran. Everything she did was for her boys. If she had to cross a line or two, then that's what she would do.

Kamran awoke in a haze and for a brief disorienting moment, thought he was still in his room at home. He expected his mother to call up in that singsong voice she usually reserved for company. On most mornings, she would pad up the stairs and hover on the landing. Kamran could hear her breathing there, loading her gentlest tone.

'Stop it,' he wanted to beg. 'Please just stop it.' He wanted his mother back: the one who would rap a perfunctory knock on the door and snappily click her fingers at him if he dared to be lazy or tardy. This softer incarnation made him feel claustrophobic.

A perverse part of him had started to push her on purpose.

As the summer drew on, he stayed in bed for longer and grew tetchier in tone, bristling visibly if she dared to touch him. He wanted to snap her out of her bovine tolerance, to force her to discipline him, to remind her to be his mother, to remember who he was.

Leaving for Hampton last night had filled him with relief. By some dark stroke of fate, the start of the trial was in the first week of term. Mr Morewood had convinced Sofia that Kamran should return to Hampton despite being called to court. Returning to school with the other pupils would make the transition smooth, he said. Kamran suspected that in reality it was easier to sequester him there, far from the lens of the press. Whatever the motivation, he was relieved to be back in school, free from the cloak of his mother's concern and the ersatz cheer of his father.

He remained in bed for a moment and listened to a series of familiar sounds: the hollow ticking of his clock, the clanging effort of pipework as someone turned a shower on. *Two days*, he told himself. *Two days of testimony and then it's out of my hands.*

He sat up and watched a blackbird hop outside his window. The autumn lawn at Hampton was still a defiant green and the trees hemming the sky bloomed in reds and yellows. *Two days and I can get on with life.*

He drew himself out of bed and went through the motions of his morning routine: a quick check in the mirror, shower, dry off and moisturise with the rich Moroccan oil his mother insist he use. He waited for his skin to absorb the moisture before he touched his clothes: a metallic blue suit and a crisp white shirt coupled with a salmon tie. He held up a waistcoat and studied it for a moment. It was too much, he decided. Zara had told him to dial back on the privilege; that the jury needed to identify with him. He spritzed on some CK One, which arrived every September like clockwork from Rana; a back-to-school hamper for him and Adam with a bottle each of the perfume, a pack of merino socks, Tom Ford boxers, a Moleskine notebook and a Cartier pen. He had four of them in his drawer.

He dressed slowly and methodically and assessed himself in the mirror. With a fresh shave and haircut, he knew he looked well groomed, but mixed with that was a frisson of fear. What if he failed to pull it off – like he'd failed at Avi's wedding that summer?

A girl at his table, Neena, had leaned towards him, her faced bathed in the flattering rose light that lined the arches of Hintze Hall, the venue of his cousin's wedding. 'Are you brothers?' she'd asked, gesturing towards Adam.

Kamran smiled, bravado kicking in like muscle memory. 'Yeah, but I'm better looking, right?'

She laughed. 'I mean, he's pretty cute too.'

'Too?' he said, with an amused tilt of his chin. It was comforting – this mindless, effortless banter – but as the tenor of flirtation grew deeper, Kamran began to flounder. He flinched when she briefly touched his knee midway through a bout of laughter and felt his stomach clench when she pressed her shoulder to his while showing him a funny meme.

When at the end of the night she suggested swapping numbers, Kamran began to stammer. She thought it cute but he pushed back his chair and walked away, leaving her mute and confused. He fled to the bathroom and locked himself in a cubicle and swallowed great gulps of air. What was this new version of Kamran Hadid that hid itself in bathrooms? That fled from pretty women and found itself seized by panic?

He couldn't succumb to that same weakness today; had no choice but to weather the weight. *Two days*, he thought as he readied to leave. *Just two days.*

Outside, he was startled to find Adam waiting.

His brother squared his shoulders. 'I'm coming with you.'

'No.'

'I am,' insisted Adam. 'I forged Mum's signature and got leave from my housemaster.'

Kamran held up a palm. 'Adam, I don't want you in there listening to what happened. I can't be thinking about you or worrying about you.'

'And I can't be *here* thinking about you and worrying about you.' He flung an arm at the window. 'You may have convinced Mum not to come but you're not convincing me.'

Kamran was surprised by Adam's conviction. He did not admit it but he was touched. 'Okay,' he said with a tight nod. 'Let's go.' He headed to the stairs, buoyed by the footsteps that echoed his own.

Zara waited on the green outside and he greeted her with a nod, never touching a woman unless expressly invited. Perhaps that's why boys liked to wrestle so much; they were touch-starved – too old for a mother's affection, too young for a serious girlfriend.

Zara led them down the winding path into her waiting car, she and Kamran in front and Adam in the back.

'How are you feeling?' she asked.

'Yeah, okay.' Kamran did not elaborate.

Zara clicked in her seatbelt. 'I'll be there for every minute of it.'

Adam leaned forward. 'I will too.'

Kamran cracked a weary smile. 'Thanks, but if Mum finds out you forged her signature, she'll kill you.'

Adam shrugged defensively. 'Well, she's hardly being honest herself right now.'

Kamran twisted in his seat. 'What do you mean?'

Adam raised his chin defiantly. 'She wanted me to search your room today while you were in court; to check your cabinet for pills.'

'Jesus Christ.' Kamran shook his head. 'She thinks I'm going to top myself.'

Zara next to him glanced over. 'Why would she think that?'

He waved vaguely at the window. 'She found some sleeping pills in my cabinet. Jimmy's dad owns a chain of pharmacies and he swiped them for me. It's not a big deal.' He waited but Zara didn't say anything. 'I haven't used any at all.'

'Okay,' she said meditatively. She manoeuvred out of the parking bay and headed to Inner London Crown Court.

Kamran watched the landscape change. It never ceased to amaze him the stark difference to be found in a two-mile radius. While Hampton was all red brick and green trees, the rest of Wembley Central seemed grey and insipid. He wondered about the boys who walked these streets. He met them occasionally at weddings with their slicked-back hair and cocky manner as if making up for something lacking.

Where did they go to spill their fears – too tough to talk to their fathers, too proud to talk to their friends?

But was it any different at Hampton? Could Kamran and his peers really confide in their matrons and masters? Weren't they all just pretending, too?

Zara glanced over as they approached the court. 'Are you okay?'

Kamran exhaled, low and soft, barely disturbing the air. He surveyed the empty concourse, relieved to see there were no reporters yet. 'I'm a bit nervous,' he admitted.

Zara parked, then reached over and tapped his hand – twice with a forefinger as if freeing a cigarette of ash. 'That's normal, Kamran, but you're tough. You can do this.'

He unclicked his seatbelt. 'Thank you.' His pressed his lips together – so tightly, the pink of them turned yellow.

Zara led him to the building, her hand on the small of his back. The gentle press of it stirred something weak inside him and he blinked hard to bat it back. He cleared his throat, raised his head like a good Hamptonian and strode into the courthouse, he and Adam flanking Zara like bodyguards, each six inches taller than her. They passed through security and were directed to a waiting room. Kamran sat in a plastic chair and stared at the grey-blue carpet, flecked by design so that marks and stains were easily masked. He felt the familiar kick of adrenaline, so helpful on the fencing piste but giddying here in this room. His words felt thick in his mouth, disjointed and unwieldy. He knew he had to be honest, but when the truth felt so murky, how could he articulate it?

There were two facts he had to convey: he did not consent

to sex and Finn could not have reasonably believed that he did. The jury would then decide the truth.

And Finn? What would become of him if they chose in Kamran's favour? He pushed the thought from his mind, not yet ready to consider the answer.

There was a knock on the door and a slight woman with a large grey bun ducked her head in the room. Zara introduced her as the usher, then left with Adam for a place in court, he in the public gallery, she with dispensation to sit by the witness box. Kamran watched them go, his heart thumping a skittish beat. In a matter of moments, he would be called on to tell the truth, a truth that wasn't clear – not even to him.

Zara sat in the courtroom and noted that Mr Morewood, the child protection officer and deputy head at Hampton, was seated in the public gallery, presumably in lieu of Finn's family. He sat primly with his knees pressed together and looked somehow small in the courtroom.

She turned her attention to Judge Charles Arden, a doughy-looking man with plump cheeks and a jowly jawline. He wore thick black glasses that framed brown eyes with something of a twinkle. Zara was not familiar with him but had done her research before the trial. Legally, she could not coach Kamran on what to say but *could* advise him on how to say it. Judge Arden didn't care for theatrics. He had little time for bombast and was accommodating to victims. 'Don't get complacent though,' she warned Kamran. 'He is still a judge so treat him with respect.'

Judge Arden welcomed the jury and the two barristers.

Andrew Leeson seemed even taller than usual in his horsehair wig and black gown. The barrister for the prosecution was Olivia Hallett, an elegant woman with dark hair, now stuffed beneath her wig. She was in her mid-forties, Zara knew, but had one of those solid fleshy faces that could be thirty-five or fifty-five, frozen with a doctor's help. Zara understood why. In a profession so tightly pegged to appearance, it made sense to cling to your looks.

To the left of the barristers sat the jury with five women and seven men. Zara studied a man in the front row, mid-twenties with a sculpted hairstyle, dressed in grey jeans and a pale blue slimline shirt that had two buttons undone. His legs were spread wide and he leaned back in his chair with a casual elbow resting on an arm. He was a picture of nonchalance. Behind him to the left was another young man, a few years older with a seam of a smile that gave him a cocky air. It was said that men were afraid that women would laugh at them while women were afraid that men would kill them. It was equally true that men were afraid of other men's laughter and so they fell into tribes, adopting language and posture to remain part of the gang. She hoped these two young men wouldn't make Kamran self-conscious.

Andrew Leeson stood for his opening speech. 'It's an ugly thing we've gathered here to talk about today.' His voice was gentle with the merest hint of indignation. 'How do you make "rape" uglier than it already is?' He paused as if waiting for an answer. 'You add the word "male" in front of it.' He studied the jury. 'We as a society hear about the rape of women in our books and on our screens and are thoroughly dismayed by it. The visceral gut punch of "male rape", however, is still largely taboo. Few of us openly know a man who has been raped, but it happens more than we might suspect. An estimated twelve thousand men experience rape, attempted rape or sexual assault by penetration in England and Wales alone every year. That's thirty-two every day – more than one every hour.

'Male rape is deeply under-reported for many reasons: shame, guilt, embarrassment. Some of us will have heard that men in the UK are three times as likely as women to take their own lives.' He paused. 'What is happening here? Could it be that the unrelenting pressure to "man up" is having a detrimental effect? Isn't it true that we as a society tell men they can't be victims? That they can't be violated?' He exhaled heavily. 'Well, they *are* violated. One man every hour. Many thousands more experience some form of sexual abuse or assault, but we expect them to "man up" and get on with it?

'No!' he said. 'No.' He stopped, then took a sip of water and softly repeated, 'No.' He gestured towards the dock. 'You are here today because of an ugly crime. It is our case that on the night of Friday the first of May, the defendant, Finn Andersen, committed a terrible crime. Caught in the grip of reckless hedonism, he entered the room of the complainant in the deep of night and crept into his bed. There were parties across the campus and Finn Andersen *knew* that his victim would be partially impaired, having indulged – as is tradition – in drinking a little bit more than he usually would.

'Our complainant, Kamran Hadid, expected to be safe in his room at his all-boys boarding school. He expected that when he retired for the night, he would wake in the morning,

171

refreshed and unmolested. Instead, he was woken in the dark by hands that were not his, a body he did not want, a body stronger than his, in bed with him, forcing itself upon him.

'Now, Kamran may not have screamed out loud but he did not consent to this. He did not consent to Finn Andersen climbing into bed with him and entering his body. That is a fact of utmost important. That is the *only* fact that matters.'

Zara watched the jurors to glean what they were thinking, but they listened blankly, giving nothing away.

'There are several things the defence will tell you: that Kamran did not say no, that he did not fight him off, that he reciprocated physically, that he may have secretly wanted it, but the fact is: Kamran did not say yes. Kamran did not consent. What happened to him was rape. What happens to *men* is rape: one every hour in the UK. We must stop treating men like their feelings are disposable, that they don't matter, that they should "man up". When they tell us that they're in pain, when they tell us that they're hurting, we must believe them. We must believe *him*. We must believe Kamran.

'Ladies and gentlemen, we have gathered here today to talk about an ugly thing. What's important is that *you* can scrub away some of this ugliness by doing the right thing: by finding the defendant, Finn Andersen, guilty of this crime. He raped Kamran Hadid and you *must* find him guilty.'

He allowed the words to sink in, then turned to Judge Arden. 'I call my first witness, Kamran Hadid.'

Kamran waited outside the courtroom, one hand pressed to his gut as if that might somehow brace him. He raised his head, drew back his shoulders and walked into the room. As he entered the witness box, he instinctively looked at Finn who sat stoically in the dock. Kamran had declined the offer of a screen, thinking it overdramatic. He did not feel threatened by Finn and to pretend otherwise seemed like a trick. It would do a disservice, he felt, to truly traumatised victims. Zara, who sat near the witness box, gave him a subtle nod. He returned it, then looked to the jury, resisting the urge to proffer a smile, decorum drummed so deeply, he had to actively swallow it.

Zara had told him to make eye contact but his gaze hovered somewhere above their heads. How could he look at these people given what he had to say? He glanced at the public gallery, grateful to see that Adam was there.

Leeson started the examination-in-chief, first asking about Kamran's background, establishing that he was an upstanding young man, not taken to flights of treachery. Kamran explained that his father owned a medical supplies company and that his mother was a housewife, not mentioning that she was also an heiress to a steelwork fortune, for fear of alienating the jury.

Leeson led him through the bacchanalian party, then traced a route across the green and up to Kamran's room. He pressed for specific details – had he locked his door, had he taken off his clothes – and though Kamran tried to answer, his memory remained punctured with holes. He could recall the black-blue haze of the night but not very much beyond it.

Leeson carefully counted up how much Kamran had had to drink: seven in total. 'Had you been taught about drinking responsibly?' he asked.

Kamran blinked. 'Yes. I gave my brother the same warning

earlier that evening. It's just that the night of the spring fundraiser is when we all let go and I thought I would be safe.' Kamran tried to modulate his voice so that it didn't come too smoothly, an effect of three years in junior debating. It was strange – he wasn't acting so why did he feel like an actor: squaring his chest, stilling his feet, fully aware of how he'd be seen?

'Is it fair to say you had a bit too much to drink?' asked Leeson.

'Yes, that's fair.'

'But only because you thought you were in a safe environment?'

'Yes.'

'Now, Kamran, I know you have already shared with the police the events of the night in question. I will now ask you to describe some of the details first hand. Is that okay?'

'Yes.'

Leeson informed the jurors where they might find the police transcripts in their jury bundles. Over the next half an hour, he led Kamran through his evidence: the warm body behind him, the hand on his penis, the drunken haze of confusion.

'In your statement, you said, "he tried to push inside me but it was strange; like he wasn't really trying." Can you elaborate?' asked Leeson.

Kamran ordered his thoughts, wanting to give a clear answer and not a twisted mass of words. 'I think my body was slack so when he tried, he couldn't get the purchase.' Kamran winced at his use of the word for it sounded so coldly clinical. He needed to stop thinking so hard.

'But he did penetrate you?'

Kamran tried to connect with the phrase but it brought no striking impact, just a vast white numbness instead. 'Yes, he did.' His gaze flicked to Finn who was rigid in his chair, his eyes fixed on a spot on the floor.

'You are certain about that?'

Kamran remembered that cleaving of himself and the unformed notion of physical pain. 'Yes, I'm certain,' he said.

'Okay, thank you.' Leeson led him through the rest of the night in painstaking detail: the strange, rubbery sensation of a penis on his flesh, the frenzied heaving of a stranger's body, the stickiness on his skin. Kamran described it with detachment, his gaze trained on the opposite wall. Only once he looked up: at the public gallery and saw that Adam was wiping his eyes. *Crying as usual,* he thought unkindly – Mack's words ringing in his ear.

When they broke for lunch, Kamran told his brother to go home, his tone unduly harsh. Adam, however, staunchly refused, insistent on seeing it through and so together they marched back into the courtroom to face the defending barrister.

Olivia Hallett stood, rising like a baleful shadow. She started with easy questions – simple fact-based queries about the night of the party: who he was with, who he saw, what he said. Kamran answered dutifully, trying hard to control his heartbeat. As a young deer stalker, he had been taught about buck fever, the nervousness of a novice hunter. His father had taught him to control it; to stay calm and view his body as a sum of parts: a skittish heart that told him to quit, weak lungs that sapped him of breath, traitorous limbs that warned his prey. He could control these parts, each with its own agenda. Olivia Hallett may have his heart racing with fear and lungs thirsty for air, but he could subdue them both and appear assured nonetheless.

She picked up a piece of paper and skimmed it for a moment. 'Hm.' She made a small noise as if realising something. 'Kamran, I'd like to ask more about your relationship with Finn Andersen.'

Kamran noticed the way her mouth curled in a corner when she pronounced the letter 'f'. He found it strangely pleasing.

'Have you ever told Finn that you would like to have sex with him?'

'No—' He reached for a title, wanting to add 'ma'am' like he might with the female teachers at school. 'I'm not gay,' he added. 'I don't like men.'

'You don't "like" men in that you're not attracted to men?'

'That's correct,' said Kamran carefully. He had heard that lawyers used confusing sentence constructions to catch out nervous witnesses.

'But you were attracted to Finn, weren't you?'

'No, I was not.'

'Because, as you claim, you're not attracted to men?'

'No.' He paused. 'Yes, I say that but, no, I'm not attracted to them.'

'Mr Hadid, do you recall signing a release form allowing the police to access your data?'

Kamran shifted on his feet. 'Yes.' He had signed it readily, knowing it would prove that he and Finn had no prior relationship.

'Part of that agreement allowed us to see the sites you accessed via the school's WiFi network. Were you aware of this?'

'Yes.'

'This includes all your browsing history including the sites you accessed by bypassing the school's parental lock. Were you aware of that?'

Kamran felt a flush of unease but did not shift his gaze. He had done nothing that the other boys didn't do. 'Yes.'

'Okay, then you will know that we could see all the URLs you visited on youporn.com?' Olivia sounded out the syllables as if she had never heard of the site before.

Kamran tried not to squirm. 'Yes, I'm aware of that.' He was thankful that his mother had agreed to stay home.

'It says here that over the course of your time at Hampton – from the ages of thirteen to seventeen – you accessed over one hundred and sixty hours of porn. Does that surprise you?'

Kamran reached for an answer. He looked at the jurors and was relieved to find that they seemed unfazed. 'I'm embarrassed but not surprised,' he said.

'Would it surprise you that forty hours of them were gay porn?'

Kamran's lips parted and while his jaw didn't quite drop, it gave the impression of astonishment. 'I... I was just curious,' he managed.

'"Just curious",' echoed Olivia. 'Forty hours of watching men have intercourse merely because you're "curious" doesn't seem logical, does it?'

Kamran looked to Zara for help.

She pressed the air, palm down, and gave him a subtle nod. *Keep calm. It's okay.*

It forced him to gather himself. 'I don't have an explanation. I was just curious. I know that's hard to understand unless you've been a teenage boy.'

Olivia narrowed her eyes. 'Yes, but you must agree that this is unusual for someone who claims to be a heterosexual male?'

'I couldn't say.'

Olivia pointed to the piece of paper. 'But you *do* agree that you have watched forty hours of gay porn?'

He kept the grimace off his face. He looked at it once in a while – suspected that all boys did – but forty hours did seem high. 'It's possible,' he admitted.

Olivia studied him coolly and Kamran held her gaze, daring himself to not look away. 'Why did you leave your room unlocked when you returned from the party?'

'I was drunk,' he said.

'Did a small part of you hope that Finn might come by? His room is only one floor down.'

'No. That would be a big assumption.'

'Would it?'

Kamran didn't answer, certain her question was rhetorical.

'Mr Hadid, when you felt Finn get into bed with you, why didn't you say anything?'

Kamran blinked. 'I was half asleep.'

'But still cogent enough to know that someone else was in your bed?'

He hesitated. 'Yes.'

'When you found him in your bed, you became sexually aroused, didn't you?'

'No, I did not.'

'You had sex quite freely, didn't you?'

'No. I did not.'

'Mr Hadid, did you tell Finn to stop?'

'No.'

'Did you – a strong, fit young man – physically resist?'

A flush of red tripped up his neck. 'No.'

Olivia feigned confusion. 'You didn't resist and yet you say you denied consent.'

'I didn't say yes.'

'But did you say no?'

Kamran felt the weight of scrutiny. 'That's not how it works.'

'Is that right?' Olivia snickered. 'So, to you, sex is like a game of "Mother, May I?". "May I put my hand on your waist? May I draw you near? May I kiss your lips?" You don't believe that sex happens naturally by feeling your way through it and that if one party does not want it, they must let the other person know?' She looked at Kamran. 'Mr Hadid, did you or did you not tell Finn that you did not want to engage in sexual activity?'

Kamran faltered. She had a point, didn't she? When he and Maya were on that cruise, neither sought consent for the things they did; they just did them, even when they were drunk. *Especially* when they were drunk.

'Mr Hadid?' urged Olivia.

He took three deep breaths, just as he would in the grips of buck fever. 'I did not,' he said.

'You did not,' she repeated. 'Isn't that because you had sex with Finn willingly?'

'No.'

'Were you ashamed about what happened?'

'No.'

'Is that why you have made this up?'

'No.'

'You were sexually aroused, Mr Hadid, and that's why you didn't say no. That's why you welcomed him into your bed. Isn't that right?'

Kamran burned with the knowledge that he was losing. 'No, that's not right.'

She fixed her stare on him. 'Mr Hadid, given what we have learned here today, I suggest that you take a long, hard look at your motivations that night. Perhaps your body knows something *you* yet don't.'

Leeson stood and began to speak but Kamran wasn't listening. A rush of sound blared in his ears. Why did he feel so guilty? He had done nothing wrong. He was only telling the truth.

Judge Arden silenced the sparring barristers. 'I can see that spirits are running high this afternoon.' He glanced at the clock. 'This might be a good time to adjourn.' He ran through court formalities with instructions to convene at 10 a.m. the next morning.

Kamran left the witness box and was joined by Adam and Zara. He found it hard to meet their gaze, ashamed of his performance, angry he hadn't been stronger. Adam hugged him fiercely, tears glazing his eyes. 'I'm sorry they did that,' he said, lower lip trembling.

Kamran pushed his brother away, gently, but with five fingers digging in his chest, enough to signal that he needed space. 'I don't want to talk about it,' he said. He looked at

Zara. 'Not yet.' In silence, they returned to her car for the fifteen-mile drive to Hampton.

Sofia watched Nevinka dart around the kitchen. She envied this woman and the easy way she moved: the dramatic flick of her wrist as she added a pinch of garlic, the absent-minded cluck of her tongue when the salt rushed out too quickly. Nothing about her was self-conscious. Sofia even envied the way she dressed: matronly skirts that cinched the fat at her waist and long, striped socks with unsightly clogs.

Nevinka turned and saw her watching. 'Everything okay, Sofia?' she asked.

'Yes, everything's fine.' It pleased her that she called her by name. She wanted the woman to feel like her equal. She hovered by the island in the centre of the kitchen. 'Nevinka, your sons, Aditya and Hiran, aren't they teenagers now?'

Nevinka placed a wooden spoon across the top of a pot of rice to stop it boiling over. 'Yes, thirteen and seventeen.'

'It's a difficult age, isn't it?'

She laughed. 'I think "difficult" is being polite.'

'What are they like?'

Nevinka corralled the skin of the garlic into a feathery pile. 'They're teenage boys: messy, boisterous, fun-loving but often moody.'

'How would you describe my sons?'

Nevinka looked at her, a subtle shadow passing across her face. 'Well, they're wonderful boys. They're polite, they're respectful. They're gentlemen through and through. You should be very proud of them.'

Sofia smiled but the answer strangely made her want to

cry. She swallowed and said, 'Thank you,' then gestured towards the corridor. 'I just need to talk to Mack about something and then we'll be ready for dinner.' She added another 'thank you' before she left the room.

She found Mack in his study fiddling with the latch on a window, pushing it this way and that to loosen it from friction. Sofia leaned against a sideboard, her fingers gathered behind her, gripping a swan neck handle.

'I haven't heard anything yet,' she said.

Mack continued fussing with the latch. 'About what?'

Sofia stared at him. 'About our son.'

'All in good time,' he replied, his tone studiedly nonchalant. He strained against the latch, wincing with the force. It refused to budge and he struck it with an open fist. 'Bastard thing!'

'Mack, will you listen to me?' Sofia failed to keep the bite from her voice. After twenty years together, she knew that defiance was the wrong approach. She softened her tone and tried again. 'I think we should be there tomorrow.'

He stilled. 'We've already talked about this. Kamran doesn't want us there.'

'He's a child, Mack. We're the parents. We should be making the decisions.'

'It *is* our decision. If we attend court, it will look like we're taking the allegations seriously.' He gestured outwards. 'Think about how it will look. Sofia and Mack Hadid photographed going to criminal court?'

'So it's all about saving face?' she asked.

'What? Because that doesn't concern you at all?' Mack's voice grew brittle. 'You're the one who invited eight hundred guests to our wedding because "how will it look if my family's gardener's nephew's wife doesn't attend?"'

Sofia's smile was Arctic. 'Well, it's nice that you got over it so quickly.'

Mack clenched his jaw. 'Don't pretend this isn't embarrassing for you. You're only pushing it because you know I'll say no and then *I'll* be the bad guy and your conscience will be clear.'

'That's not true.'

'It *is* true,' he said. 'I saw how you acted at Avi's wedding when people asked you about the case. You were practically crimson. At least *my* family has the decency to keep quiet.'

'No one was asking about the case! It was only Noreen.'

'Ah, yes, your discreet sister with her pantomime whisper. She might as well have been on stage!'

Sofia shook her head. 'It wasn't like that.'

'I'm not going to argue with you, Sofia. We're not giving this the oxygen of attention.'

'He's our *son*, Mack.'

'I know that!' he shouted. 'Don't you think I know?' His chest heaved once, then twice, with anger or emotion. 'I'm trying to—' He stopped and took a deep breath to steady himself. He drew a hand across his face, lower lip clamped between his teeth. 'It will be easier for Kamran to talk honestly if there's no one there to hurt. It will be easier for you not to hear it and I—' Mack cleared his throat with a strange guttural sound. 'I can't.'

Tears welled in Sofia's eyes. 'Oh, Mack. But you *can*.' She walked over and gripped his hand, surprised as ever by its warmth.

He pulled away from her. 'Don't.'

'Mack—'

'Don't!' The boom of his voice made her flinch. 'He doesn't want us there, Sofia. I'm doing this for him!'

She fell silent, her features stippled with anguish.

Across the hall, the dinner bell sounded and Mack slackened with relief. 'Look, we promised the Sergeants we would go to their gala tomorrow and that's what we will do. It will take your mind off things.' He gestured at the door. 'Come on, let's just try to eat in peace.' He gripped her hand and tugged her, and Sofia mutely followed.

Zara pulled into Hampton, long slants of rain catching in her headlights. Kamran offered a brisk goodbye. She knew he needed space, so let him and Adam retreat to the green. Once they were out of sight, she turned and headed to Hampton House.

There, she found Mr Lismore, the silver-haired man in rimless glasses. 'Hello, is Mr Morewood here?' she asked.

He appraised her. 'I'll see if he is available.'

She placed a hand on the countertop, a chill black-and-white marble. 'Please tell him it's to do with Kamran Hadid's case.'

'Certainly,' he said, his cut-glass accent likely hewn by a private education. After a short phone call, he escorted her up to Morewood's room, closing the door with a subtle bow.

'Did you know?' she asked, her tone sharp with challenge.

'Know what?' said Morewood.

'Did you know they would exploit Kamran's private data?'

He sighed. 'Ms Kaleel, we were simply adhering to legal requirements, as I'm sure you can appreciate.'

She could tell from the way he said it that he had known what it would reveal. 'Why?' she asked. 'Why did you do it?'

'We mean no harm to Hadid Major. He is a valued member of our student body – but if this dalliance is just that, then there's nothing more to be done here. If he is homosexual, no one here will pay that mind. If, however, he was coerced into intercourse, then that's a whole other plate of salad.'

Zara studied him. 'And it's better for Hampton's reputation if the two had a drunken hook-up. Isn't that true?'

Morewood clucked with impatience. 'We were simply complying with legal requirements.' His lips tightened to a line. 'Ms Kaleel, we would usually conduct our own investigation, which would have saved Hadid Major this public embarrassment. It would have happened behind closed doors, but you both bypassed our channels and went straight to the Met. How can we be discreet when the police are involved? We had to give up what they were looking for.'

Zara's tone grew tart. 'So you gave it up because *you* couldn't be in control of the situation?'

'That's not it at all,' he said. 'We take consent very seriously.' He glanced at his watch. 'In fact, if you were to accompany me to the Speech Room, you would witness how strongly I mean this.'

She held his gaze coolly. 'Lead the way.' He smiled, no doubt amused by this feisty brown woman who didn't understand the ways of the world. Zara gestured towards the door. 'Please.'

Morewood drew back his chair and slowly got to his feet. 'As you wish.' He led her out and down a draughty staircase.

They stepped out onto an arcade lined with a series of stone arches, a scholar's version of a hall of mirrors.

The columns cast long shadows on the floor, bisecting each pool of light. Zara followed Morewood into another building, a two-storey construction of High Victorian Gothic. Inside, they were greeted by a bronze statue of the Dying Gaul. From afar, it looked like he could be bent over laughing. They crossed an expanse of black-and-white marble to a set of double doors. Morewood pushed one open and ushered Zara in. The Speech Room was designed as an amphitheatre that could host the school's eight hundred and forty pupils and all its teaching staff in a single sitting. Currently, it was occupied by around fifty. The stage was lit and a besuited man bounced from one end to the other. His dyed-brown hair and too-dark tan signalled that he wasn't yet ready to relinquish his youth. He pointed his laser to the screen.

'Okay, so what is the right course of action if we want to kiss a young lady?' His accent was American and he had the energy of a talk-show host: vivacity tinged with artifice. 'A: Kiss her. B: Ask her if you can kiss her or C: Don't do anything.' The pupils were silent. 'Anyone want to tell me what's the right thing to do?' There was a low murmur in the room but no one offered an answer. Finally, the man said, 'B!' He circled it with his laser. 'We ask the young lady if we can kiss her.'

He bounded to the edge of the stage and pointed at a boy as if he had given the answer. 'That's right, young man. You don't just kiss her. If she hasn't asked for it, then you must gain permission.' He flipped forward a slide. 'Okay, next question. A woman is sitting alone in a library, drinking a cup of coffee. You really have the hots for her.' He grinned. 'It happens, right?' he asked with a wink. 'Okay, so what do you do? A: You join her and tell her that she's beautiful. B: You ask if you can join her or C: You do nothing?'

He waited for a volunteer. Met with silence, he raised the laser to the screen. 'C!' he cried triumphantly. 'Now, that may surprise some of you given the answer to my earlier question about the bar but there is a *difference* between a bar and a library. A bar is a social space so it is socially acceptable to approach a woman. A library is not a social space so she has a reasonable expectation to be left alone.' He glanced up at the screen. 'Let's try another one!'

Zara nodded at Morewood. 'Okay.' She didn't need to see more.

They left the room and he gently closed the door. 'So you see,' he said. 'We take clear and consistent consent very seriously. Every single one of our boys will be receiving this training.'

Zara felt ambivalent. Young people needed to learn about consent – but was this sterile, codified method the correct way to do that? 'I understand,' she said.

Morewood led her back out to the arcade. 'We regret what happened to Hadid Major, Ms Kaleel. As you can see, we are dedicated to turning out the finest young men we can.'

'Apparently so.'

'Yes, well.' He glanced pointedly at his watch. 'If there's nothing else?'

'For now.' She offered an icy thanks and let him take his leave. She felt frustrated for failing to puncture Morewood's gentility. He might say that he cared for Kamran, but what he really cared for was maintaining appearances; making sure this carefully manicured slice of life was perfectly preserved.

Even with powerful structures around him – wealthy parents, an elite education – it seemed that Kamran was still alone, all in the name of image. Zara hastened to her car, overcome with the desire to escape from Hampton. She drove past the Stepford lawns and fled into the mulch of Wembley.

It was 7 p.m. and Hampton was in full swing: juniors leaving the dining hall and seniors rushing in. In the first week of term, everyone had stores of new-year energy and there was excitement and chatter everywhere. That was one thing Kamran loved about Hampton: even the older boys seemed pleased to be there. There was none of that studied cool of university students or the aloof smiles of those in the know, just a shared enthusiasm for living a life that was destined to be great.

He spotted his friends at the far side of the hall, lit by slants of twilight beneath a latticed window: a soft beam across Barrett's hair, turning it straw-blond; a thick line across Nathan's left eye, forcing him to squint; a rose-glow across Jimmy's lips with his eyes painted in shadow. They were laughing and Kamran smiled instinctively, the weight of the day briefly lifting.

He walked down one aisle and approached them. 'Hey guys,' he said, interrupting Barrett's anecdote.

The boys broke into smiles and stood up to embrace him.

'And so the Quartet Threat unites,' said Nathan with a cartoon pump of his fist. It was the nickname they had awarded themselves when they joined the school at thirteen.

Kamran sensed the attention of spectators; saw them on the periphery, nudging each other subtly.

'It's good to see you, man,' said Jimmy.

Kamran took a seat and nodded towards Barrett. 'Did I hear him talking about Felicia again?' he asked. The name of Barrett's long-term crush was oddly soothing on his tongue. It meant that they were on familiar ground.

Barrett smiled. 'Maybe.'

Nathan winked. 'Romeo here finally sealed the deal.' He clapped Barrett on the back. 'So go on. Tell us about it then.'

Barrett ducked his head self-effacingly. 'Nah, maybe another time.'

'Come on,' said Nathan. 'It's not like you to be coy.'

Kamran caught a look pass between the boys: Barrett's eyes darting meaningfully to Kamran, then back to Nathan. He looked from one to the other. 'What?' he asked.

Barrett stiffened, caught in the indiscretion.

'What?' repeated Kamran.

'It's nothing.' Barrett shifted in his chair. 'I just thought that maybe you wouldn't wanna hear about all that.'

'All what?'

Barrett lifted a shoulder. 'You know, about Felicia and stuff.'

'Why?' Kamran waited and his friends tensed around him. He felt a strange sensation: a slipping away of something precious. 'Guys, you can talk about sex in front of me. I'm not a child.'

Barrett fidgeted. 'I just thought…' He trailed off. 'I mean, it's not a big deal.'

Just then, a hoot of laughter rose from the table next door. 'Maybe he's batty after all,' said a voice.

Kamran froze.

'I can't load it,' whined a second. 'Show it to me.'

Kamran turned and, sure enough, the tableful of boys was looking across at him. One floppy-haired senior raised his phone and read, '"A 17-year-old boy, a fencer and keen hunter". They're talking about you, aren't they, Hadid?' He didn't share the next lines with his audience, but made a great show of reading them with a loud and dramatic *woo!* 'This is making me blush!'

Kamran's heart felt like a shard of ice. He saw that Jimmy next to him was looking at his phone, eyes scanning left and right, skin paling as he read. After a moment, he shot to his feet.

'What does it say?' asked Kamran.

Jimmy exhaled a short, sharp breath. 'Let's get out of here.'

Kamran stood. 'But what does it say?' Had the papers published the events from court?

'Come on.' Jimmy physically pushed him towards the door. 'Let's just go.'

Jeers rose across the hall as Jimmy marshalled him down the aisle. Outside, Kamran turned to his friends. It's then that he realised that Barrett and Nathan had stayed inside, watching the two of them leave.

Indistinct snatches of words burst out – 'proof', 'truth', 'excuse' – but Kamran heard one above all others. 'Liar,' they said. 'He's a liar.'

*

Erin's three-tap knock broke Zara's train of thought. 'Burning the midnight oil?'

Zara glanced at the clock. 8.30 p.m. 'Hardly,' she said. 'I'm meeting someone at nine so I figured I'd get a couple of hours in.' She did not reveal that her meeting was actually a gathering of addicts.

Erin took a seat. 'You might want to look at this.' She placed an iPad on the desk. 'Tomorrow's front page of the *Morning Mail*.'

Zara felt a creeping unease. She leaned forward and read the headline.

PUBLIC SCHOOL ACCUSER WATCHED
FORTY HOURS OF GAY PORN

Beneath it, the copy read:

In the vast green acres of an elite UK boarding school, a case unfolds that has many intrigued. A 17-year-old boy, a fencer and keen hunter, has accused a schoolmate of rape. The accused is gay and the alleged victim claims that he himself is not. In court today, however, it was revealed that the alleged victim has watched over 40 hours of gay porn during his time at the school. Experts say this is a sign of latent homosexuality.

Zara felt a coursing dread. She looked up at Erin. 'Have you been monitoring Kamran's name?'

'Yes. There's no mention of it anywhere but if the pupils at Hampton see this, they'll put two and two together.'

Zara swallowed the sour tang in her mouth. Kamran spent day and night at Hampton and news like this could upend his life.

The article continued.

The accuser is from a conservative religious family, which almost certainly does not condone homosexuality, which could explain why he is reluctant to acknowledge that the encounter was consensual. The case has understandably fanned the flames of the consent debate.

Here, there was a video of culture warrior Seth Dawson who spoke in a measured tone: 'The noose of continuous consent isn't an ideological debate. It's not about feminists pitched against incels. Let's strip away the politics and look at what we have left: confused young men and women who are told that a foolish drunken hook-up was actually rape.'

He laced his fingers. 'Look, consent requires the sort of composure that's dampened by too much alcohol and so the key question is "who has consumed the alcohol?" If it's both parties, then why is one more culpable than the other? With regards to this latest case, to me it seems like an ambiguous encounter between two consenting young men, and activists have convinced one that what they did was wrong.'

Zara paused the video. Her skin felt cold but clammy, taut with trepidation. She could not have Kamran and Finn embroiled in this culture war.

'What do you make of this?' she asked Erin.

'I can see both sides of the argument.'

Zara frowned, a question on her brows.

Erin propped her elbows on the desk. 'Look, there are several layers to this. I've had sex I didn't enthusiastically want. Have you?'

Zara considered this. 'Yes,' she admitted.

'Okay, so sometimes you just do it because that's what your partner wants and I think most of us agree that that's not rape, right?'

'Right.'

'Okay, and then we move down a layer to the men who were just a little bit forceful, a little bit aggressive, a little bit close to the edge. You've had encounters like this, yes?'

Zara thought of Michael Attali and the way he used to wrap her hair around his fist. 'Yes.'

'Good sex?'

Zara hesitated. 'Yes.'

'Skirting that line can be *sexy*,' said Erin. 'Asking for consent again and again kills the visceral thrill of sex. Can you imagine being with a guy you want and him asking "can I now kiss you?", "can I now take off your shirt?", "can I now go down on you?", "can I now enter you?" Are we going to pretend that's sexy?'

Zara thought of what Olivia Hallett had said in court. 'So, to you, sex is like a game of "Mother, May I?"' Did she agree with them both?

Erin picked up the iPad. 'Look, Seth Dawson isn't the right person but there *is* a debate to be had here.'

'And Kamran? You think what happened was ambiguous?'

'No, but I understand why some might.'

Zara felt frustrated. 'If our complainant was a woman, would it be less ambiguous?'

Erin thought about it. 'Yeah, probably.'

'Then let's give Kamran the same courtesy.'

Erin studied her. 'Are you angry?'

Zara exhaled. 'Yes, but not at you. I'm angry because I fear you're right.' She waved a hand absently. 'Last week, I met this guy, Matthew, and we went for a drink. He's nice – funny, genuine, self-deprecating – but he wasn't assertive and if I'm being completely honest, what I mean is that he wasn't aggressive. I wanted him to demonstrate that he wanted me but he gave me this chaste kiss on the lips at the end of the evening and I left feeling... deflated.'

'Well, that's my point. It's more complicated than yes versus no.'

Zara nodded vaguely, unpicking a knot of thought.

Erin stood and checked her watch. 'Anyway, I've got to go and you've got your meeting.'

Zara stopped her just as she reached the threshold. 'Funny, I would have had you down as pro consent.'

Erin gestured outwards. 'That goes without saying, but I'm also pro sex.' She turned and left, the hollow click of her boots playing soundtrack to her exit.

CHAPTER EIGHT

Kamran tilted the screen of his laptop to ward off the glare of the morning sun. He cycled through the tabs, first looking at the *Morning Mail*, then the *Daily Record*, then a chaotic feed on Twitter. It was strange how such an intensely private moment could be exploited like this – a forced unfolding of a lily, revealing the anthers beneath.

There were a thousand voices, each garnering a hundred replies. There were those who believed Kamran, their rage brazed together with the hashtag #ibelievehim. There were those who believed Finn because Kamran hadn't fought him. It was the third group that distressed him most; those who said it was consensual and that Kamran was latently gay. This group assumed that he would throw Finn to the wolves to – what? Allay his guilt about what they did?

It was true that if Kamran was gay, he wouldn't breathe a word to his family, could not bear the look in his father's eyes, the stigma, the judgement, the flowers of pity from Aunty Rana as if Kamran had died a death. But to suggest that he would accuse Finn to soothe his own self-loathing was utterly absurd. You can only be what you are, so what good would it do to hate yourself?

As he asked the question, however, he felt the sting of hypocrisy. Wasn't it true that he had shuddered at the offers of other men to counsel him through his confusion; deleted their messages with an urgency that verged on unpleasant? Wasn't it possible that years of his father's homophobia had seeped into his own psyche? That while he was 'okay with gays' as a whole, the thought of being perceived as one made his scalp tighten with shame?

He closed his laptop and pushed it away to quieten the pulse of his thoughts. As if on cue, there was a knock on the door that he recognised as Adam's. His brother walked in, dressed in his cricket whites: trousers lined with a sharp crease and a shirt emblazoned with '11' on the back.

Adam fixed him with a mournful stare. 'I want to check that you're definitely okay with me not coming today.'

Kamran looked bleakly at his brother. 'I'd rather you didn't. It's easier to talk about what happened if there's no one there.'

Adam shifted on his feet. 'It's just I can't miss another match. If I get kicked off, Dad will...'

'That's fine, Adam.' He gestured at the door. 'Come on. Let's go.' Together, they walked down the corridor. Kamran placed a gentle arm over his brother's shoulder. 'You'll be taller than me soon.'

'I already am,' said Adam.

Kamran smiled faintly. 'Not yet, little brother, but soon.' He squeezed his shoulder. They walked out to the green, their melded bodies casting a shadow in the morning light. He saw that Zara was waiting and broke away from Adam. He raised a hand in greeting and headed for her with a bone-deep sigh.

Standing in the witness box, Kamran was mortified to see a faint sprinkling of sweat visible on his pale blue shirt. He crossed his arms to hide it, then immediately uncrossed them so not to seem defensive. His tie – a Hamptonian green – seemed to pinch his neck and he wished he could retie it. He swallowed, feeling his stomach roil and kick. This was his final day in court, his last chance at justice.

Olivia Hallett stood to continue her cross-examination. 'Mr Hadid, yesterday we talked about your penchant for viewing gay porn, isn't that correct?'

Kamran looked to Zara. There was something about her calm, implacable manner that helped him keep his composure. 'We talked about how I occasionally watched it.'

Leeson, the prosecutor, aimed a sigh in Olivia's direction. 'We've covered this,' he said under his breath.

Olivia ignored him. 'Can you remind me what date you had sex with Finn?'

Kamran kneaded his palm with a thumb. 'Friday the first of May.'

'And what date is it today?'

'Tuesday the eighth of September.'

'Okay, so roughly four months ago. How have you been feeling in these four months?'

Kamran studied her, unsure where this was leading. How was he meant to explain in a few succinct sentences? In the corner of his vision, he saw Zara turn and gesture to Leeson. She drew a square in the air, her forefingers sliding outward, then down. Leeson nodded and stood.

'Your honour, Mr Hadid has provided a victim personal statement but initially declined to read it in court. Given that my learned friend has specifically asked about the impact of the crime, I wonder if we might check with Mr Hadid if he would like to read out the VPS now.'

Judge Arden glanced at his watch. 'Well, it's a little out of kilter but if the complainant would like to, I would not deny him that right.'

Olivia spoke now. 'Your Honour, we don't feel it necessary to detail the statement; I was merely asking for a brief summary.'

'You're the one who asked about the impact of the crime, Ms Hallett.' He turned to Leeson. 'The complainant may read his statement if he wishes to at this juncture.'

Kamran felt a lurch of dread. They wanted him to read his statement – the one he had crafted in the deep of night with nothing left off the page. The usher handed him a piece of paper and he felt it moisten with sweat. He hadn't been prepared for this. How does one prepare to be stripped in public? He looked to Zara who nodded at him, a barely perceptible dip of her chin.

'I—' His underarms were slick with a soupy warmth and the sweat patch spread on his shirt. 'I was told to write this to tell you how I feel,' he read. His voice sounded reedy and he cleared his throat and tried again. 'I searched for other victims' personal statements so that maybe they would tell me what I was feeling. I went to the Survivors UK website and read through a list of emotions that were supposed to be normal. There were thirteen and I tried to fold myself into each one of them. Was I embarrassed or ashamed or guilty or depressed? All those words seemed empty.'

Kamran felt the pinch of his tie on his skin. 'There's a feeling – a red rush of a feeling – that happens when you make a major mistake or are caught doing something wrong. It's a single moment of panic where your scalp begins to crawl. It might be an insulting email you mistakenly sent your boss or losing sight of your child in a supermarket aisle. That panic – that red rush – is what I feel everywhere and all the time. I feel choked by sudden sounds. I scrabble for the corners in any room with a crowd.'

Kamran gripped the wooden rail of the witness box. He wished he'd been less candid. Reading the words out loud felt like a public flaying. 'I used to be a strong person,' he read. 'I had a natural joy and gentleness. I took care of my younger brother, I worked hard at school and I felt that my future was bright – but this has been distorted. It's like someone stamped in a puddle and changed my entire life.'

He tightened his grip on the sheet, making it shake as if caught in a breeze. 'I keep telling myself that it's okay; that really it's not a big deal. I wasn't out on a run in a park. I wasn't grabbed by the throat in the dark. I wasn't forced to the ground, my face pushed into gravel or grass. I wasn't violently torn apart.' Kamran blinked – rapidly as if batting away a fly. 'I tell myself that the red rush will fade but I'm constantly on edge. I feel constantly anxious and I can't find peace. I can't concentrate in class. I can hear the change in my own tone when I talk to my brother or mother. It's impatient, testy, angry, like I'm furious at them for merely existing.

'I lock my door at night and check it five times. I store spoons in the fridge so I can press them against my eyes to lessen the swelling of a sleepless night. I don't go out after dark. I know I'm missing out on life, but I feel safer in silence.'

Kamran swallowed. 'I hesitate to use that word – safe – just as I hesitate to use "victim" or "survivor". I don't feel entitled to them and yet I feel so skittish. I'm ashamed of how timid I feel, how feeble, how guarded, how weak.' His lips twisted with the last word.

'I thought the feeling would fade but it's been months and it still clings on. That's the thing that terrifies me most: that I might never again be who I was. What Finn did to me that night was something physical – it was over in a few minutes – but it took something from me; punched out a piece of me and replaced it with something frightening. I'm scared that I won't ever escape it.'

He looked up at the jury now. 'I just want to be normal again and I wish, I *wish*, I could think logically. I wish I knew that something like this will never happen again, but I don't. I feel like a different person now. I've lost the boy I used to be. And I've lost the man I was *meant* to be. I'm terrified that I won't ever find my way back to him. That's what Finn has done to me.'

Kamran finished, awash with sick relief. He locked eyes with a juror, a male in his mid-twenties. Immediately, they both looked away. Holding each other's gaze felt somehow uncouth, as if raw pain should only be expressed in solitude. Here, beating between them, it was only embarrassing. Kamran fixed his gaze on the far wall.

Olivia Hallett nodded peaceably. 'Well, that was quite

a speech,' she said, the last word heavy on her tongue as if it were a criticism. 'You mention that you can't find peace. How would you normally do this?'

Kamran, subdued by his statement, blinked in the blare of her question. Were they to snap back into their roles as if he hadn't spent the last minutes gutting himself in the witness box?

Olivia waited.

'I—' Kamran tried to order his thoughts. 'I would normally do this by fencing, spending time with friends and going on walks.'

'Interesting. I'd like to come back to that in a moment but first, Mr Hadid, I want to ask a bit about life at Hampton just to paint a picture. As far as I can see, the school runs to a very strict schedule. Is that correct?'

'Yes.'

'Very good.' Olivia ran him through his timetable, pausing here and there to add a detail or clarification. 'What time do the lights go out?'

'11 p.m.,' said Kamran.

'Are there any exceptions?'

'No.'

'What time does the cleaning usually happen?'

Kamran was unnerved by her questions. Where was she leading him? He rifled through his memory and said, 'Saturday morning.'

'What time?'

He glanced at the wall clock as if that might hold the answer. 'When we start our elective activities, so at 8 a.m.'

Olivia asked about these activities: the breadth, the length, the frequency, then she returned to the night of the party. 'Why did you leave your door unlocked?'

Kamran shifted. 'I didn't do it on purpose.'

'Oh?' said Olivia, not asking more.

'I was drunk and I forgot to lock it.'

'You knew Finn slept one floor down, is that right?'

'Yes.'

'You knew Finn was gay?'

'No. Not for certain.'

'But you suspected?'

'I'd heard a rumour last year but it was never made into a big thing.'

'You have admitted that you have watched forty hours of gay porn during your time at school?'

Kamran flushed red. 'Yes.'

'From the statement you gave to the police, you also knew that Finn would be drinking given that he was attending a high-profile party?'

'Yes.'

'Did you leave your door unlocked as an invitation?'

'No, I did not.'

'The lights go off at Hampton at 11 p.m. with no exceptions. Didn't you think there would be a chance that he might fumble his way to your room?'

'No.'

'Well.' Olivia slipped her hand into a thick folder and hefted it open to about halfway. 'According to your statement to the police, you spoke to Finn earlier that evening and when you said "see you later", he replied with "I certainly hope so". Did you take that as an overture?'

'No.'

'Did you leave your door unlocked on purpose?'

'No.'

'I think you *did*, Mr Hadid. I think you hoped that Finn might be confused enough to enter your room so you purposely left your door unlocked. And when the next day you found him in your bed, you became worried you would be discovered. You have said of your own accord that you woke up and "fled" to the showers. While you were there, or some time later, you concocted this tale to excuse yourself. Isn't that true?'

Kamran's cheeks burned hot. 'No. That's not true.'

'No? You come from a conservative family and it didn't cross your mind *once* that sharing your bed with another male might find its way to your parents?'

Kamran's palms grew slick. 'That is not what happened. He came into my room without invitation.'

'So you say.' Olivia flipped a piece of paper. 'I want to go back to your victim statement. You said that you could no longer find peace. Did you stop doing the things that brought you this peace, namely fencing, going on walks and spending time with friends?'

Kamran's jaw was rigid. 'I still fenced and went on walks.'

'But you stopped spending time with friends?'

'Largely, yes.'

'Did you go out with those friends to parties, drinking and dancing?'

'No.'

'Not once over the past four months?'

'No.'

'Forgive my repetition. But you are saying that you felt so damaged, you did not go drinking or dancing *once* with your friends?'

'Yes, that's what I'm saying.'

Olivia gestured to the usher. 'I put it to you that you *did* go out dancing and drinking with your friends. I put it to you that you were not emotionally damaged like you claim. In fact, I think you were just as *joyful* and *gentle* as before the night of the party.' She nodded at the usher. 'Please press play.'

On screen were three boys: Kamran, Jimmy and Nathan. Behind them blared some rap music with a deep bass. Jimmy was rapping along and Kamran was behind him laughing and rolling his body in waves to the beat. His eyes were bright with alcohol and the comfort and ease of being with friends.

Kamran watched under the yellow cast of betrayal. Olivia had walked him into a trap, forcing him to make maudlin statements that were ostensibly untrue.

'You told us just moments ago that not once were you able to join your friends or have fun. I presume this clip was taken before the night in question?'

Kamran's lips parted but he remained mute.

'Mr Hadid? Was the clip taken before the night of the party?'

He felt the heat of Olivia's gaze. 'No,' he admitted. There was a shift in the courtroom: a physical rearranging of bodies – a neck craned in the public gallery, an elbow slipped from an armrest – but also a less tangible change. The room seemed tense and airless, forcing Kamran to compress himself. He knew what the jury was thinking. The boy on camera was happy, confident and at ease, not at all like the person he now claimed to be.

Could he now tell them he was only pretending? That to fit in at Hampton – or anywhere in his life – you had to be happy and lively, or else you would be branded. He remembered the night that clip was recorded: spotting Jimmy en route to an impromptu party and Kamran agreeing to join him. *Siri, load program self-destruct.* Who knew it would return to haunt him? At some point in the evening, Jimmy had opened up TikTok and started a livestream: him rapping along to a song.

Nathan had cupped the back of Kamran's head. 'Come on, man. Fix up.' Kamran had instinctively fixed on a smile and stepped into view on the screen.

'Mr Hadid, does that look like the victim you described in your speech?'

'I—'

'Just yes or no will do.'

Kamran faltered.

She jabbed a finger at the screen. 'Does that look like the victim you described in your speech?' She raised her voice. 'Yes or no?'

Kamran swallowed the bile in his throat. 'No,' he admitted quietly.

'No,' Olivia repeated. She turned to the judge. 'I have no more questions, Your Honour.'

Zara's knock was light on the door. It opened with a whine and she stepped into the room: two metres by two, a high square window of plate glass and a single unused table. It held the surgical chill of correctional spaces: prisons, courts

205

and holding rooms. She studied Kamran, who sat in his chair with an unsettling calm. His posture was firm and proud, the only telltale sign of disarray a sheen of sweat above his lips, beading on bristles of hair.

Zara sat opposite him and pocketed the tissue she held in her hands. She wanted to reach out to him but feared that it might undo him – a soap bubble bursting at the gentlest touch. 'How are you feeling?' she asked.

'Okay.' He dug a thumbnail into his palm. 'I'm sorry,' he added softly.

'For what?'

'You warned me they would look at my data. I didn't tell you about the TikTok video. I didn't think it was important. It was one night, a few seconds, a silly thing. I didn't know how it would look.' His features were tense with guilt. 'I was just pretending to be happy.'

Zara felt a downy sorrow that he had been made to feel like this. She leaned in towards him. 'Listen to me, Kamran. What happened doesn't define who you are. It doesn't mean that you're never allowed to have fun; that you're never allowed, even fleetingly, to forget the pain of what happened to you.'

'But it looks bad, doesn't it?' There was a hopeful lilt in his tone as if Zara might tell him no.

She was quiet for a moment, not wanting to worry him further, but knew he deserved the truth. 'It doesn't look great.'

Kamran slumped; Jack depressed back into his box. 'People are going to say I made it up. They're already calling me gay.'

'Do you worry about that?' Zara spoke gently to draw him from his stoicism.

Kamran grimaced. 'Yes.'

'Why?'

'Because I'm scared what people will do to me.'

Zara caught the tremor in his voice and spoke with a quiet ferocity. 'I won't let them hurt you, Kamran. I promise.' She assured him that the police would chase up every user on social media that dared to name him in public; that they would stop the press from harassing his family and ensure that Hampton protected his privacy.

He received her words with a clean, blank stare and settled into a mute pliancy. Zara could see that he was exhausted though he would never admit it. 'Come on,' she said eventually, beckoning him to his feet. 'I'll drop you back off at Hampton.'

He stood and she touched him briefly on the small of his back but felt him tense immediately. She withdrew her hand and fell in step beside him instead.

As they left the court, they spotted a small gathering of men, a dozen of them wearing a uniform of sorts: smart black trousers and a white shirt teamed with dark red braces. Each wore a matching red cap. Stamped across it in bold white letters was a single mesh of words: #NotAllMen.

As Zara and Kamran approached, the men watched with an air of aggression but none seemed to know what to do.

'Snowflake,' one ventured.

'Liar,' said another.

Zara stiffened and ushered Kamran towards her car. 'Just keep walking,' she said. She glanced at the men briefly. They were in their late teens and early twenties. Why were they here, targeting this boy? What were they angry about? What were they trying to prove? By their awkward alliance, it seemed that they themselves were unsure too.

In the car, she glanced at Kamran. 'Are you okay?' she asked.

'Yes,' he replied quickly, his voice a tone too high.

'Do you have any questions?'

He shook his head.

'Okay, let's get you home.' She put the car in gear and headed back to Hampton. She was relieved that Kamran didn't ask any questions. How could she allay his fears when she couldn't even calm her own?

Finn watched the milliseconds race up on his phone. He stopped the timer just as Hugo crossed the finishing line – two seconds slower than Finn usually would. He was certain that Hampton would lose the regionals. No one on the team was as fast as Finn, even with the trial weighing on him.

He thought of the drama of the last two days. His defence team was optimistic but their so-called victories only deepened Finn's sense of guilt. He had listened to Kamran's victim statement and knew that his pain was real.

'I scrabble for the corners in any room with a crowd. I lock my door and check it five times.'

Finn wrestled with a complicated knot of emotions: immeasurable sorrow that Kamran felt this way but also a beating injustice. He just could not fathom how what happened that night could be inferred as an act of violence. The fact that Kamran felt this way made him sick with frustration.

'Finn,' called a voice, making him snap to attention. Nick

made his way to the edge of the bench. Finn scooted over to give him some space, but Nick remained on his feet. 'Listen, man, we've got to talk.'

Finn tilted his head up in hope. Perhaps they had heard about his progress in court. Might they reinstate him?

'You can't hang around here, man.' Nick nodded towards the boys on the track. 'You're making the team uncomfortable.'

Finn blinked. 'Uncomfortable?'

Nick sighed wearily. 'Honestly? It's not just them, man. It's setting me on edge too.'

'Why?'

Nick grimaced. 'You, sitting there watching us with your phone out – it just feels a bit weird and...' His shoulder curled inward. 'Creepy.'

Finn flinched as if physically hit.

Nick shifted from one foot to the other. 'Look, I know we're being unfair, but I need their heads in the race. You being here is a distraction. We'll welcome you back when your case is done but for now, I would prefer it if you just stayed away.'

Finn grappled for words to ease this blow – some show of nonchalance – but only managed to gape dumbly. He knew he must look pathetic, his pain so crass and obvious.

Nick hovered above him to make sure he would leave.

Finn waited for the strength to return to his limbs. Then, he nodded wordlessly. He stood and after the briefest moment of hesitation, turned and walked away, hearing Nick's apology whip away in the wind. He headed towards Rendale House, desperate now for solitude. Pupils instinctively split to allow him to pass, a red sea to his Moses.

He had not been bullied – bar that one whispered 'queen' through the bathroom stall, followed by the footsteps of the fleeing culprit. Instead, he'd become something of a *persona non grata*. Cast out of the track team, he now ate alone in the dining hall and was avoided in class where possible. There seemed to be no malice in this treatment, rather a genuine discomfort caused by his presence. He didn't know what was worse: boyish hijinks that verged on nasty or this strange, church-like hush that befell whichever room he stepped in. Did they really believe he was evil? A malign presence in the bowels of their house? How many Rendale pupils checked and rechecked their locks at night?

He entered the building now and cast his eyes to the ground as a group of pupils passed him by, instinctively shuffling into single file. Finn walked up three flights of stairs and walked to his room to quietly cry.

Kamran stalked to the window and back. He felt tense and agitated as if his entire body was tightly wound in a coil. He needed some form of release, was desperate for something to punch.

A burst of laughter carried down the hall, making him clench with frustration. Why was it that *they* could continue with their lives while he sat in his room like an outcast? He wondered where Finn was now. Was *he* too sitting in his room thinking about what had happened, or was he in full flight on the running track, effortlessly breaking a record? The thought of it made his stomach contract. He wanted Finn to regret this. He wanted Finn to pay. He worked himself into such a frenzy that when he heard a knock on his door, he flung it open, half expecting to find Finn as if he'd summoned him there by the sheer power of will.

Adam stood outside. His hair was dusted with rain and he swiped a brow to soak up the moisture. 'I heard what happened,' he said.

Kamran opened the door wider. His brother stood at the threshold as if waiting for an invite. After a moment, he took a seat, the chair whining beneath his weight just as it did with Kamran. He picked up a pack of Post-it notes stacked in different colours – yellow, blue, orange and green – and rifled them across his fingertips.

'I saw the TikTok video. It looks... bad.'

'So?'

Adam hesitated. 'Have you... have you thought about maybe calling it off?'

Kamran studied his brother. 'Have you been speaking to Mum?'

Adam pressed his lips together so they disappeared inward. After a beat, he admitted, 'Yes.'

'She told you to say this?'

He lifted a shoulder. 'Not in so many words, but she's worried about you.' He placed a soft hand on his chest. '*I'm* worried about you. If you call if off, then it ends on your terms but if you carry on, and it doesn't go your way, then how will you survive this?'

'Did Dad say anything?'

A shadow passed over Adam's face. 'No.' His voice was tight in an obvious lie.

'So all three of you think I should call it off?'

'It's not about us. Isn't that what's best for you? To forget it and carry on?'

'I can't do that.'

'Think about it, Kam. It could all be over tomorrow.'

Kamran felt a spike of anger. 'I want him to pay for what he did.'

'But—'

'No!' Kamran's voice was loud and it startled them both how much it was like their father's. 'I've made my decision, now leave me alone.'

Adam stood and tossed the notes back on the desk. His lips parted, wanting to speak.

'Leave me alone,' Kamran repeated.

Adam watched him for a moment, but then turned and left the room. Kamran slid onto his bed. He pressed his palms against his eyes, letting the cool flesh slow his heart, wanting to slow it right down, wanting it to stop.

Sofia Hadid glanced over her shoulder and caught her husband watching her, his features tight with irritation. She turned back to face the corner and quickly finished her call. She slipped her phone into her tiny handbag, a gold Kate Spade with a chain strap, and steadied herself on the dado rail. The pale green of the wainscot made her feel lightheaded. She really shouldn't have drunk that champagne.

She counted up to three, then turned around with a bright smile and strode towards her husband, giddily taking his arm. She felt his fingers grip her elbow, his nails digging a tad too deep. She listened intently as Elizabeth Sergeant told a story she had heard half a dozen times already.

'So he comes home with his new Maserati and the first thing he does is grab his golf clubs. Of course, they don't fit in the back, so what does he do?' Elizabeth threw her husband a red-lipped smile. 'He goes straight back to the showroom and gets the next model up!' They cawed with laughter. Mack joined in but Sofia did not.

Elizabeth caught her gaze. Her eyes, which always seemed to squint, narrowed even further. 'Because it's bigger, you see? And you can fit the golf clubs in it.'

Sofia nodded. 'I see.' Her tone chilled the laughter and it dwindled to an awkward silence.

David Sergeant cleared his throat uncomfortably. 'I – uh – I should say that we were very sorry to hear about the business with your son.'

Elizabeth raised a hand to her chest. 'I'm so sorry we haven't said anything. It's just that we heard it through the grapevine in the spring and didn't know if it was appropriate.' She shook her head. 'After all, we don't even know what happened.' There was a greediness in her tone, a barely suppressed hunger for news.

Sofia began to speak but Mack cut in. 'Don't be silly, you two. We're old friends. There's no need to tiptoe around us.' He clapped David on the shoulder. 'We appreciate it, old chap, but there's nothing to worry about: boyish hijinks that got out of hand.' He raised his glass and took a long drink, a telltale strain bracketing his lips.

'Excuse me,' said Sofia, untangling her arm from his. She headed to the bar and heard his footsteps follow her.

He held her wrist to slow her. 'What's wrong with you tonight?'

'What?' She cocked her head at the bar. 'You don't want me to have fun?'

'Fun? Being rude to my friends is fun for you?'

'Oh Mack, just give it a rest.' She pulled her hand from his grip and headed towards the French doors leading to the lawns of the stately home, the venue of the gala. She stepped into the cool night air and headed for a bench in the water garden. Mack followed, his movements jerky and urgent.

'Sofia, I ask very little of you.'

She threw her head back and laughed. The moonlight pooled on her slender neck, giving it a strange disembodied look above the black of her dress.

'What's wrong with you?' he asked.

She turned to him, feeling a rush of fury, wanting to strike out at him, wanting to tear the pearls off her throat and slam them into his. 'I never fucking liked these,' she would tell him, then tear the clip from her hair and scream in the wind like a banshee. She stared at him, her delicate jaw set in a challenge. 'Try me,' it said. 'Just try me.'

He registered the sense of threat and took a step back. 'Is this about Kamran?'

A clot of emotion rose in her throat. 'It's about everything.' She pointed at the room. 'Them. Us. Him.' She made a low, choked sound. 'Someone hurt our son, Mack, and you don't even seem to care.'

'So that's what this is about.' He folded his arms across his chest.

Sofia slid onto the bench, gazing up at her husband. 'Do you even care?'

Mack sighed heavily and sat down beside her, his hand on her knee.

She waited, then turned to him. 'Mack, do you even care?'

'Why didn't he fight him off?' Mack's tone was low and hopeless. 'I just don't understand that. Kamran is a strong boy and he's brave, and yet he didn't do anything. Why?'

'*Talk* to him, Mack. Listen to what he has to say.'

He pulled away from her. 'No father should have to listen to that.'

She gripped his arm, tethering him to her. 'He needs you.'

Mack stared at a point in the distance where the skeletal white of the garden path faded into darkness. 'I don't know how to help him,' he said quietly.

Sofia's anger cooled to embers, quelled by her husband's pain. 'By listening to him. By not ignoring what happened to him.'

Mack closed his eyes, squeezing them shut as if in physical pain. 'I can't deal with this right now, Sofia. Not here.'

'Then where? When?'

'Not now.' He looked at her, eyes glassy in the moonlight. 'Please.'

Sofia exhaled. Tenderly, she laced her fingers with his. 'Okay.'

They were silent for a moment and listened to the rumble of laughter that drifted across the lawn. Mack gestured towards the house. 'We're being rude to our hosts.' He beckoned her up. 'Come on. They invited the Hadids – let's give them the Hadids.'

Sofia took his hand and let him pull her up. She slipped

her arm around his and together they strode back, already drafting jokes and anecdotes.

Zara shifted beneath the dry press of ventilated air. Lena sat next to her on a purple mat arranged in a circle around the centre of the room. Barry, their instructor, was racing on the spot, knees swiping almost to his chin. He pointed at Lena and called her up for his final demonstration.

She stood up and flexed her neck to the left and right, laughing as she did so.

Barry grazed her shoulder with a fist. 'What you gonna do, little girl? What you gonna do?' he goaded.

Lena took a swing and Barry dodged it easily. 'Don't stretch your arm back so far. It gives me a warning of which way you'll go.'

Lena nodded and tried again, this time landing a blow, though it barely registered on Barry.

'What if I went to slap you?' he said, lightly tapping her cheek once, then twice. On the second attempt, Lena blocked his hand with a forearm and pushed it firmly outwards.

'Ha *ha!*' she cried triumphantly.

'Oh really?' Barry grabbed her arms. 'What now?'

Lena struggled in his grip, the effort creasing lines in her skin.

Zara watched cheerlessly. She didn't feel anger or concern; only a dark cynicism. If there were a secret to evading men, wouldn't all women be taught it? Wouldn't they walk the streets more freely instead of being told to tie up long hair, to cover their knees, put away their headphones and walk purposefully? Wouldn't they learn not to fear? Instead, they took classes like this to gather a shred of *empowerment*. The word was embarrassing, a slogan that should have died in the nineties.

Lena gave up the fight and Barry stood over her triumphantly. Even he – whose job it was to empower women – took pride in their submission. Zara leaned back on her palms and watched the two restart the battle. This time, Barry fell to the floor, but did so in an exaggerated, pantomime manner that made it clear he had let her win. On that note of feigned defeat, he dismissed the class for the week.

Zara retrieved her bag from her locker, the metal key catching once, then twice, before completing a turn. She showered, dressed, then waited for Lena to finish. She watched her little sister who was slim like Zara but with a pleasing softness. She loved Lena more than anyone else in the world and she liked seeing her this way: in tracksuit bottoms and a black-and-yellow crop top, her hair scraped into a high ponytail. It was such a stark change from her usual attire of long, loose dresses that swallowed her shape, worn in the name of modesty.

Zara too had dressed that way in her early youth and she remembered how it dampened her verve; made her feel ungainly. She remembered trudging to school in her *shalwar kameez*, it billowing in the breeze, making her look three sizes bigger. She still dressed modestly when visiting their mother, but swapped *shalwar kameez* for oversized cardigans that allowed space for her sense of self.

Lena closed her locker. 'Ready?'

'Ready.'

Zara drove them to their mother's home where Lena had

left her son. He greeted them with sticky lips and Lena shepherded him to the kitchen while Zara headed to the living room.

Her older sister, Salma, sat on the sofa, legs crossed at the ankle demurely. She tipped up her cheek for Zara's kiss, then glanced back down at her screen. 'Hey, I just saw this. It's not your case, is it?'

Zara felt a kick of unease as she reached for Salma's phone. On screen was the clip that had been shown in court: Kamran with Nathan and Jimmy, bobbing his head and dancing. 'For fuck's sake.'

'It's all over Twitter,' said Salma. 'They say that's the boy who accused a schoolmate of rape. It sounded like your case.'

'Can you give me a minute?' Zara was already leaving for the corridor. First, she checked that Kamran's name had not been published on Twitter. Then, she placed a call to Mia and asked that they aggressively pursue every user that dared to name him on social media. Finally, she called the CPS and asked them to contact major search engines to ensure they did not inadvertently reveal his name through their auto-complete feature as they had done with victims in the past.

Salma eyed her, amused. 'I love hearing you in lawyer mode.' She reeled off a nonsensical string of legal terms, her voice a forceful bark.

Zara handed back the phone, only half listening, her mind dwelling on the phone calls.

Salma zoomed into the screen. 'It's weird though, isn't it?' she said. 'This boy dancing and fooling around?'

Zara started to speak, but promptly stopped when their

mother walked in. Fatima set down a tray of tea and samosas, the heat rising off the parcels in waves. Zara watched her and wondered how much she knew of the case. As far as her mother was concerned, homosexuality was still taboo, let alone male rape. These things might be shared in whispers, but always in strict lanes: two aunties could discuss it, as could two sisters, but cross-generational discussion seemingly broke an unspoken code.

'You're losing weight,' said her mother.

Zara, relieved that it wasn't her work under fire, accepted the comment with ease. She picked up her cup of tea and prepared for a courteous evening in that strange space of mothers and daughters who had never really managed to bond.

CHAPTER NINE

Zara sat with Kamran in the courtroom. She had asked him not to come; told him that it was too strange a decision. Rape victims nearly never wanted to witness the trial, but Kamran had insisted. He wanted to watch Finn explain himself beneath the glare of a jury, and so they sat side by side up in the public gallery.

Kamran loomed above her and it made her recall an exchange with Javed, a sixteen-year-old cousin of hers. He heard that she had a client in Hainault and told her its streets weren't safe. Weeks later, when she mentioned in passing the very same thing, he threw her a curious look. 'Hainault's all right,' he said.

'But *you're* the one who said it's unsafe.' Zara was confused.

'Oh,' he said, remembering. 'I meant it's unsafe *for you*.'

It occurred to her that he – over six feet and bulky – could walk any street in London safely despite being sixteen. How different it was for a girl who was seen as a half-formed thing, to be treated delicately until she was complete.

Zara glanced at Kamran, who sat there rigid and perfectly still. Wasn't he at seventeen also a half-formed thing, forced to pretend he was whole?

Kamran caught her looking and offered a tight smile.

'Okay?' she mouthed.

He swallowed hard, then nodded.

'Court rise!' called the usher. Judge Arden walked in and after case formalities, handed the floor to Olivia Hallett. The barrister called her first witness: Finn Andersen.

Finn's wavy blond hair had been trimmed and he wore a white shirt with a cobalt suit, tie and pocket square. Would the jury believe that a fine young man like him could commit a crime like this?

Finn seemed calm and contemplative. His brows were faintly creased, lending him a studious manner. As he took the oath, his English accent showed a minute inflection, lending him a continental flair.

Zara felt Kamran tense beside her and she tapped his forearm gently. He nodded, but his gaze was fixed on Finn.

Olivia began her examination, first establishing Finn's background. As the scion of a wealthy Norwegian-Swiss banking family, he was the picture of respectability. She wove through his struggles with his sexuality, which was actually struggle-free. His parents were liberal, he said, and he was never made to feel 'less than' because he happened to be gay. His gaze flicked to Kamran in the gallery, then back down to Olivia.

She led him to the night of the party and his initial brush with Kamran. 'When Mr Hadid said "see you later", why did you say "I certainly hope so" when you knew your party would end late and you almost certainly wouldn't see him unless you went to his room?'

Finn shook his head as if perplexed by the question. 'It was just a figure of speech. I didn't mean that I literally hoped to see him later – at least not that night.'

'So you meant it in the same way that he had said "see you later" even though he knew he wouldn't.'

'That's right.'

Olivia asked how much he'd had to drink that night, taking pains to establish that Kamran had seven drinks while Finn had eight. 'You're slightly bigger than Kamran so taking that into account, it would be fair to say you were on equal footing.'

Andrew Leeson stood up. 'Your Honour, my learned friend couldn't possibly assert this without a scientific study.'

Olivia conceded, then turned back to Finn. 'On a scale of one to ten, how drunk did you feel?'

Finn thought for a while. 'An eight maybe.'

'So quite drunk?'

'Yes.'

Olivia nodded meditatively. She took him through the rest of the party, then down the stairs to the third-floor corridor. 'Why did you go to Kamran's room?' she asked in a quizzical tone.

Finn said the same thing he'd told the police. 'I thought I was entering my own room.'

'Did you unlock the door?'

'It was open already.'

'And you didn't think that was unusual?'

He hesitated. 'I was drunk.'

Zara watched the shift in his body, the tightening of his jaw, the way his fingertips gripped the edge of the box as if bracing for the words. She studied him. What was going on? Why had that detail unsettled him? She made a note to revisit it.

Olivia ploughed on, breaking briefly for lunch and continuing through the afternoon. Finn spoke of his murky faculties, his surrender to a natural instinct and, most emphatically, Kamran's reciprocity.

By the time they adjourned for the day, Zara could tell that Finn had disarmed the jury. His tone was clear and direct and his manner was respectful. She hoped he would fare differently under Leeson's cross-examination. For now, they would have to wait.

Judge Arden released the jury and Zara left the courtroom with Kamran. They made their way downstairs and she asked him to wait in the foyer.

He pointed at the exit. 'I'm just going to catch some air.'

Zara nodded and watched him leave, then dialled Mia's office.

The detective picked up after two rings. 'DC Scavo,' she said, her voice thick as if she had just swallowed something.

'Is this a bad time?' asked Zara.

'No, sorry, late lunch.'

Zara glanced at her watch. It was 4.30 p.m. 'So listen, the footage of Finn Andersen outside Kamran's room, do you remember if there was anything unusual about it?' Zara had not seen it herself and though she wasn't technically allowed to, she knew that Erin could secure a copy.

'Be more specific?' said Mia.

'When Finn opened the door, was he fumbling for his keys at the same time? Did he look flustered that he couldn't find them and then try the door by chance? Did he seem surprised that the door was open?'

Mia took a swallow of a drink. 'I'll have a look but as far

as I remember, he just opened the door. Hang on a minute.'
There was the clicking of a mouse as she browsed through
her files.

At that moment, Kamran re-entered the court building, his
face strangely pallid. Zara watched him and raised a thumbs
up. He mirrored it gingerly.

'Why do you ask?' said Mia.

Zara refocused on the call. 'It was the way he acted in
court,' she said. 'There's something not right about that
moment. I want to see if you spot something odd.'

Mia was silent, presumably watching the clip.

'Okay, so we're looking at Finn's profile from the right-
hand side. His left hand is in his pocket but it's not clear if he's
searching for keys. He yawns, then reaches forward and tries
the door handle, which opens without resistance. He doesn't
seem surprised, or particularly furtive for that matter.'

Zara thought this over. 'Can you send the clip to me?'

'You know I would but I can't break protocol.'

'That's all right – I thought you might say that. I'll let
you know if I think of something else.' She hung up and sent
a text to Erin to ask her to find the clip. She rejoined Kamran
who stood rigidly by the door, right hand cupped in his left.
'Everything okay?' she asked.

He nodded. 'Those men are out there. With the red hats.'

Zara felt a spike of anxiety. 'How many?'

'About fifteen. Maybe twenty.'

'Okay. They have to stay outside the court boundary so
we'll head straight to my car. When we pass them at the gates,
keep your eyes on the dashboard. Don't look out. Don't make
eye contact. Don't react. Okay?'

'Yes.' Kamran's voice was a touch too loud; courage feigned by volume.

She led him through the exit to her car. As they drove past the gates, she glanced at the men outside. They wore the same uniform: smart black trousers, white shirt, dark red braces and a red cap stamped with #NotAllMen. They recognised Kamran and began to shout in unison. She strained to make out the words.

'No means no but you have to say so.'

Kamran looked to her. 'What are they angry about?'

Zara pointed at the dash. 'Keep your eyes low,' she instructed. She turned right onto Newington Causeway and put some distance behind them. 'Men like that will always find something to be angry about.'

'But...'

Zara waited, giving him time to order his thoughts.

'Do they have a point?' He dug his fingers into the woollen jumper that lay in a mass on his lap. 'I mean, you remember that case with the American comedian a couple of years ago? The girl gave a whole interview blaming him but she never actually told him no – like, how was he meant to know she wasn't really into it unless she actually said it. That's what I thought at the time so... don't those men have a point?'

Zara kept her eyes on the road. 'I think the better way to look at it is that "yes means yes".'

'But what if yes means yes when you start out and then yes becomes no? How is the other person meant to know unless you tell them?' He gripped the jumper in his fist now, his features creased with strain.

Zara exhaled. 'I don't have all the answers, Kamran, but

I do know that what happened to you was a crime. Finn was well aware that you could not consent.'

Kamran didn't respond, only turned towards the window in a state of mute reflection. Zara did not press him and so they drove in silence along the featureless streets of West London, passing dreary storefronts towards the greener pastures of Hampton.

'Are you sure you want to be in court tomorrow?' she asked when she dropped him off.

'I'd like to finish this,' he said, lips pressed together grimly.

Zara conceded and promised to collect him tomorrow. She watched him cross the green and noted how his shoulder sagged as soon as he stepped in shadow as if he found relief only when hidden from view. He disappeared into the darkness and Zara started her car, readying for the hour's drive to St Alfege in East London.

Zara walked down the aisle beneath the grand chandelier and saw that the group was waiting: Sam the teacher, Ed the ex-con, Kerry the writer and Chris the instructor. Instead of scattering around the pews today, they sat in a circle arranged by the altar.

Chris gestured at a chair and welcomed her in. 'Today, I want to try something a bit different,' he said. He swept a strand of hair from his eyes. 'I want to talk about what I call the "Cut" and by that I mean a defining moment in your life that hurt you, that cut your life in two, that changed you into who you are from who you used to be, and to examine if you'd want to return.'

Zara shifted in her chair. She was used to dealing with people's 'Cuts'. As a barrister, she had been specifically trained to ignore them; to sift through globules of pain and excise the simple facts. Now, as a rape counsellor, she helped people through their 'Cut' in real time. Every adult carried a 'Cut' and she had seen and heard more than most – and yet she never spoke of her own outside the walls of the church. Even Safran didn't know her father's final words to her. 'Tomorrow, your brother is going to come and hack you into pieces.'

If there was a cleaving of her life, then it lay on the full stop of that sentence, two halves falling back like the edges of a paper fortune, putting everything on a slant.

'Zara, do you want to go first?' asked Chris.

She stared at a spot on the altar just to the left of Chris's shoulder. 'Yes,' she agreed. She told them more about her arranged marriage; explained that she agreed to marry a stranger to ease the pressure on her ill father. She described the strange unmooring of her wedding night and how in the desperate days that followed, her in-laws tried to remodel her, telling her to use a more respectful tone when speaking to her elders, to dress in impractical saris, to wear more make-up and jewellery, but not to laugh with relatives for it signified immodesty.

But the 'Cut'? The 'Cut' came when her father said those indelible words. Zara's voice strained to carry their force, the white-hot horror of his need for honour over her need for refuge. She blinked rapidly, her nose blushing pink with unspent tears.

'That's when I started using more regularly.'

Ed leaned forward, his swamp-green cap shadowing his face so that she only saw his lips. 'But you're so smart. How come you had a forced marriage?'

Zara flinched. 'It wasn't forced. It was arranged.'

Ed studied her. 'An arranged marriage you did not want?'

Zara felt a tightening in her throat. Her lips parted but she didn't speak.

Ed took off his cap and ran a hand through his thinning hair. 'I think you've probably dealt with something you haven't really accepted.'

His look of profound empathy made her want to sob. *An arranged marriage you did not want.* What was that if not forced? But if that were true, didn't that make Zara a victim? And what of her mother? A villain? It couldn't possibly be true. She shook her head and turned to Chris. 'So – that's my "Cut",' she finished.

Ed spoke next and Zara listened with a quiet focus that belied the wail in her chest. She heard how he – at the age of twenty-three – found himself on a bridge at night with a man he would kill in a mugging. She dwelled on how Ed had peeled away the rotting flesh of his life and uncovered something of value. If he could bear the weight of his past, couldn't Zara too?

Afterwards, she headed straight out, reluctant to stay for coffee like the others did at the end of each meeting. She was keen to go home and draw a hot bath and distract herself from thinking. As she stepped from the church, however, her phone pinged with messages. She scrolled through them one by one: a text from Stuart asking for an update on her hours, an email from a journalist writing a retrospective on Jodie's case and, finally, one from Erin who had obtained a copy of the clip she'd asked for.

Zara clicked on it now to load it. It showed Finn Andersen walking unsteadily down some stairs, pausing briefly on the third floor, then turning right into the corridor. His figure grew smaller until he paused at a door – Kamran's bedroom. His left hand was in his pocket and Mia was right, you couldn't tell if he was fumbling for keys. He yawned, his right hand shielding his lips, then he turned the door handle.

She studied his body language for traces of intent: a furtive glance down the corridor, the curving of a foot on tiptoe. There was nothing. He walked in and the door closed. Why had he bristled when Olivia asked if he was surprised that the door was unlocked? Zara rewound the clip and watched it again. There was a certainty in his action when he reached for the doorknob, as if he *knew* that it was open. She rewound it and watched it again. It was on her fourth viewing that she saw it: a subtle difference in his movement. Finn knew. Finn *knew* he was going into someone else's room. Zara closed the clip and dialled Mia's number.

The tree shielding the court entrance shed another leaf. It clung to the iron gate in the rain, bestowed like a gift. Photographers huddled nearby to take pictures of the gathered crowd, stoked by Seth Dawson who had taken an interest in Kamran's case.

'We are living in dangerous times,' he declared on the news last night. 'When people are in the grip of a moral panic, questioning the extent of the threat isn't seen as a logical step, but as threatening behaviour itself. This is and should be deeply worrying.'

The reporter held up a hand. 'But aren't you concerned that in England and Wales two women are killed every week by a current or former partner?'

Dawson shot her a withering look. 'I can't see how you can extrapolate that to the entire male population.'

'But that is a substantial number,' said the reporter, her tone confrontational.

Dawson was bemused. 'It's not nearly enough to suggest that all men are a danger or that "rape culture" is real.' He laced his hands on his lap, a deliberate action that lent him the air of a statesman. 'It's really important that we acknowledge this. Even suggesting that rape culture is unproven earns sceptics like me the label of "rape apologist". It is not "victim blaming" to suggest that a confusing sexual encounter isn't always rape and doesn't necessarily make your sexual partner a predator.'

Dawson's thoughts clearly resonated with men across the capital, resulting in this gathering. There were forty or so clustered outside the court grounds, all wearing #NotAllMen caps, some trying to whip up a chant. '*No means no but you have to say so.*'

Zara was vigilant as she drove past the gates with Kamran. A number of men crowded the car, raising in her a smeary unease. One struck a palm against her door, making her jolt in panic. In the white-hot blare of memory, she was reminded of that greater violence: the force of a palm against her mouth, its muggy, hormonal whiff.

'Are you okay?' asked Kamran with a compassion that nearly undid her.

She gripped the wheel to stop her hands from trembling. 'Yes. Are you?'

He nodded mutely.

A security guard beckoned them forward and Zara was allowed to pass. She looked in the rear-view mirror and watched the guard remonstrate with a man. She could only see the back of his head: ruddy and bald, creased at the base by a bulge of fat.

'Don't worry. They won't be allowed inside,' she said, mostly to assure herself. *Zara the Brave*, she thought darkly, *cowed by a frothing lout.*

She parked and led Kamran to the courthouse, watching for cracks in his own composure. He seldom spoke of his pain but Zara had learned to recognise it in the subtleties of movement: the tensing of his lips, the kneading of his palm, the two fine lines that dipped between his brows. For now, he seemed at ease so she led him up a flight of stairs to the public gallery in courtroom one. They took their seats at the left extreme so they wouldn't have to move for spectators. Kamran's legs touched the casing in front and he tucked them to a side, his knees dipping towards the ground. How strange it must be, thought Zara, to have an adult's body while you were still a child.

The usher asked the court to rise and Judge Arden took his place on the bench. Today, the prosecution was to question Finn. He stood stoically in the witness box, dressed in a navy suit and a pale pink shirt with a contrast collar, paired with a burgundy tie.

Andrew Leeson began his cross-examination. 'Mr Andersen, you have described in detail the events of Friday the first of May. Can you please tell me a little bit more about the spring fundraiser party? Who usually attends this?'

Finn spoke evenly. 'The faculty, some alumni, all the housemasters and their support.'

'And why is it set at West Lawn?'

'It has one of grandest event rooms at Hampton.'

'West Lawn is your house, is that correct?'

Finn nodded. 'Yes, sir.'

'You have been situated at West Lawn for three years, is that correct?'

'Yes, sir.'

'Have you ever got lost in the building before?'

Finn shifted uneasily. 'In the early days, yes. It's a big building.'

'The early days,' repeated Leeson. 'Can you explain what you mean?'

'I mean when I first started school. The first week or two.'

'And after those initial weeks, did you get lost in West Lawn?'

'No, sir.'

'Hm.' Lesson sounded surprised. 'Can you explain to me why you got "lost" on Friday the first of May? Why, after three years of living in that building, did you get lost that night? What exactly was going through your mind?'

Zara watched Finn closely, waiting to see if his composure would slip but he remained perfectly calm.

'To be honest, I've never got quite as drunk before and so I wasn't completely in control of my faculties.'

'Yes, we've heard you speak to that already.' Leeson's tone was deliberately testy, a technique Zara herself had used in court to throw off a key witness. There were many of these subtle techniques. In normal civil society, people weren't used to being chided – to being cut short, undermined or ridiculed – so when they faced such treatment in court, they often felt disoriented. Finn, who came from a world of privilege, wasn't used to being rebuked.

Leeson waved a hand in the air. 'I want to know what you were *thinking*.'

Finn considered this. 'Well, I left the party and I was walking down the stairs and I was thinking...' He hesitated. 'I suppose I was thinking "don't trip". I could tell I was giddy, so I was being careful and holding onto the bannister.'

'And then?'

'And then I got to the third floor and I guess I thought it was the second floor and I turned right.'

'You "guess" you thought it was your floor?' Leeson's tone was thick with derision.

'I *know* I thought it was my floor,' said Finn.

'Despite living in that building for *three years*, you genuinely didn't know where you were going?'

Finn grimaced. 'We rarely ever go to the top floor so I guess – I *know* – I got confused.'

Leeson arched a doubtful brow. 'Talk me through the next minute in as much detail as you can.'

'I... I'm not sure how much more detail I can offer.'

'Try.' Leeson's tone rose impatiently.

Finn floundered for a moment. 'Well, I turned right and then I walked to what I thought was my door and I went in.'

'Not so quickly,' said Leeson. 'What did you do *before* you went in?'

Finn's gaze skirted to the jury, clearly aiming to gauge their mood. 'I—' He raised a hand and mimed unlocking a door. 'I searched for my key.'

'Did you find it?'

Finn looked at the jury again. 'No. I reached forward and

tried the handle while I was searching and I realised I'd left it open.'

'Hm.' Leeson stared intently at Finn. 'And what did you do in between?'

Finn was confused. 'What do you mean?'

'What did you do in between looking for your key and opening the door?'

'I—' Finn looked to the judge for help. 'I didn't do anything.'

Leeson shook his head as if he were disappointed in him. 'Very well, Mr Andersen.' He asked the usher to play a video.

Zara tensed in the gallery, eyes darting between the screen and Finn. It showed him walking along the corridor, unsteady on his feet. He paused in front of a door, left hand in his pocket. Before he opened it, he lifted his hand to his mouth.

Leeson paused the video. 'What I'm referring to, Mr Andersen, is this.'

Zara watched Finn in the witness box and noted how his face grew strained. To the casual observer, it looked like he was yawning on the screen but Finn knew that he wasn't. Finn knew that he was actually checking his breath: a quick exhalation into the palm of his hand followed by a barely perceptible sniff. Once you knew the truth, you could no longer see the lie so, in Finn's eyes, there was nothing else he *could* be doing but checking his breath.

'Mr Andersen?'

Finn faltered.

'If you thought you were entering your own room, why were you checking your breath? Isn't it true that you *knew* you were entering someone else's room? You *knew* it wasn't yours. You *knew* that it was Kamran's.'

'No. That's not true.'

'So why were you checking your breath before going into your own room?'

Finn flicked a hand in the air, likely meant as casual but coming across as defensive. 'I'd been drinking all night and I could smell myself. I wanted to see how bad it was.'

'That's a lie, isn't it, Mr Andersen?'

'No.'

'It is a lie. You were checking your breath before going into Kamran's room because you *knew* you were planning to get close to him. You planned the entire thing, isn't that true?'

'No.' He shook his head vigorously. 'How... how could I know that his door would be open? Why would I check my breath *before* I knew I could enter?'

Zara had known he'd ask this question; had briefed Mia already.

'Isn't it true that you are the housemaster's assistant at West Lawn?' asked Leeson.

'Yes.'

'Isn't it also true that, as part of your role, you are able to access keys to every room at West Lawn?'

Finn grimaced. 'That's not what happened. I have never touched his key. I—'

'Mr Andersen,' Leeson interrupted. 'That is a very deliberate act we saw you perform on the video. We can see you walking down that corridor, pausing and *purposefully* checking your breath before entering Kamran's room. I put it to you that you had his room key on your person, but then found that his door was unlocked.'

'No, that's not true.'

'You would have entered his room whether or not it was locked, isn't that true?'

'No.'

'I think it *is* true.'

'No, sir. It's not.'

Zara watched the jury. While Leeson's evidence was circumstantial, it *had* placed a seed of doubt. The juror with the sculpted hairstyle studied Finn with the trace of a frown, his tongue wedged in the corner of his mouth.

Leeson did not let Finn rest. 'Mr Andersen, isn't it also true that, at that time, you had a roommate while Kamran did not? The layout of your rooms are different, so how on earth did you mistake the two?'

'I was drunk,' said Finn feebly. 'I didn't switch on the light. His bed's in the same place as mine.'

Leeson narrowed his eyes. 'Mr Andersen, do you often stalk the halls searching for prey?'

Olivia Hallett rose to her feet, but Leeson promptly appeased her. 'It's okay. I don't expect Mr Andersen will answer that.' He turned to Judge Arden. 'I have no more questions for this witness, Your Honour.'

Zara felt a wash of relief and sensed Kamran relax beside her. Leeson, though not as bombastic as some of his colleagues, had a distinctly authoritative manner, verging on haughty, which worked exceptionally well in court. It impressed juries and daunted witnesses, and had been used to great effect against Finn.

Judge Arden adjourned for lunch and Zara led Kamran from the courtroom.

'Do you think we can go to a café?' he asked, gesturing at the exit. 'I could do with some air.'

Zara thought of the red caps waiting outside. 'I don't think that's a good idea, Kamran. If you've had enough of court, I'll happily take you home, but I don't think we should go for a walk.'

They bought lunch from the courthouse kiosk and retreated to a secluded corner. Zara picked at her meal of cold pasta, corralling croutons into one soggy pile.

'This must be a bit different from Hampton?' She gestured at the forlorn purple chairs and plasticky floor.

Kamran swallowed a bite of his sandwich. 'Yes, it is.'

'Are you happy there?'

He glanced up at her. 'I was, but now I'm relieved it's my last year.'

Zara felt a sense of wistfulness for all that he had lost. 'Do you know what you will do after?'

He lifted a shoulder. 'Oxford, then probably an MBA in the US.'

'That's what you want to do?'

He thought for a moment. 'Honestly? I don't know. The thing with a place like Hampton is that they let you – no, *make you* – try new things. They want you to have a passion, you know? It's academic but they also want you to have a fulfilling interest – but what if you don't know what that is? I like fencing but not enough to follow it as a career, so...' He trailed off. 'Did you always know you wanted to be a lawyer?'

Zara thought back to her early years. A memory caught in her mind. She – aged six or seven – was helping Lena with homework and listening to her parents talk, as she always did when they discussed unfamiliar things. Her father was talking about a friend's daughter who had qualified as a barrister. He had said the word so reverently, weaved with a touch of disbelief, that Zara had stopped what she was doing to watch him. His mouth was set in a soft smile, a picture of borrowed pride.

That look planted something in Zara. She asked Salma how one became a barrister. Her sister didn't know but when they next went to the library, they pulled down an encyclopaedia and flicked through the pages past bank manager, barber and barman, finally to barrister.

Zara was entranced by the pictures of stern, bespectacled men in strange wigs and gowns. She knew that, one day, it would be *her* standing in a place like this with her head held high, one hand balled in a fist, and when her father said 'barrister' in that soft blush of a tone, he would be talking about her.

Zara tamped down the memory, mere compost on a heap. 'More or less. There was a career day at school,' she lied. She knew he would understand the compulsion to please a parent, but she could not speak of her father here and keep her voice from breaking.

Kamran took a sip of water, his gaze dipping low. 'Did you have a happy childhood?'

Zara balked. It was such a banal question and yet so jarringly intimate. She considered it for a moment. 'It was a childhood of two halves,' she said. 'Up to age eleven or twelve, it was very happy. I have three siblings and we were allowed to wander and roam but then—' Her lips tensed in a plaintive line. 'Then puberty hit and something seemed to switch in my parents. Suddenly, we couldn't wear shorts and T-shirts. We had to wear *shalwar kameez* and cover our hair and be modest. We couldn't be friends with boys, or shout or run or be boisterous without being told off. We were treated like fragile things, bound to be soiled or stolen if allowed out alone. We were taught to be wary and watchful and not to draw attention and so from age eleven, things felt quite… fraught.' She exhaled.

'Do you think your life would have been easier if you were born a boy?'

She made a half laugh of a sound. 'I don't think it. I *know* it.'

Kamran twisted and untwisted the pale blue cap on his bottle. 'I think you're right. I just… It feels really hard right now.'

Zara felt a keening sorrow that settled in her chest like a physical ache. She wanted to grip him fiercely and promise him he would find peace, but she knew that Kamran responded to subtlety and that drama would make him retreat. 'It's going to feel that way for a while, Kamran, and that's okay.'

He swallowed. 'I'm really trying but I—' He pressed a hand against his chest. 'I just—' He grimaced, features bleak with emotion. Then, he laughed harshly. 'Jesus, listen to me.' His voice was a veil of distaste.

'Tell me,' said Zara. The words were almost a whisper in her effort to mask their urgency.

Kamran shook his head. 'Ignore me, please. I'm—' He raise a dismissive hand. 'I'm fine.' And just like that, the walls came down.

Zara watched him with a beating pity. 'Kamran,' she said, waiting for him to look at her. 'When you're ready to talk, I'll be here, okay?'

He nodded, eyes averting to the foyer behind her. He

gestured towards it. 'I think people are heading back in.' He gathered his litter and stood, and waited for Zara to follow.

Back inside the courtroom, Olivia Hallett called an expert witness, Dr Nina Chou. She was slim and petite with delicate features and a sleek, practical bob. She was an excellent choice, given the subject matter, Zara noted with grudging respect. It always helped to have a woman on the defence team in cases of sexual assault. Finn Andersen had two.

'Dr Chou, you are a forensic medical examiner. Can you please give me a summary of your experience?'

She nodded. 'I am a medical doctor qualified as a forensic medical examiner. I have worked in this role for six years and have dealt with over five hundred cases in a private clinic in London. I am a member of the Faculty of Forensic and Legal Medicine and have published dozens of papers in medical journals including the *Journal of Clinical Forensic Medicine* and *Forensic International.*'

'That's very impressive,' said Olivia. 'Dr Chou, you have examined the results of the forensic medical exam that was conducted on the complainant after the alleged incident. Is that correct?'

'Yes.'

'Did the exam list any genital injuries?'

'No. There was no evidence of injury.'

'No muscle contusions? No lacerations? No signs of sexual violence?'

'No.'

'Huh,' said Olivia, feigning surprise. 'Is this consistent with other cases of sexual assault?'

The doctor cocked her head, neat bob swaying with the

motion. 'It's hard to say. With vaginal penetration, there is a low proportion of cases with evidence of injury – around twenty-five per cent. With anal penetration, that percentage is higher.'

'Do you know what it is?'

'Studies vary wildly. Among my cases, it stands at sixty-one per cent.'

'So in over six out of ten cases of anal rape, you find some physical evidence of penetration, is that right?'

'Yes.'

Kamran shifted beside Zara.

'And what about a teenager who isn't sexually active? Would you expect to see evidence of injury?'

Dr Chou nodded. 'The chances may be higher than sixty-one per cent.'

'But there was none with Kamran Hadid?'

'No.'

'Were there any other bruises? Anything to suggest he had been through physical trauma?'

Leeson stood. 'Your Honour,' he said, his voice artificially aggravated. 'The complainant has explained the nature of the incident. Given his evidence, we would not expect there to be bruising. They didn't have a fist fight!'

Judge Arden nodded, making his chin fat wobble. 'He has a point, Ms Hallett.'

Olivia held up a palm. 'Yes, Your Honour.' She turned back to the witness. 'One last question then: is there anything in the evidence to suggest that this was not a consensual encounter between two young men?'

'No,' said Dr Chou.

Olivia smiled. 'Thank you.'

Zara looked at Kamran and she knew that he knew she was watching him. His expression was impassive, but his fingers dug into his trousers, creating little black pools of unease. She wanted to reach out and squeeze his hand, but the gesture felt inappropriate. Strange – if it were Jodie beside her, she would not have thought twice.

'Dr Chou,' Leeson began his cross-examination. 'You said that sixty-one per cent of your cases which involve anal rape show evidence of injury. Isn't it true that these statistics are based on female victims?'

'Yes.'

'This assumes that men and women have the same physiology, which we know they do not. Do you have equivalent statistics for a male cohort?'

'Not personally. Studies vary wildly and nearly always focus on women. I believe it's reasonable to expect similar percentages in men.'

'But you can't say for sure?'

'No,' she admitted.

Leeson arched a brow. 'Okay, well, can you say this for sure: how many days after the incident in question was the complainant examined?'

'Nine days.'

'Well done,' said Leeson. He picked up a thin pile of paper, stapled in one corner. 'Dr Chou, are you familiar with a 2015 study by Ruxana et al focusing on genito-anal injury patterns in 1,472 rape survivors?'

'Yes.'

'They reported significant injuries in only forty-nine per

cent of the victims compared with your sixty-one. Are you aware of that?'

'Yes and as I said, studies vary wildly.'

'Do you know what this percentage dropped to among the victims examined more than two days after the assault?'

She hesitated. 'I would need to look it up.'

'I can tell you,' said Leeson. 'It dropped to sixteen point three per cent. This is one or two out of ten cases – *not* six.'

There was a shifting of mood in the courtroom.

'Dr Chou, isn't it true that the absence of injury does not prove the absence of force?

The doctor laced her fingers. 'That's true,' she said.

'The complainant was examined a whole nine days after the fact. If there was physical evidence of trauma, isn't it possible – *likely* even – that it healed by the time he was examined?'

'It's possible.'

'In fact, it's *so* likely that many sexual health organisations don't even conduct an examination after a cut-off of seven days. Isn't that true?'

'That's the standard cut-off, yes.'

'It's also possible, isn't it, by your own admission, that anal rape can take place without *any* evidence of physical trauma?'

'Well—'

'Yes or no will do.'

'Yes, it's possible.'

'Then all of this was a perfect waste of time, wasn't it, Dr Chou?' Leeson's voice was scornful. He turned to Judge Arden. 'I'm done with this witness, Your Honour.'

Dr Chou left the witness box, her jaw set in a line. She was a witness for the defence and yet, watching from above,

Zara felt a sense of solidarity. She knew what it was like to stand up in court and have a privileged man undercut you; to have people judge you based on your height and name and skin tone. This time, it had worked in her favour but there were dozens of times it had not and she felt empathy for the doctor as she left the court, a flush of pink rising in her cheeks.

The judge soon adjourned for the day and Zara and Kamran left the courthouse, relieved to find that the crowd had thinned beneath the darkening sky. As they walked to her car, a bespectacled man stepped in their path. His stubble dipped into a cleft chin, etching a thick dark line. The industrial tang of his aftershave made Zara wince.

'Hello, I'm Peter Ottoman from *Visor*. I'm writing a deep dive into consent culture and I was hoping to—'

'No, thank you.' Zara gripped Kamran's elbow and tugged him towards her car.

The reporter stepped closer. 'I'm sorry to approach you both like this. I promise I'll stop if you ask. I just think this is an important story to—'

'Stop,' said Zara. She let Kamran into her car, then turned to face the reporter. 'Are you harassing a child? Is that what you're doing?'

'No, I'm taking a sensitive, nuanced look at the culture of consent.'

Zara narrowed her eyes. *Visor* was one of the publications that funnelled attention towards her during Jodie's case. 'He's a *child*,' she said, straining for civility. 'Please leave him alone.' She drove off, the smell of aftershave still pungent in her nose.

Kamran next to her was coiled like a spring. He flexed

his fists open and closed as he watched the reporter shrink in the mirror.

'It was a tough day today,' she said.

He exhaled – a rough, fragmented sound. He tapped his toes in the footwell, then gripped his shin, forcing himself to stop. He took his phone from his pocket, thumbed through it, then slipped it into his jacket slung behind his seat, keeping it from easy reach. 'Sorry, I just feel a little wound up.'

Zara turned left onto Great Suffolk Street.

'Can we stop?' he asked. 'I need some air.'

'Okay, yes.'

His voice climbed a register. 'Can we stop now?' It verged on panic as he wound down a window.

Zara glanced at him and saw that he was sweating. 'Do you need to be sick?'

'I just need to stop. Please.'

'Okay, that's okay.' Zara searched for a safe place to stop but they were in the thick of London and the streets had no parking.

Kamran gasped in air through the window and a moan escaped his throat.

'Hang on, Kamran. I'm just finding a place to stop.' She turned right onto Toulmin Street and spotted an empty space. As soon as she pulled in, Kamran rushed out and ran to a corner, then doubled over with his hands on his knees and gasped in great gulps of air.

Zara grabbed some tissue and a bottle of water. 'Hey, just breathe.' She placed a tentative hand on his shoulder.

He flinched away from it. 'I don't know what's happening.'

'That's okay, Kamran. Just breathe.'

His face creased with fear; reaching for meaning but grasping nothing. 'I feel like I'm going to faint.'

'Okay, sit down on this fence.'

Kamran sat and panted for breath.

Zara knelt in front of him. 'If you need to be sick, be sick.'

He shook his head vigorously. 'It's not that. It's not nausea. I feel...' He shook his hands as if warding something off. 'I feel panicked.'

She handed him the bottle of water. 'Here. Drink this.'

He took it from her, hands trembling as he took a shallow sip. 'What's happening?' Beads of sweat dripped off his forehead and his skin was strangely sallow.

'We'll work it out,' she said. She suspected he was having a panic attack, but didn't say so, giving him space to calm himself. 'You're okay, Kamran,' she said gently. 'You're okay.'

He wiped the sweat off his brow with a sleeve. 'I'm sorry,' he said. 'It just came on suddenly, like I needed to get out of that car as soon as possible.'

'Don't worry. Just drink a bit more water.' She was about to say more when she heard a voice behind her. It hit them both like a punch in the ribs.

'Oi, isn't that that Paki fag?'

Zara stood up slowly, deliberately, registering the fear in Kamran's eyes. She turned around. Four men stood on the edge of the lot. She felt a jolt of alarm when she spotted a cap in one of their hands. It was red with the letters #NotAllMen stamped in white across it. In his other hand, he held a beer bottle, the green glass glinting wickedly as a nearby lamp blinked on. He had a pronounced widow's peak and his lips were curled in a snarl.

'It *is* that Paki fag.'

Zara felt her nerves sing out. She knew that men who employed those words so casually were desperate to be feared. Her courage wavered, cracking her shield of confidence. She had thought it would protect her once, but after that night in a dark alley metres from her home, she knew that it would not. Her eyes flicked to her Audi. The men weren't blocking her path but they were closer to the car: two endpoints in a V while she and Kamran stood in its dip.

'Kamran, get up,' she said, her voice deceivingly steady. 'Get behind me.' Her eyes began to water and she blinked rapidly. She clicked through a process of elimination: appeasement, aggression, levity or gravity. She swallowed hard and smiled brightly. 'Evening, gentlemen,' she called out. They sniggered then and she felt her stomach lurch. Civility would offer no escape. 'Where's your phone?' she asked Kamran.

'In the car,' he replied, his voice small and tight.

'Mine too.'

The men approached them, fanning out like a pack, aggression like a basic instinct.

'What's this? A dogging hotspot?' jeered one, a stocky twenty-something with thinning hair and ruddy skin. The others laughed.

'What's this fag doing out here then?'

The words made Zara blanch. 'We were just leaving actually, so—' She stepped at an angle away from them.

'Not so fast,' said another. 'Stay and have some fun.'

Zara scanned the street. Few cars passed this way and in the falling darkness, nothing would seem amiss. 'No, thank you,' she said. 'Kamran, let's go.' She moved towards the outer edge of their fan but one of them stepped in her way.

'Come on,' he said, his voice sugary.

'I said, no.' She nodded at the cap in his hands. 'No means no, but you have to say so, right?'

The men were silent for a beat and then started laughing. 'We've got ourselves a smart one here, lads.'

Zara watched them, knowing she had made a mistake in stepping forward, closing the gap between them. Her heart pulsed in her chest beneath a blooming panic.

'Hey, pretty boy,' one called out to Kamran. 'What's wrong? You decided you didn't like it up the arse after all?'

Zara held up a hand. 'All right, that's enough, gents. We've got to go.'

He stepped closer. '*We* say when it's enough. Not you.'

Zara knew they were trapped, hemmed by the fence behind them and the four thugs in front. She looked to the empty street, willing a car to pass, hoping its driver would register the threat.

The man with the cap stepped closer. 'Well, isn't this our lucky day.'

'Gents, come on. You've done what you came to do,' she said, trying to keep things light.

'Oh darling, we haven't done *nearly* what we came to do.' He grinned. 'Oh no no no no no no.'

'Be sensible, gents. There are courts and a police station literally around the corner from here. The streets are crawling with bobbies. You don't want this to escalate.'

'Yeah, but none of them are coming to this shithole, are they? You only come here to piss or puke.'

Zara knew that he was right. The street was lined with industrial units, deserted for the evening. Could they run?

Could they vault the fence behind them, or skirt around the men and make a dash for the road? No. They would be on them before they got halfway.

'No need to worry, love,' said the one with the cap. 'We're not after you. We're after him.'

She felt an eel of dread and held out a hand to steer Kamran behind her.

'You can get in your car and go home and we won't touch a hair on your head.'

She stamped down the rising panic and thought back to her defence class: a strike to the neck, a knee to the groin. It seemed utterly farcical. She couldn't fight off one of these men, let alone four. She thought about Kamran. He fenced, but did he box or wrestle? It did not escape her that she was looking to him for protection when it was *her* job to protect him.

'Just step aside and walk away,' said the ringleader with the cap.

'That's not going to happen,' she said, her voice bafflingly firm.

'Step away,' he repeated.

Zara ushered Kamran closer behind her. 'No.'

The man knelt down and smashed his beer bottle against the floor, sending shards skittering across the tarmac. He held up the jagged neck.

Zara fought the urge to run, forced herself to stay calm but in the sting of panic, one thought rang most loudly: *they're not bluffing, they're not bluffing, they're not bluffing.*

He took a step closer to her and though every instinct told her to flee, she raised her chin and faced him. He sneered. 'If you don't step away, this is going right into your jaw.'

Zara clenched her hands to stop them from shaking. He was close enough to smell now: a stultifying mix of yeasty beer and body odour. She took in his demeanour, shoulders hunched forward, knitted brows, bottle held out away from his body, on the edge of pouncing.

'I'm sorry,' she said gently. 'But I can't do that.'

He took a step closer. Then, he drew back his arm for momentum and jerked forward with a roar.

Zara cried out, a shrill, panicked sound. She drew up her arms to protect her face and instinctively closed her eyes. The rush of blood rang in her ears, making them pulse with heat.

The man burst out laughing.

When Zara opened her eyes, she saw that the bottle was still in his hands. He threw it by her feet and leaned in close, his breath pungent and hot on her neck.

'See you soon,' he said, then turned back to his friends. Casually, they strolled off.

Zara doubled over, fingers gripping her knees. The memory of her attack came flooding back. The bright white pain of a steel-capped boot and the coppery taste of terror.

Kamran next to her crumpled against the fence. 'I'm sorry,' he was saying. 'I'm so sorry. I froze.'

Zara shook as the adrenaline rushed from her body. Tears streamed down her cheeks, catching in her lips, filling her mouth with brackish relief. She fumbled for her keys and held them out to Kamran. 'Get in the car,' she said.

His eyes were wide and frantic. 'What about you?'

The keys jangled in her trembling hand and she closed her fingers around them. 'I just need a minute. Get in the car. Lock the doors.'

Kamran took the keys, his hand soft and clammy as it brushed against hers. He hesitated, his right foot stepping forward and then back as if practising a dance move.

'Go!' she shouted. She pressed her face to a forearm, trying to stem her tears. She ground her teeth to steel herself, but couldn't stop her mind unspooling. It settled on a single item: a bottle of pale yellow pills. She reached for a way to get them: plead a lost prescription at the twenty-four-hour pharmacy, get it couriered from an online service, call a friend of a friend. In rifling through her options, she felt her breathing slow. There was something soothing in surrendering her will. As soon as she made the decision, a sense of calm muscled out her panic. First, she needed to get Kamran home. The sooner she did that, the sooner she could yield, so instead of letting her face cool in the breeze, she strode back to her car.

'Are you okay?' asked Kamran.

'Yes.' She exhaled, her mouth forming a small 'o'. 'Are you?'

The bags beneath his eyes seemed soft and hollow. Could people age from trauma alone? 'I'm sorry,' he said. 'It was my fault. I shouldn't have asked you to stop.'

'It's not your fault.' Her tone was clipped, leaving no room for debate. 'I'm going to have to file an incident report with the police. They may want to talk to you too.'

Kamran nodded wordlessly.

'Let's get you home,' she said. They drove in silence, Zara preoccupied by what was coming: surrender and relief.

At Hampton, they parted with a quick goodbye, each desperate now for solitude. As soon as Kamran left, Zara's pulse began to race. She felt a rush of anticipation; ached for oblivion. She placed an online order for Diazepam and arranged to have it couriered. Then, she began the drive across London. She thought of the comforting lull of narcotic sleep and gripped the wheel too hard, feeling her skin grow sweaty. She turned on the air conditioning and goosebumps rose on her arms. She felt the tension grow, almost sexual in intensity.

As she wound through the streets of London, however, it morphed into something sombre. She felt a tug of conscience, maddeningly insistent. With a jolt, she realised that she was speeding and tamped down on her brakes, inciting an aggressive blare of a horn. She felt the urge to scream along with it: high, shrill and piercing. Instead, she started to cry – great, glassy tears of rage. She slowed the car, then parked, wheels skewed at a forty-degree angle. She picked up her phone and watched the screen. Her delivery was an hour away and she was roughly an hour from home. If she started the car now, she would meet it just in time.

Hot tears coursed to her chin, then tipped down to her collarbone. She scrolled through her phone and desperately dialled a number.

His Irish accent was gentle. 'Zara?'

'Chris,' she said through her tears. 'Chris, I'm close. I'm really fucking close.'

There was a drawing of breath. 'Are the pills on you now?' he asked.

A sob escaped her lips. 'No, but they're on their way.'

'Where are you?'

She looked out through the window. 'I don't even know. Somewhere in north London.'

'Okay, who's bringing it to you?'

'A courier from an online chemist. They're bringing it to my flat.'

Chris said something that sounded like swearing. 'Can you cancel the order?'

Zara was silent and it rose to fill the space around her, inky and black and resistant.

'Come to the church. I've just left and can easily head back.'

'Are you sure?' Her voice cracked.

'Zara, come to the church now. Right now. Okay?'

She nodded. 'Okay.' She hung up the phone, relief spreading like gel on her skin – cold, blue and surgical.

Kamran dropped his bag on the hardwood floor. The dull thud was the only noise; the rest of West Lawn was silent. He checked his watch. It seemed impossible that it wasn't even 6 p.m. The day seemed to stretch for ever. He shut his eyes to block out those crippling minutes: the grain of the man's taunt, the gut-punch of his words – 'Isn't that that Paki fag?' – the glint of jagged glass and the wrenching realisation that he would have let them attack Zara before daring to step in.

It was Thursday, which meant his fencing class was in session and though he had been granted leave, he threw open his wardrobe and pulled out his fencing bag, checking inside for his mask, sabre, lame, wires and whites. Without pausing to think, he ran across campus to the fencing salle. The doors opened with a low whine and seven fencers looked up at him – a synchronised gust of surprise.

The teacher, Mr Storr, checked the wall clock. 'You start

your first match with a yellow card for lateness, Mr Hadid. Now get changed.'

Kamran nodded solemnly and headed to the back to get dressed.

'Mr Paulson. You won't need to spar with me today. Please take your place next to Mr Hadid,' he heard the teacher say.

Kamran changed quickly, ripping a button off his shirt as he did. A memory came to him: a warm hand slipping across his skin, making his stomach flutter. He pushed it from his mind and took his place on the long metal piste.

He and Paulson came *en garde*, their sabres held ready.

'*En garde*. Ready? Fence!' shouted Mr Storr.

Kamran extended his blade, brushing it with Paulson's. They moved elegantly, like dancers on a stage, Paulson scoring first with a parry riposte. Kamran composed himself and the next point he drove forward, but his attack fell short, allowing Paulson to seize the initiative and land another touch on Kamran.

'Excellent,' shouted Mr Storr.

Kamran felt his temper flare, but kept it in tight control. He channelled it into pin-precise movements, sharpened by faultless timing. He pushed forward with a beat attack and slashed his blade against Paulson's lame, the scoring box flashing a single green light. 'Touche,' he said with an unseen grin. He landed another point and another and another until he beat Paulson by fifteen to five. He was taller, stronger, better and he would not be beaten here.

When the session ended, the two boys shook hands. Paulson slapped him on the back but in a precise, formal way like a child learning to pet a dog.

Kamran had hoped for a sense of release – a venting of his pent-up stress – and though the win offered brief relief, he was reminded how things had changed. Instead of boisterous banter and the pushing and shoving of the locker room, the boys maintained a frigid distance like one might treat a priest.

As they piled into the shower room, Kamran remained behind, his back pressed against a wall, his hair stringy with sweat. He heard voices bounce off the pale beige walls, amplified by water.

'How come you lost to a pansy, Paulson?'

'Scared he'd stick you with his *sabre*?' Guffaws echoed across the room.

Kamran felt a pressure in his stomach, the hot-coal weight of dread. It had been three days since the report in the paper and though jeers were common in the dining hall, he expected more from his teammates. Were they unaware that he could he hear them, or did they just not care?

He willed himself to confront them, but stayed rooted on the spot. Jagged green glass flashed through his mind, followed by the word 'coward'. He waited until the boys left the building, then walked into the shower room, the word stamped in his mind like branding.

CHAPTER TEN

Zara watched the blanket of rain unfurl on Canary Wharf. Cars swooshed down the A102, their wipers going full speed, the wet rush of the road rising in a symphony. Already, silhouettes moved in the windows of One Cabot Square. She wondered if they were cleaners or ambitious young men and women already at their desks at 6 a.m.

She hadn't slept – not properly, too wired from what had happened. She'd been dangerously close to surrender, *deliciously* close in fact. How easy it would have been to come home and draw a bath and sink into oblivion. Instead, Chris had forced her to go to the church; to sit in their NA circle – just the two of them – and tell him what had happened. She had sobbed as she spoke. It wasn't the physicality that had shaken her most but what it meant for her mind: to be so scared, to panic so hard. She had carried the fear for months, tamping it down so it was not the first thing she felt, but it was so tiring, like speaking in an accent that wasn't yours. She *was* scared and she *was* fearful and the self-defence classes didn't help and joking with Safran didn't help and coming to the NA meetings didn't help. She *needed* her pills, she had said.

Chris had been patient, had listened to her cry and rage, and then he had walked her home and gently taken the package the courier had stuffed in her postbox.

'Thank you,' she said, noting how the light from the streetlamp pooled on his hair, turning it an orange-brown. She was so sceptical of this NA meeting when Stuart told her to join, yet here it was, pulling her away from the brink.

She had slept fitfully and given up trying at 4 a.m. She had curled onto the windowsill to watch the world wake up, shadows of people rising and moving in the safety of their homes. She had watched them intently and imbued meaning into their pauses, deciding if they were happy or lonely. The wind rattled outside, forcing drops of rain in directions unintended. She wrapped her woollen cardigan around her and pressed her head to the pane, letting it cool her thoughts. When One Cabot Square was fully lit up, she rose and walked to the bathroom. Today was their final day in court. On Monday, there would be a verdict.

Judge Arden's purple robes fluttered as he sat. There was a low rustle as the courtroom followed suit. Zara and Kamran sat stiffly, still shaken by the evening before. They had been greeted by jeers at court this morning, the #NotAllMen protest growing, buoyed by media attention and Seth Dawson's rhetoric. These men protested the stereotype that cast them as cruel, and yet here they were, spewing threats that verged on violence.

Zara had thought that men like this only hated *women*: that their anger was rooted in sexual frustration, but now she could see that it ran somewhere deeper. These men were angry because they didn't have the life they had been promised. They couldn't buy a big house or afford a nice car or have sex with the girl they wanted. They had failed at an idealised masculinity and because they held it sacred, they hated those who had escaped its burden: women, gay men and the trans community. They hated Kamran for admitting that someone took something from him that he wasn't willing to give; for daring to be vulnerable in a world that punished them for it.

They had shouted insults this morning – liar, attention-seeker, closeted, coward – and cheered when they saw him flinch. Zara had urged him forward, her hand gentle on the small of his back until they were safely inside. The tension in the courtroom felt like a presence: heavy and close and cowing. It was the final day of the defence's case and then a weekend of waiting.

Olivia Hallett stood. 'May it please Your Honour, the next witness is James Yang.'

Kamran's friend, Jimmy, walked in, his eyes flicking to Finn in the dock. Solemnly, he took the oath.

'Mr Yang, how long have you known Mr Hadid?' asked Olivia.

Jimmy's lips twitched as he counted. 'Four years. We started at Hampton together when we were thirteen.'

'Is it fair to say you know him well?'

'Yes.'

'I believe you have described him as your "best friend"?'

'Yes.'

'Did he confide in you the alleged events of Friday the first of May, specifically that Finn Andersen spent the night in his room?'

'No.'

'Did he mention seeing Finn Andersen at all, in the days after?'

Jimmy hesitated. 'No.'

'When did you find out that he had complained to the police?'

'I heard a rumour a few weeks later.'

Olivia murmured in surprise. '"A few weeks later,"' she repeated. 'And did you ask Kamran why *he* didn't tell you about it?'

'I figured he was embarrassed.'

'Why?'

Jimmy shifted on his feet. 'Because Finn was a guy.'

'Why is that embarrassing?'

Jimmy squirmed. 'Because then people might think he's gay.'

'And?'

'And he's not.'

Olivia nodded. 'Okay, so let me just repeat this to make sure I understand it. Kamran did not tell you that Finn spent the night in his room because he would find it embarrassing if people knew. He would find it embarrassing because people would think he's gay even though he's not?'

Jimmy nodded. 'Yes, that's right.'

'Is Kamran easily embarrassed?'

'Not really.'

'So why would he have been embarrassed by this?'

'Well...' Jimmy glanced at the jury. 'His parents would have gone nuts.'

Olivia arched a brow. '"His parents would have gone nuts,"' she repeated.

'Your Honour.' Leeson rose to his feet. 'The witness cannot reliably state how Mr Hadid's parents would react to such a situation.'

Olivia smiled at him sweetly. 'It's okay. I am finished with this witness.'

Leeson scowled, knowing she had already made her point. 'I have no questions for this witness, Your Honour,' he said.

Jimmy was allowed to step down.

Zara watched from the gallery with a mounting sense of unease. What was Olivia up to? Why had she called Jimmy as a witness for a mere ten minutes of evidence? She glanced at Kamran next to her but he did not seem concerned.

Olivia stood again. 'Your Honour, we call our final witness, Mr Tom Hare.'

A middle-aged man walked in, short with a slight paunch. He had a receding hairline and a wide, meaty nose.

Zara frowned. He hadn't been on the witness list that Erin had supplied her. He must have been added later and not filtered through to Zara. She turned to Kamran and felt a stab of anxiety. He sat stiff-backed in his seat and the colour had drained from his face. She leaned towards him to find out who the witness was, but Olivia was already asking.

'My name is Tom Hare,' he answered. 'I am a site officer at Hampton College. My team is responsible for all cleaning, repairs and general maintenance of school grounds and property.'

Zara felt a wisp of dread stir in her stomach. She willed Leeson to look up, to signal that he was expecting this and knew what was coming.

'How long have you worked at Hampton?' asked Olivia.

Tom Hare pushed back his shoulders. 'Eighteen years,' he said proudly.

'Is it fair to say you know the pupils well?'

'Can name every single one of them.' His voice was soft and broad, probably originally northern but flattened by habit or force.

'As I understand it, Mr Hare, Hampton is a place of routine and regiment, is that correct?'

He frowned. 'Not entirely. We want our boys to be free thinkers so we encourage them to question authority, to challenge received wisdom and make up their own minds.'

Olivia blinked, clearly surprised by his considered answer. She rephrased the question. 'In terms of scheduling and timetabling, Hampton is fairly regimented, is that correct?'

'Yes, that's correct.'

'Can you please explain what happens at West Lawn on the first day of spring exeat – a scheduled weekend when the boys have leave?'

'Of course. The boys need to be out by 8 a.m. unless they have special dispensation from the housemaster. I am supplied with this list on the Friday night. On Saturday morning, my team and I begin housekeeping.'

'What does that entail?'

As Tom Hare went through his morning routine, Zara looked at Kamran to try to locate the threat. He sat stock-still, refusing to return her gaze.

'Mr Hare, was Kamran Hadid's name on your list of special dispensation?' asked Olivia.

'No, ma'am. As far as I was aware, he had left at 8 a.m.'

'In that case, he was on your list of rooms to clean?'

'Yes.'

'What happened when you got to his room?'

Tom Hare winced, as if his words pained him. 'I saw Hadid Major in bed with Finn Andersen.'

'What were they doing?'

'They were asleep.'

'Were they touching?'

'Yes. Mr Andersen had his arm around Mr Hadid.'

'What happened next?'

'Well, I started to shut the door when Kamran turned around and opened his eyes.'

A hush of noise swept across the courtroom. Zara turned to Kamran, but he fixed his gaze on the witness box.

'Did he see you?' asked Olivia.

Tom Hare thought for a moment. 'We didn't make eye contact but I'm fairly sure he saw me. It was one of those moments where you're looking at someone and then they look up at the very same moment that you look away, but you're sure they saw you watching. Does that make sense?'

Zara noted that members of the jury were nodding.

'Indeed,' said Olivia. 'How certain are you that Kamran saw you?'

Tom frowned. 'I can't be certain that he saw me, but as I said he looked up just as I was leaving and I'm one hundred per cent certain he saw the door closing. He would have put two and two together and inferred that it was me.'

'So, to confirm: you are one hundred per cent certain that Kamran saw someone leave his room that morning?'

'Yes.'

'And he would have logically inferred that it was you?'

262

'Yes.'

'Mr Hare, is it feasible that Mr Hadid had a consensual encounter with Finn and then concocted a story of rape to pre-empt you revealing what you saw?'

Leeson was on his feet. 'Your Honour, my learned friend knows that that's a question the witness cannot possibly answer. He cannot know what Mr Hadid was and was not thinking.'

'I'm asking if it was "feasible", which is perfectly answerable, particularly given that the witness knows the involved parties so well,' said Olivia.

Judge Arden raised a placating hand. 'It's a reasonable line of enquiry, Mr Leeson. Ms Hallett, you may continue.'

Tom Hare cocked his head. 'It seems rather rash.'

'Yes, but is it feasible?'

'Yes, it's feasible.'

'Thank you, Mr Hare.' Olivia turned to the judge. 'I have no more questions for this witness.'

Zara swallowed. This is why they told rape victims not to attend the trial. The vagaries of the law did not treat subjects kindly.

Leeson stood now to address the witness. 'Mr Hare, you agreed that Hampton is a place of routine and regiment when it comes to scheduling. Are the pupils aware of this routine and regiment?'

'Yes, of course.'

'So Kamran would have been aware that you were due to prepare the rooms from 8 a.m. on the morning of Saturday the second of May, is that correct?'

'Yes.'

'Do boys often forget to vacate their rooms?'

'Occasionally, but they usually have parents or drivers picking them up so they don't oversleep.'

'If – as my learned friend suggests – Kamran was so terrified about being discovered in bed with a man, why would he be so careless when he *knew* you would be entering the room?'

Tom blinked. 'I don't know.'

'Does that sound characteristic of him? To throw caution to the wind like that?'

Tom shook his head. 'It does not.'

'If he were having a planned, consensual rendezvous with Mr Andersen and did not want to be discovered, doesn't it follow that he would be extremely careful about avoiding you in the morning?'

'Yes.'

'Thank you.' Leeson turned to the judge. 'I have no more questions for this witness.'

Olivia Hallett stood. 'The defence rests, Your Honour.'

Judge Arden nodded peaceably. 'In that case, I suggest we adjourn for the day for closing speeches on Monday. I advise that everyone take a good rest this weekend. We will reconvene in three days.'

Zara exhaled a long, soft breath of air. 'Let's get out of here,' she said to Kamran. She led him from the courtroom and out onto the concourse. They drove through the gates without trouble, the protestors absent on this Friday afternoon. She rolled down the window to let in a slash of air and headed to Belsize Park where Kamran was to spend the weekend.

She didn't speak until they were halfway there. 'Do you want to tell me what happened?'

Kamran's cheekbones cut two sharp lines across his delicate face. 'He's right.'

Zara waited. Her grip was tight on the steering wheel and she forced herself to loosen it.

'I didn't see him but I saw the door close. I was still half asleep and thought I had imagined it.'

'But Leeson was right,' said Zara. 'You knew Tom Hare would check your room, so surely you realised that you *hadn't* imagined it.'

'When I woke up properly, I forgot all about it. I was shocked to find Finn in bed with me and everything else just... faded.'

Zara considered this. 'It never came to you in the ensuing months?'

'No,' he said fretfully. 'I only remembered when I saw him walking into the courtroom.'

Zara drew a deep sigh. It wasn't her style to coddle her charges. What was the point of assuring them justice if she knew it wasn't forthcoming? 'Kamran, you are aware that this might call into doubt your motivations? Before, there was no reason for you to lie about Finn. Now, Olivia Hallett will try to position it as if you got caught and were so worried that you made up this lie.'

Kamran grimaced. 'But who would do something like that?'

'Someone who was afraid of being outed.'

A thick silence settled in the car.

'I'm not gay,' said Kamran.

265

'Would you tell me if you were?'

He started to speak but then stopped. He watched the road, eyes darting back and forth with each passing car. 'Honestly? No.'

'Why?'

'For so many reasons. Would you tell *your* family if you were gay?'

Zara thought of her mother who had been so angry when she had left her arranged marriage. When a slight deviation had brought such heartache, would she really tell her mother she was gay? She, Zara the Brave, wanted desperately to say yes, to claim enlightenment on behalf of her family, but she knew that she could not. She would not tell them the truth; would have to wait until her mother passed away to come out to her siblings.

'Yeah, thought so,' said Kamran.

Zara swallowed. 'Okay, I get it,' she said softly.

They reached Belsize Park and turned into Kamran's street. She cut the engine and realised she could hear nothing – no rush of traffic, no low whine of a closing gate or a bin being wheeled over concrete. The silence was almost oppressive in a city as busy as London.

She gave him a plaintive smile. 'Go and be with your family this weekend.'

'Yeah. Sure,' he said with the trace of a scoff.

Zara let him out with a twist of concern. In the few months she had known him, he had been impeccably well mannered, tamping down his pain with civility. Today, she had glimpsed something else: a snap of cynicism that twisted his features in frightening ways. What would happen on Monday if the jury acquitted Finn?

Zara watched him slink up the stairs, literally dragging his feet, looking like home was the last place on earth he wanted to be.

Sofia heard the key in the lock and snapped to her feet. It was Friday evening and both her boys were coming home. She had accordingly asked Nevinka to prepare a family feast.

She hugged Kamran tightly and noticed a new gauntness in the curve of his waist. 'Come and eat,' she said. 'We've prepared all your favourite dishes.'

Kamran ducked out from under her arms. 'I'm not really hungry.'

'Oh,' said Sofia, a solitary note of sorrow.

Kamran closed his eyes for a beat and she could tell that he was biting something back. 'But I could definitely eat,' he added. His tone was light and it made Sofia want to cry. She wanted to weep for her son – her handsome, confident, intelligent son – who still tried to please her; still pretended he was the boy he used to be; pretended that he still could be. She wanted to gather him in her arms, kiss the soft down on his neck and tell him over and over that it would all be okay.

Mack walked in and the moment was gone. 'There he is,' he said, his voice booming across the space. He strode over and clapped Kamran on the back.

'Hi, Dad.'

'Come, come,' he said. 'Your mother has prepared all your favourites: *haleem, nihari, biryani.*'

Sofia called up to Adam and the four of them sat in the dining room, gathered at one end of a table that was big enough for twelve. Kamran took a helping of *dahl makhani* and rice along with a spoonful of salad. He picked at it politely under Sofia's gaze.

'What's wrong, son?' asked Mack. 'Stop picking at that rabbit food and eat some meat.' He shoved a dish of beef at Kamran and watched as he dutifully took a helping. Mack's tone grew tetchy. 'Well, don't just have it because I'm telling you to. Have it because you want to.'

Sofia tried to catch Mack's eye to tell him to ease off. It would be simpler if her husband were an out-and-out bully who reaped pleasure from inflicting pain, but his thousand cuts of criticism were always well intentioned. He wanted his sons to be strong and confident, moral and upstanding, but instead of teaching them a lesson and letting them practise, he would stand over their shoulders and comment on every mistake. It made her sons not *nervous* exactly but constantly wary. They were acutely conscious of disappointing him and so they sat, head up, shoulders back, poised like aggressors.

Mack embarrassed her sometimes with his sweeping statements served with a bullish confidence. Last year, he told their friends, Elizabeth and David Sergeant, that gay men came to be gay because they had an erotic homosexual experience before they came of age. Sofia had trilled in that placatory way that embarrassed even her. In failing to confront her husband though, hadn't she also failed her children? She looked at them now, sitting shoulder to shoulder, each as rigid as the other.

Kamran forked an enormous piece of meat, slopped it in thick gravy and jammed it in his mouth, barely able to chew. 'Mmm,' he said with overblown enthusiasm.

Adam looked up at him, his doe eyes wide in surprise.

Sofia tensed. It was unlike Kamran to be impudent. She couldn't remember the last time he had rebelled against his father, no matter how small the infraction.

Mack set down his fork and stared at his son, a furrow creasing between his brows.

Kamran held his gaze and chewed audibly.

'Is there something you want to tell me?' asked Mack. Sofia interjected but he held out a finger. 'Just a moment.' He pushed back his chair with a purposeful scrape. 'Is there something you want to tell me?' he repeated.

Kamran's bravado dropped off in a blink. 'No, sir.'

Mack placed his cutlery together and leaned back in his chair. 'Mr Morewood called us earlier. He said that Hampton's caretaker gave evidence in court today.'

Kamran's gaze slid to his plate.

'He said that the caretaker walked in on you with that boy. Is it true?'

'Mack,' Sofia tried gently.

He held up a hand. 'Sofia, if my son is a queen, I want to know, okay? I want to know what happened to make him that way.'

'For God's sake, Mack. Not at the dinner table.'

He ignored her. 'Look me in the eye, son, and tell me it's not true.'

Kamran set down his fork.

'Well?'

'I'm not, Dad. I swear.'

'Your mum said there were condoms in your bag. Some of them gone.'

Kamran startled and looked across to Sofia. She flushed with guilt, feeling the rush of dissolving trust.

Adam spoke now in a rapid burst. 'He's not gay. He was sleeping with that girl on the cruise last year. The ballet dancer with the long hair. They were sneaking around, telling me not to knock on his cabin. That's when he bought the condoms. I saw him in the ship pharmacy.'

Mack and Sofia stared at their sons, from one to the other. 'Is that true?' asked Mack.

Kamran shifted in his chair. 'Yes, sir.'

Mack exhaled audibly. 'Then *why* didn't you fight back?'

Sofia felt the air drain from the room. 'Mack, please.'

'No. I want to know how that happens. A boy climbs into bed with you. You're not gay, so why didn't you fight back? You're a strong boy, so I can't understand why you would just lie there.'

Kamran's jaw was set in a line. He didn't collapse beneath the salvo; only sat up straighter.

Mack's voice grew urgent. '*Why* did you just lie there?'

Kamran turned to Sofia, a hard scrape in his features. 'May I be excused?' he asked.

'No, you may not.' Mack raised a finger at him. 'Not until you answer my question.'

A tense silence fell across the room; a freeze-frame snap of turmoil.

'I don't know,' said Kamran quietly. 'I don't know why I just lay there.'

Mack closed his eyes and took a long, slow breath as if quieting a violence inside him. When he spoke, his voice was cold and hard. 'You're excused. Go on. Get out of here.'

Kamran stood and tucked his chair beneath the table. 'Thank you.' Calmly, he turned and left the room.

'Can we talk in private?' asked Sofia.

Adam stood with his plate. 'I'm done anyway.'

Sofia nodded, granting him leave. She turned to Mack, choosing her words carefully. She wasn't afraid of him, but knew he had to be manoeuvred in slow and subtle movements. 'Mack, we need to talk about how you're treating Kamran.'

A vein twitched in his temple. 'I just don't understand it, Sofia. You keep telling me to talk to him, but when I ask him questions, I don't get any answers.'

'Maybe you're asking the wrong things.'

'Then what are the right things?' He placed a soft fist on the table. 'Tell me, Sofia, because I can't seem to find them on my own.'

'Oh, Mack.' A choke in her throat surprised her. 'You have to be gentler with him. Stop pushing him so hard.'

He shook his head. 'You don't know what it's like, Sofia.' He drew a palm across his face. 'I push him because I *have* to.' He fixed his gaze to the far wall, his voice growing soft and wistful. 'I never told you this story but when I was younger – ten or eleven maybe – I saw this boy on my way to school one day and I think I must have smiled at him. A few days later, I saw him again and out of instinct I smiled. Do you know what he did? He came up to me and punched me in the face *so hard*.' Mack sucked in a breath. 'He must have gone home and said something to his dad about a boy smiling or laughing at him. His father must have told him – as a lot of men did with their children back then – to go up to that boy and hit him as hard as he could. Neither of us wanted to be in that situation but his dad or maybe an uncle or a brother told him to do it. These things come at you from such an aggressive angle, it... daunts you.' Mack squared his jaw. 'I taught him how to fight, Sofia, so that nothing like this would happen to him; so that he could get on in this world.' He met her gaze. 'So please don't blame me for making our son into a man.'

Sofia's eyes filled with tears. 'But you never allowed him to be a child.'

Mack flinched, his features mottled with hurt. 'I won't be made to feel guilty about this,' he said quietly. He drained his glass and set it down. 'Now if you'll excuse me, I'd like to finish my meal.' He picked up his fork and pushed it into a hunk of beef. He bit into the meat and chewed it resolutely.

Sofia watched him. How was it possible to love this man so fiercely yet dislike him so intensely? 'You're excused,' she said finally. She pushed back her plate, still half full with food, and left Mack alone at the table.

Safran pushed away his wine glass. 'We were just too different,' he said, lamenting his failed second date with the doctor. 'On paper, it was perfect but we'd spend our lives trying to change each other, so we decided to call it a day.' He gestured at Zara. 'What about you? Have you seen that guy again? Matthew?'

She shrugged a shoulder. 'No. It was a bit of a non starter.'

'Why?'

'He was just a bit... meek.'

Safran was amused. 'Ah, yes. We need an alpha specimen of a man to tame Zara the Brave.'

She frowned. 'Is that wrong?'

'No. You like what you like,' he said.

'But is that because I'm *told* to like it?' Zara gestured at him. 'And what about you? Are you alpha because you naturally are, or because you were taught to be in youth?'

Safran puckered his lips in thought. 'A bit of both, but it's hardly unique to men, is it? Look at you.'

'What about me?'

He studied her for a moment, picking his words carefully. 'When's the last time you spoke to someone about your dad?'

She flinched. 'That's not the same. That was a specific trauma; not a general, widespread malaise.'

'Drop the lawyer-talk for a sec, Zar.' Frown lines creased his forehead. 'I'm looking at you and I can see all the things you're doing to keep yourself from crumbling. I see the squaring of your shoulders and the lifting of your chin. I see the pressing of your lips and the curling of your fist. I see the way you steel yourself and every time you do it, a piece of that stays inside, hardening you from within. You talk to me about men forcing themselves to be strong. Well, what about you? When do you allow yourself to cry and flinch and be weak?'

Zara reached for a quip or a way to leaven the weight of his words, but Safran pre-empted this.

'Even *we* dance around the subject. It's been three years and you still can't talk about it.'

Zara's arms flushed with goosebumps. 'I will in my own time.'

'That's what I used to think.'

She swallowed. 'You know I'm going to NA meetings, right?'

He nodded.

'We've been talking about the "Cut": a thing that happened in your life that sliced it in two.' Zara grimaced. What felt insightful in the meeting now felt earnest and callow. Still, she persevered. 'For example, your "Cut" was probably when your mum got cancer.' She noted the shadow pass across his face. 'I know she recovered but the horror of that time changed you, right? My "Cut" was when my dad died after our estrangement. Framing it as a clear and tangible thing has been...' She lifted a shoulder. 'Helping.'

'But, Zar,' said Safran softly. 'It's an NA meeting. Should you see a real therapist?'

She exhaled. 'I'm not there yet.'

His lips curled in one corner. 'Because you're a little bit alpha?'

She smiled cheerlessly. 'I get it, Saf. I know there's a lot I don't talk about but... it takes time.' She traced a burl in the tabletop. 'Sometimes years, but I'll get there.'

'I hope so.' Safran raised his glass. 'To Zara the Brave,' he said.

'Zara the Brave,' she echoed.

CHAPTER ELEVEN

It seemed obscene that such a monumental day would look so perfectly ordinary. The mid-September sky was a damp-towel grey and there was no breeze or chill in the air, only a humid closeness that lay heavy on his cheeks. Kamran waited for Zara to pull on her blazer. She wore her hair in a bun but there were no loose wisps grazing her chin the way he liked in the girls from the nearby comprehensive.

Together, they walked from the car to the courthouse. As they passed through security, Kamran wondered if he had truly meant what he said when he told his mother to stay away. A part of him had thought she would show up regardless.

He felt a kick of unease with each click of Zara's heels against the floor of the foyer. As they climbed the stairs, he fought a sudden, desperate urge to raise a palm and slap himself; to somehow shock his body into a tougher gut. His hands began to tremble and he pushed them in his pockets, then – thinking this too casual – took them out again and held them by his thighs. Is this what it meant to be a victim? To second-guess your every movement: the set of your shoulder and tilt of your chin?

He cupped one hand in the other and followed Zara in. He took a seat in the front row, hoping that today was a day of closure. Below, Andrew Leeson stood to give his closing speech. Fine wisps of blond hair peeked from beneath his wig. He turned to the jury and started gravely.

'This is a case involving two people: the complainant, Kamran Hadid, and the defendant, Finn Andersen – but there's a third presence in this case we haven't fully addressed and that is Hampton College. It plays an important part because it has done several things. Its privilege and exclusivity has helped construct an air of respectability around Mr Andersen that he would not be afforded if he were, say, living on an estate in Lewisham. Hampton College is also responsible for constructing an air of intimacy. Because these boys live in close quarters, we imagine them to share spaces, which blurs the line between the public and the private – but this is a trick. Kamran's room at Hampton is his and his alone. It is as sacred as your own bedroom at home, your own four walls, your front door on which you have a lock. Don't be fooled into thinking that the collegiate air of the school bled back those boundaries. The pupils at Hampton know very well that they cannot enter a fellow pupil's room without his express permission. So what are we left with?'

Leeson combed the jury. 'We are left with a young man who essentially walked into Kamran's home uninvited, *knowing* that he was inebriated. He climbed into bed with him and initiated sexual contact *without his consent*. I will not ask you to put yourself in his shoes. Instead, put him in *yours*. Have him sitting in the office you work in, taking the same Tube as you, unlocking the door which is yours to unlock and going to sleep in *your* home. Now, imagine, at night, someone creeps into that home, climbs the stairs, opens your bedroom door, gets into your bed and initiates sex without your consent. What is that if not rape?'

Kamran watched from the gallery, jarred by Leeson's words. Even he had been lulled by Hampton's culture. Presented this starkly, it felt like a different beast.

'Now, there are several things I want to address. First, the defence has made much of the fact that Kamran viewed some hours of pornography during his time at Hampton. To brand a seventeen-year-old boy as deceitful based on the fact that he has watched some pornography is simply preposterous. Boys are curious. Kamran was simply exercising this curiosity in a safe, non-judgemental forum.

'The defence has sought to establish what they call "a lack of physical evidence" but as you have heard, physical evidence of injury is found in only a minority of sexual assault cases. It is the exception, not the norm.

'The defence also claims that Kamran Hadid levelled this accusation after being spotted by a site officer because of some outsize fear of being exposed. This, ladies and gentlemen, is where your judgement plays an important role. You have to ask yourselves: does Kamran Hadid, an exemplary member of Hampton's student body, strike you as the sort of character that would make up a life-destroying lie to escape some imagined form of opprobrium?

'It is the prosecution's case that Finn Andersen had sex with Kamran Hadid without his consent. The fact that they were drunk is irrelevant. Finn Andersen penetrated Kamran Hadid without invitation or consent. That is the very definition of rape. Finn Andersen is guilty. You *must* return a verdict of guilty.' Leeson's chin dipped forward, a half bow to the jury. 'Thank you,' he finished soberly.

Kamran took a quiet breath as if anything louder than a whisper might draw the court's attention. They might spot the way his chest rose and fell in a frantic rhythm, or the way sweat beaded on his upper lip and his fingers ached to scratch his skin, convinced that it was burning.

How would life change if Finn was found guilty? He would be put in prison to repent for what he did – and Kamran? Kamran would pick up his life and seal it back together: two cables being connected, driving home with a click, putting a pin in all his suffering. And what if Finn was freed? Would he move back to West Lawn, in the room below, the devil beneath Kamran's feet?

Olivia Hallett now stood for the defence's closing speech, the final word in the case. 'Ladies and gentlemen of the jury, you have heard a number of conflicting accounts over the course of this trial. It is a confusing process, that is true, which is why I want to highlight the clarity of one simple fact: there was no force. That bears repeating: there was no force. These are the facts of the case: Finn Andersen was at a party at West Lawn. Mr Hadid was at a party at the Batts. Both of them drank a little too much, enough to impair their judgement. Mr Hadid returned to his room at 1 a.m. He either did or did not lock his bedroom door. He cannot remember and therefore we cannot trust his recall. He entered his room and – according to him – he went straight to sleep. Some time later – what we know to be 2 a.m. – Finn left the party at West Lawn. We have seen him descend the stairs and turn right on the third floor. What we know is that Finn's room is on the second floor. What you have to ask yourself is this: is it feasible that a drunk person descending from the sixth floor might mistake the third floor for the second, particularly in a building in which all the floors are identical?'

Kamran thought about the time he had gone up to see his housemaster in the staff common room and had turned right at floor five instead of six. He knew that the answer was yes, it *is* feasible.

Olivia Hallett continued. 'Finn turned right, walked along the corridor and paused outside what he thought was his own room. You can see on the video that he searched for his key with his left hand. The prosecution has made much of the fact that he checked his breath but who among us hasn't been unpleasantly surprised by ourselves after a night of drinking and checked just how bad the damage was?'

Kamran shifted in his seat. Olivia Hallett with her statuesque frame and glowing skin was consistently immaculate. It was difficult to believe that she had ever been drunk, let alone checked her own breath like Finn.

She continued. 'By instinct, Finn reached forward and tried the doorknob – again, a perfectly natural instinct – and found that it was open. He entered what he thought was his own room, undressed and climbed into bed. When he realised there was someone next to him, his body began to react and the two of them had consensual sex. There was no force, no aggression, no premeditation. These young men were simply following a natural instinct.'

Olivia's voice grew grave. 'Now, if one of them had woken up just half an hour earlier, perhaps there would have been a sheepish hello and an awkward goodbye and that would have been that. What happened, instead, is that Tom Hare, a site officer at Hampton College, walked in at 8 a.m. as he was scheduled to and found them in bed together. Kamran stirred and saw this – and then he panicked. He panicked that someone had seen him; he panicked that his parents and classmates might find out; and he panicked that it might mean that he's gay. So, instead of accepting it for what it was – a drunken late-night romp – he decided to label it rape. He decided that this was the course of action that would earn him the least blame, and so that's the direction he chose.'

She gestured outwards. 'This is nothing more than a case of post-coital regret. Finn Andersen is an upstanding young gentleman with the brightest of futures ahead of him. Do not rob him of it because of one night's misunderstanding. There was no force. There was no aggression. There was no rape. Finn Andersen is *not* guilty. You must find him *not* guilty. Thank you.'

Olivia sat down, not with her usual flourish but with a slow, deliberate sinking to her chair, a visual manifestation of the gravity of the case.

The courtroom was silent and Kamran felt a tightness in his gut. This was it. There was nothing else to be said other than the verdict. After months of waiting, could it really be over in the space of a week?

He stood giddily.

'Easy.' Zara gripped his elbow. She stood too, hand firm on his arm. 'Are you okay?'

He gave her a tight smile, feeling like a spring about to snap. 'I'm fine.'

Zara guided him out to the meeting room she had wrangled from the staff. Kamran sat on a hard plastic chair, his hands crablike on his knees. Zara handed him a bottle of water that he accepted gratefully. He took three neat sips and replaced the cap.

'What happens now?' he asked.

'We wait. Sometimes it takes minutes. Sometimes it takes hours.'

'It's good if it's quick, right? It means they think he's guilty?'

'There's no way to know, Kamran. What you see in the movies isn't always true.'

Kamran traced one edge of the table, his thumbnail digging in the cheap Formica filling, picking out small beige flakes. 'What if it's not guilty?'

'Then we focus on recovery.'

Kamran's mouth twisted in one corner. 'Recovery?' He grimaced. 'It sounds so... American.'

Zara leaned forward. 'That may be, but it's an intrinsic part of the journey. You can't brute-force your way out of this, Kamran. You can't simply tough it out. Do you understand? If you try to do that, the trauma will stay with you for years.'

'I understand,' he said, not adding that he disagreed. 'Recovery', 'trauma' and that indulgent word 'survivor' were not in the Hadid vocabulary. And Zara was wrong: he *had* to brute-force his way through it no matter what happened next. There was no other choice. Not for a Hadid.

Sofia pressed the pedal with her foot, bedecked in a soft white plimsoll. She held the white lilies over the bin and then sighed exasperatedly. She released the pedal and then took the flowers over to the counter. She carefully snipped the string, unwrapped the rich cream sheath of paper and slipped off each of the petal guards. She dutifully pulled away lower-reaching leaves and any rotting petals, then cut two inches off each stem. She took out a crystal vase and filled it with lukewarm water, then snipped a corner off the plastic sachet and sprinkled in the flower food. Carefully, she placed in each stem, arranging and rearranging as she progressed. Finally finished, she took the flowers to the stool by the French doors, knowing the sun would hit it just so. She stood there, watching the way the light shone through the white translucent petals. What she really wanted to do was sling the vase across the room. How satisfying it would be to watch the rivulets of water drip down her immaculate wall, to see the shards of crystal lie among the thorns – two shades of the same sharp pain. She imagined pressing the pad of a finger into the head of a thorn, feeling it pierce her skin, and then vibrant drops of blood on the pristine marble floor. Instead, she took photos of the flowers, being sure to press the button for high definition. She flicked through the pictures, selected the best one and sent it to Rana.

Thank you so much for these, it read. **So thoughtful of you**.

She set the phone down on the oak wedge of her dinner table, then watched the sky outside as if it might offer some clue as to what was happening to her son.

She had woken this morning, determined to go to court, but Oliver was running an errand for Mack and she hated to drive in London. She preferred not to travel by cab; couldn't abide the thought of strangers heaving into the back seat with all their sweat, wet and odour. She had asked Mack to send her Oliver, but he had blankly refused; told her not to get hysterical. 'It will be easier for Kamran without you there,' he said. 'Besides, do you *want* to be photographed walking into criminal court?'

'But it's not our son on trial,' she said.

'That's not how people will see it,' said Mack.

Sofia pressed her head against the French door. She wondered how many times she had acceded to her husband over the course of their marriage. It was true that in social gatherings or matters of the home, he would submit to her with performative deference – 'she's the boss,' he liked to say, adding a pantomime wink – but behind closed doors, Mack always had the final say.

When had her girly coquettishness devolved to this docility? Sofia had assumed that all the things she did to charm him – her demure inability to choose a movie, her doe-eye gratitude when he settled the bill – would stop when their relationship matured. Instead, it changed to something else. Mack would subtly reverse every decision she made, always with a mollifying 'hon'. 'The movie sounds great, hon, but the reviews are terrible.' 'It's cute you want to pay, hon, but I've already got this.' 'Our son was raped, hon, but don't you worry about it.'

In the glass pane, Sofia watched herself open her mouth and though her features twisted in a scream, there was only a sibilant sound like the rush of gas waiting for a flame.

The knock on the door startled Kamran and he instinctively rose to his feet.

The usher looked in. 'The jury has a verdict.'

Kamran willed his legs not to buckle beneath him.

Zara nodded at him, the gesture markedly sombre, as if calling him to arms. 'Ready?' she asked.

His stomach coursed with nerves. 'Yes.'

Zara squeezed him, just above the elbow. He closed his eyes for a moment, his Adam's apple contracting once, then twice, before he followed Zara out.

The courtroom held an iron-like smell, the radiators left on too long. In the gallery, Kamran felt a desperate need to take off his blazer and pull off his tie. With its knot fastened around his neck, he felt the stirrings of panic, like what he had experienced in Zara's car. He bent over, elbows on his knees, and took a series of shallow breaths, sweat now coating his skin.

Zara leaned forward too and stroked his back in long, firm movements. 'Kamran, look at me,' she said. 'Look at me.'

He shook his head, scared that averting his gaze might spur the nausea churning inside.

'Just breathe. You're okay. You're fine.' She started breathing along with him, taking deep lungfuls of air. He copied her but it did not assuage his panic. He shut his eyes and imagined his father standing there, watching with utter bafflement. 'Head up, shoulders back,' he would say. 'Head up, shoulders back.' Kamran took three deep breaths, a hunter with buck fever. *Head up.* He swallowed the rising bile, the acid tang of it coating his throat. *Shoulders back.* He opened his eyes and straightened, shrugging off Zara's hand.

She leaned in to talk to him but he flinched away. 'I'm okay,' he said.

'Kamran—'

'I'm *fine*.' He slid a few inches away from her. *I'm fine.*

The usher opened the door and allowed the jury inside. Kamran swallowed, tasting his own stale mouth. He searched the jury for clues. He saw the young man with the buzz cut glance at Finn in the dock. Was that compassion on his features?

'I believe we have a verdict, jury, please,' said Judge Arden.

The clerk asked the defendant and foreman to stand. 'Mr Foreman, have the jury reached a verdict upon which you are all agreed?'

'Yes.'

'Do you find the defendant guilty or not guilty of rape?'

The courtroom seemed to tilt and contract, making Kamran weave.

The foreman smoothed his tie. 'We find the defendant not guilty.'

Finn in the dock cried out with relief. He took great gulps of air, his chest rising, then dipping concave – a hollow of vindication.

In the gallery, Kamran was stunned by the verdict. He had known that it was likely but he wasn't prepared for this feeling. The raw exposure of the moment – like driving into a sunbeam, blinking for your bearings – opened something inside him: a vast chasm of fury. If Finn was not guilty of rape, then what did that make Kamran? A liar? A fantasist? A coward? He rose to his feet. 'I'm going to be sick.'

Zara stood too.

'I need to get out – now.'

Zara led him out and guided him to the nearest bathroom.

She entered with him and he rushed to the toilet, knelt by its bowl and then retched. His stomach emptied and he trembled with the effort. Zara stood over him, one hand on his shoulder, the other holding a fistful of tissue.

Kamran retched and vomited again. When he was certain that he was finished, he pushed himself away from the bowl and slumped against the door. 'They think I'm a liar.'

Zara knelt by his side. 'No, Kamran. They don't. It's just a game of proof.'

'They think he's innocent.'

'No.' Zara sat on the floor.

'Don't,' said Kamran. Even in a state of distress, his manners kicked in like a first language, urging him to beckon her up, to tell her not to soil her skirt, to find her chair, to be a gentleman, but she was already on the floor, her legs stretched out on the cold white tiles.

'Kamran, it's not that they think he's innocent; it's that his guilt can't be proven beyond a reasonable doubt.'

Kamran's anger gave way to profound fatigue. 'What do I do now?' he asked. His voice was unfamiliar: hoarse and strangely plaintive.

'You sit here with me for a while and then...' She looked at him with a sad smile. 'Then, you get up.'

'And if I can't?'

'Then we'll sit here awhile longer.'

Kamran's face creased, a mixture of grief and gratitude. 'Okay,' he said softly. 'Thank you.'

It was half an hour later when they heard a knock on the door.

Mia Scavo looked in. 'I was told you were in here.' Her

plain black shoes made slight squeaky sounds as she crossed the tiled floor. She reached out a hand to Zara and pulled her to her feet. They both reached for Kamran, but he was already standing, swiping at the seat of his trousers.

'I'm sorry things didn't go our way.'

Outside, there was a rabble of cheer and a chant emerged from the noise: 'Not Finn! Not all men!' – the 'Finn' distorted to 'fenn' to form a clumsy rhyme.

'I'll walk you to your car,' added Mia.

Zara heard the cheers grow louder. 'Is it bad?' she asked.

'It sounds worse than it is.' Mia beckoned them to follow her.

Outside the courthouse, Kamran saw that Mia was right. The crowd was louder than its numbers: two dozen men dressed in the now-familiar uniform of black trousers, white shirt, red braces and of course a red cap stamped with #NotAllMen. He scanned the faces for the thugs from the car park but saw only an angry mass. *Not all men but certainly these ones.*

Kamran thanked Mia for the escort and watched her shrinking figure in the mirror as they sped away to his parents' home. Zara was talking – 'care programme', 'recovery centre', 'weekly appointments' – but Kamran wasn't listening. He was thinking of the hours and days ahead: how he would face his father, what he would tell his mother, the inevitable flowers from Aunty Rana. The grieving of his eligibility, the perpetual whispers at family weddings: 'There's the boy who—' There's the boy who got caught red-handed, there's the boy who cried rape. It made him feel mad and manic, on the cusp of catastrophe. He squeezed his eyes shut and chanted like a mantra: 'Head up, shoulders back. Head up, shoulders back.' He fought to keep his composure as they neared his parents' home – a fencer on the piste, a hunter on a stalk.

Zara parked and they both looked up at his house, the light warm and woolly through the white gossamer curtains. 'I'll walk you in,' she said.

'There's no need,' he replied.

'I'd like to.' Clearly, she knew how hard this would be.

Kamran walked up the steps first and unlocked the door. It yawned open and he wondered how many times his mother had complained that she 'already told' Julio to fix it but that man just 'does not listen'. He waited for Zara to enter and closed the door behind her. In the living room, his parents were gathered on the sofa. Adam was still at Hampton, granted reprieve from this family drama. Kamran stepped inside the room, Zara trailing behind him.

'Hi,' he said tentatively. His mother's eyes brimmed with tears but his father was inscrutable.

'Sit down,' said Mack.

Kamran did as he was told but when Zara moved to follow, his father pointed a finger at her. 'You're not needed.'

Zara held his gaze. 'I'll stay all the same,' she said coolly. 'It's no trouble.'

His father studied her for a moment and evidently decided not to challenge her. 'Mr Morewood called earlier. He said they found the boy not guilty.'

'Yes, sir.'

'So?'

Kamran felt a lick of uncertainty. He knew his father

would be angry – but what was this? 'So?' he repeated unsurely.

'So what are you going to do about it?'

Zara, still standing, began to speak but his father cut her short. 'One minute, Ms Kaleel. I would like to talk to my son. You're in my home and I ask that you respect my right to speak.' To Kamran, he repeated, 'What are you going to do about it?'

'I—' He faltered. 'I don't know.'

His father pinched the skin between his brows and was silent for a moment. Then, his expression softened. 'We're going to get you some help, son.'

Kamran watched him, unsettled by his tender tone and the plaintive slant in his features.

'There's a place you can go. A facility for boys like you.' He reached into his breast pocket and took out a business card of a pale, watery yellow. 'You can go there next week.'

Kamran searched his father's face for clues. 'What kind of facility?'

Mack traced the edge of the card. 'They help boys like you who might be confused.'

'Confused? About what?'

'About who you are. They help you find clarity and get you on the right path.'

Kamran froze. 'Are you talking about a *conversion* centre?' His words were packed tight with horror.

'I wouldn't call it a conversion centre.' His father raised the card to the light. 'It's a private mental health hospital and rehab clinic.'

Kamran stared at him, astounded.

Zara cut in. 'Mr Hadid, I know this is upsetting for you but the best place for Kamran is school.'

'The best thing for Kamran is to work out what and who he is,' his father said acidly.

Zara regarded him evenly. 'Can I suggest someone that you and Mrs Hadid might want to talk to? They help parents navigate situations like this.'

His father's face flushed with pink. 'I don't need help.' He stood up and took a step towards Zara. 'To be frank, Ms Kaleel, I don't even know what you're doing here. Is this an official capacity or because you just like being in the centre of controversial cases?'

'Mr Hadid, I'm trying to help your son.'

He sneered. 'Is this some form of Munchausen by proxy? You convince impressionable young people to complain about rape so you can bathe in the limelight?' He jabbed a finger at her. 'I don't want you seeing my son anymore.'

'I understand that you're angry.'

'Oh, I don't think you understand anything.' His words were tight and short. 'I have worked my whole life to even the odds for my children; to give them the tools to counter this skin.' He slapped his forearm. 'You think a brown man can walk through this world comfortably?' He smirked and took another step towards her. 'You're a woman. You walk through the world knowing that should you fall into trouble, people will come to your aid. What happens when my son gets beaten in public? You think people will help him? A tall, strong boy like him? No one will come to his defence, so *I* must defend him.'

Kamran thought of the car park, a jagged glass bottle in an outstretched hand and Zara standing between them.

'I know you have Kamran's best interests at heart,' she said. She reached forward to calm him, but he smacked her hand away with enough force to spark a frisson of shock.

Kamran watched Zara's demeanour change. She was like a praying mantis unfolding, rearing on its hind legs. 'Mr Hadid, if you want your son to be a man, learn to be a better one.'

His father stared at her in shock. 'Get out of my house,' he snarled.

Zara stood for just long enough to let him know she was not daunted. Then, she glanced at Sofia. 'I apologise for disrupting your evening.' To Kamran, she said, 'I'll be in touch,' then turned and left the room. Her footsteps echoed down the hall and the door yawned open, then closed, leaving behind an electric silence.

Kamran felt a churning tension. He flexed his shoulders to ease it, making the movement affectedly casual as if he were unperturbed.

'I don't want you seeing her again,' said his father. 'In fact, you're not going anywhere this week.'

Kamran balked. 'But Oliver's driving me to Hampton today. I can't miss more school.'

'You can follow along online. I want you at home so we can decide what to do.'

'But, Dad,' said Kamran quietly. 'It's over.'

'It's not over,' he shouted. 'If that boy forced you, he should pay for what he did.'

'I just want to forget about it.'

'No!' He held up a finger. 'If you forget this now, it will *weaken* you. Do you understand that? It will make you forget the next insult and the one after that. A man should have more pride.'

The words landed like a slap. Kamran had spent *years* trying to prove that he was all the things a man should be. The fact that his father would question him now felt like a butchering.

Kamran dug his nails into his palm, rerouting the ache in his heart. *This* pain was physical, tangible and therefore solvable. He cleared his throat. 'I won't see that counsellor again. I don't need her.' His tone was crisp but hollow. 'I'll stay home this week and we'll work out what to do.'

His father nodded but remained mute.

In the silence, Kamran seized his chance to leave. 'I'll tell Oliver we don't need him,' he said. He stood and headed to the door, fully expecting his father to stop him – a barked command like a bullet to the kneecap – but he made it safely outside. There, he crumpled against the bannister, head pressed against the handrail, hands gripping the balusters. The thought of being at home for a week filled him with desperation. How could he escape this morass of fury, this tide from pulling him under?

He heard movement in the living room and snapped upright, then bounded up the stairs, his footsteps light and jaunty, emotion quickly aborted.

Zara set down her phone with a prickling worry. It had been three days since she had left the Hadids' and still there was no word from Kamran. The case was officially over and she had no reason to continue contact unless he sought her help.

She sifted through her options again. She could pursue

a legal route to ensure that Kamran saw a counsellor, but this felt unduly combative. She could try to meet Mack on neutral ground and convince him to change his mind. For this, she needed a way to disarm him and had enlisted Erin's help.

A third option nicked her conscience: you *could* leave him alone. Zara knew she was often forceful and didn't always know when to give in – but could she really leave Kamran at the mercy of his parents? What had happened to him had left a wound and if he closed it up without cleaning it out, it would slowly corrode him. Zara *had* to find him help.

She texted him now and said she would visit tomorrow. **Don't worry about your father**, she wrote. **I'll speak to him when I get there.**

She shut down her computer and readied to leave.

Erin appeared in the doorway and whistled to catch her attention. Her pitch-black hair was freshly dyed, making her skin seem paler. 'Are you on your way out?' she asked.

Zara glanced at her watch. 'Yes. I've got dinner at my mother's but you can walk me out?'

Erin nodded and together they walked to the stairwell – the lift still out of order. It held an industrial chill and Zara walked quickly, her boots echoing off the bare walls.

'So I've looked into Kamran's father.'

'Anything interesting?'

Erin shook her head. 'Sadly, no. Mustaque "Mack" Hadid is a second-generation Pakistani. His family owns a medical equipment company. They hit a big contract with a Chinese firm which builds roads in places like Ethiopia and Djibouti. He was a high-performing student. Four As at A Level, is an Old Hamptonian, got a PPE at Oxford, then entered the family business and "worked his way up" to CEO.'

'So far so boring,' said Zara.

'Yes. I did a deep dive and the only blip is that his girlfriend at university – now a presenter at the BBC – had an abortion at the age of nineteen. Other than that there's nothing of note.'

Zara paused by the exit. 'So why is he so angry?'

Erin shrugged a shoulder. 'People want their kids to be perfect.'

'So there's nothing I can use?'

'Sorry.'

Zara sighed and reached for the door.

'There's something else I want to talk to you about,' said Erin. 'You know who Julia Harker is, right?'

'The Downing Street spin doctor?'

'Yeah. She's setting up a crisis management company. I'll be doing some freelancing for her but she's asked if I know anyone that might head up the firm for her.'

Zara arched a brow. 'And?'

'And I thought you'd be perfect for it.'

Zara laughed. 'To work in PR?'

'It's not PR. It's crisis management: a mix between lawyer, investigator, strategist and agitator. Think Stephen Lawrence or Amanda Knox; false accusations, police brutality, cases that change the status quo.'

Zara narrowed her eyes. 'And you'll be working there?'

'Not full time but yes.'

Zara pushed open the door and stepped into the biting wind. 'I'm not really sure it's for me.'

'I thought you might want to practise law again.'

Zara blinked. 'I guess I always thought I'd go back one day but not in this capacity.'

Erin raised her collar against the cold. 'Okay, well, just have a think.' She raised a hand in parting.

Zara headed to her car and mulled over Erin's proposal. She had worked at Artemis House for two years now, burrowed in a tiny office with its sun-bleached carpet and leaking ceiling. She did miss the buzz of chambers. Could this be a mix of the two? She folded it into a corner of her mind. For now, she had other things to consider.

She drove towards her mother's home, feeling the familiar beat of nostalgia as she passed Thames Magistrates Court. She turned left before the bridge and parked at the end of the road. She noticed the green glass bottle shattered by the wheels of a recycling bin. She thought of the men in the car park and the overwhelming urge to flee. It was strange: courage wasn't always striking or strong; sometimes it was watery-faint and might buckle at the knees if you didn't hold still. It was found in the split second between action and retreat, easily replaced by cowardice.

She stood over the shards of glass, then kicked them together in a neat, shiny pile, careful not to let one bed into her sole. She headed to her mother's house. The homes here always stirred a sense of poignancy. People tried so hard and cared so much. You could see it in the trim astroturf, the tree with a square of pebbles at its feet, the wheelbarrow positioned just so to make it less imposing. She loved and pitied the people on this street. In some ways, they were her kin but she had left them far behind, so many of them with their stunted dreams. How many writers or poets or artists would this street ever produce?

A curtain twitched in her mother's kitchen. Fatima beckoned to her, then disappeared from view. Moments later, she opened the door.

'*Asalam Alaikum*,' said Zara.

'*Walaikum Asalam*.' Her mother ushered her inside. 'Your sisters are in the living room. I'll be in in a minute.' Behind her, hot oil bubbled on the cooker and the smell of fried pastry wafted across the hall. Zara kicked off her shoes and nudged them into a neat row.

'You came straight from work?' asked Salma, tilting her head up for Zara's kiss.

'Yes.' It was always obvious when one of them came from work, for their outfit was less modest. In Zara's case, a pair of jeans and a loose silk blouse in a rose-gold hue, covered by a long black cardigan. On a weekend, she would have opted for a long tunic over trousers, a Western take on the traditional *shalwar kameez* that Salma was now in.

'Is Rafiq here?'

'No, just us,' said Lena, giving Zara a peck on the cheek. 'How was work?'

Zara sat down with a heavy sigh and poured herself some tea.

'We saw the news,' said Salma.

'Yeah, it hasn't been my favourite week.'

Salma sipped her cup of tea. 'It said the verdict was not guilty, so did something happen or not? I read that the caretaker walked in on them, which is why the boy said it wasn't by choice.'

Zara sighed. 'Don't believe everything you read.'

'Will they both stay at the same school?'

'Yes. The accused can't be forced to leave and the victim shouldn't have to.'

'God, that's so weird.' Salma grimaced. 'I don't think I could do that.'

Their mother walked in and placed a plate of samosas on the table. As she bent, the fabric of her sari slipped off her shoulder into a nylon pile on her wrist. She righted it with an efficient flick. The movement, so minute and familiar, stirred something in Zara: a sense of wistfulness mixed with a dark remorse.

'Eat,' said Fatima. 'I'm making more.' She headed back to the kitchen.

As Zara watched her go, a question rose in her mind: *An arranged marriage you did not want?* She remembered Ed's profound empathy. *I think you've probably dealt with something you haven't quite accepted.* The words churned in her mind like a wheel. After a minute, she stood and walked into the kitchen. 'Mum, can we talk?' she asked.

Fatima scooped a samosa from the boiling oil and held it in the slotted spoon. 'Why? What's wrong?'

Zara reached for a way to ask it without sounding combative. She leaned against a counter and kept her tone light and gentle. 'When I got married, did you think it was the right thing for me?'

Fatima flushed with surprise. She placed the samosa in the drainer, the stain blooming yellow in the kitchen towel. *'Oneh khene mathreh itar kotha?'* she asked. *Why are you bringing this up now?*

Zara shifted on her feet. 'Because I want to understand what happened.'

Her mother waved a dismissive hand. 'The past is in the past.'

'But is it?'

Fatima didn't answer, busied herself instead. Zara watched her move around the kitchen: the slow and steady movement of her body, the way her two gold bangles – one on each wrist – fell up the length of her forearm when she reached up to open a cupboard. So much of this woman was familiar and yet so much was strange. Why couldn't they talk to each other? Zara willed herself to say more, to press her mother further, but the ink-dark pain of that time and the murk of what it meant – *an arranged marriage you did not want* – was almost too great to bear.

Fatima shut the cupboard and placed three plastic pouches on the counter. 'Go and eat the samosas before they get too cold,' she urged.

Zara watched her put a bay leaf, a stick of cinnamon and two cardamom pods in a ramekin. She lingered to see if she would turn to face her. Then, after a full minute of waiting, she slipped out from the kitchen.

CHAPTER TWELVE

Finn Andersen lay on his bed in state of frigid stupor. It had been five days since the verdict and Mr Morewood had invited him back to West Lawn. Finn had agonised over the decision. Should he move back to the house he loved and be among friends and comrades, or struggle on in a temporary home in which he felt untethered?

He had opted to return, but found himself ill at ease, flinching at every sound he made lest it reach the room above his. He no longer listened to music or did his morning stretches, wary of drawing Kamran's attention multiple times a day. Instead, he crept out of the building, round to the side and out of sight, for his pre-run warm-up each day. He hadn't yet rejoined the track team but wanted to be prepared. With his headphones on, starting with the Choir of Young Believers, he set out on the trail each morning, doing the same circuit again and again until his muscles threatened to tear and his mind stopped churning with Kamran.

Alone now in his room, it was all he could think of. There were many things for which he felt guilty. The act – though pardoned in a court of law – haunted him nonetheless. The fact that those heady moments still made him flush with erotic warmth only deepened his sense of guilt. How bewildering it was to be accused of violence but to remember only beauty: the curve of his shoulder blade, the dip of his waist, the feel of his sleep-softened skin.

How could Finn have got it so wrong? If only he'd asked, 'Do you want it? Do you want me?' none of this would have happened.

He sat up and for a mad moment, considered leaving his room, walking up one flight of stairs, turning into that fateful passage and knocking on Kamran's door. What would he say to him? 'I'm sorry? Forgive me? Please understand.' No – it was far too late to say sorry. Far too late for the truth.

Kamran scraped a thumbnail over his cuticle, drawing it back and forth until the tiny piece of skin came away, leaving behind a sediment of white. Adam had joined him at Belsize Park and sat now at his desk. He swivelled the chair to the left and right, working a nervous tic.

'That night with you and Finn,' he said. 'Would you have said anything if Tom Hare hadn't seen you?'

Kamran looked up sharply. 'What do you mean by that?'

Adam hesitated. 'It's just… it changes who you are, doesn't it? In the eyes of others, I mean. Would you have told people about it if you weren't worried that Tom would tell them himself?'

Kamran felt a flare of temper. 'Of course I would have. And I don't give a fuck what I am in the eyes of others.'

Adam blinked. 'But that's not true, is it? We all care.'

'What's your point?'

'I just… I wonder if you would have looked at it as rape if the caretaker hadn't seen you.'

'You think I made it up because I was scared of a tattletale?'

Adam stopped swivelling. 'No. I... I don't know.'

'Get the fuck out of my room.' Kamran's tone was vicious and took Adam by surprise. He sat rigidly, his eyes wide and doe-like. 'I said, get the fuck out of my room,' Kamran repeated. When Adam didn't move, he leaped to his feet, strode over to him and clipped him on the head just as Mack used to. 'Don't make me tell you again.'

Adam, stunned by the action, was rooted in his seat.

Kamran raised his hand again, but froze when the door flew open. Their father stood at the threshold, dressed in his Ridgeline smock. 'It's prime weather for some hunting, boys. Go and grab your things.'

Kamran stared at him dumbly. A week at home had felt like a slow suffocation. Spending more hours with his father would surely drive him insane. 'I'm not feeling well,' he said, knowing the excuse was weak.

'Some fresh air will do you good,' said his father. 'Come on. Chop chop.'

Kamran tried to find a way to negotiate this. A straight-up refusal would fail, as would whining or pleading. He made a show of looking out the window and frowning at the forming clouds. 'I don't know, Dad. It looks like it's going to rain. Remember how our wheels got stuck last year?'

He guffawed. 'That was certainly an experience, but don't worry. I've checked the weather and it's due to be the best weekend we've had for weeks.' He rapped on the door. 'Go on. *Tempus fugit.*'

Kamran gestured at the window. 'Perhaps we should leave it till tomorrow. There's meant to be better weather.'

301

'Oh-wee!' His father made a loud, high-pitched sound. 'Never have I met a boy so scared of the rain. Come on. Get your gear on.'

Kamran felt the tension harden and knew that if it sent his father into a mood, there would be no quick reversal. He had always been forceful in nature but since the day of the verdict, had veered into something nastier.

'Yes, sir,' said Kamran, buckling beneath the mounting pressure. He gestured to Adam. 'Come on. Let's go.'

Together, the boys filed out and headed to the utility room at one end of the garden. It smelled of cold concrete and the musk of damp tarpaulin. Kamran pulled out his camouflage smock, feeling pinpricks of anger. He looked at Adam. 'Maybe you could butt in once in a while.'

Adam flushed red. 'He never listens to me.'

'Because you're weak,' spat Kamran. 'If you stood up to him, he'd listen. Why is it always all on me?'

Adam's wide-eyed hurt drained quickly into shame. He turned his back to Kamran and grappled with his boots.

Kamran watched him sway on one leg. Part of him wanted to prop him up and the other to shove his shoulder and make him topple over. He closed his eyes to stem the fury beating behind his brows. He wanted to fall to his knees and scream – a sharp line of pain that would beam into the sky, high and bright like Batman's sign. He wanted to beat his palms into his own eyes and tear at his own hair; scratch at the world till he bled and then cry and cry and cry.

'Are you ready?' His father's voice boomed across the garden.

Kamran turned towards it. 'Yes, sir,' he called and grabbed

his rifle. He joined him in the garden and together they strode to the car without looking back for Adam.

Zara rang the bell and waited, preparing to clash with Mack who had banished her from his house. The door whined opened and a stout woman greeted her with a smile. She wore a boxy black dress with a scallop-hemmed white apron tied around her waist.

'Hello, I'm Nevinka. How may I help you?' she asked. Her accent was Estuary London hewn flat by years in service.

'Hello. I'm Zara Kaleel. I'm here to see Kamran Hadid.'

'Ah, yes. He said you might be coming today.' She opened the door wider and gestured at the stairs. 'Kamran said that if you came, to tell you to go straight up. His bedroom's to the right on the second floor.'

'Okay, thank you.' Zara kicked off her shoes, a habit formed in childhood; whenever they entered a relative's home, they would take off their shoes as a sign of respect. She padded upstairs, taking in the lushness of the carpet and the immaculate white walls. It was strange how this intrusive feeling of being in others' spaces never dissipated whether it was a rundown council flat in Barking or a multi-million pound home in Belsize Park. She reached the second landing and paused by the door. She knocked, hand resting on the brass doorknob.

'Kamran? It's Zara.' She waited. After a few seconds, she tried again. When there was no reply, she said, 'I'm coming in, okay?' She twisted the knob and opened the door. Inside was a tastefully decorated room: a king-sized bed made up with a quilted duvet and four thick cushions.

A French dresser with a mirror and a button-back chair. There were only a few signs of use – a stack of books on the dresser: Ursula Le Guin, Isaac Asimov, Philip K Dick. Next to it, a glass of water atop a pad of paper, the base of it bleeding moisture that turned the pale blue an inky colour. Two hangers were hooked on a wardrobe door, the first held a formal pink shirt; the second, a cricket white, the number '11' stitched on the back.

'Sorry, miss, that's Adam's room,' called Nevinka from the foot of the landing. 'It's the next one you want.'

'Oh, I'm sorry.' Zara hastily shut the door. She pointed at the next one. 'I'll try again.' She knocked and called Kamran's name. When there was no response, she gave him the same warning and twisted the doorknob. Inside, the room was even neater than Adam's. There were no books on the dresser or half-drunk glasses of water. It was minimal and tasteful like a high-end hotel room.

'Kamran?' she called, scanning the room to see if there was an en suite. She glanced down the stairs at Nevinka who stood expectantly on the landing. 'Do you know where they are?' she asked.

'No, miss.' Nevinka frowned. 'They were here this afternoon. I popped out to Waitrose to get some last bits for tonight's meal. I can't think where they would have got to.'

Zara walked back down. 'Can I speak to their mother?'

Nevinka smoothed her apron. 'I'm afraid not. Mrs Hadid is at the Ladies Guild. They frown if you miss a month.'

Just then, a key turned in the lock, a low metallic clatter followed by Mack's baritone. He stopped in the doorway. 'Nevinka, what is that woman doing here?'

'I've come to see your son,' said Zara.

He stepped into the hall. 'My son doesn't need to see you.'

Zara looked past him to Kamran. He turned away from her, masking the haunted cast in his features. 'Mr Hadid, if I could just have a moment, I—'

'Please go,' said Kamran. He raised his gaze to her but instead of a covert apology, there was only a blank stare. 'I'm fine.'

Zara was dismayed. 'Mr Hadid, it's really important for Kamran to talk to someone. If you prefer another counsellor, I can arrange that but ceasing—'

'You heard the boy,' Mack cut in. 'You are trespassing in my home – now go.'

'Mr Hadid—'

'Go!' he repeated, the word echoing in the hall.

Zara knew there was no reasoning with a man like Mack. 'Okay,' she said softly. She locked eyes with Kamran and asked him a silent question – are you okay? – but he shot her a look of contempt, as if angered by her presence. She nodded at him sadly, then thanked Nevinka and left.

Outside, she paused and looked at the house, the two pillars flanking her frame. For the first time in her professional life, she felt truly helpless. She thought of Mack and the ferocious guarding of his son. *What damage we do to the ones we love.*

She told herself it was time to give up; to trust that Kamran knew his own mind and would ask for help when ready. She wrapped her coat around her and headed to central London, her mouth sour with the tang of defeat.

*

Pelirocco was a tiny Italian restaurant with a cover of eight people. The chef, once the head of a Michelin-starred restaurant, had retired but still cooked because he loved to. Squeezed behind Regent Street, it was as yet undiscovered and catered mainly to curious walk-ins.

Zara watched Safran joke with the owner. They feigned punches, a strange custom only men seemed to practise. Even in jest, there was violence. He shook the man's hand and headed to Zara, squeezing past two tables.

Zara stood and they shared a hug.

'You look well,' he said.

She raised a doubtful brow.

'No, honestly. This weather suits you.'

'"This weather suits you"?' she repeated. 'It's miserable outside.'

'No, I mean big scarves, autumn colours, dark hair under comfy berets. It's made for the Brooke Shields, Jennifer Connellys and Zara Kaleels of the world.'

She smiled. 'Well, in that case, I won't complain.' She poured him a glass of water.

He nodded his thanks. 'So – I saw the verdict.'

'I thought you might.'

'You want to talk about it?'

'Yes and no.' Zara sighed. 'I knew it was the likely outcome, but it still feels like a punch in the gut.' She gestured helplessly. 'I don't know what to do, Saf. Professionally, I know I should leave him alone, but that's the problem, isn't it? We abandon victims when they need us most. I'm worried he's going to suffocate if left in that house alone.'

Safran took a typically practical approach. 'You can't do

everything,' he said. 'With some cases – like Jodie's – you have to go that extra mile but from what I understand, this boy comes from a good family. He's getting the best education he can and he's got teachers around him that care. Your job was to guide him through the court case, which you've done.'

Zara shook her head. 'I don't buy that, Saf. What you're saying is that because he's rich and privileged, he doesn't need the help that Jodie did. Those things don't magically inure you to the aftershock of rape.'

Safran set down his glass. 'That's not what I'm saying. I'm saying he already has a support system around him to help.'

'I'd like to talk him one last time and make sure he's okay. It seems that everyone wants him to ignore what happened and that will only make things worse.'

Safran frowned. 'I don't think you should press the issue, Zar. I think it's time to let go.'

She made a low, frustrated groan. 'I just hate leaving him like this.'

'That's what it means to be a professional.'

She slackened in her chair, feeling thoroughly deflated. 'You're right,' she said. 'I need to let go.'

Safran let her brood for a moment. 'How are the NA meetings going?' he asked.

'Yeah, they're good but...' She gripped the stem of her glass.

'But what?'

She made a harsh cough-like sound as if shaking something free. 'They send my mind wheeling.' She fixed her gaze on the table. Then, softly, she said, 'I miss him, Saf. But how can I remember him when I can't bear to think of it? Of what he said to me?' Her lips curled inward, pressed together in a tight line, the pink of them paling to white.

Safran reached forward and grabbed her hand, his grip hard to the point of pain. The act tethered her and she clung to him, letting her breathing slow, letting her blood stop beating.

'Zar,' he said. 'It's okay to love and hate our parents at the same time.'

She shook her head vehemently. 'No. I've never hated my father.' Her voice wavered. 'I don't hate him. I—' She paused to steady herself. 'I just wish we had done things differently. I wish I'd had the backbone to tell him that I didn't want to get married. Mum has come to accept it. Perhaps he would have too.' She twisted the glass by its stem. 'If he had lived, we would have reconciled and what happened that day would have been one awful thing in a sea of happy memories, but it ended there so suddenly and blackened everything before it.'

Safran was silent, letting her speak.

'I remember when Salma and Rafiq joined nursery and Lena was still too young, Dad and I would go to Chrisp Street Market. It was a half-hour walk but I'd insist I could do it. He would hold my hand and every time I tripped on the pavement, he would gently tug me up, just enough to right me. That feeling of being secure, of knowing he'd pull me up, was so... precious.' Zara exhaled. 'I haven't thought of that for the last three years because thinking of him feels like acid in my throat and I don't know, Saf, I don't know if he hated me in the end. I will never know if he hated me.'

Tears spilled onto her cheeks, cutting two wet lines down her matte make-up.

Safran eased his grip on her hand and she withdrew it to her lap. 'What made him happy?' he asked.

Zara blinked. After a beat of silence, she said, '*Natochs* made him laugh.' The farcical comedies from the subcontinent were aired infrequently but when they were, her father would sit in his favoured spot on the sofa with a cup of tea and a plate of digestives and would roar with fulsome laughter. Zara didn't share his humour, but would laugh along anyway at the slapstick falls and silly mix-ups.

'Which were his favourite?' asked Safran.

Zara felt a rush of affection for her friend, this man who would never feed her platitudes or tell her to be strong; would instead march her out of enemy territory, always covering her back. 'Thank you, Saf. You're a good friend.'

He smiled. 'Well, Zar, you need one.'

'Yes, I do,' she said softly, blinking the last of her tears from her lashes.

Sunday church bells rang across the sky, announcing a stranger's wedding. Kamran pictured the newlyweds laughing, the husband plucking confetti from her hair and lacing his fingers with hers. It seemed absurd they could be so happy.

At home, the Hadids play-acted their own version of bliss: a mother and a father and their two strapping sons gathered for a Sunday roast. Kamran ate in silence. The thick gravy had soaked the potatoes, giving them a soggy, tasteless texture. Still, he carefully cut them apart and put them in his mouth, forcing himself to swallow. Adam next to him stared absently through the French doors and crunched a coin of carrot.

Their mother walked in from the hall with a lavish bouquet of flowers. 'From Aunty Noreen,' she said brightly. She placed it on the kitchen table, then noting that Kamran and his father could no longer see each other, lifted it again and placed it on a stool. 'She's thinking of coming and seeing us next weekend. I've spoken to Hampton and they said they're willing to be flexible until Christmas.' She rearranged the flowers. 'So nice of them to offer to come.' Her tone was bright but the strain in her voice was clear. A visit from her older sister meant a six-course meal, hiring extra staff, coordinating transport and buying all of them presents, for Noreen always brought gifts.

'They just want to come and rubberneck,' said his father.

His mother stilled. 'That's not fair.'

'Look, Sofia, I think highly of your sister, but she's like a magpie when it comes to crises. Can't keep away.'

'That's what families are meant to do: support you in difficult times.'

His father smirked. 'She comes to spectate, not to support.'

She sighed and righted the stem of a flower.

'You know what she'll be like: dragging Kamran to a corner of the garden for one of her *heart to hearts*. That's the last thing he needs. He shouldn't be cosseted.'

'Maybe talking to someone would help.'

'If he wants to talk to someone, he can do that, but I won't have him spilling his guts to your family.'

'I won't,' said Kamran, interrupting. 'I won't talk to her.'

His father pointed the tines of his fork at him. 'That's

good, son. You need to remember that she's not doing it for your benefit.'

He nodded.

'How you act around people is important.' His father set down the fork, warming to his theme. 'In fact, how you act tomorrow will set the tone for the rest of your time at Hampton. After what happened, people will treat you differently but don't you dare let them do it. If you do, your life at Hampton will be over.'

Kamran recognised the tow of his father's anger. He smoothed his voice so it was bright and clear, keen to escape while he could. 'I still need to finish packing. May I be excused?' He drew his chair back.

'Wait a minute.' His father pointed a finger at him. 'Listen, if that boy comes anywhere near you tomorrow, you floor him, okay?'

'Dad, I can't do that.'

'What do you mean, you can't do that?' His face was pinched in a scowl. 'Do you *want* people thinking that you took what he gave you?'

Kamran flinched and felt the air in his chest desert him.

'Mack, let him go,' said his mother.

He turned on her. 'Do you understand what's at stake here? Every student in that school thinks that our son lay like a fish and took it. He needs to prove that he didn't or he can forget about his life at Hampton.'

Sofia grabbed Kamran by the arm. 'Get up. Come on. Go and finish packing. Go.'

There, beneath the pull of his mother's grip, Kamran felt something break: a rupturing of his sense of self, an ungluing of his heart as if it might slip its chambers and sink somewhere unseen. He let her push him from the room, an expelling that felt more than physical, and when the warmth of her fingers left his skin, he felt as if he were falling. He braced himself against a wall. Tomorrow, he was back at Hampton. Tomorrow, he would be free.

CHAPTER THIRTEEN

Kamran sat in his favourite corner of Hampton Library: an elevated cubbyhole tucked beneath an oriel window. He checked his watch: 5.30 p.m. All day, his thoughts had clamoured and climbed and pinballed off the walls of his mind. He tried to order the weight of his pain. Perhaps he could deal with each piece in turn: lay it out in the sun until it was leached of emotion. First, the failure of the court to return the correct verdict; second, the aggression of Hampton's pupils who now saw him as a fair target; and third, his father's insistence that he somehow prove his manhood.

He had sat in classes all morning, mute and impassive. It was in period three, listening to Mr Folkestone detail the Treaty of Vereeniging, that he felt his resolve cave in. His pain, compartmentalised so carefully, now swelled in a single mass: sharp and yellow and discordant, a stultifying resin that seemed to bleed from his ears, as if his very brain were leaking. Each torturous minute seemed cleaved in two, the halves as long as the whole.

The jeers and jibes of the dining hall calcified to something crueller: a gleeful mix of scorn and mockery. 'There goes the boy who cried rape,' a label sanctioned by a court of law. It made him pulse with fever – not a red-hot fury but a tar-black storm of something frightening.

He checked his watch. It was now 5.40 p.m., ten minutes since the track meet ended. He would wait for ten more minutes – allow for showers and locker-room banter – then head back towards West Lawn.

Zara turned her phone to silent as she ascended the steps to St Alfege Church en route to her NA meeting. It was by luck that she caught the flash of the screen just as she reached the building. She answered the phone and huddled by a wall to shield it from the wind.

'Zara?' Mia sounded breathless, as if she might be jogging.

'What's wrong?'

'There's been an incident. At Hampton. DC Dexter and I are there now. Shots have been fired.'

The air around Zara seemed to still: the wind dropped in an instant and the cars on the street stopped moving, their muffled lights held frozen. Then, her breath came rushing back, propelling her into action. 'Are you in danger?' she asked.

'No. There are first responders on the scene, but we need to disarm the assailant.'

Zara's heart seized. 'Do you know who it is?'

'No confirmation but he's been described as Asian, five feet ten, athletic but lean.'

'Oh God.' Zara turned and ran down the steps. She rushed back to the main road and frantically scanned the street. 'I'm on my way.' She hailed a cab and jumped in, reeling off a postcode. She felt her hands begin to shake, her body's reaction to adrenaline but also a cry for something chemical. She clasped them together and took a series of long, deep breaths. Her first thought had been suicide but Mia said they had to disarm the assailant. *Asian, five feet ten, athletic.*

She glared at the street outside, willing the traffic to ease, fighting the instinct to get out and run as if that might somehow be faster. The driver made small talk but where Zara would normally engage, she gave him only distracted answers that ended in ellipses.

'Don't worry, Madam,' he said, noting her distress. 'I'll get you there as soon as possible.'

She wedged her hands beneath her knees. 'Thank you,' she croaked, trying to slow her thoughts, praying that Mia had made a mistake.

An agonising hour later, they pulled up to the gates of Hampton. There was no guard on duty, likely directed to the crime scene. Zara slipped through the pedestrian entrance and, from memory, ran towards West Lawn at the leftmost extreme of campus. She spotted lights in the distance and heard a commotion of voices.

'Zara!' Mia called from West Lawn's doorway. She beckoned her closer. 'We have a situation.'

'Is Kamran okay?' she asked, the words one breathless rush.

'He's upstairs in Finn's room.'

'And?'

Mia's voice was grave. 'He's hurt Finn.'

Zara felt a lance of fear. 'Badly?'

'We don't know yet. He won't let us in.'

Zara's response was immediate. 'Let me talk to him.'

Mia shook her head. 'We have an experienced negotiator talking to him.'

Zara looked at her watch. 'It's been over an hour since you called.'

'I know but negotiation is delicate work.'

'Finn could be bleeding out on the floor.'

Mia flushed. 'It's not my call.'

'Let me talk to him, Mia. He trusts me. I'm his counsellor. A feasible case could be made that this was the least dangerous course of action.' Met with silence, Zara's voice grew forceful. 'Mia, come on. This could turn into murder. Do something!'

She grimaced. 'Okay, I'll try. Give me a minute.' She turned and began speaking calmly but rapidly into her radio.

Zara paced along the concrete path.

'No,' Mia was saying. 'After an initial threat to shoot at the door, the assailant has been silent.'

Zara looked up at the building, her pacing now growing panicked. She felt a coursing adrenaline and fought the urge to snatch the radio and start shouting into it.

After an eternity, Mia looked up. 'Okay, you're in but you have to wear a vest.'

Zara shook her head. 'It's better if I don't. I—'

'You wear a vest or you're not going in,' said Mia bluntly.

'Okay, fine.' She motioned an officer closer, keen to get moving. After a hurried briefing, she entered West Lawn and walked up the stairs to the second storey. She turned into a passage and paused in front of Finn's door, identical to Kamran's above.

'Kamran, it's me, Zara,' she said softly, one hand on the door.

There was only silence on the other side.

'I'm going to gently open the door. Is that okay?'

'No! Go away.' Kamran's voice was teary and panicked.

'Kamran, I'd like your permission to come in, please.'

'No!' he shouted. 'If you do that, I'll shoot.'

Zara swallowed. 'You have a gun? Where is it?'

'It's in my hand.'

'Is Finn okay?'

Kamran voice was shrill. 'I don't know.'

'Is he still breathing?'

'I don't know!'

'Where did you shoot him?'

He was silent for a beat. 'The throat.'

Zara sucked in a breath. 'Kamran, please listen to me. I have two paramedics here with me, people who go to work to save lives. They would like to come in and check on Finn. Would that be okay?'

He was silent.

'Listen, I'm going to open the door. I will be standing in the doorway, okay? Please point the gun at the floor.' She waited, then warned him again. 'I'm coming in, Kamran. Please point the gun at the floor.' She turned the handle and opened it slowly.

Kamran sat at the opposite end of the room, his back pressed against a wall, a long-barrelled pistol pressed to his chin, tears pooling around the muzzle.

Zara's breath seemed hollow in her throat. 'Kamran, you and I are going to talk. I'm going to sit by you and talk but first, two paramedics are going to come in and take Finn, okay? I'm going to stand right here in front of you so no one can get to you, okay?'

Kamran's eyes were wild – but he nodded. 'Help him. Please help him.' His chest wracked with sobs.

Zara signalled behind her and the paramedics rushed in. They moved with a mechanical efficiency. 'He's alive!' one shouted and Zara felt a surge of relief. She let them work behind her and held Kamran's focus. She knelt, two metres in front of him.

'Is he going to die?' Kamran was visibly shaking.

Zara shook her head. 'Not if they can help him.' She inched closer to him. 'Hey,' she said, holding his attention. 'It's going to be okay.'

Kamran sobbed uncontrollably. 'I'm sorry,' he said. 'I'm sorry.'

'It's fine. He's fine.'

'We need to get him out of here,' said a paramedic.

'Okay.' She held up a hand. 'Kamran, is it okay for these gentlemen to take Finn out of here?'

He nodded, his eyes red and bleary.

'Go,' she told the paramedics. She let them exit without turning around, keeping her gaze on Kamran. 'Listen to me. I know it's hard to think logically right now, but please try.' She pointed at the gun. 'It doesn't have to go that far, Kamran.'

'That's what everyone will say!' he cried. '"It didn't have to get this far," but it *did*. They say I wanted it, but I *didn't* and now they know.'

'I believe you, Kamran.'

'But no one else does!'

Zara tried to work out what he wanted. Revenge? Redemption? Respect? 'They will believe you now. I promise you.'

His arm slackened somewhat, the barrel no longer creasing his skin. 'Will he be okay?' he asked.

'I think he will.'

'I'm sorry.' He repeated it like a mantra.

Zara sensed motion behind her and raised an arm, warding off intruders. 'Here's what's going to happen, Kamran. You're going to put down the gun and push it aside. I'm going to let in some officers who will escort you to the station. I will meet you there and together we'll explain what happened, okay?'

Kamran sobbed.

'Okay?'

He nodded through his tears.

'Okay, so the first step is to put down the gun.' She kept her hand raised behind her, warning off the police. 'Put down the gun, Kamran.'

He hesitated, then with shaking hands, set the gun down next to his knee.

'Now please push it aside.'

He shoved it hard. It skittered across the floor and hit the far wall with a dull thud.

Immediately, officers stormed in, flowing around her like a river round a rock. Two officers cuffed Kamran and lifted him to his feet. Another pulled up Zara and pushed her towards the door. She saw the blood-splattered spot on the floor, red and vivid amid teenage banality: a chair laden with clothes, the Hampton uniform hooked on one notch and a crumpled white shirt on the other, a corkboard pinned with ticket stubs and postcards, a loopy 'Finn' on a blue envelope, its serifs curled with flourish. The normality didn't compute.

Zara felt a hand on her shoulder, guiding her outside. There, she doubled over and took heaving gasps of air. DC Dexter stood next to her, but she struggled to hear him speak. Then, the volume seemed to turn back on and come to her in sharp relief: the jarring stretch of police tape, the persistent burr of a camera, the sigh of booties on wood.

'Mia's gone ahead,' Dexter was saying. 'But I can give you a ride.'

Zara held up an index finger, the blood too loud in her ears as the adrenaline left her body. She braced herself against the wood panelling and tried to regain her breath. She pictured Finn's body and the way his limp arm lay askew on the floor. He looked as close to death as the living could be.

In that moment she learned that a barrister's famed composure was merely convenient myth. These lauded men and women performed well in court and on panel debates on political shows, but removed from the lap of civility, they found themselves exposed. It's true that some faced aggression – from defendants, reporters and protestors – but real peril was rare and shocking. When those men attacked Zara in that alley last year, hadn't she grown leaden with dread? And now, wasn't her heart pulsing so fast, she thought she might keel over?

Dexter stood next to her, his feet placed too far apart as if he were bracing his nerve. When Zara's breath came back, she pushed herself away from the wall, forcing herself to stand. Dexter steadied her and together they walked down the two flights of stairs and across the lawn to his car.

Zara sat in the passenger seat and tried to chart her next steps, but her mind pitched backwards instead. She thought of Saturday evening, only forty-eight hours ago, she by the base of the stairs facing off with Mack as Kamran stood aside with that strange blank stare. Did she see the turmoil coursing in his brain? Could she have stopped this nightmare?

She turned to Dexter. 'Do you know what hospital Finn's been taken to?'

He raised a finger off the steering wheel. 'No, I don't.'

Zara sent a message to Erin, asking her to find out. To Dexter, she said, 'Do you think they'll let me see Kamran?'

They were in different territory now: this was no longer a rape case to be handled by Mia and Dexter. Kamran was looking at attempted murder.

'After you're processed, maybe,' he said. 'Mental health is important in the Met, so if you tell them you're his counsellor, you might have a shot.'

Zara gripped her phone, willing Erin to answer. If Finn was okay, there was a possibility that Kamran wouldn't be sentenced too harshly. If the worst happened, however, then he was looking at a minimum of twelve years in prison. Zara was already hewing his defence from a set of mitigating factors; a brick-by-brick argument to explain Kamran's actions. First, a sexual encounter that was rape as he saw it; second, the experience of giving evidence in court; third, the impact of the verdict; fourth, the pressure from his family; fifth, the cultural taboo of having had sex with a man. These were all factors that contributed to his unstable frame of mind. Fragments of sentences formed on her tongue. *Debilitating pressure from his parents, intolerant stance on homosexuality, intense shame and guilt.*

She put herself in his shoes, imagined a man stripping her of dignity. Wouldn't she want to hold a gun to his head?

No. She knew her answer was no. She might cry and rage and thirst for revenge, but to hold a gun to skin and bone and be able to pull the trigger? That would require a dehumanisation – of the victim *and* herself. How desperate he must have felt, how lonely, how powerless, to be driven to pick up a gun and use it on another.

Zara's phone pinged with a message.

At Northwick Park Hospital. Will update you when I know more.

Zara felt some tension ease. Knowing that Erin was there made her feel less restless. If there was news to be known, Erin would find out. As they drove on, Zara pictured Kamran in an interview room. Had he just destroyed his life?

Dexter parked outside Wembley Police Station and escorted her to a waiting room. She took a seat, feeling the foam of the chair sink to its base with her weight.

Dexter explained that she would be interviewed by a member of the Major Investigations Team. She nodded mutely. She had worked with them in the past and found them to be skilled and thorough, but bogged by a rigid bureaucracy that allowed for few concessions. Dexter handed her a coffee which she held to her lips but didn't sip, letting the steam warm her.

It was a long time, hours maybe, before she was collected. Zara kept her answers short and factual, not wanting to incriminate Kamran. 'No, I didn't see him shoot the victim.' 'No, he did not threaten to shoot anyone else outside the room.' 'No, he did not seem in a lucid state of mind.'

None of it was lies, but she did introduce more ambiguity

than she had seen first hand. Trials were based on what could be proven and if Finn was okay, then perhaps both lives could be saved. If Finn did not survive, however, then that was a different matter.

When Zara was released, she returned to the waiting room and found that Dexter was gone. A message explained that he was still on the clock and had no excuse to be there. His sudden departure was strangely affecting, the room suddenly cavernous. She slid into a chair and looked at the clock. It was nearing 11 p.m. She wondered if Kamran's parents were there; if Sofia with her elegant pearls and neat chignon was sitting in a similar room, dabbing her eyes in grim disbelief. An uncharitable part of her wanted to see Mack's face and the realisation of what he had caused. She pictured herself nodding; confirming that, yes, you were the one who drove Kamran to this. 'You did this,' she would say. 'You are to blame.'

The door whined open, pulling her from her thoughts.

'We're taking the suspect to his cell,' said an officer. He was young and male with a shock of dark hair. 'DC Dexter said you'd want to be informed.'

Zara rose to her feet. 'I'd like to speak to him.'

He frowned. 'Um, I'm sorry but I don't think that's—'

'I'm his counsellor,' she said, knowing that this did not grant her any automatic rights. 'He is vulnerable and I am concerned for his state of mind.'

The officer hesitated. 'Look, I didn't even have to tell you. I only did it as a favour to Dexter.'

'All I'm asking for is ten minutes. Please.'

He studied her for a moment and took in her barefaced plea. Then, he sighed.

'Okay, I'll ask the custody sergeant and we'll see what we can do.' He returned a few minutes later and beckoned her forward.

'Thank you,' she said, her voice a whisper. She hurried after him, her heels slipping on the shiny floor.

Kamran startled when Zara entered. Whatever resolve had seen him through his interview collapsed in this safer space. The sobs came from deep within as if his very chest were cracking open.

'Kamran,' said Zara softly. She sat at the table opposite him.

He swiped at his eyes with the jerky anger of a child that cannot yet speak its mind. He turned from her, twisting his body sideways, pressing his face into his hands and sobbing with a keening pain.

Zara watched, allowing him to cry. She thought of the last client that had affected her so much. Jodie too had broken down, but with the slow-release catharsis of short and frequent cries – never with this gut-wrenching, soul-crushing torment.

'Kamran,' she repeated. 'It's okay.'

'No,' he said, shaking his head, cloudy tears streaming down his face. 'It's not okay.' He leaned over and laid his head on the sheet-metal tabletop. His sobs sent small reverberations across it, making the metal bend and contract.

'You're okay,' Zara repeated, waiting for him to calm.

'What did I do?' he asked, his voice low and mournful. His eyes were veined with red, bloodshot from hours of crying. 'What will I do?'

'You will survive,' she said gently.

A shadow passed over his features. 'And Finn? Will he?'

'I don't know,' she admitted. 'I'm trying to find out.'

Kamran crumpled in his chair. 'I should have shot myself.'

'No.' Zara's tone was far more forceful than her training allowed. She swallowed all the words she wanted to say. *Don't you dare. Don't ever say that. Don't ever think that.* Instead, she asked, 'Why do you say that?'

He looked at her with anguish. 'Then I wouldn't need to think anymore.' He pressed a hand against his temple. 'I shouldn't have started this. Finn would still be fine and I could look my father in the eye.'

'Is that how you feel?'

His face blanched with sorrow. 'I've always tried to make him proud but since the night of the... Since the night it happened, I can't look him in the eye. It's like something has burst between us.' Kamran's voice was hoarse and he swallowed in an effort to clear it. 'I thought about it. I thought about going into the shed and loading my rifle but...' He shook his head. 'I couldn't leave like that. I couldn't let him win.'

Zara exhaled. 'You planned it?'

Kamran closed his eyes and nodded. 'Yes.'

'When?'

'Yesterday.'

'Why?'

He blinked. 'Because he hurt me.'

Zara waited.

'I was so *angry*.' His voice dropped to a growl. 'I felt like if I didn't do something, I would explode. I hated him. I hated him for what he took from me, what he did to me.

I hated him for being freed. I hated him for what he said to me – "I had *fun* the other night" – and I hated him for keeping his perfect life.' Kamran thumped his chest. '*I* was meant to have a perfect life. *I* was meant to be happy, but I couldn't see that in the future for me. He could go back to Switzerland or get a job at his dad's company or do anything he wanted – and me? What would *I* do? What could *I* be? If everyone knew what I was, could I ever be anything else?' His face twisted into something ugly. 'I couldn't let him get away with it.'

'So you took a gun to school?' Zara's voice was calm, factual.

Kamran nodded. 'Yes. I took it to school and I waited until I knew he was in his room.'

Zara recalled the image of Finn lying in a pool of blood, his arm twisted at that awful angle.

'I knocked on the door and he opened it, and even that made me angry.' Kamran made a small choking sound. 'I lock mine every day and night.' He looked up at a corner of the ceiling, his thoughts somewhere further. 'He opened it with this big smile on his face, like he was expecting company. It dropped off his lips when he saw me. And the *fucked-up* thing?' Kamran's tone turned bitter. 'He pulled the door open wide, welcoming me in.'

Zara waited. 'What happened next?'

Kamran's eyes took on a glazed, faraway look as he relayed to Zara what followed.

He walked into Finn's room and neither of them exchanged a word. Kamran waited for him to speak, comforted by the cold gunmetal pressed against his belly.

'I've been hoping to speak to you,' said Finn. 'Will you sit down?' He pulled out the desk chair for Kamran and took his own seat on the bed, his right foot stacked on top of the left. After a moment, he spoke. 'I never meant to hurt you. Please believe me.'

Kamran almost laughed at the banality of the apology – absurd given the scale of his crime.

Finn kneaded the edge of his blanket. 'I consider you a friend and I never meant to hurt you. It was all a terrible mistake. I don't know if you want to hear my side, but...'

'But what?' Kamran's voice was cold and demanding.

'But I honestly thought it was consensual. When I touched you for the first time...' Finn paused as if testing to see if Kamran would halt him. When he didn't, he continued. 'You made this sound that I recognised. It was... desire.'

'What sound?'

Finn shifted in his seat. 'A moan. Like you wanted it, like you were enjoying it. I was drunk and I didn't stop to think. I just reacted.' He grimaced. 'Please believe me. Please forgive me.'

'Forgive you?' Kamran made a sharp, sour sound. 'You think I'll ever forgive you? You have no fucking idea what you've taken from me and now you sit there and try to convince me that I *wanted* it?' He stepped towards Finn. 'Get this through your thick skull: I am not a faggot.'

Finn flinched. 'Don't.'

'Don't what? Why are you so scared of that word when that is what you are? Faggot.'

Finn rose to his feet. 'I'd like you to leave now.'

'Make me, faggot.'

'Please.' Finn's voice broke in a hairline crack. 'This isn't who you are.'

'Don't tell me who I am!' Kamran felt a feverish flare of insanity. 'Is *this* who I am?' He drew out his gun and raised it.

Finn froze but there was no panic in his face, as if confronted by a toy gun or an absurd version of reality. Then, the peril hit him and instead of trying to talk him down like Kamran had expected, Finn charged for the door. By instinct, Kamran traced the movement like he would a fleeing deer and without time for rational thought, pulled back on the trigger. The bullet grazed Finn's neck and he dropped instantly to the floor, hitting it with a dull thud that did not do justice to the gravity of the fall.

Kamran felt a sick flare of victory, a mere split second of pleasure, before his world caved in. He dropped the gun and it seemed obscene that its clatter to the floor should be louder than Finn's. Kamran lost the strength in his knees and buckled, engulfed in a smoke-like horror. He scrambled backwards on his seat until he hit the wall. A wail escaped him that made him fear he was possessed: a banshee scream of disbelief. His mind broke away from his body and soared not to the ceiling but through it, shooting through the West Lawn common room and the grey-slate roof above it. He raced towards the night's first stars, careening in the wind. He screamed and the scream was endless and there was no name to put to it. It wasn't horror or terror or pain but a boundless feeling that kept on swelling. In this black-twine morass, his mind threatened to snap and he scrabbled for the gun and raised it, pressing it to the dip of his temple.

His instincts begged for a clean resolution; screamed that he pull the trigger.

When he found that he could not, he slammed the gun down in defeat. It broke the dam he had guarded so long and he doubled over and sobbed. When the sirens began to wail, he picked up his gun again, now slippery in his grip, but he knew he had lost his nerve. Whatever was on its way, he would now have to face it. He cried in anguish and disbelief, unable to name the texture of his grief. It wasn't fury or regret or penitence, but a vast and nameless dread.

The first voice was male, a deep and commanding baritone that urged him to open the door. The second was also a man, but more measured and calm, as if he'd just learned the lines of his script and hadn't yet practised emotion. His clinical monotone served to balance Kamran but he still refused to open the door. It was half an hour later, only when he heard Zara's voice, that Kamran truly decided that he would not put a bullet inside him. Zara was the sound of real life rushing back to tether him.

He looked at her now across the sheet-metal table. 'I think you saved my life.'

Zara drew in a long and quiet breath. '*You* did that, Kamran.' She laced her fingers on the table. 'Can I ask you something? Will you keep yourself safe tonight?'

He nodded, tears gilding his eyes.

Zara was about to say more when her phone pinged with a message. It was Erin. Her heart was a pellet of ice as she opened the text and read.

Finn Andersen was pronounced dead at 23.59.

Her face fell and without saying a word, Kamran

understood. He wilted in his chair and began to sob – not loud and panicked as they were before, but low and mournful like a trapped animal that had lost all hope. Zara stayed and let him cry and cry and cry.

CHAPTER FOURTEEN

Sofia Hadid studied her husband and tried to divine his thoughts. He had always been stoic, that was true, but lately it had taken on a harder cast that she found unassailable. His confidence, his gusto, his sheer force of being, was a protective layer around her family that had calcified with time. Now, in the same way that others couldn't pierce their way in, Sofia could not punch her way out.

In the early hours of the morning when they received a call from the police, Mack was calm and controlled with little sign of anything wrong. He relayed the news in a series of factual sentences, his tone barely changing. 'Our son has been arrested. He shot the boy he accused of rape. He is in jail. The boy he shot is dead.'

Sofia was seized by a vice-like horror. She started to hyperventilate and Mack threw her a quizzical look as if he could not fathom the fuss. His bemusement seemed to belittle her, as if she were going too far. Never had she felt so much distance between them.

She dressed quickly and obsessed over a defiant strand of hair until Mack barked at her to leave it. They rushed to the station, Mack behind the wheel, Sofia tense and rigid. The custody sergeant told them that Kamran was asleep and they would have to wait for morning.

'How did this happen?' she kept asking, her voice in a panicked register. Her boy, her fair and strong and gentle boy, had fallen so hard and so far that he had bundled a gun in his suitcase and taken it to school with lethal intent. Was this the son that they had raised? She told herself that maybe it was a psychotic break but knew it couldn't be true. Kamran was calm and staid and thoughtful, and the sober truth was that he had planned this. He had decided, in the depths of one cold night, that his life was no longer salvageable and had planned this act of violence. This is the son they had raised.

When they were finally allowed to see him, Sofia cradled him in the crook of her arm, shielding him from view. Kamran shook with sobs that soaked into her white silk top. Mack stood a metre away, turning his head and averting his gaze as if the scene embarrassed him.

'Don't worry,' he said when Kamran's tears finally ceased. 'Nothing will happen to you.'

'Stop,' said Sofia. 'Just stop. Something has already happened to him, Mack. Look at him.'

Kamran's hair stuck on its ends as if in cartoon-shock. There were deep bags beneath his eyes and his jawline seemed to sag. How was it that so much damage could be wrought overnight? Or had this started five months ago and they'd just chosen to ignore it?

Mack moved closer to Kamran and tried to smooth a tuft of his hair, but it sprang stubbornly up. He bit his lower lip and made a thick, glottal sound. 'Son.' He seemed to be reaching for words and Sofia prayed that he would find the right ones. *I love you.* That's all he needed to say. *I love you.*

'I will get you whatever you need,' he said. 'I'm going to call Charlie Blackstone in Whitehall and see what he can do. I don't want you to worry.'

Kamran closed his eyes and though his face crumpled, he seemed to have no more tears. 'I don't want help, Dad.' His voice was hoarse and pleading. 'I killed him. I killed Finn.'

Mack grabbed a fistful of Kamran's sleeve. 'Don't you dare say that, do you understand? Don't say that in front of anybody!'

Kamran pulled away from him, his features taut with anguish.

Mack spoke in a rapid burst as if the sheer velocity of speech could keep their world from caving in. He spoke of the 'best lawyers in the country', 'contacts in the Cabinet', 'full political force'. Sofia listened but she knew they could not help him. That time was over. Now was the time for repenting.

They drove home in a state of stunned calm, two soldiers returning from battle. Inside, Mack handed her a bouquet of flowers.

'It's from Rana,' he said and asked her to write a thank you note.

'No,' she replied tartly.

Mack looked at her. 'Okay. It can wait.'

Sofia shook her head. 'No.'

'What do you mean "no"?'

'I'm tired, Mack. I'm tired of this.'

'Why don't you get some sleep?'

'No. I'm tired of *you*.'

Mack started in surprise. 'I understand you're upset but there is no need to act like this.'

'Who are you, Mack?' she asked. '*What* are you?' She flung an arm out at the room. 'Do you love these things? Do you care about them? Do you think about them when you go to sleep at night? Because *I* don't. I think about our children. I think about Kamran. I think about what he's going through. Do you?'

'Of course I do.'

Sofia struck out at the bunch of flowers, sending them flying across the room. 'Then why the fuck are you asking me to write a thank you note?'

Mack's jaw dropped open.

'Why are you standing there so calmly? Aren't you sad? Aren't you angry? Aren't you feeling *anything*?'

Mack's eyes drew narrow. 'Please don't swear, Sofia.'

She cried out in frustration, a rough bellow of a sound. 'I *will* swear, Mack!' she shouted. 'I will swear at you and everything, every day, until my son is free.' She swiped at the waiting vase, which toppled over and then rolled towards the edge of the counter.

Mack caught it just as it tipped over and replaced it on its base. It made Sofia cry out with fury. There was no cathartic shattering, only Mack's insistence on fixing everything.

'This is your fault!' she screamed at him.

He shook his head. 'I keep all the guns locked up.'

She laughed derisively. 'Oh, you stupid man. It's not what you put in his hand.' She struck her temple. 'It's what you put in his head.'

'No.' Mack pointed a finger at her. 'I've done everything I can to raise a good son.'

'And what if we had a daughter? Would you force her to learn to shoot? Shame her for crying when hurt? Shove her the way you do Kamran? Masculinity is a *cage*, Mack, and you put him in that cage and I—' Sofia's voice broke into a sob. 'I helped you.'

Mack's lips parted but he did not speak.

'That's what you have to say?' Sofia aped a shrug. 'What else, Mack? What else do you have to say?'

A vein twitched in his temple.

'What else?' she urged.

Mack's chest heaved once, then twice, his chin dimpling with distress. He watched Sofia cry and reached out to comfort her, but his hand drifted from her shoulder to her hip as if unsure that he could touch her. His features creased with effort, unable to find even the start of a sentence. Defeated, he stepped away from her and left her to cry on her own.

Zara paced the length of her office. It was Tuesday afternoon and Kamran had been in custody for nearly twenty-four hours. She spoke fast: 'Chase up his solicitor and get me a meeting. Go over Finn's records with a fine-tooth comb. Make sure you don't miss a thing. If there is anything in his medical history that could have contributed to his demise, I want it. If we can prove that he—'

'Hey.' Erin waited for her to still. 'You know that Kamran's guilty, right?'

Zara scowled. 'What's your point?'

Erin propped one boot on top of the other. 'My point is

that he's guilty. He did the crime so maybe this is where you bow out.' She pointed at the hall outside. 'Maybe it's time to turn your focus back to the people who need you.'

'I can't just leave him, Erin. He still needs help.'

'To do what?'

'To recover. He's still a victim.'

Erin rolled her eyes.

'What?' Zara asked testily.

'There's enough help out there for men like Kamran. I didn't get in this game to help a murderer.'

Zara struck her desk with a palm. 'But he was *made* into a murderer, Erin. He was *made* that way by his bully of a father and his feeble mother and a system that won't let him fail. He was made that way by the messaging that tells him to rise up, strike back, head up, shoulders back. He was *made* into what he became.'

'But why do you care?' pressed Erin. 'There are enough women to help here without getting distracted by problematic men.'

Zara exhaled. 'Because without fixing problematic men – without changing the systems that make them that way – we can't improve things for women.'

Erin considered this for a moment, then made a weary huff of a sound. She uncrossed her ankles and leaned forward. 'And you want to start with Kamran?' she asked.

'I want to start with Kamran.'

Erin stood and brushed down her trousers as if she had sat in something soiled. 'Okay. Fine.' She waved a yielding hand. 'I'll see what I can do.'

'Thank you.' Zara watched her leave with bitter relief. Erin was right: they were helping a murderer, but she remembered the wrench of what Kamran had said – 'I think you saved my life' – and in recalling the plaintive cast in his eyes, she knew that she had to help him. If she abandoned him to his parents, there was a chance he wouldn't survive.

Kamran stared at the blue strip of paint that cut its way across the shiny white walls. The room was so narrow, they seemed like half walls. Half a room for half a life, not in length but breadth. Isn't that what this room was for? Half lives stifled by poverty, crime and abuse. A room that housed half men. Isn't that what he was now? Isn't that what he had been since the night of the party?

A dark part of him rejected the thought. After all, he had taken back control. No one could claim that he had consented, not when Kamran had shot his rapist.

He thought of Finn's reaction: a moment of cool disbelief and then a white-hot flash of panic. Why had he run? He had forced Kamran's hand. Maybe Finn would still be alive if he'd only stayed in his spot. Or maybe it was better this way. Maybe he should thank his hunter's reflex. Without it, maybe he wouldn't have pulled the trigger at all.

A rap on the door made him flinch. A uniformed officer looked in. 'You have company,' he told him, then stepped aside for Zara.

In catching the lift of her perfume, Kamran felt his stomach lurch. It brought a memory into sharp relief: Zara crouched down next to him, speaking to him gently, Finn behind her, his life fast ebbing away. He felt the taste of bile in his throat and he swallowed, feeling something solid go down. It made him want to retch and he curled his arms around his stomach. His plastic mattress squeaked from the movement.

Zara sat in the sole chair. 'How are you doing?'

He stared at the floor in silence. After a moment, he said, 'I'm sorry, I don't mean to be rude. I just…'

Zara waited.

'I'm feeling a little stunned.'

'Do you need anything?' she asked. 'Tea? Coffee?'

'No. Thank you.'

Zara explained that he would attend a court hearing and enter a formal plea. If he wasn't granted bail, he would be housed in a young offender institution until the date of his trial. She would stay in touch, she promised, and liaise with his legal team.

Kamran listened, but his mind was elsewhere, playing a maddening reel: Finn smiling and saying 'I certainly hope so'. Finn telling him 'I had fun the other night'. Finn claiming it was consensual. Finn welcoming him into his room. Nothing had changed for this boy who had taken so much from Kamran and, yes, last night he was crazed with guilt but today he could think more clearly. Finn was a rapist and Finn deserved it. Kamran was glad he did it. He *had* to be – because otherwise what did that mean?

Zara watched him intently. 'Kamran?'

'What?'

'I asked if you've spoken to your family?'

He nodded. 'Yes. I saw Mum and Dad this morning and Adam came after school.' He gestured at a pile of books. 'He brought me homework. Went to all my teachers and made notes.' Kamran laughed, a harsh sound that held a bitter note. 'Soppy bastard even wrote me a letter.' Kamran tossed aside the envelope, a pale blue with cursive black writing.

Zara smiled softly. 'What did he say?'

'Just sentimental stuff about staying strong. Adam's read a lot of Paulo Coelho. He's always perched beneath the sycamore tree, contemplating the great questions of life.' Kamran stopped, knowing his tone was bitter.

'And how are you feeling?'

'I'm fine.' He paused, then added, 'I'm glad I did it.' Zara balked and Kamran almost smiled. It felt good to be transgressive – ugly but thrilling like a shot of sour tequila. He held her gaze and said it again: 'I'm glad I did it.'

Zara studied him. 'Is that the truth?'

He raised his chin and said, 'Yes.'

'Is it really?'

He felt his skin prickle with heat. 'Yes.'

'Is it?'

'Yes,' he insisted but his voice wavered with the weight of the word.

She held his gaze. 'Is it the truth, Kamran?'

He closed his eyes, feeling the nearness of tears. 'No,' he said finally. Beneath the blinding white of denial, he understood the truth: if Zara hadn't arrived when she did last night, he would have put a bullet in his head. 'I think I need help,' he said. Glassy tears now fell from his eyes. 'Zara, I need help.'

She sat down next to him, the plastic squeaking crudely. She put an arm around him and he turned his face to her shoulder and wept with horror and grief.

*

The cavernous space of St Alfege Church was even colder than usual. Zara pulled her woollen scarf tighter and breathed on her hands to warm them.

'I'm glad you came,' said Chris. He had texted her last night to ask where she was. She had failed to reply so he had called this morning to press the importance of the weekly meeting. 'Complacency,' he said, 'was a killer,' and though she wanted to laugh at the platitude, instead she solemnly agreed.

She now took a seat at the back of the gathering, hoping to just observe. Since leaving Kamran, she had felt a sense of unease that stubbornly refused to quieten. What was it that stirred in her brain? She sifted through their conversation; walked through it step by step.

Chris was addressing the meeting now. 'It's at our lowest ebb that we need people the most,' he was saying.

What was it that bothered Zara? She rewound the day further and paused on Erin. Was she preoccupied by their earlier meeting?

'That's when we need the support of the people we love,' said Chris. 'A phone call, a text, a letter.'

Zara's mind snagged on the word: a letter. She pictured the envelope on Kamran's plastic mattress, a pale blue with loopy black writing. Where had she seen it before? The answer came to her easily: when she had mistaken Adam's room for Kamran's, she had seen a writing pad and envelopes of the same pale blue, stained by the half-drunk glass.

As she listened, however, her mind pawed and probed at the image, trying to remember if she'd seen Adam's writing: the flourish of the serifs, the cute crook of the letter 'n'.

Then, another image flashed in her mind and she felt her breath desert her. An image of an envelope just like Kamran's – the same pale blue and loopy black writing – but this time the name was Finn, stuck on a corkboard above a bloody floor.

Another image followed: a white shirt hooked on the side of Finn's chair, the twin peaks of the number '11' visible in a crease. She had seen that shirt before: in Adam's room hung on a door handle.

The hall seemed to sway for a moment. Without apology or explanation, Zara stood and ran down the aisle. Bursting into the cold outside, she ran to her car, cursing the twenty-mile distance to Hampton. She placed a call to Erin and asked her to send her Adam's schedule. Her mind churned with questions but failed to grasp the answers. She raced along the A40, changing lanes erratically.

It seemed an eternity before she arrived at the gates of Hampton. There, she raced to the cricket field only to be told that Adam was absent. Zara recalled Kamran's jibe. 'He's always perched beneath the sycamore tree, contemplating the great questions of life.'

'Is there a sycamore tree here?' she asked the coach.

He frowned, confused, but said, 'Yes.' He pointed vaguely south-eastwards. 'It stands on a knoll on the southern tip of the lake.'

'Thank you,' she said breathlessly. She turned and did all she could do not to run. It took her a full fifteen minutes to find the tree. Sure enough, as she approached, she spotted Adam's lone silhouette. From behind, she could swear that it was Kamran. There on the knoll she froze, her mind connecting the dots.

Kamran in his police interview: 'I was supposed to spend the weekend at a friend's.'

Adam telling Kamran: 'She wanted me to check your room today' – which meant he had a key.

An image of Finn checking his breath, turning the handle like he knew it was open.

Sofia on one of Zara's visits, affectionately telling Kamran: 'You should have been Adam.'

Zara felt her stomach drop. She must have made a sound for Adam turned and looked at her. He seemed unsurprised, as if he had been expecting her.

'You,' she said, her breath shallow and fractured. 'It should have been you.'

Adam's faced blanched with emotion. 'Me and Finn,' he said quietly. 'It's always been me and Finn.'

'How?' Zara tried to catch her breath. Adam turned to the lake and skimmed a stone across the surface. She walked to him, the grass soft and mossy underfoot. She sat, knees in the grass, ankles tucked beneath her. 'Adam,' she said. 'How?'

He shook his head. Where Kamran's eyes were delicate and knowing, Adam's were sad and soulful. 'Where do I even start?'

'What happened on the night of the party?'

He skimmed another stone across the surface and it emerged four times before sinking. 'Kamran wasn't supposed to be there,' he said. 'He was supposed to be at a friend's house.' He exhaled and the warmth of his breath misted the air. 'Finn and I are juniors and we share our room with others. I have a key to Kamran's room so I asked Finn to meet me there. It was a rare chance for us to spend the night together.' He cleared his throat. 'Kamran found me at the party and told me he wasn't leaving after all. I was crushed and knew Finn would be too. I sent him a text.' Adam made a small bitter sound. 'I still have it in my phone. I think I've read it a thousand times.'

'What did it say?'

Adam gestured outwards, as if the lake might extend an answer. He recited the words in a bleak monotone. 'F, I'm gutted but Kamran's not going away after all so don't come round tonight. I'll see you soon.' He closed his eyes. 'I love you. I'll miss you.' His voice cracked with grief. He pressed his hands into the grass as if that might somehow brace him. 'Finn didn't receive the message. West Lawn is a black hole and the text wasn't delivered.' Adam's mouth curled in a corner. 'I didn't realise what happened. I was so *stupid*. I even saw him the next day and he kissed me in secret and he said "you smelled so good last night". I thought it was strange because I saw him after cricket practice when I was awful and sweaty but I thought he was being silly and sweet because that's just the way he is. But he meant at *night* – in bed.' Adam blinked and his tears spilled over. 'Kamran wears CK One – the same scent as me.'

Zara's mind raced with questions. They clamoured and clashed in a turbid mass that momentarily struck her mute. She tried to sift through them; to pick out each black filament and arrange it in a logical order. 'Finn thought he was coming in to see you?'

Adam watched the corrugated surface of the lake. 'He didn't rape Kamran,' he said softly. 'He had sex with me just as I asked him to. That's what he thought he was doing.'

Zara absorbed this. 'But why did he tell Kamran he "had fun the other night"?'

'He was just making small talk!' Adam's voice grew bitter. 'Stupid, banal small talk about the spring fundraiser. They'd spoken about it getting "tired and emotional" and Finn was riffing off that. He only meant he had fun at the party.'

Blood pulsed in Zara's head. Could it really be true? She recalled walking into court with them, two brothers identical in height, weight and manner. Could a drunken teenager have mistaken one for the other? 'And you believe him?' she asked.

'Yes. You don't understand. Finn was in love with me and I was in love with him. He would never cheat on me.' Adam wiped a cuff across his cheek. 'He didn't even know what he did until the police spoke to him.'

'But that's not true, Adam,' said Zara gently. 'Finn spoke to Kamran before the police interview. He even told him that "it takes two to do what we did".'

'He was talking about me!' Adam thumped his chest. 'When Kamran confronted him, Finn thought he'd found out about us; that maybe someone had spotted us. The "we" was Finn and me!'

Zara struggled to fit the pieces together.

'You have to understand something. Finn didn't know. He didn't know what he'd done. It was only when the police asked him a question – "Did you obtain Kamran's consent?" – that he realised they weren't talking about me.'

'Then why didn't he tell the police?' cried Zara.

'Because he didn't want to out me!' Adam made a hoarse bark of a sound. 'You've met my father! If he found out I was gay, it would be the end of me and Finn. He did it to protect me.' His voice took on a desperate lean. 'I begged him, "Please just tell the truth," but he begged me to wait. He promised that he'd be acquitted. He said he'd read the stats and in a few months' time, we could forget this and move on.'

'And Kamran?' said Zara. 'You let him think his rapist walked free?'

Adam's face clouded over. 'I thought he would come to understand that what happened was a drunken mistake.' He blinked. 'Look, I've had sex with Finn and he's the gentlest, kindest person I've ever met. What happened between them was not violent.' His chest heaved with a sob. 'I didn't know that Kamran would do what he did. I didn't know it would end like this.'

Zara felt a glassy shock. 'Oh, Adam, why didn't you say something?'

'I wanted to!' he cried. 'But Finn wouldn't let me. He wanted me to come out on my own terms. He would *never* let someone out me.' Adam gestured hopelessly. 'Besides, who would have believed him?'

Zara exhaled. She wished she could have spoken to Finn and told him there was precedent. She had studied cases like this; could recite them even now: 2015 in Santa Rosa, California; 2014 in Bolton, UK; 2011 in Calgary, Canada; 2009 in New Plymouth, New Zealand; 2005 in Sydney, Australia. The list went on. The fact that they were brothers of the same weight and height would have earned Finn reasonable doubt. Zara thought of this boy who she had cast as a villain, he with his sunny blond smile and continental flair, which she had interpreted as entitlement. In the grip of inebriation, Finn had made a grave mistake. The darker forces of serendipity – a text that failed to send, a door left unlocked – made it seem less likely. She imagined his panic on discovering the truth and the urgent instinct to protect his lover.

She remembered Mack's reaction to Kamran – his casual offer of conversion therapy, his needling and verbal bullying. If he found out that Adam was gay, who knows what he would do?

Adam pressed his face to his knees, wrapped his arms around them and softly began to weep. Zara watched with a profound sense of sorrow and the feeling that matters were beyond her control. If there was a dark force at play, then it wasn't serendipity but hyper-masculinity. It was this that told Adam to hide who he was; that made Finn lie to protect him; that drove Kamran to lethal violence. How toxic it was to teach these young men to dominate, to dangle that haunting phrase – *beta male* – above them like a guillotine.

Zara thought of her own brother, Rafiq, and the imperious note in his speech that developed in his teens. She thought of the aggressive square of his shoulders and how he refused to even make a round of tea as if that might diminish him.

Zara listened to Adam cry, the fractured weeping of a boy who was lost. She mirrored his stance – arms wrapped around her knees, a bulwark against the buffeting wind – and waited for his tears to dry.

As they sat, a swan swam to the lakeshore and traced a graceful figure of eight. They watched her, and the beauty of that moment held them in silence. The wind raged against the swan and yet she remained by the shore, regal and serene.

'You can't tell Kamran,' said Adam.

Zara was silent for a moment. 'I think *you* should.'

Adam shook his head. 'Finn died trying to protect me. If I tell the truth now, then what was it all for?' He swallowed. 'Kamran can never know. It will kill him.'

Zara thought of him, already on the brink. 'Can you live with this, Adam?'

'I have to.'

'I don't think you do.'

'I know why you're saying this. You think it will eat me up inside but it won't.' Adam watched the movement of the swan. 'I will remember Finn and I will love him every day for the rest of my life and that is enough.'

'And Kamran?'

'Kamran is tough. He will survive. And so will I.'

Zara felt the weight of a dark melancholy. *And so this is your 'Cut',* she thought. *This is the knife in your heart that you will try to heal around. But the edges will stay livid and shiny until one day in the future, it hurts so much, you have to pull it out.* 'And if you can't?'

Adam's lips curled in a strange, detached smile. 'My father likes to say *faber est suae quisque fortunae.* Every man is the architect of his own fortune.' He tipped his face to the sky. 'Kamran and I believe that and we'll both decide to survive.'

Zara studied him. 'And so you remain in the cage,' she said.

He gave her a sad smile as if she couldn't possibly understand. Together, they watched the swan glide across the surface, her furious thrashing hidden underneath. The breeze picked up and they sat still, tears skimming off their eyes in the wind.

ACKNOWLEDGEMENTS

Thank you to Jessica Faust who took a chance on a Tower Hamlets kid from halfway across the world. You walk the walk and for that I will always be grateful.

Thank you to my editor, Manpreet Grewal. You're not sentimental and neither am I, but I hope you know what you've done for me. I'd go to war for you.

Thank you to the indomitable Lisa Milton and the team at HQ: Janet Aspey, Sophie Calder, Lily Capewell, Laura Daley, Rebecca Fortuin, Georgina Green, Melanie Hayes, Sammy Luton, Fliss Porter, Lucy Richardson, Joanna Rose, Darren Shoffren, Georgina Ugen, Kelly Webster and the tireless design and production teams. I love your innovative ideas and am continually surprised and delighted by how far you will go for your authors.

Peter Borcsok and the team at HarperCollins Canada, I am so thankful for your support. I hope we get to hang out in Toronto when I finally make it there.

Thank you to the generous authors who championed *Take It Back*: Nazir Afzal OBE, Christina Dalcher, Lisa Hall, Louise Jensen, Christina McDonald, Sarah Morgan, Alex Khan and Roz Watkins. Your support has been invaluable.

I would be lost without the help of Matthew Butt (now QC!), barrister at Three Raymond Buildings. As ever, I hope you will forgive the creative licence I've taken with your meticulous advice. Thank you, also, for warning me against photographing Inner London Crown Court and possibly stopping me from getting arrested.

Lee Adams, I will always be grateful for your time and generosity. Let's try to grab another coffee when you're not too busy fighting crime.

Thank you to all those who so patiently helped with my research: Dina Begum, Rob Cawdron, Sara Crofts, Dr Sanjeev Gaya, Simon Green, Peter Holt, Victoria Hughes, Hiren Joshi, Jack Knott, Imran Mahmood, Mike McKay, Jane Nickels, Tania Rahman, Jacqueline Redikin, Neville Young and, finally, Francis Rossi for what became Mack's story.

A special thank you to my early readers for your precious time and feedback: Lottie Gross, Ariane Sherine, Diederik Stolk and Serena Wong.

I will forever be grateful to Colin Giles, the first person who said I could write for a living, and to Kashif Ali aka Sensei for the 24/7 tech support.

Thank you to Priya Patel, Rabika Sultana and the friends I've named above: Dina, Ariane, Josh and Serena. Did someone say squad goals?

Thank you to my sisters Reena, Jay, Shiri, Forida and Shafia. (Shaf, you get this one; Fro will get the next one.)

Finally, thank you, Peter Watson, for making every day better (and for support that never wavers).

Read on for an extract from the explosive and
gripping novel by Kia Abdullah, *Take it Back…*

CHAPTER ONE

She watched her reflection in the empty glass bottle as the truth crept in with the wine in her veins. It curled around her stomach and squeezed tight, whispering words that paused before they stung, like a paper cut cutting deep: colourless at first and then vibrant with blood. *You are such a fucking cliché*, it whispered – an accusation, a statement, a fact. The words stung because Zara Kaleel's self-image was built on the singular belief that she was different. She was different to the two tribes of women that haunted her youth. She was not a docile housewife, fingers yellowed by turmeric like the quiet heroines of the second-gen literature she hated so much. Nor was she a rebel, using her sexuality to subvert her culture. And yet here she was, lying in freshly stained sheets, skin gleaming with sweat and regret.

Luka's post-coital pillow talk echoed in her ear: 'it's always the religious ones'. She smiled a mirthless smile. The alcohol, the pills, the unholy foreskin – it was all so fucking predictable. Was it even rebellious anymore? Isn't this what middle-class Muslim kids *did* on weekends?

Luka's footsteps in the hall jarred her thoughts. She shook out her long dark hair, parted her lips and threw aside the sheets, secure in the knowledge that it would drive him wild. Women like Zara were never meant to be virgins. It's little wonder her youth was shrouded in hijab.

He walked in, a climber's body naked from the waist up, his dirty blond hair lightly tracing a line down his chest. Zara blinked languidly, inviting his touch. He leaned forward and kissed the delicate hollow of her neck, his week-old stubble marking tiny white lines in her skin. A sense of happiness, svelte and ribbon-like, pattered against her chest, searching for a way inside. She fought the sensation as she lay in his arms, her legs wrapped with his like twine.

'You are something else,' he said, his light Colorado drawl softer than usual. 'You're going to get me into a lot of trouble.'

He was right. She'd probably break his heart, but what did he expect screwing a Muslim girl? She slipped from his embrace and wordlessly reached for her phone, the latest of small but frequent reminders that they could not be more than what they were. She swiped through her phone and read a new message: 'Can you call when you get a sec?' She re-read the message then deleted it. Her family, like most, was best loved from afar.

Luka's hand was on her shoulder, tracing the outline of a light brown birthmark. 'Shower?' he asked, the word warm and hopeful between his lips and her skin.

She shook her head. 'You go ahead. I'll make coffee.'

He blinked and tried to pinpoint the exact moment he lost her, as if next time he could seize her before she fled too far, distract her perhaps with a stolen kiss or wicked smile. This time, it was already too late. He nodded softly, then stood and walked out.

Zara lay back on her pillow, a trace of victory dancing grimly on her lips. She wrapped her sheets around her, the expensive cream silk suddenly gaudy on her skin. She remembered buying an armful years ago in Selfridges; Black American Express in hand, new money and aspiration thrumming in her heart. Zara Kaleel had been a different person then: hopeful, ambitious, optimistic.

Zara Kaleel had been a planner. In youth, she had mapped her life with the foresight of a shaman. She had known which path to take at every fork in the road, single-mindedly intent on reaching her goals. She finished law school top of her class and secured a place on Bedford Row, the only brown face at her prestigious chambers. She earned six figures and bought a fast car. She dined at Le Gavroche and shopped at Lanvin and bought everything she ever wanted – but was it enough? All her life she was told that if she worked hard and treated people well, she'd get there. No one told her that when she got there, there'd be no *there* there.

When she lost her father six months after their estrangement, something inside her slid apart. She told herself that it happened all the time: people lost the ones they loved, people were lost and lonely but they battled on. They kept on living and breathing and trying but trite sentiments failed to soothe her anger. She let no one see the way she crumbled inside. She woke the next day and the day after that and every day until, a year later, she was on the cusp of a landmark case. And then, she quit. She recalled the memory through a haze: walking out of chambers, manic smile on her face, feeling like Michael Douglas in *Falling Down*. She planned to change her life. She planned to change the world. She planned to be extraordinary.

Now, she didn't plan so much.

*

It was a few degrees too cold inside Brasserie Chavot, forcing the elegant Friday night crowd into silk scarves and cashmere pashminas. Men in tailored suits bought complicated cocktails for women too gracious to refuse. Zara sat in the centre of the dining room, straight-backed and alone between the glittering chandelier and gleaming mosaic floor. She took a sip from her glass of Syrah, swallowing without tasting, then spotted Safran as he walked through the door.

He cut a path through soft laughter and muted music and greeted her with a smile, his light brown eyes crinkling at the corners. 'Zar, is that you? Christ, what are you wearing?'

Zara embraced him warmly. His voice made her think of

old paper and kindling, a comfort she had long forgotten. 'They're just jeans,' she said. 'I had to stop pretending I still live in your world.'

'"Just jeans"?' he echoed. 'Come on. For seven years, we pulled all-nighters and not once did you step out of your three-inch heels.'

She shrugged. 'People change.'

'You of all people know that's not true.' For a moment, he watched her react. 'You still square your shoulders when you're getting defensive. It's always been your tell.' Without pause for protest, he stripped off his Merino coat and swung it across the red leather chair, the hem skimming the floor. Zara loved that about him. He'd buy the most lavish things, visit the most luxurious places and then treat them with irreverence. The first time he crashed his Aston Martin, he shrugged and said it served him right for being so bloody flash.

He settled into his seat and loosened his tie, a note of amusement bright in his eyes. 'So, how is the illustrious and distinguished exponent of justice that is Artemis House?'

A smile played on Zara's lips. 'Don't be such a smart-arse,' she said, only half in jest. She knew what he thought of her work; that Artemis House was noble but also that it clipped her wings. He did not believe that the sexual assault referral centre with its shabby walls and erratic funding was the right place for a barrister, even one who had left the profession.

Safran smiled, his left dimple discernibly deeper than

the right. 'I know I give you a hard time but seriously, Zar, it's not the same without you. Couldn't you have waited 'til mid-life to have your crisis?'

'It's not a crisis.'

'Come on, you were one of our strongest advocates and you left for what? To be an *evening volunteer*?'

Zara frowned. 'Saf, you know it's more than that. In chambers, I was on a hamster wheel, working one case while hustling for the next, barely seeing any tangible good, barely even taking breath. Now, I work with victims and can see an actual difference.' She paused and feigned annoyance. 'And I'm not a *volunteer*. They pay me a nominal wage. Plus, I don't work evenings.'

Safran shook his head. 'You could have done anything. You really were something else.'

She shrugged. 'Now I'm something else somewhere else.'

'But still so sad?'

'I'm not sad.' Her reply was too quick, even to her own ears.

He paused for a moment but challenged her no further. 'Shall we order?'

She picked up the menu, the soft black leather warm and springy on her fingertips. 'Yes, we shall.'

Safran's presence was like a balm. His easy success and keen self-awareness was unique among the lawyers she had known – including herself. Like others in the field, she had succumbed to a collective hubris, a self-righteous belief that they were genuinely changing the world. You could hear it dripping from the tones of overstuffed barristers, making demands on embassy doorsteps, barking rhetoric at political figureheads.

Zara's career at the bar made her feel important, somehow more valid. After a while, the armour and arrogance became part of her personality. The transformation was indiscernible. She woke one day and realised she'd become the person she used to hate – and she had no idea how it had happened. Safran wasn't like that. He used the acronyms and in-jokes and wore his pinstripes and brogues but he knew it was all for show. He did the devil's work but somehow retained his soul. At thirty-five, he was five years older than Zara and had helped her navigate the brutal competitiveness of London chambers. He, more than anyone, was struck by her departure twelve months earlier. It was easy now to pretend that she had caved under pressure. She wouldn't be the first to succumb to the challenges of chambers: the gruelling hours, the relentless pace, the ruthless colleagues and the constant need to cajole, ingratiate, push and persuade. In truth she had thrived under pressure. It was only when it ceased that work lost its colour. Numbed by the loss of her father and their estrangement before it, Zara had simply lost interest. Her wins had lost the glee of victory, her losses fast forgotten. Perhaps, she decided, if she worked more closely with vulnerable women, she would feel like herself again. She couldn't admit this though, not even to Safran who watched her now in the late June twilight, shifting in her seat, hands restless in her lap.

He leaned forward, elbows on the table. 'Jokes aside, how are you getting on there?'

Zara measured her words before speaking. 'It's everything I thought it would be.'

He took a sip of his drink. 'I won't ask if that's good or bad. What are you working on?'

She grimaced. 'I've got this local girl, a teenager, pregnant by her mother's boyfriend. He's a thug through and through. I'm trying to get her out of there.'

Safran swirled his glass on the table, making the ice cubes clink. 'It sounds very noble. Are you happy?'

She scoffed. 'Are *you*?'

He paused momentarily. 'I think I'm getting there, yeah.'

She narrowed her eyes in doubt. 'Smart people are never happy. Their expectations are too high.'

'Then you must be the unhappiest of us all.' Their eyes locked for a moment. Without elaborating, he changed the subject. 'So, I have a new one for you.'

She groaned.

'What do you have if three lawyers are buried up to their necks in cement?'

'I don't know. What do I have?'

'Not enough cement.'

She shook her head, a smile curling at the corner of her lips.

'Ah, they're getting better!' he said.

'No. I just haven't heard one in a while.'

Safran laughed and raised his drink. 'Here's to you,

Zar – boldly going where no high-flying, sane lawyer has ever gone before.'

She raised her glass, threw back her head and drank.

*

Artemis House on Whitechapel Road was cramped but comfortable and the streets outside echoed with charm. There were no anodyne courtyards teeming with suits, no sand-blasted buildings that gleamed on high. The trust-fund kids in the modern block round the corner were long scared off by the social housing quota. East London was, Zara wryly noted, as multicultural and insular as ever.

Her office was on the fourth floor of a boxy grey building with stark pebbledash walls and seven storeys of uniformly grimy windows. Her fibreboard desk with its oak veneer sat in exactly the wrong spot to catch a breeze in the summer and any heat in the winter. She had tried to move it once but found she could no longer open her office door.

She hunched over her weathered keyboard, arranging words, then rearranging them. Part of her role as an independent sexual violence advisor was filtering out the complicated language that had so long served as her arsenal – not only the legalese but the theatrics and rhetoric. There was no need for it here. Her role at the sexual assault referral centre, or SARC, was to support rape victims and to present the facts clearly and comprehensively so they could be knitted together in language that was easy to digest. Her team worked tirelessly to arch the gap between right and wrong, between the spoken truth and that which lay beneath it. The difference they made was visible, tangible and repeatedly affirmed that Zara had made the right decision in leaving Bedford Row.

Despite this assurance, however, she found it hard to focus. She did good work – she knew that – but her efforts seemed insipidly grey next to those around her, a ragtag group of lawyers, doctors, interpreters and volunteers. Their dedication glowed bright in its quest for truth, flowed tirelessly in the battle for justice. Their lunchtime debates were loud and electric, their collective passion formidable in its strength. In comparison her efforts felt listless and weak, and there was no room for apathy here. She had moved three miles from chambers and found herself in the real East End, a place in which sentiment and emotion were unvarnished by decorum. You couldn't coast here. There was no shield of bureaucracy, no room for bluff or bluster. Here, there was nothing behind which to hide.

Zara read over the words on the screen, her fingers immobile above the keys. She edited the final line of the letter and saved it to the network. Just as she closed the file, she heard a knock on her door.

Stuart Cook, the centre's founder, walked in and placed a thin blue folder on her desk. He pulled back a chair and sat down opposite. Despite his unruly blond hair and an eye that looked slightly to the left of where he aimed it,

Stuart was a handsome man. At thirty-nine, he had an old-money pedigree and an unwavering desire to help the weak. Those more cynical than he accused him of having a saviour complex but he paid this no attention. He knew his team made a difference to people's lives and it was only this that mattered. He had met Zara at a conference on diversity and the law, and when she quit he was the first knocking on her door.

He gestured now to the file on her desk. 'Do you think you can take a look at this for the San Telmo case? Just see if there's anything to worry about.'

Zara flicked through the file. 'Of course. When do you need it by?'

He smiled impishly. 'This afternoon.'

Zara whistled, low and soft. 'Okay, but I'm going to need coffee.'

'What am I? The intern?'

She smiled. 'All I'm saying is I'm going to need coffee.'

'Fine.' Stuart stood and tucked the chair beneath the desk. 'You're lucky you're good.'

'I'm good because I'm good.'

Stuart chuckled and left with thanks. A second later, he stuck his head back in. 'I forgot to mention: Lisa from the Paddington SARC called. I know you're not in the pit today but do you think you can take a case? The client is closer to us than them.'

'Yes, that should be fine.'

'Great. She – Jodie Wolfe – is coming in to see you at eleven.'

Zara glanced at her watch. 'Do you know anything about the case?'

Stuart shook his head. 'Abigail's sorted it with security and booked the Lincoln meeting room. That's all I know – sorry.'

'Okay, thanks. I'll go over now if it's free.' She gestured at the newest pile of paper on her desk. 'This has got to the tipping point.'

Carefully, she gathered an armful of folders and balanced her laptop on top. Adding a box of tissues to the pile, she gingerly walked to 'the pit'. This was the central nervous system of Artemis House, the hub in which all clients were received and assigned a caseworker. It was painted a pale yellow – 'summer meadow' it had said on the tin – with soft lighting and pastel furnishings. Pictures of lilies and sacks of brightly coloured Indian spices hung on the wall in a not wholly successful attempt to instil a sense of comfort. The air was warm and had the soporific feel of heating left on too long.

Artemis House held not only the sexual assault referral centre but also the Whitechapel Road Legal Centre, both founded with family money. Seven years in, they were beginning to show their lack of funds. The carpet, once a comforting cream, was now a murky beige and the wallpaper curled at the seams. There was a peaty, damp smell in the winter and an overbearing stuffiness in the summer.

Still, Zara's colleagues worked tirelessly and cheerfully. Some, like she, had traded better pay and conditions for something more meaningful.

Zara manoeuvred her way to the Lincoln meeting room, a tiny square carved into a corner of the pit. She carefully set down her armful and divided the folders into different piles: one for cases that had stalled, one for cases that needed action, and another for cases just starting. There she placed Stuart's latest addition, making a total of twelve ongoing cases. She methodically sorted through each piece of paper, either filing it in a folder or scanning and binning it. She, like most lawyers, hated throwing things away.

She was still sorting through files when half an hour later she heard a gentle knock on the door. She glanced up, taking just a beat too long to respond. 'May I help you?'

The girl nodded. 'Yes, I'm Jodie Wolfe. I have an appointment?'

'Please come in.' Zara gestured to the sofa, its blue fabric torn in one corner, exposing yellow foam underneath.

The girl said something unintelligible, paused, then tried again. 'Can I close the door?'

'Of course.' Zara's tone was consciously casual.

The girl lumbered to the sofa and sat carefully down while Zara tried not to stare.

Jodie's right eye was all but hidden by a sac of excess skin hanging from her forehead. Her nose, unnaturally small in height, sat above a set of puffy lips and her chin slid off her jawline in heavy folds of skin.

'It's okay,' misshapen words from her misshapen mouth. 'I'm used to it.' Dressed in a black hoodie and formless blue jeans, she sat awkwardly on the sofa.

Zara felt a heavy tug of pity, like one might feel for a bird with a broken wing. She took a seat opposite and spoke evenly, not wanting to infantilise her. 'Jodie, let's start with why you're here.'

The girl wiped a corner of her mouth. 'Okay but, please, if you don't understand something I say, please ask me to repeat it.' She pointed at her face. 'Sometimes it's difficult to form the words.'

'Thank you, I will.' Zara reached for her notepad. 'Take your time.'

The girl was quiet for a moment. Then, in a voice that was soft and papery, said, 'Five days ago, I was raped.'

Zara's expression was inscrutable.

Jodie searched for a reaction. 'You don't believe me,' she said, more a statement than a question.

Zara frowned. 'Is there a reason I shouldn't?'

The girl curled her hands into fists. 'No,' she replied.

'Then I believe you.' Zara watched the tension ease. 'Can I ask how old you are?'

'Sixteen.'

'Have you spoken to anyone about this?'

'Just my mum.' She shifted in her seat. 'I haven't told the police.'

Zara nodded. 'You don't have to make that decision now. What we can do is take some evidence and send it to the police later if you decide you want to. We will need to take some details but you don't have to tell me everything.'

Jodie pulled at the cuffs of her sleeves and wrapped them around her fingers. 'I'd like to. I think I might *need* to.'

Zara studied the girl's face. 'I understand,' she said, knowing that nerve was like a violin string: tautest just before it broke. If Jodie didn't speak now, she may never find the courage. She allowed her to start when ready, knowing that victims should set their own pace and use pause and silence to fortify strength.

Jodie began to speak, her voice pulled thin by nerves, 'It was Thursday just gone. I was at a party. My first ever one. My mum thought I was staying at my friend Nina's house. She's basically the daughter Mum wished she had.' There was no bitterness in Jodie's tone, just a quiet sadness.

'Nina made me wear these low-rise jeans and I just felt so stupid. She wanted to put lipstick on me but I said no. I didn't want anyone to see that I was ... trying.' Jodie squirmed with embarrassment. 'We arrived just after ten. I remember because Nina said any earlier and we'd look desperate. The music was so loud. Nina's always found it easy to make friends. I've never known why she chose me to be close to. I didn't want to tag along with her all evening – she's told me off about that before – so I tried to talk to a few people.' Jodie met Zara's gaze. 'Do you know how hard that is?'

Zara thought of all the corporate parties she had

attended alone; how keen she had been for a friend – but then she looked at Jodie's startling face and saw that her answer was, 'no'. Actually, she *didn't* know how hard it was.

Jodie continued, 'Nina was dancing with this guy, all close. I couldn't face the party without her, so I went outside to the park round the back.' She paused. 'I heard him before I saw him. His footsteps were unsteady from drinking. Amir Rabbani. He— he's got these light eyes that everyone loves. He's the only boy who hasn't fallen for Nina.'

Zara noted the glazed look in Jodie's eyes, the events of that night rendered vivid in her mind.

Jodie swallowed. 'He came and sat next to me and looked me in the eye, which boys never do unless they're shouting ugly things at me.' She gave a plaintive smile. 'He reached out and traced one of my nails with his finger and I remember thinking at least my hands are normal. Thank you, God, for making my hands normal.' Jodie made a strangled sound: part cry and part scoff, embarrassed by her naivety. 'He said I should wear lace more often because it makes me look pretty and—'. Her gaze dipped low. 'I believed him.'

Jodie reached for a tissue but didn't use it, twisting it in her hands instead. 'He said, "I know you won't believe me but you have beautiful lips and whenever I see you, I wonder what it would be like to kiss you."' Jodie paused to steady her voice. 'He asked if I would go somewhere secret with him so he could find out what it was like. I've never known what it's like to be beautiful but in that moment I got a taste and ...' Jodie's eyes brimmed with tears. 'I followed him.' She blinked them back through the sting of shame.

Zara smarted as she watched, dismayed that Jodie had been made to feel that way: to believe that her value as a young woman lay in being desirable, but that to desire was somehow evil.

Jodie kneaded the tissue in her fingers. 'He led me through the estate to an empty building. I was scared because there were cobwebs everywhere but he told me not to worry. He took me upstairs. We were looking out the window when ...' Jodie flushed. 'He asked me what my breasts were like. I remember feeling light-headed, like I could hear my own heart beating. Then he said, "I ain't gonna touch 'em if they're ugly like the rest of you."' Jodie's voice cracked just a little – a hairline fracture hiding vast injury.

Zara watched her struggle with the weight of her words and try for a way to carry them, as if switching one for another or rounding a certain vowel may somehow ease her horror.

Jodie's voice grew a semitone higher, the tissue now balled in her fist. 'Before I could react, his friends came out of the room next door. Hassan said, "This is what you bring us?" and Amir said he chose me because I wouldn't tell anyone. Hassan said, "Yeah, neither would a dog."'

Jodie gripped her knee, each finger pressing a little black pool in the fabric of her jeans. Her left foot tap-tapped on the floor as if working to a secret beat. 'Amir said, "She's got a pussy, don't she?" and told me to get on my knees. I didn't understand what was happening. I said no. He tried to persuade me but I kept saying no ...' Jodie exhaled sharply, her mouth forming a small O as if she were blowing on tea. 'He— he told his friends to hold me.'

Zara blinked. 'How many were there?' she asked softly.

Jodie shifted in her seat. 'Four. Amir and Hassan and Mo and Farid.'

Zara frowned. 'Do you know their surnames?'

'Yes. Amir Rabbani, Hassan Tanweer, Mohammed Ahmed and Farid Khan.'

Zara stiffened. A bead of sweat trickled down the small of her back. Four Muslim boys. Four Muslim boys had raped a disabled white girl.

'I—' Jodie faltered. 'I wasn't going to tell anyone because ...' her voice trailed off.

'You can tell me.' Zara reached out and touched the girl's hand. It was an awkward gesture but it seemed to soothe her.

'Because if a month ago, you had told me that any one of those boys wanted me, I would have thought it was a dream come true.' Hot tears of humiliation pooled in her eyes. 'Please don't tell anyone I said that.'

A flush of pity bloomed on Zara's cheeks. 'I won't,' she promised.

Jodie pushed her palms beneath her thighs to stop her hands from shaking. 'Farid said he wasn't going to touch a freak like me so Hassan grabbed me and pushed me against the wall. He's so small, I thought I could fight him but he was like an animal.' Jodie took a short, sharp breath as if it might stifle her tears. 'Amir said he would hurt me if I bit him and then he ... he put himself in my mouth.' Jodie's lips curled in livid disgust. 'He grabbed my hair and used it to move my head. I gagged and he pulled out. He said he didn't want me to throw up all over him and ...' A sob rose from her chest and she held it in her mouth with a knuckle. 'He finished himself off over me.'

Zara's features were neutral despite the churning she felt inside. 'What were the others doing?' she asked gently.

Jodie shook with the effort of a laboured breath. 'I— I couldn't see. They were behind me.' She clasped her hands together in her lap. 'Hassan pushed me and I fell to the ground. He tore my top and undid my jeans and then ... he started.' Jodie's features buckled in anguish. 'He— he came on my face, like Amir.'

Zara closed her eyes for a moment, stemming the weakness knotting in her throat.

Jodie's words came faster now, as if she needed them said before they broke inside. 'Hassan turned to Mo and said, "she's all yours". Mo said he didn't want to but they started calling him names and saying he wasn't man enough, so ... he did it too.' Jodie's voice cracked, giving it a strange, abrasive texture. 'Mo has sat next to me in class before. He's helped me, been kind to me. I begged him to stop, but he didn't.' She swallowed a sob, needing to get through this.

Zara listened as the words from Jodie's mouth fell like black spiders, crawling over her skin and making her recoil. The sensation unnerved her. Part of Zara's talent as a caseworker was her ability to remain composed, almost dispassionate, in the face of the painful stories told between these walls. Today, the buffer was breached.

'Jodie.' Zara swallowed hard to loosen the words. 'I am so, *so* sorry for what you went through.' Her words, though earnest, rang hollow, echoing in a chamber of horror. 'We're nearly there. Can you tell me what happened after?'

'They just left me there.' Her words held a note of wonder. 'I wiped everything off me using some old curtains. I tucked my top into my jeans so it wouldn't keep splitting open and then I walked home.'

'Did you see anyone on the way? Any passing cars or revellers from the party?'

Jodie shook her head. 'I stayed off the path. I didn't want to be seen.'

'Were you injured at all? Bleeding?'

'No.' Jodie took a steady breath, appeased by the simplicity of this back and forth questioning.

'What time was it when you got home?'

'I walked for fifteen minutes so around twelve I think.'

'Did you tell your mum?'

'Not that night. She was in bed and I let myself in. I went to my bedroom and then I cleaned myself up.' Jodie pointed at her backpack, a bare and practical navy so she couldn't be teased for signs of personality. 'I've brought the clothes I was wearing.'

'Washed?'

'No. I didn't want to be stupid like you see on TV.'

Zara blinked. 'Jodie, nothing you did or didn't do could be called stupid. Please understand that.'

The girl gathered her perfectly formed hands in her lap but gave no sign of agreement.

'Did you tell Nina or anyone else what happened?'

'How could I?' Jodie's voice was soft but bitter. 'How could I tell her that a boy who doesn't even want *her* wanted me? How would she ever believe that?'

Zara looked up from her notes. 'Hey,' she said, drawing Jodie's gaze from her lap. 'No matter what happens, I want you to know that I believe you.' Zara studied her for a moment, noting the dozen different ways in which she kept control: the tensing of her jowls and the squaring of her jaw, the curl of her fists and feet flattened on the floor. 'I believe you,' she repeated.

Fresh tears welled in Jodie's eyes. 'So you will help me?'

'Yes, I will help you.' Zara watched her wilt with relief. 'Is there anything else I need to know? Anyone else who was involved?'

'No. That's everything.'

Zara drew two lines beneath her notes. She watched Jodie dab at her dripping nose and wondered how a jury would view her. A rape trial usually hinged on power – one person stripping it from another – but in this case, it would be difficult not to consider desire. Zara believed Jodie – had seen too much devious behaviour, met too many appalling men to doubt the young girl's story – but felt a deep unease at the thought of her facing a jury. Could they imagine four young men wanting to have sex with Jodie even in some twisted gameplay?

Zara reached for her box of tissues and handed a fresh piece to Jodie.

She took it with a quivering hand. 'What happens now?'

Zara's lips drew a tight line, a grimace in the guise of a smile. 'We would like to conduct a medical exam. All our doctors here are female. After that, if you're ready, we can help you make a formal statement with the police.'

Jodie blanched. 'Can we go to the police tomorrow? I want to think about it for one more night.'

'Of course,' said Zara gently. 'We can do the exam, store the samples and see how you feel.'

Jodie exhaled. 'Thank you for being on my side,' she said, each few syllables halting before the next.

Zara offered a cursory nod.

'No, I mean it.' Jodie hesitated. 'I told you it was hard to be at that party alone. The truth is it's hard to be anywhere – *everywhere* – alone.'

Zara leaned forward. 'You won't be alone in this – not

for any of it.' She gestured to the door. 'If you want me in the exam room, I can sit with you.'

Jodie considered this but then shook her head. 'I'll be okay.'

Zara led her to the exam room and left her with the forensic medical examiner, a brisk but matronly Scotswoman who ushered Jodie inside. Zara shut the door with a queasy unrest. A small, delinquent part of her hoped that Jodie would change her mind, that she would not subject herself to the disruptive, corrosive justice system that so often left victims bruised. The law stress-tested every piece of evidence and that included the victim – probing, pushing and even bullying until the gaps became apparent.

Beneath her concern, however, she knew that Jodie needed to pursue this. A horrifying thing had happened to her and only the arm of the law could scrub the stain clean and serve justice.

ONE PLACE. MANY STORIES

Bold, innovative and
empowering publishing.

FOLLOW US ON:

@HQStories